# HUBRIS

## THE ICHOR SERIES
## BOOK FIVE

## TRISH D. W.

*This book is dedicated to Nora Grace. For the sake of spoilers, I will not divulge why until the acknowledgement section. But thank you for everything you've done for me, Nora. I love you so much.*

# TRIGGER
# WARNING

This story contains mature topics that may trigger some readers and can be inappropriate for a younger audience. These triggers include excessive gore, torture, PTSD from previous wars/battles, self-sacrifice/suicide, and a magnitude of beloved characters' deaths. Out of all my books that I have written, and will write, Hubris has the most casualties of characters I ardently love. This book tore me apart, and I haven't been able to stitch myself back together yet.

If you are like me, then collect tissues for chapters 16, 19, 27, 34, 35, 36, 37, 38, 40, 46, 47, 49, & 50

# THE PROPHECY

On the eighty-eighth night of the
    eighty-eighth year
When crimson shifts to gold,
A prophecy will unfold.
From the ashes of time,
Eight figures will rise.

Eight, the sacred number of
    immortality,
Seals the destiny of a seer and a
    savior,
A heart and a hammer,
A singer and a seeker,
And a hero and a huntress.

A river of black will cease to exist,
Unless the one with sight sees
    through the mist.

# THE PROPHECY

A world of hatred and oaths will
    prevail,
Unless the oracle can see the truth
    and can derail.

The ultimate fate is decided when
    the heart twice fails,
And from the savior, a terrible
    scream will wail.
The sound will echo forevermore,
And from the scream, spawns a war.

Hatred and Sight,
Oh, how they will fight.
The winner is untold,
But one thing is known.

Whichever side has the hammer
    which swings,
The hero who knows he must bleed,
The muse who no longer sings,
The seer, who sees the future with
    great speed,
The huntress who clips the
    monster's life strings,
The heart whose life will cede.
The savior with death she brings,
The seeker with life he leads,
Will be gifted the role of eternal
    queens or kings.

The world will crumble like
    Pompeii,

But the seeker will guide fallen
    friends away.
To safety, the seeker will find the
    ashes he will revive.
The world will be unlike any other
    and will eternally thrive.

Unless the hatred wins,
Then the seeker and the seer, the
    hero and the hammer will
    surely die.

# PROLOGUE

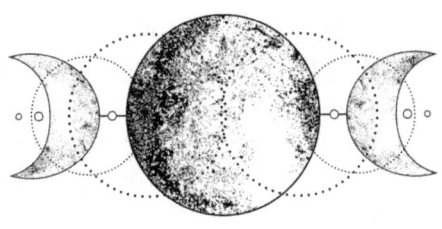

## HECATE

*The Day the Underworld Died*

Many of the dead run when confronted with the reality that they chose the losing side. They claw through the Underworld's broken ceiling by climbing on the backs of their fallen friends, hoping to clamber their way back to the real world. Debris falls like cataclysmic raindrops upon the once-again living souls of the Underworld, who do not realize that their afterlife ceases to exist.

As my rage grows, so does my magic.

It festers, spreading and destroying everything in its wake. I decimate the Fields of Punishment until the former heroes of ancient times are dead once again, but their souls do not have a place to go. There is no longer an Underworld to carry the souls towards. The gates are ripped apart. The ceiling gone. So, when my magic steals the lives of Odysseus, Theseus, Oedipus, and so many others, their souls glow like white orbs from their chests, and they beckon to my command.

I'm the closest divination to life anew, as the goddess of necromancy. I could bring them back to life, but they are just numbers for Saffron's side. They are just instruments the opponents will play so that I lose it all. So that I lose *him*. My Mastiff. My hopes and dreams of Mastiff alive again will all fade into nothingness without Styx, so when they die a second time and their souls gravitate towards me with futile hope for reanimation, I create another world of complete oblivion within the depths of my decaying soul.

I embrace them whole. Each soul tries to fight for an afterlife or a second chance at life. I absorb each orb-like soul like they are the world's most painful pleasure, and they sink into the bottomless pit I've created just for them. Pain wiggles itself through me, momentarily scarring my flesh and making it anew, but it is all worth it. They seep into my skin, fluttering like butterflies towards me. They don't want to die. I can feel as much, but hope is for the weak. I was once weak, believing my life would become better simply because I asked it to be. My hope relied on my friendships and their loyalty to me, but Mastiff would still be dead if I continued wandering down that path.

I refuse to give into the hopes of the weak.

Just as Styx taught me.

The corpses pile up in the Underworld as I strike down another hero and another necessary causality. I destroy the kindhearted souls who live in the castle on my rampage towards *her*. The false queen who refused me, who I once saw as my greatest friend. With each soul that enters my body, I become more powerful, teetering on omnipotent. I invite them all and use their strength to strike down another soul. Kill another maid and soldier and smiling face until I'm in her throne room.

Persephone and Thanatos wait for me.

Styx already informed me Hades would not be with them, and that's why I had to strike now. That's why my army destroys the remnants of the Underworld today, because I could never defeat Hades again. But Persephone and Thanatos? As this newfound magic bubbles up inside of me, turning my veins a sickly dark green that pushes against my skill; I can destroy them both.

*Keep them alive.* Styx's order rings in my ears, betraying the raging hatred I feel for my two former friends.

A swirl of my magic creates a tornado around my body, spinning my hair in a thousand directions, and I know I'm losing control. Whatever words Styx whispers in my ears over the decades has infested me.

For a single, sane moment, I realize that I'm as much of an experiment to Styx as her human monster, Gareth. Her power of hatred has seeped into me, metamorphosing the fabric of myself until I'm also a monster, but I don't want to relinquish it.

I hate Persephone for never giving Mastiff to me back when I begged. Cried and pleaded for mercy when I still had goodness in my heart. I hate Thanatos for being a friend, but not choosing me instead of Persephone and Hades, who stole so much from me. There's only hatred in my wake, blurring my vision to anything else but the all-consuming need to destroy.

I step towards Persephone as my tornado of magic grows. The framed portraits and torchlights rip from the walls, scattering towards me and the wind I command. A scream breaks all the glass in the room, and it takes me a belligerent moment to realize that I am the source of this scream. It is me who shatters every glass, then commands them like spinning daggers towards my enemies.

Towards my former friends.

Persephone falls first, with hundreds of glass shards pinning her to the ground. She yells, but it isn't louder than my enraged cries, as my tornado and I run towards Thanatos. His body bears the consequences of my hatred, with almost a dozen pieces of glass embedding his body, but he stands tall. He grips his scythe with both hands, even as rivulets of ichor slither down his arms and torso; he waits for me to strike.

We meet in a blazing array of anger, hatred, and remnants of regret. He swings his scythe at the exact moment I duck my head. I throw more green-tinted glass shards his way, but he doesn't dodge them. They slip inside his cheeks, shoulders, and stomach, but he continues to dance with me. He swings; I shoot. He begs me to see him rationally, and I hurt my former friend in return. This level of abhorrence has made me strong, but it's made me blind, too.

I do not see Thanatos's scythe until it is a moment away from cutting off my head. It wouldn't kill me, but it would stop the magic that's destroying the room we stand in. Thanatos hesitates, even though his weapon cannot kill me. The blade rests underneath my chin, and I silence the surrounding storm within me. The tornado disintegrates, and the glass falls to the ground, until it is just Thanatos, the scythe, and me.

"This isn't you," he says.

"I asked you all to save him." I do not realize I'm crying until dark green droplets hit the floor. *Since when did I cry green?* "You all refused me. All I wanted was him, and you all said no. How could you do that to me?"

He follows the path of that dark green droplet, which sizzles like acid the moment it hits the floor, before slowly drawing his gaze back to me. To my eyes that burn a darker shade. To my pale arms infected with obsidian green veins pushing against the flesh, trying to break free.

"What has she done to you?" Thanatos gutturally asks, his voice scratchy with emotions.

At the same time, I say. "And now I must refuse you your lives. Your happiness."

I wrap my hand around the scythe's blade, puncturing my skin as I turn his sacred weapon into ash. Obsidian green ash. He watches with astonishment, and while he sees my hand coming, he doesn't stop me. I wrap it around his throat, stealing his airway. But he does nothing, only clamps one hand on top of my wrist with a pleading expression.

"Death is essential to life. I thought you understood that." His words vibrate against my hand, circling around his throat, but I don't stop squeezing. Don't stop wishing he would die. "It was Mastiff's time. He understood that. Why can't you?"

More newly dead souls in the form of glowing orbs rush towards me, sinking into my skin, and only now I realize how much it hurts. Stealing their life force gives me strength, but it rips apart my flesh every time. In the blaze of my hatred, I almost didn't realize the razor-sharp sensation, or the now-green blood dribbling down my arm instead of the familiar golden ichor.

I let out an ear-piercing scream when he collapses unconscious, but I don't stop hating him and Persephone as they lay on the floor. I snap my fingers, and they both vanish, joining Styx in the prison of my design. The same prison that kept Saffron captive many, many years ago, when she was still a naïve, human girl.

I stroll out of the castle that putrefies around my feet, not daring to look back at the world I have destroyed. A world I once coveted. Each step I take down the staircase causes decay in the form of scattering, uncontrollable green magic. It slithers like snakes from my body, sinking its venom into every fissure of the castle I once loved. The ground quakes beneath me, knowing that I no longer belong here; or because I steal death and pocket it for myself, and the ground hates me for my actions.

Maybe if hatred didn't steal away my breaths, I would hate myself too. But I don't. All I care about is that Mastiff is back at the prison, safe and sound. He won't die again, not when I have control of the souls' fates. That must be enough.

It will be enough…right?

I step out of the castle, and the entire infrastructure collapses. Whoever remains inside screams one last time, then their souls swarm towards me, burrowing inside my skin where they will never find a reprieve. It is not my choice if they swarm towards me, hungry for any vestige of life, but I have no choice but to accept them all the same. It is Styx's plan that I readily concede to. They join many others in their abysmal new afterlife. The remnants of the castle sit above a hill, and I have a full view of the carnage below me. My army, with swords glinting with crimson blood, slashes into anyone who opposes our side. They kill humans who have just begun to live again.

I collect useful humans on the journey down the hill and towards the Underworld gates. Plucking friends and family members of Saffron's who haven't yet died again. Letting the rest perish. I watch as nameless souls, who I've seen wander these halls for centuries, fall victim to my armies' bloodlust. All the while, I capture those I know by name.

Shackle Angel, Saffron's first friend from their time as imprisoned children.

Subdue Sika, the huntress who first taught Saffron how to fight.

Incapacitate Panda and Pyro, the first human couple to show Saffron what unadulterated love looked like.

Chain Willow, a huntress who Saffron idolized from her time in the prisons.

Steal Hypnos, a god who fought on the Underworld battlefield with more compassion than most immortals but winces every time he's in Saffron's company.

By the time I reach the Underworld gates, where Gareth has Diam and Zig unconscious and bloodied on the floor, I have enough presents for Styx. So she may grant me a chance to see Mastiff again. While I know he is safe, Styx keeps him from me. Locks him away until I have earned the right to see him, but that's alright. At least I have him for a little while. At least he's safe.

My captives, Gareth, and I disappear in a puff of my smoke back to the prisons where Saffron's story began, and hopefully, will end.

# ONE

SAFFRON

The Fates are equally cruel and benevolent, curse-mongers and wish-givers; they grant Hattie a second chance at life, but there is only one minute separating our reunion with irreparable travesties. She is an ominous warning of the Underworld's unraveling and the effects this has on our world forevermore.

Her body trembles beneath my guiding hand as Cerberus and Ares join us inside our home.

We built the interior of this home together, with Diam and Zig, and I've changed almost nothing. The walls are still painted the same almond wisp color Hattie found eighty-eight years ago, with minor touch-ups. I still have the rustic wagon-wheel chandelier that Zig loved, hanging from the ceiling above the staircase, which was glossed by Diam. Everything is just how she left it. Her eyes bounce around the home without leveling on a single item.

She's physically here, but a fragmented part of her remains in the Underworld. Witnessing its ruination.

Watching our loved ones fall as Cerberus runs away with her to safety.

Ares and I share a look.

My arms stay wrapped around her, as he and I have a conversation without words. We have both seen Hattie in the thicket of wars, with a manic grin and fearlessness in her eyes. We watched her face Kronos with stoic determination. I saw her on the precipice of death in the Underworld closet when we were both humans, complicit with her unfortunate fate. In our friendship, it has always been me who freezes with fright as she pushes me forward.

To see Hattie like this, unable to stop shivering and staring at nothing-yet-everything, says more about our predicament than any words could convey.

I help Hattie sit down on the loveseat. She wraps her hands in mine, stopping any notion that I'd leave her side, and Cerberus sits at our feet. The three-headed dog tries to warm Hattie, with his fur covering her bare feet, but she still shivers. Still trembles with memories of the Underworld's deterioration.

I nod my head towards the blanket slung over the back of the neighboring sofa, and Ares listens. The only sound in the room is Hattie's chattering teeth as he picks up the blanket, but when he tries to drape the material over Hattie's shoulders, she flinches. Finally, her eyes focus on one thing: him.

Daggers form in her eyes, hoping to slice Ares into a thousand miserable pieces.

With that withering look alone, she reminds us why she hates Ares. I forgave him for his past after that night in Poseidon's jail cell, when he told me Morpheus had polluted his mind, but Ares didn't kill my sister. He killed Hattie's, and that type of loss does not lessen. It shouldn't lessen.

He sets the blanket on the arm of the loveseat nearest Hattie, then hurriedly murmurs. "I'll inform Zeus and retrieve my sons." His gaze lands on where I stand, lingering on my face for a beat too long, before whispering ever so softly. "Stay safe, please."

He hesitates on leaving, waiting until two words leave my lips as quietly as his plea did. "I promise."

Only then does he leave.

And only then does Hattie speak. "It started like a storm. The ceiling rumbled, dark green clouds forming above us, and we knew. Diam and I recognized that sickly green color, and we knew danger had found us again, but the older members of Elysium Fields laughed at the sight. They saw a storm, and the many children of Zeus thought their father was playing a parlor trick. Even as Diam grabbed my hand and ran with me to Elysium's gates, I heard their echoing laughter."

She pauses, and I know she can hear the echoes of that sound. Remembering how quickly their amusement turned to horror. I reach for the blanket, pulling it over her shoulders, but it doesn't lessen the shudders that leave her. She's not fully here with me, and the Underworld is so, so cold.

Words cannot escape her lips again. She sits beside me, but she's a thousand miles away. I try to jostle her back to my reality. Squeezing her hands in mine. Repeating her name until my throat scratches. Nothing works until a sheen of gilded light streams down into my living room.

Apollo and Hart materialize. They stand together with their hands clasped. While Apollo's eyes widen with shock at the sight of Hattie, or the version of her that remains, Hart removes her hand from Apollo's and walks towards us. Immediately, I notice a shift from the paint-splattered girl I met a few months ago in my office. She walks with too much grace. Stares with too much knowledge.

She kneels on the floor beside Cerberus, and she holds her hands palm-up towards Hattie. "Let me tell your story for you." Even her voice sounds different. Like her raspy baritone is the coalescence of a dozen voices. Her eyes are the same blazing brown-gold, but they brim with more understanding than ever before.

Perhaps that is why Hattie stops shivering. She removes her hands from mine, slides them out from underneath the blanket, and lays them flat on Hart's. The oracle closes her eyes for a moment, and every hair on both their arms rises like an electrical current. There's a whoosh of air. Then Hart opens her eyes. Suddenly, they are Hattie's. Dark like midnight.

Hart speaks, but it's Hattie's genuine voice which carries through the room. And with those words, I'm suddenly brought to the Underworld, running through Elysium with Diam's hand wrapped tight around mine. I am Hattie, living this harrowing experience in her perspective. Hattie's fear becomes my own, stitching itself into the fabric of my mind. My living room ceases to exist, and in its place is the darkness of the Underworld, which now holds an ominous moss green hue.

*Green lightning slashes the ground with rueful intent, splintering the floor Hattie and Diam run across. Their fear is palpable, filling the nearby air with a putrid stench that only worsens with each hurried step and anxious leap. Hattie wonders if they will make it to the gates before whatever storm Hecate creates collapses the Underworld and takes them whole.*

*But they reach the gates, barreling through them with unbalanced determination.*

*Zig stands in his ferry at the bank directly across from Elysium Fields, waiting for them. His hands are tight against the oar, and his face is as white as a sheet. Her close friend normally smiles in her company, but not today. Today, Zig shows the trepidation of this* moment with more clarity than Diam and her. He removes one hand from his oar for Hattie, and she doesn't hesitate. He hoists her onto the ferry as Diam jumps on. It rattles with the sudden weight, but with ease, Zig spins their transportation around.

Hattie has never seen Zig move at such speed before. His biceps bulge with each erratic movement, slashing the oar through the clear blue water that replaced the River Styx upon Styx's escape. He moves like this is his personal mission in life, steering them away from Hecate and Styx's vengeance. Lightning reaches the river, but it's not made of electrical currents. Not like Zeus's. Instead of the lightning smiting them down, the bolts create waves of staggering heights. Water splashes on them with every row, to where Hattie can barely see.

When the lightning breaks the ground on a hill to the far right, it reaches the Fields of Punishment with brutal accuracy. The Fields of Punishment are a place in the Underworld where only the worst occupants of the world spend their afterlife. Men like Sisyphus, who attempted to cheat death, and Tantalus, who killed his sons and tried to feed their meat to the gods, reside there. Now, Hecate has freed them from their chains. Without being able to see the truth, Hattie can hear it. A thousand chains clattering to the ground at the same time, forming their own thunder.

A sea of mostly men clambers down the hill, now holding weapons made entirely out of Hecate's green magic. As they run down the hill, they kill any human within their vicinity. Soon, hundreds of nearby humans scream with a frightening realization that they are about to die twice. Not even Zeus's children believe this is a practical joke any longer. The fear of trillions of people hits a crescendo until it becomes too much for Hattie to bear.

The water is so cold, slapping against her face and bare arms, but she knows better than telling Zig to slow down. She must quiet her fear because if she does not, then how will she ever survive? To persevere, survival must be the precipice of all thoughts. Hattie does not have time to be afraid as Zig nears the front of the river, where his dock lays splintered in a thousand pieces. She only has time to escape a place she thought she'd live forever.

And how she will miss *Elysium Fields*.

The little cottage Diam and her have made for themselves, where everything and everyone ceases to exist. She misses her friends, Saffron, most of all, but she was happy in her cottage. She was at peace with her garden and her neighbors and her afterlife. Now, in a storm of calamitous witchcraft, it's gone.

The ferry smashes into the riverbank, and Diam's hand returns to hers. He pulls her off the ferry, and they sprint towards the Underworld's gates. She doesn't have time to question why Zig only saved her and Diam, instead of the other dead souls screaming under the torment of Hecate's army and the freed prisoners from the Fields of Punishment. She doesn't have time to ponder anything except how all three will escape.

They're almost there, at the onyx gates that separate the Underworld from the world of the living, but Cerberus is not the only one at the gate. There's a man there, with dark skin destroyed by a malicious blade, who stands at six and a half feet tall. His left arm is gone, replaced with a mechanical instrument that has one of Cerberus's heads pinned to the ground. He whimpers, unable to move away from a human with unnatural strength.

The mechanical arm, which has gifted this human unparalleled strength, almost looks like a creation from Hephaestus himself. Yet Hattie knows Hephaestus would not create a weapon of mass destruction against them and Cerberus. Hephaestus has a love for invention, but he is not cruel. Only someone truly monstrous could destroy this man, who is more robot than human, in such a fashion.

Hattie knows he is human because of the three slash marks across his neck from Cerberus's attack that bleed painstakingly red; otherwise, she would question if he was real at all. Metal pieces litter his body, drilled into parts of his leg and welded into his right cheek. The mechanical arm fuses into his flesh, and all the surrounding skin blis-

*ters with the first signs of infection. The arm gifts him strength, but it is also slowly killing him.*

I recognize the man as Hattie's experiences project into my mind. His name was Gareth French. The heartbroken man, whose wife and child died by Oizys's hand under Styx's command. The same heartbroken man who watched as I exacted his justice. He stands at the Underworld's gates, with a missing arm replaced by a mechanical one that can pin down Cerberus. Now, with eyes that no longer blink. With lips that no longer open and continually bleed. Almost every inch of his remaining flesh is in deep cuts and slashes, worse than Epiales's when subject to Zeus's torture.

I know Styx is the only one cruel enough to create such a creature from a man who already suffered enough by her hand. The sight of him, a man who only wanted his wife and daughter back, brings bile to my throat. I want to vomit and apologize to him for not saving him from a fate worse than death.

*Cerberus whimpers, paws thrashing to be let go. The head under the monster's hand has blown out pupils, and his eyes are ready to burst. Hattie lets out a gasp for her favorite pet, and the sound turns the monster's head towards them. Unblinkingly, he sees Hattie first, then Diam, then Zig. He drags his haunted, blanked stare back at her, and it's like staring into the depths of Tartarus.*

*Zig runs towards Gareth while Diam turns Hattie's body to face him. Tears blur Diam's eyes, but his grip on Hattie's shoulders remains firm. He stares at her for a few seconds, but it feels like a millennium. He opens his mouth to speak once, twice, but it takes a third time for words to escape.*

*"I love you more than the stars and the moon and all that comes after. You are my soul, Hattie Pyro. My absolute soul."*

*Diam moves his hands to cup each cheek, and he pulls her into a kiss that speaks goodbye. She doesn't want a goodbye. She wants a promise of forever. That's what she earned. She's fought the battles and won, so she deserves him as her prize. Him, forever. These kisses, forever. They aren't supposed to end. This was not meant to be a limited affair.*

*He pulls away from her, and she can taste his tears on her lips.*

*Or perhaps hers, she's not entirely sure.*

*He turns and runs from her. Correction: runs towards the monster. Diam dives towards death, so that she can be led to a second chance at life. Tears constrict her vision, but she watches the moment Diam's head hits the monster's stomach and they both crash to the ground. She sees the moment Cerberus's airway is no longer restricted by the monster, and how all three of his heads swivel towards her. Hattie doesn't understand why her life holds more precedence than Zig's or Diam's, who fight side by side against the monster. None of them have weapons, but that mechanical arm is a weapon that will strike them both down.*

*She climbs onto Cerberus's back the moment he reaches her, and she sobs as Cerberus runs away without Zig and Diam. She doesn't know how long she cries for her husband, her soulmate, her everything as his fate lays in the mottled hands of a creature designed to kill. But she knows when she stops. The moment Saffron's mansion comes into view, where some of her happiest moments played out, the tears finally dry. For if there is anyone who can save Diam, if there is anything left of him to save, then it will be Saffron. Her best friend and sister.*

The living room returns in translucent spots until the Underworld ceases to exist once again. It's daunting, returning to the quiet living room after watching heartache and death, followed by endless screams.

Hattie rips her hands from Hart's, shoving them back into the blanket, but she's no longer shivering from the river's cold water. She no longer wears the sheen of fear as she said goodbye to Diam, whose fate teeters with uncertainty. Instead, my friend, who chooses anger over fear, takes back the reins.

"What in the gods did Hecate do?" Hattie asks this question through gritted teeth.

Instead of a straightforward answer, in an eerily melodic tune, Hart speaks.

"It is not Hecate who wields the blade of war.

The manifestation of hatred is evil at her core.

Hatred destroys the worlds of death and afterlife,

But all around her are pawns under her smite.

Hecate will fall, that much is true,

But most of all, Hatred must too.

For deaths to be avenged,

And the wars to finally end,

The Savior must cry,

For the heart, that must die.

Twice alive,

But twice cannot survive."

There's more Hart wants to say, more of the prophecy that must be told, but the Fates have other plans. The same three fate-spun women who give the prophecies also stop them from being told in their entirety. For before Hart can say more, reveal more, the living room ground splinters in half.

And a bony, decayed hand juts through the floor in search of human flesh.

# TWO

LAMB

To be invisible is to be the best at consuming one's surroundings. I have spent centuries in the background, fading into the shadows even on the brightest of days, whilst in the company of most immortals. In the beginning, this unwavering truth devastated me. Realizing my invisibility was realizing my mundanity, even in the company of other humans.

Now, I see it for the blade it is.

In my place in the background, nestled around a handful of other huntresses, I get to openly watch those around me. I get to use their facial expressions as teaching tools to fully understand the range of emotions and notice even the most subtle changes. Once upon a time, far before my confidence existed, I hated my shadows; now, I love them. I crave discovering the truths of others before they have a chance to open their mouths and vocalize their own thoughts for the rest of the room.

Zeus has noticed me the least over the centuries. If he does not find someone powerful or beautiful, then he forgets their existence. Casts them aside in his mind like they never shared the same air as him. I am forgotten by Zeus, despite being the oldest living huntress in Artemis's regime. Regardless of holding the coveted spot of Artemis's closest friend, he still forgets me. Yet, it is because he forgets I stand in a room of only a few that I can brazenly assess him.

And I dislike what I see.

The king of the gods does not mask his emotions well, even when he plays a charade with an open-mouthed grin. He wears his fear like a stain on his sleeve, unable to be erased. Zeus walks into Artemis's home on Mt. Olympus without knocking, but his gait is faster than usual. He tries to walk into the home casually, but it's a poor performance. As is his too perfect smile amid the drums of war.

I understand now why he has never been successful in his trysts outside of his marriage. Hera is not an exceptional sleuth; Zeus is a sub-par liar.

Naturally, with only Dýnami, Vee, and me in the room, Zeus's attention snags on the prettiest. Vee stiffens ever so slightly under his watchful gaze and that leeringly fake smile, barely turning her body to acknowledge him. "What can we do for you, King Zeus?"

Dýnami sits nearest Vee with a stack of cards in her hand, with only a small circular table separating the two girls. She, just like I, have witnessed Zeus's lecherous comments towards the prettier members of our huntress clan. For many centuries, Willow was his primary fascination. Zeus has never laid a hand on a huntress, but Dýnami angles her body towards Vee just in case today begins a daunting new tradition.

I watch from my shadows with the certainty that Zeus will not approach Vee for any other reason than Artemis's whereabouts. It isn't because Vee isn't beautiful. She's gorgeous. A kind of pretty that takes a second to process. On any other occasion, Zeus would try every option to lead Vee away from the huntress clan and towards his bed.

But not today.

The gods can change their appearances at the drop of a hat, and I wonder if Zeus knows he has changed the color of his eyes from an electrically sharp blue to the darkness of an upcoming storm. His hands remain at his sides, but he continuously clenches and unclenches them. Most importantly, he didn't immediately answer Vee. Zeus always talks. Even if there is a minimal audience and no question has been asked, Zeus talks. And talks. And talks.

But not today.

I spin my attention towards Vee. My whispered demand clamorously echoes in the too-quiet room. "Go get Artemis and the other huntresses."

Vee quickly leaves the room, choosing the side door not occupied by Zeus's hulking frame. Only upon the sound of my voice does Zeus's attention deviate from Vee and latch onto me. It's not with the same appraisal as he gave Vee, but in the hundreds of years with Artemis, this is the longest he's looked at me.

"What is it you require, King Zeus?" Only when the question leaves my lips, do I wonder if he's ever heard my voice before today. Or, if he has heard me speak before now, has he ever cared to listen?

He clenches and unclenches his fists, over and over. So much so that Dýnami spares me a questioning glance. With only a stare alone, we ponder the same question. What danger has arrived on our doorstep that frightens even the king of the gods?

"I'll wait for my daughter," is all he says.

We linger in the tensest of silence for nearly five minutes, and in this time, Zeus stares only at the floor. He does not dawdle with small talk, as is customary of him. He does not ask where Artemis is, or joke that we sent away the prettiest of the huntresses. For the first time in hundreds of years, Zeus is eerily, frighteningly mute.

When Artemis walks into the room, the remaining huntresses are a step behind her. Iris stands hip-to-hip, hands interlocked with the goddess of the wild. Zeus does not bother with pleasantries. He sees their hands conjoined, the first open declaration of their relationship, but he doesn't make one of his typically lewd comments. There's no teasing joke about stealing Iris from her; he only stares at his daughter, clenching and unclenching his fists.

Something is very, very wrong.

"You and your huntresses need to go to the gates between the Underworld and the living world immediately."

Artemis's brows knit together, a crease forming between them. "Good morning to you too, Father. Any reason we need to the Underworld?"

"Because I am your king and that is what I ask of you." He clears his throat and takes a deep exhalation before adding. "Hermes and Athena are already at the entrance, waiting for you all."

Younger huntresses, like Shikari, subtly roll their eyes and believe this is the typical behavior of Zeus. The totalitarian leader, who doesn't expect questions, only blind obedience, but they do not know him with the same complexity that Artemis and Iris do. The younger huntresses do not understand that just like all the gods, Zeus is complex, with a thousand layers to peel away. Dýnami and I share another glance, another unspoken declaration of our unease with his suddenly rigid, almost frightened behavior.

Zeus hasn't looked his daughter in the eyes since she has walked into the room. Since he gave his order, he hasn't looked at any of us. Even Vee or Iris. His attention remains fixed on a bare wall, or the fan whirling atop the ceiling. Even the floor catches his fascination, but not us. Not his daughter, who he has always been brisk with but never silent.

There's something amiss, and it's waiting for us at the Underworld's entrance. I stare at Zeus, willing him to look in our direction. To look at any of us. But he doesn't. Zeus emanates raw guilt and fear, and suddenly, the last place I want to go is the Underworld's entrance. What awaits us there that has Zeus so frightened? That has him unwilling to look at his own daughter?

Iris manifests her rainbows, which shower over each of us. Before I'm sent away, I hear a deafening scream from Ares's instantly recognizable voice.

"Father!" he yells.

But I'm gone before I hear the rest.

I have a sinking suspicion that whatever Ares tells Zeus, I will discover on my own in the form of this onyx gate. As promised, Hermes and Athena are already standing watch. He grips his six-foot tall Caduceus, and she holds her spear, to prepare for a battle. The rest of us follow suit. I never venture far from my god-anointed weapon, which Iris created specifically for me. The green gleam of my four-foot-long sword glints off the remaining sunlight not covered by growing clouds, and I turn to face the gates with uncertainty.

The rest of the huntresses follow suit. Artemis materializes a bow and arrow. Iris grips her rainbow-colored staff, while a recently healed June grips her cyan-hued axe with her last remaining hand. Dýnami spins her magenta spear. Shikari tightly grips her blood red crossbow. Vee's throwing knives glint the brightest yellow in her grasp, and Jamila points her plum-shaded bow-and-arrow at the gates with rueful anticipation.

Hermes glances at his youngest daughter, now sheathed for battle alongside him, and inches closer to her. She notices his closer proximity and releases a small, almost distressed smile. "Fancy meeting you here, Dad."

He kisses the top of her curly head. "This will take some getting used to. Seeing you in danger."

"And what danger should we expect?" Artemis asks, her voice as lethal as a blade.

"There are remnants of paw prints on the ground." Athena points to the muddy floor beneath us, where an almost foot long paw print sits. "If Cerberus ran from the Underworld instead of fighting, then danger is all we can expect."

I have never known Cerberus to flee from battle. He is the largest, most ferocious dog in history. Only gods and the then-demi-god Heracles have been able to defeat him. So, for him to run, most likely in defeat, then how can we survive? I grip my sword tighter, sweat forming on my brow.

My conversation with Hart on the arena pew returns. I asked her if I was going to die before the end of this war, and she never responded. Yet, that silence was my response. Death waits for me on a battlefield between now and the war's end, but is today the day? Will I fall with my sisters now, or will I survive until the prophetic moment we face Typhon?

Is this when we face Typhon?

With death comes a surplus of emotions. I never feared it when I knew where I was going, but even I can hear the screams echoing from the Underworld. If death is no longer peaceful, then I struggle with accepting my fate.

Death is as unavoidable as the changing seasons, but after evading it for so long, it's coming for me. Today, tomorrow, or next year. It looms closer with each rising moon.

Am I ready for the fall?

The gates separating the Underworld from the living world lay decimated on the floor. Undoubtedly, Cerberus broke through these gates in his mad dash away from the carnage, but now there's no barrier between us and them. The dead and the living.

The screams grow louder as hurried footsteps *pound, pound, pound* against the ground. We all know what comes next. A dozen blood-drenched humans' barrel through the opening, brandishing weapons that glint the darkest shade of green. Hecate's darkest shade of green. Some are instantly recognizable, like the fallen and traitorous huntress, Roxie. Her red hair, a fan of flames, billows in the air as she screams and barrels towards us, but she only makes it three steps before Artemis's arrow plunges into her eye.

Roxie collapses, dead once again, but the strangest occurrence happens after her heart ceases. A white orb exits her chest, and it flies away. Was that her soul? If so, why didn't it go to Hermes, who carries all the souls to their eternal resting place? I glance at Hermes, and he stares at Artemis with widened, confused eyes.

May the gods save us because something is very, very wrong indeed.

Hart's former fiancé, Lowell, who tried to murder her, rushes towards me. He holds a sword in the air, ready to try to strike me down, but I'm quicker. I slide down onto my knees as he clumsily swings his sword towards where my head once was, and then I drive my blade upwards. A sea of intestines spills from his stomach, and he makes a terrible gurgling sound before he collapses onto his knees.

Our eyes lock for a millisecond, and then he falls backward. Dead once again. And just like Roxie, a white orb escapes his chest and flees far, far away from the Underworld.

"They're from the Fields of Punishment." Athena confirms all our suspicions as she fights against one of the Fields of Punishment's longest residents: Sisyphus.

Sisyphus, a man who tried to escape death, has finally succeeded. He fights against Athena for a few minutes of life anew before she decapitates him. His head bounces on the floor, as his soul joins the others in a place unknown, and lands at my feet.

Hermes fights against another long-term occupant of the Fields of Punishment, Tantalus. He suffered without eating or drinking anything for all of eternity after killing his own son, chopping him up into pieces, and trying to feed him to the gods. A few seconds after Sisyphus's head falls off his neck, Hermes hits Tantalus so hard in the head that before his body reaches the ground, his brain matter spills from his skull.

The escapees start in a slow rivulet of bodies, which we quickly cut down, but soon they emerge in tsunami-sized waves. Some have the dark green weapons that declare their allegiance to Styx, but there are innocents floating through, too. Whimpering humans who want a second chance at life, or an escape from all those who try to kill them in their once-peaceful Underworld.

It becomes the cruelest game, deciphering the good from evil amongst thousands, then millions, of swarming bodies. I can scarcely process anything besides the gnawing need to survive a little while longer. I try to focus primarily on those with green-colored blades because they need to die first. The sun drenches us in sweat as we dodge swords, strike with our own, and run to aid another. We fight for so long; the sun falls to slumber and the moon rises.

There's no break, even as my body screams for reprieve. The other huntresses and I are moving slower and slower with each passing hour, but our opponents remain the same in strength and speed. My newest opponent, a burly male with a scar dragging diagonally down his face, elbows me in the nose.

I hear the unmistakable crunch of my nose breaking, and I stumble backwards. Before I can see past the blur of blood across my face, he's back. His fist comes next, hitting me in the same spot, and I crumble onto the floor. My entire face pulsates with pain, originating at the bridge of my nose and scattering around my forehead, cheeks, and mouth. I swear I can taste the pain on my tongue, sharp and coppery.

My sword lays limply in my hand, but with the scraps of remaining strength I possess, I thrust it upwards. I hope, but am uncertain, that I will pierce flesh. He blocks it easily with his own sword, and I know this is it.

This is where I die.

Not on the battlefield against Typhon, who is nowhere in sight. I'm about to die at the hands of a nameless human when all my other sisters continue to fight, mostly unscathed. I don't know if it is tears or blood that obstruct my vision, but for a delirious moment, I think I see a ghost running towards me as this nameless man's sword moves to puncture my heart.

Except, the ghost tackles the nameless man to the ground when the tip of his sword is a breath away from my chest. The ghost grabs my sword and effortlessly drives it into the nameless man's eye. His scream is loudest of all until he is forever silent.

The ghost spins to face me, and only one word escapes my lips in pure disbelief. "Reaper?"

Reaper was one of the first huntresses in Artemis's regime after Willow, Raven, and me. She was endlessly fearless, always grinning in the face of battle, just like she is now. She was the huntress who started the monologue of the day, which I have continued to uphold centuries after her death. Reaper walks towards me, grabbing my hand and hoisting me up to my feet.

Wearing that manic grin I have missed so, so much, she says. "It's been a while, little sheep."

Death surrounds us, but I smile at the nickname I forgot over the years. Reaper looks the same as the day she died, except she doesn't wear the bear's claw marks that stole her life too soon. They once covered the expanse of her arms, chest, neck, and face, but that's gone now. She still has a buzz cut, with the shortest red locks trying to stand at attention. Still has the most crooked teeth I have ever seen, which she loves so much that she smiles twice as much as anyone else I know.

"You're alive again." My words come out in a breathless gasp.

"Hold on a second." Reaper, using my sword, pushes me out of the way, and impales the man running at me from behind. He lets out a gurgling noise, then falls to the floor, and she spins back to face me. "After we kick some butt, we have a lot of catching up to do."

She gives me back my sword, and I pass her my spare knives, holstered on either side of my hip. Together, back-to-back, we slash down anyone holding Hecate's magic-infused weapons. Blood turns the floor into a river, and we slosh our way to victory. Eventually, the waves of bodies turn into a slight stream, until there are no more people escaping from the Underworld. Some escaped from our crusade, for there were too many waves of humans to fight, but at least five hundred lay dead around our feet.

I drop my sword in exhaustion, but Reaper runs and collapses me in a hug. I fall flat on my back, but I don't care. Wrapping my arms around Reaper, I can't help but laugh with joy. The laughter hurts my broken nose more than words can accurately describe, but I can't stop the sound from escaping my lips. She's alive again. One of my oldest friends. And if she's alive, then that must mean…

"Willow." Her name comes out with hope for the first time in nearly a century.

Reaper pulls away from the hug at the mention of our other friend. She stands up, and she holds her hand out for me. But that signature, all-encompassing smile she always wears is gone. I take her hand, letting her help me up again, and I stare at the macabre scene around me.

Everyone on our side is still alive; in fact, my broken nose seems to be the worst of the damage. Dýnami has a black eye, and Athena is doused in ichor, but that's it. We're fine, and we have two huntresses back from the dead. Hound, alive again, stands beside Shikari. The latter openly sobs at the return of her lost friend and holds a battle axe drenched in our enemies' blood.

But there's no Willow or Sika.

I face Reaper, who still wears a crestfallen expression. "We were running away together, and one second, we were holding hands, but the next…"

She doesn't finish her sentence. Artemis steps forward, standing shoulder-to-shoulder with me. "But the next second, what?" Artemis sounds angry, but I hear the fear underneath the rage. "Where is Willow?"

"Hecate got her." Reaper stares at the blood-soaked floor and audibly gulps. "She plucked her out of thin air. I couldn't do anything to save her."

Hecate has Willow. Those three words ring with dreadful promises, and I bite back my fear for my friend as I ask. "But she's alive?"

Reaper nods her head, but there's no elation from this truth. Sometimes, death is more merciful than life in the wrong hands.

"Sika was taken, too." Another voice dreadfully admits.

I spin to face Hound, who wears the same solemn expression as Reaper as she stares at Dýnami. "I'm sorry."

"Don't apologize, because we will get her back." Dýnami white knuckles her spear, bouncing her gaze from Artemis, Hound, Reaper, and me. "We will get them both back, no matter the cost."

I nod my head and repeat. "No matter the cost."

Finally, Artemis whispers. "No matter the cost."

# THREE

## HART

When the decomposed hand of a hapless soul reaches out of the splinter in the center of Saffron's living room, Apollo places me behind him. He unsheathes a blade so bright it glimmers like the sun, but he doesn't rush towards the hand. Neither does Saffron, who places Hattie behind her in a similar position to Apollo and me.

I could tell them that neither Hattie nor I will die from this single hand sprouting from the ground, but if they do not focus on the human who crawls their way to the surface, then who knows how much the future will shift in Styx's favor. I understand the power of words as much as the strength in silence.

Every future death plays like a melancholy violin, cursing my ears with its symphony. The only solace today is the certainty that none of those deaths will occur in this room. Except, perhaps this human whose head peaks out from the fissure.

He's alive again. That much is clear in the way his eyes blink with awareness, but he isn't fully back from the Underworld. His skin still peels with signs of decomposition, slowly stitching itself back to normalcy. This newly alive soul is innocent as he clambers his way to the top, his lithe body trembling in fright as he inspects Apollo's sword and the fierceness behind Saffron's undivided attention.

He takes one step towards Saffron, then another, but that's all he has the chance to do. While he is innocent, a poor soul who wanted to escape the carnage of the Underworld's deterioration, the others who rip through the ground aren't as benevolent. In only a few seconds, joining this shivering man are seven more souls clawing to the surface. A few hold dark green swords glinting with malicious intent, and one thrusts his blade into the innocent one's back.

He only had a few seconds of fresh air after months, years, decades, or centuries below ground, but he is gone as quickly as he arrives. The man opens his mouth in a gasp; no words tumble out. Only rivulets of blood. He stumbles to his knees, a few feet from Saffron.

So close to safety.

The nearly resurrected, with their glowing green weapons, multiply. There is power in numbers, but all it takes is a lingering glance towards Hattie and me, and the room electrifies with power that could crumble worlds. Destroy realms. Obliterate existences. If Saffron did not carve out a portion of her heart for humanity, if she didn't use their existence as a tether to her own consciousness, then everyone would bow to her. She could hold control of Earth within her palm with almost no exertion. Her power has shined across a thousand stories and has played out in front of a thousand eyes, but it's only a sliver of what she's capable of.

Saffron has never erupted. She has never shown the world the end of her power's potential, but when she does eventually explode, the ground will tremble with fright. All her enemies will dissolve into ash or fall into a pit of fiery doom. These humans, with malice in their stance, only get a miniscule sliver of her potential. She lifts two fingers, and the room freezes under her control. The only part of their bodies that Hecate's undead army can move are their eyes, which widen with dreadful realization.

But she hesitates to rip their bones from their flesh.

The skies and the ceiling disagree with her benevolence. They want the enmity brimming on the surface of her boiling rage, and they demand the bloodshed. It starts with a single, fallen piece of plaster, landing a foot away from me, before the entire ceiling collapses under the weight of the earthquakes.

Saffron sees the piece of the home crumble before the rest crash in sharp clumps to the ground, and she leaps towards Hattie. Her desperation plays evidently on her face as she sees Hattie, who only recently returned, near death's embrace again. She tackles Hattie, and they crash onto the floor. She wraps her body completely on top of her friend. Correction: her sister, in truer words than any goddess she shares parentage with. A sister of the heart, who she already lost one too many times in her eternal life.

Her quickness saves Hattie as a jagged piece of the ceiling cuts through Saffron's back. A pool of ichor spills onto the floor, momentarily distracting Saffron from the army she keeps frozen. Their paralysis dissolves, and Apollo isn't as fast as Saffron. He leaps on top of me with the same fevered need to protect me as Saffron did with Hattie, but the undead rush towards us. They are not here for Hattie, Saffron, or Apollo.

Their orders are to kill me, the oracle, with the ability

to see everything we need to sacrifice to defeat their ruthless queen.

Apollo's body curls into a fetal position on top of me as he takes the brunt of it all. The pieces of wood that slide into his skin. The undead that climb on top of him and pierce him with swords before the home's fallen pieces can crush them to death. Ichor spills in several locations, but Apollo cradles my head in both hands, shielding me from the worst. His and Saffron's blood permeates the room with its sickly scent as they absorb all the pain for us.

Outside, the screams worsen with the onslaught of debris. Humans of every age, race, shape, and size climb out of the now mile-long cracks. From my angle in between Apollo's bloodied arms, I cannot see the severity of the ground or how many desperate hands grasp for their life anew. I can only see the multiplying numbers of newly re-surged souls roaming around the splintered floor, wearing the garb designated for the citizens of the Underworld.

Apollo and Saffron stay on top of us, hesitant to re-introduce us to the surrounding carnage, even once the ceiling completely gives way. I tap on Apollo's shoulder. "I'm alright." The two words come out muffled, as his shoulder presses against my mouth, but he hears me.

He shivers above me, his hesitance clear, but he slowly rises. As soon as I remove the pieces of the ceiling embedded in his flesh and the two daggers still piercing the back of his arm, his injuries immediately heal; the blood remains. Golden streaks decorate his face, clinging to the blonde locks sticking to his cheeks. Still, he reaches a hand for me to accept. Still, he treats me delicately, like I was the one who accepted the pain of a collapsing ceiling instead of him.

Saffron brushes debris off her pants, as if there isn't dust and ichor covering eighty percent of her body. Hattie helps her remove the one piece of ceiling embedded into her back as soon as Saffron helps her to her feet.

"Hecate lived in the Underworld for eons," Saffron says. "Those aren't the only humans she gathered at her side. More will come, so we must prepare."

All the members of Hecate's first round of human attackers are dead on the floor, or moaning in agony as death quickly comes to collect their souls. The ceiling, walls, and its accessories stole their lives before Saffron could. It was the Fates giving her a reprieve from obliterating more human lives.

Saffron's entire roof lies on the floor, with shattered glass from the chandeliers creating a battlefield of pain. Her walls collapsed with the ceiling, and now there is nothing. She wears her love for this home in a slash of grief across her eyes, but now there is only war. There is no time to mourn the inanimate objects and the memories they carry with us. There is only the living and the fight that must continue.

Apollo sweeps me up in his arms. But when Saffron tries, Hattie swats her away. "I can handle a few pieces of glass."

We are in a battle of unprecedented size, but Saffron still smiles. "Fine, but I'm not hearing you complain about the cuts for the next week while I'm perfectly healed."

Hattie groans. "Ugh, you win. But you better not hold me like that." She points to Apollo, who has me swept up into a honeymoon position. "I better be slung over your shoulder like a sack of potatoes."

Saffron's smile widens, and I've never seen it as genuine as today.

Have I ever seen her smile?

She slings Hattie over her shoulder like a sack of pota-toes, as requested. Apollo places a tender kiss on the top of my head before he and Saffron walk out of the crumbled remains of her mansion. They accept every slice of glass and ricochet of pain. They wince as each piece slides into their flesh, wiggling its way through with each advancing step. Neither Saffron nor Apollo can heal until after someone removes the glass embedded in their skin, so they attempt to suppress their growing discomfort until we are on the front lawn.

The surrounding land mirrors a plethora of leafless trees. The branches of broken earth are two feet in width and length. It spans for a mile, but the trunks are deep fissures of irreparable damage. They stretch as far as the eye can see and are ten feet in thickness. As far as I can tell, at least a dozen tree-shaped, destructive cracks decorate every inch of the once pleasant neighborhood.

But I know more than a million desecrates the world.

Screams erupt from every direction, never ceasing but always growing. There are no more houses, except for the crumbled remains that either lay on untouched ground or fall into the fissures. The inhabitants are dead and buried beneath the destruction, or they are running from the newly resurrected souls climbing out from the cracks in endless waves. Some of them are innocent, baring no weapons, but a majority of the undead wield dark-green blades shrouded in mist and malevolent intent.

Murder colors a world of previous peace, and Saffron delicately drops Hattie to the ground. She takes a step away from us, facing the destruction encircling us, and her anguish is palpable. Styx has destroyed a world that Saffron rebuilt, brick by brick. She destroyed a portion of her soul with each green sword that strikes down another one of her neighbors.

Saffron kneels to the ground, her hands roaming the decayed remains of a world once bursting with peace. "I swore I would never do it again," she says, more to the ground than us, but we all watch the moment she lifts her head to face the miles' long cracks ahead of her. "I swore I would never kill another human again."

Hattie flinches beside Apollo and me.

From where I stand, I can see the glints of green blades in the distance. I can hear the screams of innocent lives snuffed out by those swords, but I do not have the strength to save them. My abilities lie in seeing the future and determining how to control the right outcome. Saffron's power lies in her magic, which is the only guarantee that those with dark-green misted swords will die for good.

She opens her arms, palms facing the screams of humans, and she whispers. "Come to me."

The bones hear their queen's command, and they obey. Every single human with a green blade erupts in an explosion of guts, blood, and skin. I don't know how far her power stretches, but it's as far as I can see. Even the tiny blips of humans, who are barely visible with a green-glinted sword, explode. Her strength spans several miles, but her mass murder delivers peace to the innocent.

The screams come to an abrupt stop. Saffron paints the sky in human bones. She saves hundreds of thousands with this one action, but I can see the tears that trek down her face. I know she promised herself that she would never have to kill another human, and now she must shatter her promise. She only kills the deserving, but Saffron's heart does not have the innate desire to destroy. She has only wanted the role as the humans' savior, but her powers demand bloodshed and sometimes she must deliver.

Carefully, Saffron brings the bones of thousands of rebellious, murderous humans towards us. She creates a new home from their bones. Not one that she loves, but one she needs. She uses every ribcage and skull and tibia to protect us all from the onslaught. There are no more homes in this world; all of them have crumbled to dust, except for the one built on the bones of murderers.

Hattie and I are the two safest humans at this very moment, with a door that swings shut and locks, but our savior feels no pride. Saffron stares at me, tears never stopping, as she mourns the lives she took to protect everyone else. Her bottom lip wobbles as she tries to stop her anguish.

"What is happening?" Each word Saffron releases comes out clipped and so broken.

There are only two windows in this home she built. Each bone compacts so tightly, like bricks, shielding us from the truth before we go for another fight. Accept another battle with more bloodshed. The screams stopped, but not for long.

Saffron asks me, not Hattie and Apollo, because she isn't looking for a friend's consoling words. She asks the oracle if her greatest fears have come true, and if they have, what she must do to stop this war once and for all.

The most powerful oracles, who lived in the ancient times in Delphi and first spoke this prophecy, died by Styx's hands. My ancestor, Aashritha, and several other oracles were burned alive in their temple, but they live again within me. Their corporeal forms exist in my mind. They imbued me with their abilities, so I can become as close to omnipotent as possible. All the most powerful oracles bring me the words that Saffron needs to hear most of all.

Our voices tumble together in a symphony of chaos.

"Hatred's reign begins today,

Upon the ground that trembles with death and decay.
While the skies believe they still sit upon the throne,
The world is hers alone.
Red will stream endless rivers where there are now cracks,
And screams will reach their climax.
Unless the hammer and the huntress find each other and forgive,
And thievery helps the hero and the singer live.
Unless the heart says their goodbyes for the final time,
And the seeker makes his dire climb.
Only then will Hatred crumble like Pompeii."

I tell her everything she needs to hear, but it's spoken in a language only I can fully understand. To her, I spoke in riddles, but to me, I was crystal clear. She stares at me with a whorl of emotions. Rage for my riddles. Sadness for what comes ahead. Hopeless for the heart that must die, who she knows she loves dearly but cannot save. Confusion for the roles that have not revealed themselves.

But the rage wins out on this day.

"You must know who they are," Saffron says through clenched teeth. "We are the savior and the seer, but you must know who the rest are. Why can't you just tell me?"

Because if Saffron learns all their identities before the heart dies, then we will lose the war. I have seen the version of this war if I tell Saffron right now who the heart is, or the hunter, the seeker, and the hero. If I spoke those words right now, then Saffron would bend the world to save her heart. So many would die in Saffron's crusade to do what she thinks is right, and Styx would sit upon an ivory throne.

Only one other soul can know the truth, and he sits on the throne of Mt. Olympus. There cannot be anyone else I confide in. The others will unwittingly fall into Styx's trap and inadvertently kill us all. Apollo stares at me, imploring for the same answers as Saffron that I cannot give him. He can never know, not until Styx is gone.

Fervent knocks on the new home's door rupture their probing gazes, but this will not be the first time I evade this question. The world's survival relies on me to lie to everyone I love.

"Saffron?!" Ares's voice booms through the closed door. "Saffron!" He yells again.

She flicks two fingers, and the door made of bones swings open. Ares barrels into the room, with Phobos and Deimos directly behind him. Hattie flinches upon his arrival, her glare vicious, but he ignores it. His focus is only on Saffron as he runs across the room, clasping her face in both of his hands. I watch Hattie as she sees the tender way Ares brushes away the smear of ichor across Saffron's cheek, and the way his entire body relaxes when he realizes she's safe.

I wonder if Hattie realizes what Apollo and I have known for so long about Saffron and Ares. That Epiales is not the reason Saffron's marriage to Hermes was destined for ruination the moment they said, "I do". I wonder if Hattie stares deep enough into Ares and Saffron's embrace to realize that it is more than lust guiding Ares's actions. Despite his terrible past, he is actively changing for her.

He exhales in her proximity, like he doesn't know how to breathe when she's away, but the only person who does not realize his obsession is Saffron. She takes the hand on her cheek with both of hers, pulling it away from her with a softening expression. It isn't a smile, but it's a look of content when her eyes meet his. She doesn't realize her own emotions towards the brutish god, who is no more aware of his feelings for her.

His unwavering, life-altering love for her.

"I'm alright."

But she's not.

None of us are not until I ensure all eight members of the prophecy play their role with precision.

And it all starts with Hermes and Hecate.

# FOUR

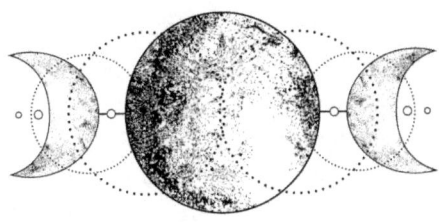

## HECATE

*One Week Later*

There is a disease running through my veins, darkening my already nefarious thoughts until all I crave, all I need, is the color of gold and red. Styx gifts me this obsidian desire with a prison full of our enemies. Ten foes stand forcibly pressed against the walls, chains connecting their slumping bodies to the bricks. The weaker humans, like Panda, only have chained cuffs on their ankles and wrists, but powerful goddesses like Persephone wear their imprisonment like gowns. Serpentine chains slither around her waist, clinch tight around her throat, and squeeze her thighs and calves.

Persephone wears the most chains and blood because she is the best chance Styx and I have at answering the most important questions. She is the wife of the godly king who trained Hart, honing her skills as a formidable oracle. The mother of the savior, who defeats all the monsters we throw her way. The daughter of the king of the

Olympians, who undoubtedly wields a deadly role in the ensuing war. Persephone bleeds the darkest gold, and with each infraction against her body, her skin stitches itself back together a little slower. Her screams become a little louder.

Gareth and I stand side-by-side in front of the former queen, whose head remains upright only because of the cuff around her neck. What started as a puddle of gold around her ankles has become a steady stream of interconnecting rivers spilling around the prison floor. The stench of her blood is so strong that I almost do not smell the urine and feces. Her screams are so loud that I almost do not hear the sobbing pleas from Panda or the spattered threats from Sika.

Gareth, the once grievous human, holds a dark green scythe meant to mock the deterioration of Thanatos's scared weapon. It drips with my former queen's ichor, staining the weapon that looks eerily similar to her loyal friend's. Gareth wears apathy on his face like a mask. I did not know him before Styx toyed with his mind like a marionette doll, but whoever he once was, it evaporated with months' worth of torture and mutilation. He's a void, committing torture to others with the blankest expression.

Persephone tries, and fails, not to flinch as Gareth places the curve of the scythe's blade against the bottom of her chin, tilting her face so that her bloodshot eyes land on me. I never thought this would be the journey the Fates led me on, staring into eyes so broken from someone I once loved so dearly. I wonder what she sees when she stares back at me. A shadow of indifference veils my truth so expertly, but can she see the kernel of regret that grows smaller by the day?

"Who are the other members of the prophecy?" I

repeat this question once again, my voice more devoid of emotions each time I speak the words aloud.

It has been a week since I destroyed the Underworld, and we took Persephone and the others as prisoners. In this week, I have watched Persephone lose limbs beneath Gareth's blade, heard Thanatos's chains clatter in helpless rebellion against his friend's pain, but I have only spoken the same eight words. Uttered the same question without a sufficient answer.

A quarter-size splat of saliva hits my cheek, and Persephone hisses. "I don't know who the huntress is in the prophecy. I don't know the gods' damned singer, seeker, hero or hammer. On the gods, I am not even certain who my daughter's heart is. You can have your creature torture me for months, years, or eons. He can take my limbs. Bleed me out. Steal away all my screams. But that answer will not change."

She stares at me with anger, but I move my attention onto Gareth. There are no words that pass between us, mainly because Gareth hasn't spoken since Styx experimented on him. I could ask him to slit her throat or lop off her head, but the words scratch too painfully against my throat.

I have become a monster; one I scarcely recognize in the fleeting seconds when I deign to glance at my changing reflection. Guilt worms through my chest, scarfing away every morsel of...anything, really. Anything except hatred, which Styx pumps through my veins like the worst drug. But I still do not have the heartlessness to say any damning words for Persephone's torture. I only nod my head, and Gareth does as he wishes.

This time, when I nod in his direction, Gareth swings his scythe backwards, the tip almost hitting the ceiling light, before arching it down towards her arm. It only takes one precise movement, and the sharp blade slices through bone and flesh. Her arm, from the elbow down, falls onto the ground next to the other limbs Gareth has amputated throughout the week.

Persephone screams as her blood spurts out of the wound, but Thanatos's bellows are louder. He thrashes in his chains, the wall trembling under his might, as he tries to rush towards his queen. There will be no god as loyal as Thanatos is for Persephone. He strains against the hundred magic-restricting cuffs around his sinewy build, but he doesn't have the strength to free himself. He screams her name with raucous pain. Slowly, piece by piece, her skin stitches itself together, but that does not ease Thanatos's rage. It will be another day before the arm re-materializes, and Persephone closes her eyes with exhaustion.

Others must receive a nightly reprieve, but never Persephone. She has not slept since she woke up in this prison cell. Gareth places the blood-dripping scythe below Persephone's chin again, lifting her face in an endless loop of terror that we've played for seven days. Persephone's purple-rimmed eyes find mine again.

With the back of my hand, I wipe her spit from my cheek. To her credit, she does not flinch when I step over her severed arm and touch her. I wipe the back of my hand across her tattered gown, now soiled with both fresh and dried ichor. "Your daughter is the Savior-"

"The same daughter you tortured in this very place." Persephone pins me to the spot with her withering glare. "I should have known never to trust you again after what Saffron told me you did to her. You promised me it was for her benefit, and I stupidly believed you. It is the greatest regret of my life. Trusting you. Believing you." I drop my hand from her clothes, but I don't retreat. I stare right back.

The past repaves itself here in this prison. This is the same prison I reigned over with Phobos and Deimos. Human blood painted my lips and fingernails, and the role of the humans' villain fit me well between these walls. I've slipped into the role once again; except I no longer leer over Saffron. It's her mother who lives in agony under my watchful eye.

"Your husband trained the Seer, and your father is Zeus, but you pretend ignorance? I do not believe your falsities, and neither does my queen."

"Your queen." Persephone scoffs, finally turning her gaze away from me. "Dictators try to wear crowns, no matter how little they fit their enlarged heads."

I'm not too deeply drowned in the river of hatred; I know Persephone's words ring with undeniable truthfulness. Styx is a dictator, stealing a throne and forcing a crown upon her head, and she is the queen. The world will quake beneath her feet, begging for forgiveness for allowing any other monarch to grace their ground. But I will be an exception to her tyranny, and Mastiff will live peacefully amidst the chaos. The others may scream similarly to Persephone and Thanatos, but not the one I love most.

"Zig or Thanatos?" It is the first time I have deviated from my original question, and Persephone's blanketed fear arrives instantaneously. The chains rattle as she fights against her entrapment, and the weight of helplessness finally rests upon her shoulders.

Gareth looms over me, casting a shadow over my figure as I ask the question. The bloodied scythe drips down onto my shoulder, and it paints the most believable picture. A daemon of witchcraft, threatening to destroy everything for a single answer.

Will she sacrifice Zig's body to torment? A male who

took Charon's role as the ferryman, who has become a close ally in recent decades. He still bleeds red and still dies like a human, but he is not her dearest friend. He has not sat beside her for eons, lending a listening ear for all her worries. Zig is a closer friend to Saffron than her. Despite that, the right amount of blood stolen from his veins will kill him.

It won't kill Thanatos.

So, will she sacrifice Thanatos to the blade, who is her closest friend? They have been each other's confidants for eons. They're more like siblings. He will suffer beneath another's scythe, and it will rupture Persephone's strength. The power of sibling love, whether its biological familiarity or a role tethered through time and resilience, is a powerful thing. Perhaps it is enough to destroy Persephone once and for all.

"I have already told you, I don't know who the other members of the prophecy are!" Fear revitalizes the sleep-deprived goddess. Her chains rattle as she tries to move towards me, but I take retreating steps until Gareth and I are shoulder-to-shoulder once again.

"And I don't believe you. Thanatos or Zig?"

Persephone flinches at my question, while Gareth takes a thunderous step towards both men. They chained Thanatos and Zig onto the same wall, separated only by a furious Sika. Gareth stands next to Thanatos, but he angles himself in Zig's direction. The latter stands limply against the wall, his face gaunt with malnutrition. His cheeks have hollowed in the week since being brought to the cells, and he mirrors a skeleton more with each passing day.

Styx has ordered me to feed the humans with just enough food to survive, except Zig. The ferryman, who thwarted her attempts to see Saffron for decades, has incurred her wrath, and she wants him to suffer. His friends, like Diam and Sika, scream for reprieve for his sake. Two days ago, when she was receiving her food, Sika almost broke her wrist to free one of her hands and feed Zig her meal.

He got one bite before I intervened, and she hasn't received food since.

Persephone gives me no answer. Instead, she stares at me. After eons together, I understand her expressions well. There's hope that I will give mercy and that our past will pave this future. Sika screams threats at Gareth and me, thrashing in her chains with energy she shouldn't have in her malnourished state. She spits phlegm at both of us, spatters hitting Gareth in the face, but he doesn't react. The robotic murderer waits for further instruction, the rest of the world fading away into nothingness.

"Hasn't Zig suffered enough?" a male voice asks.

Diam does not need to scream, like Sika, to be heard. His question comes out as a growl, and power ripples from the human male. I remember his day in the arena well, despite the decades that have passed since. Diam fought Ares himself in the arena in a valiant, yet futile effort to stop the god of war from claiming a young girl who looks eerily like his wife, Hattie. Diam drew blood that day, splitting a bone in Ares's nose until his ichor spilled on the arena floor.

Many gods could not make the great Ares bleed, but in a fit of a human's rage, Diam broke his nose. I have been foolish enough to underestimate many humans, but never Diam. If I had not seen his red blood splatter the arena the same day Ares took him and the girl, then I wouldn't believe he was fully human. Something festers inside of him, and when it erupts, I do not wish to be in his vicinity.

"He hasn't eaten and can barely stand upright," Diam continues. "He can't handle torture."

I refuse to look at the raging human as I answer his plight with an emotionless. "His death means nothing to me." Persephone bites back her sobs as the weight of helplessness becomes heavier than her chains. "Choose. Zig or Thanatos."

The jail cell creaks open a second after Persephone's first tear falls. Other than Gareth and me, there is only one other deity who enters this room. I turn my entire focus onto Styx, who siphons away any fragmented warmth with her proximity. Beauty has never looked more frightening than my queen, whose feather-light movements carry an ominous echo in the suddenly silent room.

She is not alone. Two men stand on either side of her. One wears the face of a creature I never thought I'd see again, while the other is a mystery shrouded in wheat-blonde hair and cherubic features.

The male I recognize, who hasn't existed on this plane in many eons, wears the same electric blue eyes as his son and grandchildren. His lips are fuller than most women, and they wear a smile of malice, just as I remember fearing the first time I met him in the depths of Tartarus. When I freed Kronos and the titans, I purposely left him to fester down in the pit. He is the child of Chaos and the largest regret of Earth's infinite existence.

Uranus, the original ruler of the skies, has clawed his way out of his prism of darkness.

There are few I fear in this world, but Uranus is a deity who chills my blood and makes me wonder if death is preferable to his proximity. If I was not intimately aware of who the god of nightmares is, then I would have assumed Uranus bore the affinity to scare all with their greatest frights. He rarely blinks, and to avoid his probing stare, I focus on the unfamiliar male with round cheeks and unruly blonde hair.

"Who is this?"

"You and Uranus's entryway into Dionysus' house." Styx places her hand in the center of the blonde male's back, pushing him towards me. The male, barely older than twenty, yelps as he collides with my awaiting grasp. I curl my nails into his shivering shoulders as my queen orders. "Bring me the Dagger of Chains and fill it with some friends."

She turns around, but at the doorway, she pauses. As if I need a reminder of why I commit every treasonous act in her name, Styx turns around and pins me with her depthless stare. "Give me three gods within the Dagger of Chains, and you can have your human lover for the night."

The door closes behind her with a thunderous finality.

Mastiff is always just out of reach until now. I do not know who the cherubic human is, who shivers underneath my touch, but I suddenly do not care. Mastiff is finally in reach, and if I must claw through humans and gods alike to grasp him, then so be it.

My magic swirls around Uranus, the human, and I while I lock gazes with Gareth. "I miss the zig-zags that once covered the ferryman's face. Bring them back."

Gareth removes a knife from its sheath, and as I teleport away, Zig's screams follow me.

# FIVE

HERMES

After the world crumbles around us and the dead resurge, I instantly think of Epiales. Is he dead? Has the newly reanimated corpses, wielding Hecate's blades, sliced off his head? Did someone else get to bleed him dry instead of me? Right after my fight alongside Athena, Artemis, and the huntresses at the Underworld gates, I fly to Epiales.

I search for him with the sole purpose of killing him before the dead have a chance.

Rubble opens its frigid arms, inviting me to the apartment I left Epiales in as the memory-devoid Erik Oneiroi. I came here to kill him, yet a jagged chill claws down my spine when the former bricked building sandwiches together corpse after corpse. I throw off every brick, scarcely feeling the sharp edges slicing my skin and bleeding gold atop dead human after dead human. There is enough blood on the ground to bathe in, and I haven't figured out if the reason I don't want to see Epiales beneath the rubble is because I want to be the one to kill him or because I fear he is Saffron's prophesied heart.

There are no survivors in the carnage. Only crushed skulls and broken spines. Empty, glazed eyes staring at nothing. But Epiales isn't here. His corpse doesn't lie amongst the others, and I don't know if it's relief or dismay that roils my stomach, threatening to spill out all its contents. Noise surrounds me, echoing from the deteriorated streets from all the frightened and confused humans, and I don't know where my next steps should be.

How can I find him amongst all the carnage? Will there be anything to find?

Within a mile radius, I can only make out three partially intact buildings. In the hours since the dead rose and death raged havoc, only one of those buildings covers its broken ceiling with a tarp. As I walk closer to this edifice, I see that the structure isn't indicative of a former home. It was a restaurant only hours ago, now barely kept upright through sheer will, the Fates' benevolence, and threadbare maintenance.

The door is no longer connected to the fractured frame, and I easily walk into the establishment. As soon as I enter, raucous bellows surround every corner. Bodies writhe with pain as others loom over them, putting bandages on wounds. Tarps cover most of the missing pieces of the ceiling and walls, but there isn't a way to swiftly fix the foot-long cracks in the ground. Carefully, I step over the threshold and deeper into the place where survivors collect and try to persevere another day.

I find Epiales easily enough.

He is the only one in the room of destruction that has curly, raven black hair. Surprisingly, the now-human Epiales is also one of the few unscathed in the room. He leans over a woman, whose sobs echo loudest in a room of wailing victims, but he's not adding to her misery. I forever see him as a tormentor, but today he wraps bandages around the woman's arm.

The closer I prowl, I hear his soft apologies for the onslaught of pain before pouring alcohol over her wound. She screams as he stitches up the wound, but he talks to her throughout the ordeal. The monster behind my anguished past tries to console this woman, one stitch at a time.

I came here with every intention of slitting his throat until I see the bone, but then he smiles down at the woman whose life he just saved, and I begrudgingly change my mind. Instead, I watch as he jumps to another injured human and repeats his kindness. Eventually, as the night bleeds as richly as those who suffer the wounds of Styx's reign, I join him and the others in helping the injured.

I place broken arms in slings, suture slashes, and console the ones destined to die alongside the man I came to murder. There are others who are mostly unscathed, who run around the room with us to tend to the injured. Most do not spare me a second glance. I cover Caduceus well, and with human blood splattering my body, I do not appear god-like. Only one healer, a woman with dark brown skin and a chin-length hair, glances my way with a quizzical expression.

Epiales doesn't look at me, but she does. A woman who has never seen me before questions my presence. I'm certain she doesn't know most of the people in this bar, and those she helps are as much a stranger to her as I am, but she continually finds my gaze from across the room. She continually questions my presence with her doe-shaped eyes that take over most of her small, round face.

I try to avoid her gaze, even when I feel the tingle of it every few minutes, like a caress of static electricity down my spine. My focus bounces between whoever my patient is, writhing in pain, or Epiales. I wait to see the moment that his smile drops and his kindness wavers. He's been a part of my existence for eons, but I only correlate him with my time as Kronos's prisoner on Mt. Olympus. So, I watch him, and I wait to see that same monster, scars and all.

That version of him never rebirths, even as the sun peaks up from the sky.

*Tonight,* I decide. *I'll come back tonight and kill him.*

The healer woman walks towards me, a question poised on her full lips, before I leave for the day. She doesn't follow me out of the bar, and I fly back to Mt. Olympus with a promise to return the next night.

I spend the entire day, as others fret about Styx's next steps, fantasizing about how I will kill Epiales. It might be an arduous task with so many humans present, but maybe when he goes to the bathroom, I'll follow him. I'll bash his head against the concrete until puddles of brain matter and crimson blood confirm he's gone for good.

I will-

"Hermes." My name jolts me out of my reverie, and Zeus leans forward on his throne with a narrowed gaze. His elbows rest against the top of his knees as he watches me with a subtle, disappointing scowl. "Did you hear what I said?"

"Why do you ask a question when you are certain of the answer?"

Zeus ignores the sarcastic quip. "For the foreseeable future, you are banned from Mt. Olympus. You are one of the gods most familiar with the modern world, and I need you down there to keep the peace."

"The peace?" the scoff escapes my lips faster than I can retract it. "Styx stole peace. Pried it out of everyone's chest. There is only fear now."

"Fear that your presence will lessen. You're dismissed."

I'm definitely killing Epiales tonight.

Anger at Zeus's dismissal, which has been the precedence of our entire relationship, boils my blood. The rage sends me down to the bar with every intention of ripping out Epiales's spine. I do not care who sees my winged sandals and Caduceus, recognizing me as a god as I decimate someone they foolishly believe is a kind human.

I walk into the bar, or what's left of it, with my mind settled on this action. But on the second night here, I don't see him first. It's the woman, and her eyes lock on mine instantly. I cloak the wings on my sandals and Caduceus, and I walk towards her. She stands behind what's left of the bar, leaning forward on her elbows as she waits for me to take the only empty stool across from her.

I sit down, and her question comes out sharp as a whip. "Who are you?"

"Someone who needs a shot. Preferably, tequila, but I'm not picky."

"That'll cost you."

For the first time since wandering into this ruinous establishment, I look around at the other patrons. They are all survivors of this town. Men, women, and children who found the first place not completely capsized to call a temporary haven. Every other stool is occupied by one dirt-and-blood covered human after another. They do not stand up straight, but they slump like the last morsel of their energy goes towards lifting their drink for one more sip.

"I doubt anyone else paid with money."

"Everyone else stayed throughout the day, and everyone else still bathes in blood and dirt. While you, stranger, left like you had a bed to sleep in and a shower to enjoy." The woman's eyes peruse me as she pours a shot of tequila, as I requested. "You're awfully clean, given the circumstances."

That's why she kept staring at me yesterday. Nobody else noticed, but she did. I was fighting in a battle against the newly resurrected minions of Hecate, but I wasn't on Earth when everything crumbled. I had no soot on my clothes or dirt on my cheeks. Blood covered me from my hands to my toes, but that was all.

"You're observant." I slap a dozen gold drachmas on the bar.

It speaks to everyone else's exhausted state that nobody looks over. It's like they did not hear the clatter of coins, or they simply do not care.

This woman doesn't care about the money, either. Why would she? This new, destroyed world does not run on currency. She doesn't touch the drachmas or glance their way. Her gaze stays locked on mine. She keeps her distance, one hand wrapped around the shot glass.

"And you're suspicious."

"Does that mean I won't get my drink?" I counteract.

I'm certain that my challenge is the only reason she walks towards me and sets the shot glass on the table. It is a chipped glass, but I'm more surprised than anything that it is still intact. I lift the shot glass, knock it back, and bite back my grin as she scoops up the dozen coins. She doesn't give a damn about those coins, but she takes them anyway.

I like that.

"Who are you?" she asks once more.

"Someone who likes tequila."

She grabs the shot glass from my grasp, ripping it free. "Can this male who likes tequila get everyone else that fancy shower you got in the hours since you left?"

"That'll cost you." I snap, but she doesn't recoil. Whoever this woman was before the blooming war is all daggered grins and stealthy glares. A fighter without the blades.

"What about food? Can the male who likes tequila get some food?" She walks towards the bottle of tequila, pouring another shot full. "This was a dive bar before everything crumbled. We had half a dozen frozen pizzas and a few boxes of chips, but that was it." She walks back and slams the shot glass on the counter. Droplets spill out, landing on my hand as she glowers at me. "The kids already went through that."

I reach for the glass, our fingers grazing, and I stare into those doe-shaped eyes. They are a dark shade of brown, and they are endlessly beautiful. She leans in closer, her nose a ghost of a breath against mine, but she doesn't look away. She lets me see every raw emotion brewing in her hypnotic stare until I'm the first to look away.

I shoot back the drink. "Don't let anyone take my seat while I'm gone. I'll only be a minute."

"No promises."

I slide off the stool, but I choose not to leave. "What's your name?"

"You think I will answer that after you've ignored that same question twice?"

"A male can hope."

One corner of her mouth twitches, fighting back a smile. "Get us some food, and I'll tell you."

Three hours later, I bring enough food to feed the two hundred people crammed into this dive bar for the next month. I see a glimpse of curly black hair on a tall, heavily tattooed man, but I only focus on the woman at the bar. She expected me to bring in food, but her eyes still widen with disbelief at the quantity.

Everyone else runs to the food, but she stays behind the

bar. I take a seat on the same stool, where a fresh shot of tequila waits for me.

"My name is Maressa Holliday."

On the second night, I decide not to kill Epiales because I only pay attention to Maressa Holliday.

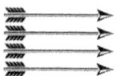

ON THE THIRD NIGHT, IT ISN'T BECAUSE OF MARESSA THAT I spare Epiales's life.

A new influx of injured humans runs into the bar, and Maressa is busy tending to their injuries and supplying food portions. Epiales helps heal them, too, with that same compassion as the first time I entered the bar, but I expect the smile this time. I choose to kill him despite the kindness because it's an act. It must be an act, because if it isn't...

Then I stole something real from Saffron.

And I don't know how to cope with that yet.

I have a plan tonight. The moment he takes a break to go to the bathroom, I will follow him. I'll break his neck and make it look like an accident. Maressa might guess that I'm behind it. She's too cunning for my own good, but losing her quick wit is a consequence I will bear.

I sit at my stool, even though there isn't a shot glass full of tequila in front of me, or a beautiful, smart-mouthed woman. The spot gives me a perfect view of Epiales, who tends to the injured nearest me. He's helping a young woman with a bone protruding out of her leg, and he distracts her with questions.

*What was your job?* She was a senior in college.

*What is your favorite dessert?* Chocolate cannoli.

"I'm single," the woman says. She stares at him with hope, even in a world this desolate. The bone protruding from her leg could get infected and kill her, but she stares at Epiales with a sense of wonderment. It looks too much like how Saffron stares at him, and my need to kill him triples. "Are you single?"

"I'm flattered. You are a beautiful woman, but I'm waiting for someone."

Until he says that.

Epiales doesn't remember Saffron, even when I am tainted with the memories of the love that I have for her. But he acts as if he does. He rejects this woman, and I know it is because of Saffron. He does not remember her, but he remembers something. The love he feels for her, maybe? The imprint of their relationship, perhaps?

"Is she lost in the rubble?" The woman asks Epiales.

He gives her a warm smile, but it isn't authentic. I've watched him enough to know the difference between his wide, full-toothed grin and this one. It's sad, his expression, but he tries to pretend her question does not rattle him.

"She is lost, or maybe I am, but I'll find her again. Until then, I must politely decline."

Before Maressa blocks my view of Epiales and the injured girl, I know I won't kill him tonight.

"Are you just going to sit there, pining after alcohol, or can you actually help?" Maressa Holliday is barely five feet tall, yet she is an imposing woman. Her hands rest on her hips, and although she must crane her neck up to see me, she doesn't stand down. "We need medicine."

"I wasn't aware that I was an infirmary. Maybe I need help too."

Her glower worsens, scrunching her small, round face. "You smell like mint and soap. If you think you need help, then you better hope you find a functional insane asylum amidst the rubble."

I can't help it, I laugh.

Gods, when was the last time I laughed?

"Give me a list of the medicine, and I'll get it done."

Maressa has a list of fifty different medications that she extends to me as soon as I agree. I raise a brow as I look over the list. "Didn't you say you were a bartender at this dive bar before everything happened? How in the gods' names do you know all these medications?"

"Does it matter?"

"Yes. Consider it my payment for the medicine." Curiosity prickles me, and that is a rare feeling. I'm the cunning god, known for deciphering secrets as efficiently as I weave them, but Maressa only displays two expressions: anger and annoyance. Neither one tells me how she's a bartender who knows medicine.

That readable scrunch of annoyance brings a crease between her brows. "I like to read about the world, and I'll pick up any book about any topic. Books are a pleasant escape from reality, and I spend all my time within different stories, learning about different things. I figured when I found a college book about pharmaceutical drugs that it would come in handy one day. Turns out I was right."

"I'll be back soon."

I almost leave, but I pause when I notice the college girl hitting on Epiales. He doesn't know how to put the bone back in her leg, or how to help her, and his hesitation shows from across the room. The selfish part of me, which screams loudest in my ears, wants him to suffer. Yet, that tiny part of me that fell in love with humanity throughout my relationship with Saffron makes me walk over to them. I lean down on the girl's other side, and I place a hand on top of her forehead. The other goes to her leg.

"This will hurt," I tell her. "But then you are going to feel a lot better."

With my hand on her forehead, I imbue healing properties. Not enough to announce me as a god, but enough to give her a chance to survive. I glare up at Epiales, but he doesn't balk at the clear rage I cast his way.

"How can I help?" He asks, his voice sickly sweet.

I instruct him on what to do. We work together to set her bone and wrap it in a temporary cast of duct tape and a piece of wood. Internally, I add more items to Maressa's list. I don't remove my hand from her forehead until her screams lessen, and I feel the bone fitting back together.

"Thank you," Epiales says.

*I hate you;* I want to say back.

Without another word, I leave. An hour later, I return with everything on Maressa's list, a few extra items, and a bottle of tequila.

ON THE FOURTH NIGHT, I LIE TO MYSELF AS I WALK INTO the bar. I tell myself that I'm here to kill Epiales, but I don't search him out when I enter. My stool is empty, and Maressa is already pouring a shot glass full of tequila.

I tell myself the same lie on the fifth, the sixth, and the seventh night. I swear to all the gods that I will finally end Epiales's life, but on the seventh night I realize Epiales might be dead. Erik Oneiroi is the male who stays in this bar with other survivors, smiling and laughing and helping people. I still want to break his neck, but on the seventh night, as I sit at the same stool and laugh for the millionth time, I want to spend time with Maressa a bit more than I want to kill him. That's why I will not kill him.

"Are you ever going to tell me your name?" Maressa leans against the counter, casually eating a bag of chips and biting back a smile. She's been doing that more lately, smiling in my company. The sight sends a zap of electricity straight into my brain.

"You get three guesses."

"Just three?" That gorgeous smile widens. "There are billions of names, and you expect me to get it right with only three guesses?"

"You're smart. I have faith you can figure it out."

"Hm." She contemplates as she pops another chip in her mouth. I can see every gear turning in her mind, trying to solve a riddle with no clues. Almost a minute passes as she concludes. "Frederick."

I let out a roar of laughter. "Do I look like a Frederick? I'm insulted."

"Frederick is a popular male's name!" She outcries, offended.

"Maybe in the early 1900s before the second Titanomachy War."

She tries to smother her laugh with another chip. "You don't like the name Frederick, got it. What about Rufus?"

"That's worse!"

"Maybe I should just call you Rufus until it drives you so insane that you finally give me your real name."

"That is-"

The words die on my lips, along with the laughter. The bar's doors slam open, rattling the walls; extinguishing all the noise. Around two hundred people call this bar their haven, and none of them speak. They barely breathe.

I turn around on my stool, my hand curling around Caduceus holstered on my hip. Seven men and one woman stand in the doorway, all brandishing the darkest green-misted weapons. The man in the middle has an eyepatch covering one eye. A long, curved sword rests in his hand. It hosts the same obsidian green mist as his accomplices' weapons, but his blade is slick with red blood. The blood drips from the tip and is the only sound in this room.

*Drop.*

*Drop.*

*Drop.*

The others have axes, swords, and spears, but Eyepatch is in charge. Acne scars cover most of his face, and he is so thin that his shoulder bones poke from his blood-drenched shirt. This human, who I recognize from the pits of the Fields of Punishment, is not here for food; he hungers only for blood.

Epiales- sorry, Erik Oneiroi- takes a step forward. Others cower, but he stands in front of the human. Yesterday, I brought weapons for everyone, and Erik's hand wraps around the handle of his sword. I almost didn't give him a weapon. I almost told Maressa that he is the worst villain of them all and exiling him is a better option than brandishing him with a sword, but I hesitate. Instead of admitting the gruesome truth of Erik Oneiroi, I let him play the hero a little while longer.

"You need to leave. *Now.*" Erik Oneiroi's voice booms with authority, sounding too similar to his former godly state.

"Aww, don't be like that." Eyepatch walks towards Erik until they are chest-to-chest, grinning wolfishly at the challenge in front of him. "I thought this was a place of protection, and I'm starving."

Erik moves to take out his sword, but he's too slow. I came here with a rational plan: Epiales must die. It will be so easy to let the events unfurl in front of me. Eyepatch is faster and quickly unsheathes his sword. He swings his weapon with quick efficiency towards Erik's neck, and it will kill him. Epiales will finally die, and I won't wear the blame like a sash across my chest.

Saffron could forgive me. She could finally see that Epiales is not the one for her, but I….

Am I?

I look at Maressa for a moment, just one flickering second, and I register the fear across her face. She screams out one name, "Erik!" and I make my decision.

I unsheathe Caduceus, and I let my wings erupt from my sandals. Faster than the blink of an eye, I push Erik Oneiroi to the ground, and my weapon meets Eyepatch's blade. I can feel Maressa's stare on me, like a thousand bolts of lightning, but I focus solely on my opponent. A smirk pulls over my lips as I look at the pirate who recognizes me, almost instantly, from his days in the Fields of Punishment.

From when I took his soul to the Underworld the first time he died.

"Lord Hermes." Eyepatch, and another very feminine voice, say the words at the same time.

I don't look back at Maressa, but I say. "I knew you'd get it right on the third try."

# SIX

SAFFRON

A week has passed since the Underworld erupted, and all its once-dead inhabitants reacquainted themselves with the world of the living. In these seven days, I have understood all too well the games played at the humans' expenses. The webs the gods weave bleed crimson. And I am one of them, a god that strums the strings of misery.

On the first day, nothing but melancholy battles surround us. I kill more humans in this single night than I ever have before, and each bone I pull from their flesh tears something out of me, too. With each murder, I remind myself that I'm only killing the corrupt. There were so many destructive souls in the Underworld, and now many wield green-misted weapons against the inno-cent. I end their lives forever with such ease, destroying them so thoroughly that their faces are no longer recogniz-able, but I do it to protect the benevolent who scream for a hero. Yet, by the end of the first night in a newly destroyed world, I stare at my blood-soaked appearance and only see a monster.

The power that thrums through my veins is a gift from the Fates and my lineage, but it is also a curse. On this first night, I do nothing else but murder and mourn. Hattie helps me wipe away the carnage, but it seeps into my skin. I look at my reflection; I see the destruction on an unmarred face.

ON THE SECOND DAY, I PREPARE MYSELF FOR ANOTHER miserable day on the new battlegrounds, desecrating every square inch of the world. I'm one step out of my house of bones when Iris and the huntresses find us. Their clothes are as bathed in blood as mine were the night before, but their haggard appearances do not draw my primary attention. First, it is my daughter, Jamila, who smiles proudly at me. Although she is just as bathed in blood as the other huntresses, I have never seen her happier than beside Artemis.

I run to her, and although the cloying scent of copper invades my nostrils, I clasp her in a tight hug. She lays her head in the crook of my neck, squeezing me with the same vigor. "I'm so proud of you," I murmur against a kiss in her hair.

She pulls away, still smiling. "Sorry for the mess. We had a long night, and then this morning, King Zeus called for us and…"

"He has orders for you." The second person to draw my attention is Iris, who is the only one not covered in carnage. She holds a pristine white, rolled up parchment with Zeus's seal stamped in the middle.

I drop my arms from Jamila, but she takes my hand with a sense of comfort that tells me they all know what Zeus's orders are. "I'm not reading it. Just tell me." There's a pause, then I add. "Please."

Behind me, Hattie, Apollo, Ares, Phobos, and Deimos stand ready for another day of fighting for the humans. I never bother to ask Apollo where Hart is within this new house. All that matters is seeking peace. I want this war to end, and I want this to be achieved as peacefully as possible, but my aspirations seem to be an insurmountable mountain that continues to grow taller by the minute.

The room is deathly silent as Iris breaks the seal and unrolls the scroll with Zeus's royal demands. Iris doesn't need to look down at the scroll to know what it says, but she stares anyway. It is to avoid my gaze, I realize, which sends a sinking feeling to the pit of my stomach.

"He's forcing me back to Mt. Olympus, isn't he?"

"No," Iris says. "He's forcing you to stay inside the house and wait for further orders."

"Stay in my house of bones? As innocent humans beg for me to save their lives?" My voice cracks at the end. "He won't let me leave?"

The screams are less audible than the night before, but they come from every direction. I killed hundreds of Hecate's newly re-animated corpses the night before, but there are still thousands or millions of others following her command.

"The undead aren't the only escapees from the Under-world. Hecate freed every occupant from Tartarus, too." Iris stiffens as her words register, and every god surrounding me mimics her.

"Uranus." The name is a curse upon Ares's lips.

Epiales told me that my nightmare on the eve of his death was with Uranus. The original ruler of the skies is so malevolent that other deities deemed Kronos kind in comparison. Kronos, who started the world's enslavement of humanity almost six hundred years ago. The same Kronos who I killed after he manipulated me and so many others to fall prey to his whim. That Kronos is benevolent compared to his ruthless father, Uranus, who now stands beside Styx.

"You are all forbidden from returning to Mt. Olympus or leaving these walls until he says otherwise." Iris wanders her gaze to those behind me.

"And if we defy him?" Ares asks as he steps forward, so we are shoulder-to-shoulder. "Do you not hear the humans right now? They're dying faster than ever before. Faster than when we ruled over them with an iron fist. Faster than the war with Kronos that almost wiped them from existence. They're dying and we're supposed to just sit, listen, and accept it?"

"Why do you care?" The sound is quiet, almost imperceptible, but we all hear Hattie.

Almost as quiet as her, Ares responds. "Because this time, my mind is my own. This time, I'm trying to be better than my past actions. I am the god of bloodshed and war, but even this is too much."

He did not tell many, but in the times of human enslavement, Morpheus wormed into his mind. Morpheus stole Ares's sanity, one dream at a time. One stolen night of sleep at a time. Ares remembers some days when he was especially cruel, but he forgot most in his maelstrom of paranoia and carnage. Now, the god of bloodshed hates his own moniker because of the blood he spilled through the agony of so many humans.

Most dastardly, the murder of Hattie's sister in a blind act of insanity.

He turns to face Hattie, and he opens his mouth, but

no words escape. I know what he wants to say, though. He recognizes Hattie's sister within her, and he knows the source of Hattie's rage. An apology tries to worm itself out of his throat, but there is a gaping silence fueled by fear and uncertainty.

Hattie scoffs, looking away from him and facing Iris once more. "So, what is the consequence of defying Zeus? A lightning bolt-sized scolding?"

"Zeus wants to only protect his favorite children." Shikari, one of Artemis's more vocal huntresses, chimes in with a rueful sneer of her lips. "The scroll says that we are his shields once more."

"Shikari," Jamila hisses the huntress's name between clenched teeth.

Shikari rolls her eyes, but silences.

"What is she talking about, Jamila?" I ask, but there is no immediate response.

There's silence as Hart walks into the room, holding three drawings. While I cannot see the bottom two, the top drawing is of a male with a scar that starts at the top of his forehead and stops by his chin. Hart barely glances at Apollo or me as she breaks through the tension and presents the drawings to Artemis.

Artemis accepts.

"You can't leave the house," Jamila says. "But King Zeus ordered us to find whoever Hart draws and kill them. He says it's essential that they die before the last battle."

"But I can't leave?" I don't ask Iris, who holds the scroll with Zeus's decree, but I whirl on Hart.

It feels like eons ago when Hart was that paint-splattered girl who stumbled nervously into my office. Something ancient about her has taken over, and I know these are her orders written in Zeus's scraggly letters.

"Why? I cannot die, and I'm stronger than all of

them." I don't spew my strength as a gloating matter; It is a fact that nobody can dispute. "Why should they risk their lives when I'm right here?!"

Hart looks at me, and there is an absence of the innocence I used to see in her. Instead, she stares with an immortal dullness, like she has suffered a thousand lives. She is the second youngest in this room, other than Jamila. Yet, she stares like she is a thousand souls crammed in one body.

"All stories begin and end on different pages. Theirs begins now, and yours when the rivers bleed red."

"That doesn't make any gods-damned sense." Ares says for me.

Hart focuses back on Artemis. "You have today to bathe and rest, then you must leave in the morning."

"μέλι." Apollo reaches for his soulmate, trying to grasp her, but she's more like the wind than anything real.

"I have too much work to complete," is all she says as she leaves as enigmatically as she entered.

Her newly assigned room on the second-floor closes with a soft click of the door.

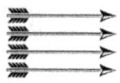

ON THE THIRD DAY, JAMILA AND THE OTHER HUNTRESSES leave, and I wish I could tell her to stay. I wish I could protect her a little while longer, but this oncoming war is not one I control. Hart and Styx are the strings behind it all, tugging the ends in hopes it falls in their favor, and I'm only collateral in a war against the seer and the goddess of hatred.

There's nothing but melancholy thoughts on this day. Hattie doesn't elevate the mood with jovial antics, and Ares avoids her presence, and therefore mine, for the rest of the day.

And the fourth, fifth, sixth day.

Now, a week after the war began, I am a prisoner in a home I built through grief and decay. My windows do not have bars, but they feel as if they do, caging me in once more. Almost a million times a day, I must stop myself from storming out of these doors and disobeying Zeus and Hart.

Each day, I stand atop the staircase, staring at the front door, and each day Apollo guides me back to my room. I know he does not agree with Hart, but he follows her decisions with certainty that she is right. He reminds me that the screams will eventually end, but the thought doesn't comfort me. The screams will only end when death claims their souls, and no souls are returning to the Underworld. They escape bodies in white orbs that travel somewhere nobody can find.

Only Iris's daily visits tether me to sanity, so I do not spiral in the feelings of inadequacy as the screams outside grow louder and louder. She informs me of what occurs outside these walls, confirming some truths while revealing new mysteries.

I assumed correctly that all those chained within the Fields of Punishments escaped their captivity with Hecate's help and now stand dutifully at her side. The worst monsters within humanity wield weapons and murderous intent for those who imprisoned them to the worst immortal punishment. The Olympians, and all who follow them, are victims of the monsters who were once prisoners in the Fields of Punishment.

Those humans are the ones Hart draws and gives to Iris during her visits. There are always three portraits, drawn with eerie accuracy, and they all belong to the worst humans to wander the world across the eons.

Hecate did not free only the evil souls. Most occupants in the Underworld wandered aimlessly without recollection of their mortal lives, and they fluttered onto an earth most do not recognize. Iris informs me that their memories come back, little by little, each day they are on Earth. That is, if they survive long enough to get their memory back.

Mania takes the siege of many reanimated humans, especially those who lived in the time of human enslavement. Many of the revived humans carve into their own bodies, giving themselves another scarification mark. The huntresses mercy-kill whoever is so far distorted from reality that they mutilate any human they find without a scarification mark. Other humans have searched for the gods responsible for their deaths in a bloodthirsty desire for revenge. And a rare few act like the gods who enslaved them by murdering in the name of their masters.

The Underworld is empty, all except for its sorrowful king who waits for souls that will never arrive at his gates. My father sits on his decaying throne and waits for humans to enter. Mostly, he waits for his missing wife, and with each day that passes, he grows more and more sullen. I've asked if I could see him every day when Iris comes to the house, and each day Iris gives me a sorrowful expression before answering the same.

"You still can't leave the house. It's King Zeus's orders."

We all know it is Hart's orders, but she plays the king like a puppet. They won't even let Hades leave the Underworld, but I doubt he'd leave even with permission. Every day, right after Hart gives Iris the portraits, and she leaves, I demand answers that never come. Each day, she says the same vague line.

"It's not time for you yet."

Every night, Hattie joins me in my room with snacks. Cerberus always lies on the foot of my bed, waiting for the treats Hattie brings him. We share stories of the past, too. Sometimes, it's tales surrounding Diam or their children together, but most of the time, she avoids mentioning her children who are wandering somewhere in this new, daunting world. Or Diam, who let himself be captured in exchange for her freedom. Just as I am forbidden from leaving this house, so is everyone else under this roof. Hattie distracts herself from her fears with memories, and I accept a sliver of distraction.

Tonight, she sits in my bed with a bowl of sugared strawberries between us, but Hattie doesn't smile. She stares at the bowl like it can swallow her whole. "I never thanked you for what you did for me in my first life."

She means when I killed her.

We have avoided this conversation for a week now, but it's here with gnarling fangs. It was one of the worst days of my life, ending hers. I can still feel it, see it darkening the tips of my fingers like a disease rotting them away. I know I gave her peace, but in exchange, I sacrificed any fragment of solace within me. For years, I didn't smile. Didn't truly live because when night fell, I still heard her bone piercing her heart.

A bone I commanded to move to a fatal location.

"You would've done the same for me if I could actually die." I shrug with nonchalance, like that day still doesn't traumatize me.

It was naïve, but before that day, I never expected to live in a world without Hattie. She isn't just my best friend, but she is more of a sister than anyone I share paternal lineage with. She gave me her strength when I had none, and when she died, I didn't think I could survive it.

I did, just barely.

"And I'm sorry."

"Sorry?" I look at her, even though her focus remains solely on the bowl. "Why are you sorry?"

"Because I couldn't have done it if you asked. There's no way I could have killed you, mercy or otherwise, without guilt swallowing me whole, but I still made you save me in the worst possible way. I was so scared of forgetting everything about myself again, and I was so selfish." Tears drop into the bowl of strawberries and she hiccups. "I'm sorry for making you do that."

She holds the bowl with a white-knuckled grip until I place my hand on hers. I intertwine our fingers, squeezing them the same way I did many years ago in the closet in the Underworld, when we thought we waited for our deaths. "Haven't you realized that I'll do anything for you?"

Hattie finally looks up at me, and her eyes are bright with tears. "I would do anything for you too, Saf, just not that. There's not a world where I could live without both of my sisters." She squeezes my hand and cracks the tiniest smile. "Except deal with the two dumbest gods in existence. That's asking too much of me."

Phobos and Deimos stand on either side of my bedroom door. In the week since Zeus ordered us to stay here, Ares has avoided me while demanding that his sons never leave my side. They are always on guard, waiting for the ceiling to crumble atop us. The first few days were only slightly unbearable with those two, but each hour, they get progressively dumber. Hattie started calling them Brain Cell One and Brain Cell Two because that's all they have collectively.

They hear Hattie's comment and Phobos spins his head to glower at her. "We can hear you."

"Good, I was hoping I insulted you loud enough."

I laugh louder than I have since she was alive the first time. She looks at me, her grin growing wider by the second, and soon she joins me in the humor. For the rest of the night, we ridicule Phobos and Deimos and entertain ourselves until we fall asleep.

# SEVEN

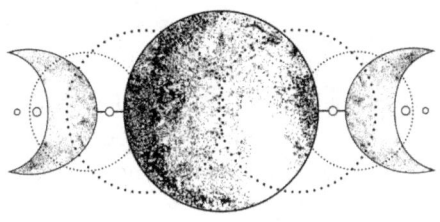

## HECATE

Zeus swears to the heavens and all the immortals who will listen that he is the rightful ruler of Mt. Olympus. It is his birthright to be on the throne as the other gods bend their knees, yet he does not guard his land the way a king should. It is too easy to transport Uranus, the frightened human, and me to Mt. Olympus. We land upon the ground of clouds without a rush of guards stopping us. There are no bolts of lightning threatening to smite us down, or a rueful Saffron with her hands up in demand of our bones.

Mt. Olympus is quiet at night, not suspiciously so, but with a veil of misplaced peace. Faintly, I can make out the hushed voices of gods in their homes, believing they will fall asleep tonight and awaken to another harmonious day. There's laughter coming from one dimly lit building, and as Styx's hatred trails dark veins through my skin, I thirst to silence that gleeful sound.

I teleported us right in front of Dionysus's home, where the sound of giggling females accompanies his instantly recognizable, bellied chortle. Uranus grins ferally at me, then at the boy beneath my sharp, blood-drenched nails. I lay my hand atop his shoulder as a gentle warning that he must complete his job, or else.

"Let's break a god's heart. Shall we?" the primordial being says with glee.

The wheat-haired boy flinches at Uranus's cruelty, but when I give him a tame push towards the door, he stumbles dutifully forward. There is a moment of hesitation as he lifts his knuckles towards the door, but as Uranus and I slink into the shadows for the moment to strike, the human knocks.

Dionysus's voice breaks through in a joking cadence on the other side of the door. "Dear Ariadne, is that you? Excuse me, lovelies." Women giggle almost on command, and he adds. "Ariadne, you are a goddess. How is it you still need help to open doors?"

The door swings open to a smiling, yet slightly inebriated Dionysus.

I do not know who this human is, but I'm certain he promises the breakage of one godly heart. Dionysus cannot see me, but from my angle, I notice the exact moment recognition enlightens his face. I have known Dionysus for eons, with a charming smile that hides any genuine emotions, but today, his joyful relief is as clear as the cloudless night sky.

The Fates gift everyone, humans and gods alike, with three great loves. The first love is based on passion that threatens to incinerate you. Mine was Hermes, who shared arguments and the greatest blights of ardor I have ever experienced, but we doomed ourselves from the moment our eyes locked. Passion cannot solely drive a relationship.

The second love is more of a friendship that tries to bloom into something more, but it is nothing more than a falsity. There is love, but not the kind that takes your heart and makes it tug. My first husband, who I grew to hate with such fervor, was that second love.

But then the third love is the truest one. The Fates' given soulmate, who has an extension of your heart within their own. Mastiff is that soulmate for me, and as Dionysus's face grows into the most genuine smile, I am certain this wheat-haired, trembling boy is Dionysus's soulmate. I never knew it was possible to deceive your own soulmate for the sake of surviving another day, but Dionysus breathes out a single word like a prayer.

"Claudius."

And Claudius enters the home with every intention of imprisoning his soulmate.

In Dionysus's disbelief, the door remains ajar. Uranus looks at me, his feral grin never wavering, but I do not spare him a glance. I slink towards the entrance, just as two scantily clad nymphs rush out. The females do not notice us, too absorbed in their wounded pride at Dionysus's quick rejection.

Uranus leans against the doorway on the right. Dionysus is oblivious to his surroundings. His focus solely lands on Claudius. His back is to us, and his hands thread into Claudius's hair. They fall into a kiss that speaks of their eons apart. Claudius, for a moment, forgets that he is betraying Dionysus for our benefit, and he kisses him back with the same fervor. I sneak into Dionysus's house, gaze flickering between them and the glass case holding the Dagger of Chains.

"Claudie," Dionysus breathes the nickname against Claudius's lips. "It hasn't been the same without you. Every day, I have missed you. Every day, I have mourned you."

Claudius pulls their mouths together again, ending

their words as I carefully lift the glass casing. The Dagger of Chains' immense power roils off the dagger in steady waves, beckoning me to prick my skin and invite myself to its prism. It's a sumptuous thought, escaping this declining war and falling into the dagger's prison, but I accepted my role as a villain a long while ago.

I wrap my hand around the handle, and with Dionysus's side profile in clear view, I throw the dagger. Claudius sees the spinning blade before Dionysus, and he pulls away from the kiss. They stay close, and in the precarious seconds before Dionysus is gone from this realm, Claudius places his hands on either side of Dionysus's face and utters one word.

"Sorry."

Confusion crinkles Dionysus's brows before the dagger sinks between his shoulder blades, and clarity quickly widens his eyes. There's a moment when he recognizes Uranus's relaxed frame against the open door, feels the sharp twang of the dagger in his shoulder blades, and sees Claudius's crestfallen expression.

"Why?" is all he can ask before the Dagger of Chains sucks Dionysus inside.

Claudius collapses to his knees, audibly sobbing at the loss he contributed to. The dagger clatters to the floor. I stroll towards the inconsolable human, plucking the dagger from the ground.

"We need to deliver the dagger to Queen Styx."

"Not yet." Uranus kicks himself off the doorframe, eyeing the dagger with merciless intrigue. "There's one queen I want to see first."

"But-" I say.

Uranus cuts me off. "Remember, little witch, Styx wants three gods in this dagger before you can see your human."

When I first aided Styx in freeing Kronos from Tartarus, I used every scrap of my magic to keep Uranus tethered to the prison while the others escaped. Even then, I knew that while Kronos was a malicious force; he was tame compared to his father. Uranus is a sociopath, enlivened only by malice and bloodshed.

But he's right.

"Fine. Who are we seeing first?"

"I heard that many of the gods do not share a resemblance to my wife and I, except for the current queen of the Olympians. Hera is regaled as Gaia's mirror, and I would love to see any visage of my wife *destroyed*." He snarls the last word, the feral grin dying for a flickering second to give way to rage, then it returns as big as ever. "Be right back."

He blinks, and he's gone.

Uranus was so feared in his time as the original king of the skies that his own wife and mother, Gaia, orchestrated his demise. Uranus understood the power of children, and he was the first primordial being who feared what his offspring could do to his reign. Every pregnancy was predestined for failure. Uranus, while she was in childbirth, shoved the babies back into her body, refusing them freedom from her womb. This form of torment caused the titan children and their mother excruciating pain, so Gaia worked with one of her sons, Kronos, to defeat Uranus.

Kronos, while in the womb, received a blade, and he castrated his father the moment Uranus approached his wife in the marital bed. Infamously, his castrated appendage fell into the ocean and formed Aphrodite, but Kronos threw the rest of his body into Tartarus as its first prisoner.

Saffron stole Uranus's chance to kill Kronos and receive justice for his castration, and Gaia is too powerful and too well hidden for Uranus to seek retribution. So, when Uranus materializes back into Dionysus's house with three women from Hera's past, I understand his motives. His dark eyes illuminating with a form of anger only associated with vengeance.

"Lead the way, little witch."

# EIGHT

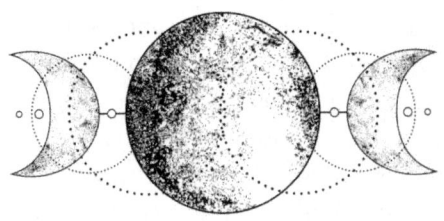

## HECATE

This isn't a wise idea.

No part of Styx's orders includes Hera's torment at the hands of women she scorned eons ago, but my once rational mind isn't present.

Semele, Dionysus's mother, stands nearest Uranus.

Any newly reincarnated soul who escaped from the Underworld through aligning with us shows the lingering appearance of their moment of death. I recognize Semele by the clumps of her hair that have grown back, but she's not fully human. Her once golden blonde hair, which she passed onto Dionysus, is matted atop her skull. Her purple eyes have returned, so she doesn't stare with empty sockets, but most of the skin on her face hasn't healed. She's more charred bones and muscle than flesh. Still, I can see the snarl where her lips should be, as she considers inciting vengeance against Hera.

Long ago, Hera saw the godly son that Semele bore with Zeus, and she vowed for the mistress's death. She told

Semele about the beauty of Zeus's true godly form. She polluted Semele's mind until all she wanted to see was Zeus's godly form, and after much convincing, Zeus agreed. It was foolish of the king to agree to Semele's delirious request, but he did, knowing the sight of a god's true form was death for any human.

Semele still smells of ash thousands of years later.

On Semele's other side, there stands Echo.

When she was human and alive the first time, she was a notorious gossip. Echo did not have an affair with Zeus like Semele, but she did aid Zeus and a nymph in their illicit rendezvous. Hera asked Echo for Zeus's whereabouts, and she lied to the powerful goddess. Eventually, Hera learned about Zeus's affair with the nymph, but the nymph was not the only woman who suffered her wrath for this indiscretion.

She decided that Echo's name would inspire her punishment. Echo could no longer speak lies or unfamiliar words; Hera forced her to only echo the words of those around her. She forfeited her autonomy the moment she lied to Hera, and she spent the rest of her mortal life hiding in a cave, hoping nobody would find her. Eventually, she died of dehydration.

Echo's skin has grown back faster than Semele's, but it is a dark gray, inhuman shade that sags against sharp bones. While she appears more alive than Semele, her appearance is daunting. Her mess of red curls hangs over a gaunt face and rows of black teeth. She stares at me with eyes devoid of anything and repeats Uranus's last words.

"Lead the way, little witch."

Last, and far from the others, stands Lamia.

After Hera's particularly cruel punishment against Lamia, Zeus's extramarital affairs diminished, fearing her retribution. Not even Aphrodite would get near Zeus for decades in fear of Hera because, compared to Lamia, Semele and Echo received light punishments. Lamia had never died in the thousands of years since Hera cursed her. Monsters do not live mortal lives, they suffer until a hero slays them, and even then, they might come back once again to live out their torment.

Lamia was one of Zeus's most beautiful mistresses. Artists painted her gorgeousness, which incited a level of jealousy within Hera that unrivaled any lover before her. From the first rumor of Lamia's affair with Zeus, a new form of rage overtook Hera. She vowed to give Lamia a punishment more severe than death itself.

Throughout their years-long affair, Lamia gave birth to three children, and Hera stole them from her. It is unknown what happened to these demi-god children, but considering how many times Hera tried to kill a baby Heracles and a baby Saffron, most of us gods assume Hera killed Lamia's children. These losses turned Lamia mad, and she clawed out her own eyes. In this fit of madness, she begged Zeus for death.

Hera heard the prayer first.

Instead of death, where she would have an afterlife to spend with her children, Hera gave Lamia a brutal deformity. Lamia was once a Libyan queen, but after Hera's wrath, she became a vicious creature. A ten-foot-long serpent's tail replaced her long legs. Her white teeth fell from her mouth, and in their place came razor sharp canines that feasted only on children's flesh. Streaks of scales slashed her once beautiful face, and the eyeless monster roamed the earth for thousands of years. She only thirsts for children's deaths, which reminds her of her own slain kin, and it spirals her further into her fit of insanity.

It's the cruelest cycle, and seeing these women once again reminds me why I loathe the gods so ardently. We are all cruel monsters, wearing the faces of heroes. We feast and laugh as humans cry and crumble, and we deliver the worst of their torments. It is our magic that blackens their fates, and it is our blades that slice the deepest into their flesh. I may hate myself and the acts I do in the name of desperate love, but I hate the other gods more. Just a little more, but enough to glower at Uranus and snap my fingers.

I transport us in plumes of smoke to Hera's home in Mt. Olympus. She sits on her bed, wearing a simple purple nightgown. Perched on her lap is an open book. Unlike Dionysus, Hera notices our arrival instantly, but she doesn't immediately look up from her book. The queen waits until she finishes her page, then calmly closes it and glances at us.

She darts her attention to me first, where the Dagger of Chains rests bloodied in my tight grasp, but she doesn't dawdle on the sight. Instead, she peruses over the faces of the women she's scorned throughout the eons, before leveling on Uranus.

"Grandfather." Hera calmly sets her closed book on the empty side of her bed, then slides out of the covers. Her feet plant on the ground, eyes never wandering from where he stands and simmers with barely kept rage. "I heard the vermin released you from your cage. You look a lot like the son that cut off your-"

"You killed me." Semele steps forward, weaponless but fueled solely by eons' worth of rage. "You bitch."

"Technically, my dear husband ended your life. It isn't my fault that you were dim-witted enough to listen to my advice. Really, dear Semele, why would you listen to your lover's wife's claims? That was hardly wise."

Uranus unsheathes a curved sword from its holster. His silver eyes dance with ruthless mirth as they lock on Hera. "It is such a shame that we have to deprive the world of your beauty."

Quickly, Hera's attention jumps back to the dagger in my hand, and the song of its imprisonment that she's heard once before. She takes a step backward, her calves hitting her bedside table, but there is nowhere else for her to turn. Hera has never been an expert fighter. Uranus prowls towards her with the same grace as a panther nearing its prey. She blindly opens the drawer behind her and removes a small, foot-long dagger with a peacock-styled handle.

She points the dagger at Uranus. "Not a step more."

Uranus doesn't obey. The other women and I stand back, but Uranus prowls closer with a slow, yet lethal precision. He hasn't yet asked for the Dagger of Chains or opened his hand in invitation. He's playing with his meal first, testing how far he can push her before she ruptures.

"I could save you from the Dagger of Chains and tell Styx that you devoted yourself to me."

He doesn't stop moving until their bodies are nearly flush against each other. There is just one foot between Hera and Uranus, separated only by the tip of her dagger, that she presses against his stomach. Hera cranes her neck upwards to stare at the imposing deity, seeing her demise in his eyes. Uranus has one hand on his sword, which rests against his hip, but the other reaches for her chin. She barely flinches as he grabs it and leans down to her. Their noses brush one another's, but Hera never baulks.

She only glowers like her eyes alone can deliver death.

"You could be mine," he muses. "My betrothed, and eventually my wife, once we dispose of your current, useless spouse." Almost tenderly, he runs his thumb across her bottom lip, vexed by her beauty. A beauty that reminds him so much of his first wife, without the torrid past severing them. "No harm would come to you, and I'd be faithful. Isn't that what you've always wanted? Faithfulness in a marriage? A god who will worship you?" There's a pause as he lets her taste the words, like the first sip of aged wine, then he tenderly whispers. "I can be that."

This time, she flinches.

Not at his touch, as his hand on her waist becomes more possessive, but his words hold a daggered tone. It punctures every vital organ. All Hera has ever wanted was a loyal husband. An actual marriage. She is the goddess of marriage, and yet hers is the most false. Uranus promises her a version of a future she might prefer. She will lose the diadem from her head, but she might gain more.

If she' chose Uranus, Hera would gain a faithful marriage and safety in a world run by Styx. She would avoid persecution and eventual death when Styx wins the war, while the rest of the Olympians would die. Perhaps best of all, Hera would finally watch her adulterous husband's demise.

Uranus is an attractive male. He looks so much like his son, Kronos, with golden locks and eyes of blinding blue. Slight stubble caresses his sharp jaw, and when he smiles at Hera, it almost appears genuine.

"And what would you have me do in exchange?" Hera asks, voice softer than I have ever heard before.

"Only names." He still caresses her, guiding his thumb in gentle circles around her waist. "Tell me who the heart, the hammer, the singer, the seeker, the hero, and the huntress are, and I am yours forever. Your protector, your faithful husband, forever."

The women beside me, who have been scorned by

Hera's rage, remain eerily silent. They watch the exchange with quiet, contemplative expressions like me. I stand to the side, a silent observer to the manipulation Uranus spills from his lips. Curiosity prickles the back of my neck because earlier, Uranus vocalized a desire for revenge, but now he acts like a reverent lover. I watch without interruption because I have never been a victim of Hera's anger, but why can the other women?

Lamia is a monster because of Hera, Echo cannot speak her own words because of Hera, and Semele never got the chance to watch her son become an Olympian because of Hera; yet they all watch without argument.

Hera reaches up a hand and places it atop his, which cradles her face. "It is no secret that I am unhappy. Each morning, I wake only to watch another god leave my husband's room with ruffled hair and wrinkled clothing. Each day, I talk to my husband and hope he will finally look at me with the same reverence as his lovers. But each night I come back to my room, which becomes more and more empty. I have a void in my heart where love should be, and I wait for him to finally acknowledge me. Finally, love me. Instead, I go to bed and watch another walk into his room. Instead of receiving his love, which is all I have ever truly wanted, I hear him love another through the walls, which are regrettably too thin. My love, as distorted and grotesque as it is, stops me from taking out this anger and defeatism on him. So, it's his bastard children I harm. It's the men and women who enter his bedroom instead of me, who I harm."

Hera's attention deviates from Uranus, who never looks away from her, and she stares at the three women around me. She guards her emotions, building a wall over her features, so I cannot gauge her feelings. I do not know if she regrets her actions against these women, and by the visible confusion on the women's faces, they are equally perplexed.

She finally looks back at Uranus. "I never faulted Athena for being her father's favorite. She was born before I was his wife, but I hated the others who were born after my children. Most of all, I hated Heracles and Saffron. I thought that if I could not be my husband's great love, then at least I could be the mother of his most powerful children. Maybe if I gave Zeus the strongest god and goddess, then he would only love me."

The last words come out like cracked glass.

"I wanted both to suffer more than anyone else in this world. For the longest time, I thought the only way I could reach peace was if they both suffered so much pain that they'd beg to escape their immortality. I almost ruined Heracles once. Many eons ago, I had him writhing in agony, but when his mortal flesh burned off, he became a god. Worse, he married my daughter, Hebe. Fate forced me to realize that as long as he lived, my daughter would be happy. So, I buried my anger and need for his suffering for her."

"I can make Saffron suffer for you," Uranus makes the prettiest promise that makes a slow, wide smile grow on Hera's lips. "Tell me who her heart is, and I'll make sure they die. I'll do it for you. Just tell me their name."

"If you made that promise to me a few decades ago, then I would have given you the world. I would tell you every name you would want to hear, but the Fates are especially cruel to my rage. I gave Zeus three children- Ares, Hebe, and Ilithyria- and they are the most important beings in my life. There isn't a secret to this confession, but I am not a perfect mother. Hephaestus's burdens are proof of my misgivings as a mother, but for them all, even

Hephaestus, I will destroy the world. Especially for my favorite child. My Ares."

All at once, upon her son's name, her emotions finally bleed through the wall she built over her face. Resilience stares back at Uranus. A queen of anger that only comes with motherhood oozes from her dark, fearless gaze.

"Telling you anything about this prophecy will cause Saffron harm, and until recently, that was all I wanted. I wanted her to suffer so much pain, but the Fates are especially cruel when it comes to my rage."

I suddenly become all too aware of the knife in her hand, which rests against his belly. She moves her arm ever so slightly, and I know she's about to stab him. I reach forward with my magic. Green smoke whirls around Hera's wrist, stopping her weapon. Uranus tilts his head towards the weapon, then surprises the room with laughter. It starts softly, but it becomes a deep-bellied laugh that reverberates off the walls.

He drops Hera's hand and retreats, but he doesn't look away from her. As he joins our threshold once again, situating himself between the three women scorned by Hera, he stares only at the goddess who denied him with a maniacal grin.

"Such a shame. We would have had fun together." He extends his arms wide, inviting chaos into the room. "Instead, the girls get to have their fun with you."

"Fun with you," Echo repeats as I materialize a sword into her awaiting hand.

Uranus glances at me. "Let go of Hera's hand, little witch. Let's have a show before we entomb her."

I drop my magic from Hera's hand as I materialize a sword into Semele's awaiting hand. Lamia does not require a weapon; a monster of her magnitude is the weapon. The moment her hand wraps around the sword's handle, Echo does not hesitate. She runs with an open mouth that tries to scream, but no noise escapes. She rushes towards Hera, but Hera readies herself.

Uranus stands beside me, and I wordlessly pass him the Dagger of Chains. Hera replaces her knife with a newly materialized staff, and she slams the royal weapon against Echo's head. The cursed woman flies across the room, crumbling several feet away with a shattered skull. Quickly, her blood mingles with her fiery red hair, with no sign of stirring awake.

Only a second after her body hits the floor, I see her orb of life flutter from her body. It rushes towards me, destroying my body along with every other corpse's soul across the world. Echo's soul rips open the flesh in my forearm, worming its way through my bloodstream. She gives me strength, but she also gives me agony.

Hera smiles at the two remaining women- Lamia and Semele- and she wolfishly grins. "Who is next?"

Semele and Lamia race towards her before the question can fully leave Hera's lips. For a blinding moment, as Hera yells, Lamia bellows, and Semele's sword clatters loudly against Hera's staff, I wonder why nobody checks on Hera.

None of her attackers are silent, except for Uranus and me, who watch the ordeal with a mask of indifference. Only gods live on Mt. Olympus, and they can hear the screams and the clattering swords, but no one seems to care about her peril. Zeus's room is only a wall away, but he does nothing.

Why isn't anyone coming to her aid?

Hera isn't the most skilled fighter, but with relative ease, she wraps her hands around both sides of Semele's head and breaks her neck. The woman crumbles onto the floor while Lamia tackles Hera to the ground. The impact is so hard the floor splinters; still, there aren't any gods rushing to her cause. Where are her children she loves so ardently? Or the husband who turned her into a puddle of rage and resentment?

Uranus stays beside me, but as Lamia and Hera thrash on the floor, he spins the Dagger of Chains around in his grasp. "Where should I hit her? The chest or shoulder? Maybe the neck?"

Hera punches Lamia across the face, but the monster digs her claws into Hera's arms, eliciting a bellowing scream.

"Did you truly believe Hera would have the answers and readily give them?" I ask.

"A deity could hope, but no. I just wanted to play for a bit." He lifts the dagger, aiming it where Lamia and Hera tousle on the floor. "The forehead it is."

He throws the Dagger of Chains, and the few seconds between Hera's freedom and her captivity move in slow motion. As the blade slices through the air, nearing Hera, she wraps her hands around Lamia's throat. The monster lets out a whimper, sounding so human, as Hera snuffs the life out of her. The dagger pierces Hera's forehead, but not before she ends Lamia's life.

Hera grins victoriously before the Dagger takes her whole.

I retrieve the Dagger of Chains from the floor and whirl to face Uranus. "Why did you bring the women? We could have easily taken Hera down ourselves. Why drag these women to their deaths?"

"Because I could."

I force myself to look away from him and see his eerie calm, even in the face of so much bloodshed. He led three women, who were loyal to our cause, to their death for no other reason than amusement. How many more of our loyal fighters will he kill because of his insatiable bloodlust?

"We need one more god in this blade before we go back to our queen."

Uranus theatrically opens his arms and thrust them toward the doorway. "Lady's choice."

One god's name rings loudest in my ears. He's not here on Mt. Olympus, and while it would be easier to continue our carnage upon the clouds, where no one is coming to aid the gods screaming in peril, my hatred focuses on the male I once cared for. I swirl us in dark green mist, and I take us to the Underworld.

The place I once called home is a graveyard without the bones. All the rivers have dried up, the ground is no longer filled with dead souls forever wandering. The homes, once filled with happy after-lifers, lie as crumbled remains. The Underworld once bustled with constant noise, but now as I step towards the ruinous castle, my stilettos echo too loudly.

Uranus follows, whistling along the way, but when we reach the first step towards Hades's castle, I turn to face him. "I let you dispose of Hera. This one is mine. Stay put."

I expect Uranus to argue with me, as his glee towards carnage consumes him, but he plops a seat on the first step. He continues to whistle from his spot as I walk the remaining distance separating me from Hades.

In a place as quiet as the Underworld's desecrated remains, Hades hears our arrival. Even as I enter the castle and journey to the throne room, Uranus's whistling plays a haunting tune. I materialize two swords forged from my magic, anticipating the moment Hades removes his helm of darkness and attacks.

But the moment never comes.

Hades sits slumped in his obsidian throne. He does not look up at me, but he knows who enters the room. "Was it all worth it?" he sounds a breath away from tears.

The clinking of my heels against the black floor reverberates in the too quiet castle.

"I haven't decided yet," I answer truthfully.

I have not seen Mastiff since I destroyed the Underworld for Styx. She promised me three souls in the dagger in exchange for him, and here slumps my third god. There are three steps separating Hades's throne from the floor, and he flinches when I take the first step.

"My old friend," Hades finally pierces me with his electric blue, bloodshot eyes. "If you do not know with unwavering certainty that your decision is worth it, then it is not. You damned those who loved you for one soul. A soul that you got to see every day in the Underworld. A soul that was content with his afterlife. You damned the world for a soul that did not need saving."

"He didn't deserve death." My voice wobbles as each of Hades's words strike my heart with a fatal blow. Perhaps I was wrong. Perhaps Mastiff preferred his fate down here, where I could visit a corporeal version of him.

But I did not prefer that ghostly version of him.

I glower at Hades, who stares almost sympathetically back. "My old friend, don't you see what Styx has done to you?" He does not swat the Dagger of Chains out of my hand; instead, he plucks up my free hand to flip it, so my palm faces the ceiling. He stares at the black veins that are slowly polluting my golden ones. "You let Styx poison you with so much hatred that you do not see that you made the gravest mistake of them all."

Tears blur my vision because even when I am moments away from imprisoning him, he still speaks to me with such calmness. A hint of compassion like we are still friends.

"Shut-up." My words break apart, unraveling before our eyes.

He traces one of the black veins with one frigid finger. "There's no saving you anymore. I will mourn your loss where I go." He finds my eyes again. "Is my wife waiting for me, or must I suffer without her a moment longer?"

"That's the cruelest irony of it all. Isn't it?" I press the tip of the Dagger against his chest, not yet puncturing the skin. "I betrayed you and Persephone to be with him, and in the crossfire of my actions, I separate you and Persephone forever. For that, I am sorry."

His eyes widen as true betrayal weighs down any vestige of hope. He doesn't fight as I slide the blade into his chest, even as he knows Persephone does not wait for him. The last sight I have of my former friend is a tear rolling down his cheek before oblivion takes him whole. The moment he is gone, I collapse onto my knees in front of his throne, and I sob.

I do not know how long my body racks with guilt and sadness, but I do not move until every ounce of water escapes my body. Only when I cannot cry any longer, I stand up, walk out of the castle, and join Uranus at the bottom step. He tilts his head up curiously, taking in my tear-streaked cheeks, and holds out his hand for the Dagger of Chains.

"No."

Without another word, I transport us away from the Underworld and return to the prison where Styx waits for us. I never make assumptions about Styx. Everything I predict is far from actuality. She is a goddess of mystery, shrouded in the realm of unpredictability.

The mist clears upon Uranus and my arrival back at the prisons.

Styx stands at the top of the staircase garbed in armor.

She swears a diadem made of black crystals and jagged wire. The material cuts into her pale, almost translucent flesh, causing rivulets of ichor to slither down the sides of her cheeks like snakes.

Styx is a petite woman, barely weighing over a hundred pounds. Her armor, which is made from the scales of a hundred snakes, threatens to swallow her whole. The material is as black as her crown. In the center of her chest plate, an emblem of a pomegranate struck in the middle by a dagger that looks nearly identical to the one in my hand, ominously rests. Her sharp mouth wears lipstick the same shade as the tarnished pomegranate, but on the corner of her lips is a streak of ichor that careens down to the jut of her chin.

Beneath Styx is her army of monsters, humans, gods, titans, and nymphs. They all wear black armor, and they are all sheathed with weapons on the ground floor of the prison. Rage and hatred contort their faces, staring back at me like a mirror image. Styx is the only one who does not acknowledge my presence. She merely holds out her hand expectantly, and I drop the Dagger of Chains into her palm.

"Tonight, we take Mt. Olympus for ourselves. I have waited for eons to claim my crown and sit on my throne on Mt. Olympus, and now my time is here. Our time to take the throne and the accolades and make it ours. We will march to Mt. Olympus's gates, and we will destroy them all."

Styx never raises her voice. She always speaks in a soft, almost whispered cadence, but her voice carries. It takes on an ominous tune that undulates throughout the space until every single one of her followers hears it and sings the same melody. One by one, they raise their swords or hammers or axes and clamorously cheer for their chance to shine. To take away the rights of the gods who damned them.

Styx's appearance remains stoic, like she is not orchestrating a seamless coup that will make her queen. "By the time the sun rises for a new morning, I will be the queen, and you all will be Olympians in this world. The old will die and the better will rise."

# NINE

## LAMB

I am no stranger to bloodshed.

Over the centuries, battles have blended in a cluster of fired arrows, bellowed cries, strangled throats, and bodies permanently collapsing. I have killed more souls than I dare to count. I try to remember all their faces, weaving a tapestry inside my mind, but not because they need to be immortalized. Almost all of them were corrupt souls; damned to the Fields of Punishment the moment I stopped their hearts from beating. I try to remember their faces because it tethers me to my humanity. Seeing their faces in the darkest pits of my mind reminds me I do not kill for sport or amusement; every action is methodical and necessary.

But last night, as I slit the throat of a second man this week, I now question my actions.

All those who I have killed this week have been Hart's needs, spoken as Zeus' commands. She sketches their faces with eerie accuracy on a piece of parchment, and by the time the sun sets, all those faces have wear red slashes. A prettily drawn death sentence us huntresses must execute.

Each morning, as the sun just begins its steady rise into shimmering shades of pinks and oranges, Iris leaves our temporary encampment. She finds Hart, who always greets her with ominous warnings as she presents three pieces of artwork. There are always three faces, differing in weight, race, age, and gender, but they all wear gray Underworld garb. They all wield a dark green-misted weapon, and they all die by nightfall.

Each morning, Hart asks Iris to relay a message. It never varies. Every word is the same from the day before. She rains doom upon us, hoping we shield ourselves from the onslaught in time. Yet, danger slinks around every corner like a steadily growing shadow, and Hart ensures we never forget the looming war surrounding us in the darkness.

*Kill these humans and we might win the war.*

That is the warning Hart delivers every morning to Iris, who repeats it in the same ominous tone as the enigmatic oracle. Most often, the humans on the drawings have blood splattered across their faces. It is never their own, but the victims they collect along the way like tokens. Maybe Hart draws them this way to absolve us of our guilt because none of us has killed without a battlefield in front of us, except the goddesses.

For the first time, we are the executioners without fulling understanding the crimes of the executed.

Today is the seventh day since Hart set us out on our journey, with our nineteenth, twentieth, and twenty-first victims in a neat pile atop Iris's hand. We are little more than assassins for hire, and try as I might, the faces blur. My resolve blurs with them.

Hart knows more than she lets on. I have known this

since our day together in the arena, where she watched Hermes strike Saffron, an almost hidden smile on her face. Hart knows everything, engorging herself on knowledge, but she only feeds us crumbs.

Why?

Why does Hart send us to kill twenty-one humans in a single week with no provocation? She promises they must die, but why are humans so valuable in a war against gods? The Olympians are omnipotent, but we are not killing gods. We are slaying humans who have already fallen in defeat once before.

Why, why, why?

"Who should we go after first?" Reaper's mournful sarcasm breaks through the silence brought on by three more sketches. The endless barrage of murders dilutes her normal fearlessness. Her voice crackles like marble, her color dimmed by unexplained yet necessary carnage. "I vote we dispose of the woman first."

Iris sets the sketches on the floor around our circle of huntresses. Athena stays with us, and I think she stays out of mercy, so we do not have to deliver as many killing blows. Or this could be another unexplained request from Hart that turns into a command from Zeus. Regardless of the reason Athena is here, gratefulness seeps into the humid air from all of us huntresses.

Athena kills the most, with Artemis close behind her, out of sympathy for the other huntresses and me. They are more familiar with murder than we are, especially when there isn't a battlefield and spiked adrenaline involved. They never admit why they wield the last strike more often than us, and none of us bring it up.

Out of the eighteen we have killed thus far, Athena has disposed of ten of them, Artemis has killed four, and both Vee and Dýnami ended one life. I have killed two humans in the past week, their faces woven into the threads of my mind forevermore, but those who I help kill blur together. I can scarcely tell them apart from one another in this war that has only begun.

How many other faces will I forget, cast aside in my journey towards apathy?

Athena quickly glances at the sketch in the middle of a long-faced woman with a scar across her cheek. "I agree. She's farthest from our current location, so it'd be wise to terminate her first."

I glance back down at the woman we agree to kill. Whoever this woman recently murdered fought back by that scar and the claw marks around her neck, but she was victorious. A dark green gleam surrounds the woman from the axe she holds in her hand, identifying her as a loyal subject to Hecate and Styx.

On the bottom right corner, there are sketches with the coordinates to their locations. Iris slouches where she stands, fatigue weighing heavily on her shoulders, but she does not have time to rest. Her sole job in this cursed game is to retrieve the drawings and drop us off at the designated location. In this past week, I have only seen Iris sleep once for an hour. She laid her head on Artemis's shoulder, but the sun rose too quickly, and Iris left once again at Hart's beckoning.

As if reading my thoughts, Artemis interjects. "We will have time to kill the three before nightfall. We need a little while longer to rest and eat."

Athena opens her mouth to object, but Jamila jumps in first. "I agree, I'm starving."

Athena clamps her mouth shut.

For the past week since Athena joined us, Jamila has been the mediator of the two strong-willed goddesses. Artemis and Athena have rarely agreed on anything during our weeklong trek, and Jamila is the only one who can stop an argument before it manifests. Iris, Dýnami, and I have tried a few times, but our attempts have been in vain.

On the second night, when we nearly lost one of our targets in Bhutan, the two goddesses screamed so loud at each other that one mountain trembled. I tried to speak to both Artemis and Athena, trying to quiet them, but pieces of the mountain collapsed amidst their rage. If Iris didn't jump in and teleport Shikari, Hound, and I away, we would've been buried alive beneath the rubble.

After that night, it became Jamila's sole job to mediate her two aunts. Artemis cares for Jamila like she cares for all her huntresses, so she would listen to any of us, but Athena is different. She cares for some of us, but only a little. Jamila holds a tender part of Athena's heart. It was Athena who first trained Jamila as a child and gifted her with her first weapon. Athena is one of the three virgin goddesses who will never bear children of her own, but she found a kinship with Jamila.

Artemis told me one night, when the rest were asleep, that after Athena trained Jamila for the first time, she bestowed her grace onto the young girl. Many believe Athena loves Jamila because she is the only daughter of Athena's closest sister, Saffron, but she loves Jamila wholly for her wisdom and courage. When Jamila speaks, Athena listens, even if she quiets the rest of the world.

"Just a quick nap." Iris collapses at the empty spot next to Artemis. She curls herself into Artemis, resting her multi-colored hair atop her shoulder. Artemis wraps an arm around Iris's shoulder, and within less than a minute, the goddess of rainbows is fast asleep.

Every morning, when Iris returns with the three drawings, she brings bags of food, too. I only open one bag, which has piles of bread and fruit, while the huntresses create a line. It is the only food we eat throughout the day, unless Artemis or Athena have enough strength to materialize more, or we have enough time to hunt for game. Everyone gets a loaf of bread and one type of fruit. The fruit always changes, and today we have a bag full of green grapes.

Dýnami typically complains that she doesn't get three loaves of bread, but today we remain as silent as possible for Iris. As I pass out the food, Shikari grabs extra to place on Artemis's lap. She doesn't eat it, though. Her sole fixation is Iris, who now has a blanket draped over her body.

I sit between Dýnami and Reaper once everyone else gets their servings, and the first bag is empty. No words that transpire, but there is a sense of peace within the silence. The three of us clink our bread together, cheering like we have a glass of wine in our hands. We celebrate a new day like we are at a party rather than a deserted town in the middle of Europe.

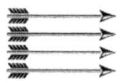

An hour later, a bleary-eyed Iris transports us to a little town in Italy. None of us know what to expect when the rainbow dissipates, and our mission becomes clearer. Sometimes, our target is on a murder spree and the dead bodies create our trail. Those are the easiest targets to kill because there's an obvious need for their death. Other times, we find our targets scared, with tears falling down their faces. Those are the hardest to kill. Some are regretful, unsure, or enraged. It all depends on when we find them, but we always find them.

Hart's coordinates are specific to when we materialize in front of them, which speaks of the oracle's power. She not only knows where we will find them, but when we find them in this exact location. Most of the humans on Hecate and Styx's side are constantly moving from one place to the next, but we always find them at the opportune time.

The long-faced woman is easy to find, just like the eighteen targets before her. We materialize inside a cottage house, where she sits with a cup of ale around a circle of corpses. There are eight bodies, hacked into smaller parts, all around her. For the sake of my sanity, I refuse to stare at them for long. I refuse to see if there are smaller body parts once belonging to children. Instead, I glower at her.

She stiffens ever so slightly upon our entrance, but she otherwise does not react. Without looking in our general direction, she lifts her cup and takes a sip. The surrounding huntresses unsheathe their weapons, but I wrap my hand around my sword's handle and stop myself. Athena is the first to take an advancing step, her shield glinting in the poorly lit room. A sliver of sunlight peeks through the tattered curtains.

The long-faced woman sets her cup down with a soft clank. "They killed me. Twelve years ago, they got me drunk, and they butchered me." She reaches for the half-empty bottle of whiskey, then pours her cup to the brim. "If the Furies walked into this room instead of you, they would find this divine justice. They cut up my body and chucked it in the nearest body of water, but you, Lady Athena, have decided that I am the villain for returning payment."

It's a sour sound, her laugh, as she tilts back her drink and gulps down her victims' whiskey.

"If you are truthful, I consider it justice, too." Athena takes another step forward.

She sets her cup down again, then wipes the residue of alcohol off her lips with the back of her hand. She still doesn't look at us. Her focus is solely on the cup of whiskey. "But you're still going to kill me. You understand my plight, but I'm still a dead woman. Why?"

She doesn't ask in a desperate plea to survive another day. Her voice is too monotone to truly care about her life. I realize she is merely curious. Life means nothing to a woman who breathes revenge once it's exacted.

Athena doesn't answer her question until she stands directly behind her, sword unsheathed. "Your axe glows green."

The woman picks up her cup again. "They said we fight for them, or we die a second time." She shrugs her shoulder and takes another drink. "I don't care about what you gods do with your never-ending lives. You can try to kill each other a thousand and one times, it doesn't bother me none. I only wanted to cut those men up like they did to me, and I was going to agree to anything the witch goddess asked to achieve it."

Almost every target who spoke to us in their last moments sounds like her. Most of these humans do not care about the gods' wars. They have their own reasons for joining Styx's side, and only a few choose their path because of their allegiance to Styx. They want revenge for their past or a second chance at life, after squandering their first one. These humans, who Hart tells us to murder, rarely care to fight on the battlefield alongside Styx and Hecate. They have human wants that are only achievable with a little white lie and a glimmering dark-green weapon.

"Do you want to finish your drink before you die?" Athena finally asks.

Athena cannot see it, but the long-faced woman gives a tight-lipped smile. "I prayed little in my first life, but I pray a thanks to you now, Lady Athena. I would love to finish my drink."

We all wait in silence as our target looks around the room at her murderers. The woman seized the justice she deserved, and she lifts her cup in a silent cheer. She downs the rest of the cup, gulping it like the whiskey doesn't burn a trail down her throat. She slams the cup down with ferocity, then looks back at us.

Her eyes land on mine when Athena swings her sword and decapitates the long-faced woman.

Crimson splatters across Athena's pale face, but the goddess does not wipe away the carnage. She stands amongst the death cloying the room and faces Iris.

"Who is next?"

Before searching for our next target, we spend our time going through this small town and deliver the second bag of food to any survivors. Unfortunately, as every day passes in this new, tormented world, we find less and less survivors. It used to take us only a few minutes to empty our bag of food; now, we take a little over an hour to find living people who need food. Corpses are a more common company nowadays.

She transports us to an island, where a robust man in his late sixties argues with the young woman he's robbing. He has his hand wrapped around the young woman's throat when Artemis releases an arrow. It spins through the air, and the robust man's only warning of his impending doom is the young woman's widening eyes at the last second. The arrow pierces his neck, sprouting out of the other side like a blooming flower.

His hand lets go of her throat, moving to his own. He stumbles back, obsidian green sword clattering to the ground, clutching the wound that will never stitch back together. He falls with a loud thud onto his back, gripping his neck until his body stills. The woman bites back a scream as she looks at him, then us, then the moldy piece of bread she holds. The same piece of bread that he nearly killed her to get.

Vee goes into the third bag, and she produces a piece of fresh bread and fruit. At the sight, the young woman collapses onto her knees and cries so hard that her entire body shakes. Vee tentatively walks towards her; hand outstretched with the food, and lays it gently beside the woman. She doesn't immediately leave once the young woman picks up the food and tears into the bread. Vee waits ever so patiently as the woman sobs, takes a bite, and repeats the process.

We all wait until the woman stops crying and registers who we are. "Huntresses," the woman says with a sigh of relief. "Thank the gods." She carries her attention to where Iris, Artemis, and Athena stand and her bottom lip trembles. "My people and I will pray to all three of you every day for years to come. Thank you."

Artemis carries the last bag of food to the young woman, dropping it beside her. "Give this to your people, and when you need more, pray to us and we will come. You have my solemn vow."

The young woman stands on wobbly legs, but she is quick to wrap her arms around Artemis's neck. "Thank you."

Artemis hesitates for only a second, then wraps her arms around the woman in return.

We stay here longer than we should because this assassination is the first in three days where we know why Hart wanted us to kill him. More often than not, we kill targets like the long-faced woman, whose crimes are more gray than black-and-white. There is no gratitude in murders like hers, but when we carry the bag of food for the young woman and meet her townsfolk, they speak of the man's terrors.

We stay a little longer here than we should because they thank us for saving the young woman's life, and every other townsfolk who would have died by this man's hand. Every day since the Underworld died, this man has killed one of their people. This is the first meal they have had in seven days, and they cheer on our entrance. It is difficult to feel like my actions are just when we surround ourselves with uncertainty; today, we stay a little longer because we need to know that we are the heroes in this story.

Iris transports us away when the sun sets, but our last image is of smiling faces. It rejuvenates us, reminding us why we follow Hart's daily orders. We chose to be huntresses because we wanted to protect the women of this world. We wanted a purpose in this life, and after saving that woman, our purpose is clearer than ever.

"Who is last?" I ask the moment we land in a new place.

Much of this surrounding land is rubble, but amidst the debris, there is one remaining building. Makeshift tarps and pure luck keep this establishment going, but it is a haven when the rest of their land is wreckage.

"Some guy with an eyepatch." Iris passes me the last drawing as we walk towards the last operating business because it is the only place the man with the eyepatch can be.

I glance down at the drawing as we walk. He is a very thin man, with a litter of acne scars around his sunken cheeks and underneath his scraggly goatee. In his hand is a curved sword, glinting green like everyone loyal to Hecate and Styx.

"Erik!" A female lets this single name slip from her lips, laced with pure terror, and we sprint towards the source as we unsheathe our weapons.

Just as we round the corner, I hear the clash of two

weapons, and I imagine what I will see once I enter this doorway. Yet, nothing prepares me for who joins the man with the eyepatch inside this former bar.

Eight humans with green weapons block the door, ready to kill whoever takes solace in this place, but in the middle of the bar, I can make out Hermes fighting the man with the eyepatch. His caduceus gleams inhumanely bright in the dark bar as it clinks against Eyepatch's curved sword. Hermes smirks as a sword nears his boyish face, like war enlivens him.

"I knew you'd get it right on the third try." His gaze wanders from Eyepatch, and he sees us in the doorway. "Care to join me in the fun, sisters?"

I slice my sword down on the nearest male, and as their blood splatters my face, a battle ensues.

# TEN

HERMES

I don't allot myself time to wonder why my sisters, Athena and Artemis, are here with a horde of huntresses. I refuse to look back at Maressa, whose eyes feel like a thousand lightning bolts against my flesh. As a battle bleeds both gold and red around me, I can only focus on my opponent. The same man whose soul I carried to the Underworld hundreds of years ago.

Long ago, this man was a ruthless pirate who would promise peace, only to murder those who made deals with him so he could rob their corpses. When he died from an outbreak of smallpox, he tried to fight me when I reached for his soul. In his addled mind, he believed that if he defeated me, then he defeated death. I am neither the god of death nor its king, but he still deemed me his opponent.

On the day I dropped his body off in the Underworld and suggested the Fields of Punishment for his eternal soul, we dueled for his right to stay alive. In his first life, he was as foolish as he is during this second chance. I disemboweled him with one clean swipe of my blade against his

113

stomach when we first fought, and now as he lazily swings his sword towards me, I duck and crash Caduceus against his jaw.

Every tooth in his mouth flies across the room, and he stumbles to the floor. His jaw hangs from his mouth, utterly useless, but he still raises his sword. On any other man, this would appear valiant, but he already lost a fight against me. He knew the outcome from the moment he saw me sitting on that bar stool, and still he tested the Fates for a second time.

I knock his sword aside with a soft brush of Caduceus against his blade, and it flies out of his hand. "It's almost too easy, Eyepatch."

He growls at me.

Actually, growls like a dog.

"Mysshnameishdennish."

I raise an eyebrow. "What in the gods did you just try to say?" I point my weapon towards his mangled jaw. "You need that to speak properly, Eyepatch."

Again, he tries speaking without a working mandible. "Mysshnameishdennish."

"I'm the god of languages, and even I don't understand you."

Anger enlivens his one eye. "Mysshnameish-"

An arrow breaks through his skull, silencing his undecipherable sentence. Artemis stands on the other side of his corpse. "It's not nice to play with your kills."

I grin. "But it's so tempting."

She's not smiling, and I do not need to ponder why. I can see Epiales, now Erik, from my peripheral. He's helping an extremely confused Dýnami to her feet, not understanding she wants to impale him. She rips her hand away from his as fast as possible, and she wipes it on her tattered pants, like he's infected with a deadly plague.

Suddenly self-conscious, the clueless man glances down at his hand. Flips it over to see if there's anything but grim attached.

"I can explain," I say.

Artemis crosses her arms, unamused. "Can you?"

Maressa runs up to Epiales shortly after Dýnami storms away, still wiping her hand on her pants. Maressa wraps her arms around the back of Epiales's neck, squeezing him tight, and he returns the sentiment. They pull away quickly, but they remain close. A sting of jealousy, sudden and unwarranted, hits me. She's so tiny next to him, and for a belligerent second, I wonder how much tinier she would look next to me. While Epiales is tall, an inch above six feet, I am six and a half feet tall. As she talks with her hands gesticulating in the air, I imagine how they feel wrapped in a hug like the one she gave him.

"Hermes." Artemis's rough voice draws me back to her. "I'm waiting for that explanation."

"It's a terrible explanation."

The huntresses carry the eight corpses out of the room with Iris and Athena.

"We have a few minutes," Artemis says.

*I came here to break my word and kill Epiales.* The words bounce against my skull, begging for release. *But I couldn't find the monster any longer, even when I stared right at Erik Oneiroi.* I urge the words to escape my lips, so Artemis can hear my truth, but I'm only capable of honesty when the only ears hearing it are my own.

My eons' old rage for Epiales stops any admission. I hate Epiales, and this boiling, discordant rage is not solely because of Saffron. He was instrumental in my torture on Mt. Olympus. He watched as Typhon inflicted the worst kind of pain upon me. Epiales is one of the four immortals responsible for my suffering. He is one immortal I blame for my sleepless nights, and he is one of the last remaining vestiges of my torment whose heart still beats.

Artemis waits for an answer that will never come. I know what to say, but as the answer grows louder in my mind, I look away. "Let's go make a fire. It's getting too cold for the mortals." I spin around and walk towards the back door of the bar.

Artemis does not initially follow me out of the bar. I step out alone on this night, with only the stars and the chilly winds as company. I lean over a stack of newly materialized wood, create the first strike of fire, and stoke it until a blazing inferno ignites the obsidian night. It is because of the bright oranges and yellows that I easily make out Maressa's silhouette in the bar's doorway.

She's so tiny, barely five feet tall, but she consumes the surrounding space. Demands its sole attention. Slowly, Maressa walks out of the doorway and approaches me.

"So, you're Hermes." There's a pause, then. "You're a god."

She doesn't need an answer to the question she already knows. Instead of pleasantries, I show her the truth she wants to see once more. She wants the undeniable proof that I am a god. I stand to my full height, and the wings on my shoes emerge from their hiding spot. Maressa's eyes immediately drop to the two white wings, flapping in greeting.

Maressa is a mortal, and yet I do not receive instant gratification from her reaction. Normally, when a human meets a god for the first time, there's a look of awe upon their face. Their jaw threatens to fall on the floor, and they suddenly lose the ability to speak. Yet, Maressa looks at my godly gifts, and she seems…bored.

That won't do.

"Be right back."

I move at the speed of lightning, disappearing from the roaring bonfire and the beautiful bartender. I run to the other side of the world. Across the globe, there is strife, but the severity is most prominent in North America. Styx focuses all her hatred and manipulation on the continent where Saffron's home and building are located, so in the Middle East, there is enough food to share. I grab as much food as my hands can carry, and I run back to the place where I left Maressa.

It has only been ten seconds, maybe fifteen, since I left her. Now, I stand with enough food to feed everyone at our site. Carefully, I lower all the bread, fruits, and meats on the sole table in the backyard, but I keep an apricot. I throw it at Maressa, and she catches it. Slowly, she lifts the apricot to her mouth and takes a hearty bite. A line of juice falls down her lips and drops from her chin.

I have never loved the sight of apricots more.

She waits to break the silence once she finishes chewing the apricot. "Where'd you go to get this?"

"Iraq."

Finally, disbelief shines across her enormous eyes. "You were only gone for eleven seconds. I counted." She whispers the last two words with disbelief.

Several feet separate her and me, and for reasons I refuse to question, I need to move closer. I break the distance, one hesitant step after another, until I loom over her. She cranes her neck to stare up at me. I'm so close, I can smell the partially eaten apricot like it's an extension of her. She doesn't balk by my nearness, and she doesn't look away from me. We stare at one another in the charged, closed space.

"You wanted to see proof of who I am." My voice is softer than usual. Huskier, too. "So, I gave it."

Her gaze flickers from my eyes to my lips, to Caduceus

glowing at my holstered hip. She looks everywhere, as if by staring at me longer, she can unravel all her questions. "You are one of the more powerful gods on Mt. Olympus, but you've spent almost every night here for the past week. Why would you do that?"

Her question at the end becomes breathless, and all I can dare to do is stare at her lips. They're still wet from the single bite of the apricot, and I take that last step. My chest is a breath away from hers, and that charged feeling grows. A thousand bolts of electricity have taken over my body, and only this sensation and her proximity matters. I forget about Epiales and Saffron. Forget about my situation and the war surrounding us on all angles.

I only see her glossy lips, feel her nearness, and understand I need more of her.

The bar's back door opens with a loud thud, and Maressa jumps away from me. The huntresses stand in the doorway, and Dýnami, who is in the middle, yells out. "I heard you got us some food. I'm starving!"

A wave of huntresses, gods, and humans filter outside. They sit around the bonfire I made and eat the food I provided, but Maressa moves away from me. She sits by the bonfire, with a nameless human on her right and Epiales on her left. The latter glances at the huntresses with a confused crease in his forehead while they openly glower at him.

Maressa takes another bite of her apricot, and only then does she glance up at me. I feel a presence standing beside me, but I only stare at Maressa until she looks away.

"You didn't answer my question," Artemis says. "Why are you here?"

"I don't think I know anymore."

# ELEVEN

## SAFFRON

S leep is a friend lost at sea, never to rise again. Hattie slumbers to my right, her snores loud enough to rumble the walls, but I have not found escape in my unconscious void yet. Instead, I lay here, my head resting on the softest pillow, and I am a victim to my own whirling thoughts.

I created a single window in this room, no longer than a foot and barred with bones, but I can see the stars all too well. They are the beacon of light against the midnight sky, illuminating the room enough to capture my attention. It is when I stare at the twinkling lights in the night sky that I think the most about Epiales.

Regardless of the miles between us and the years we spent in turmoil, I always find him in the constellations. Our stories flourished within these stars. I stand upon my balcony, and his words become one with the whispers of the wind. His touch is the chilly breeze against my cheek. When I look up at the stars we stared at for countless nights on the island, I imagine he is looking up at them as well. When I smell the crisp night air, the smallest sliver of electricity slides down my spine and makes me believe he is here; even for just a second.

He is alive somewhere on Earth, and for anyone who listens, I pray he has found more happiness as a human than he ever found as a deity. I hope he will become a baker when the war ends and he can truly flourish with the humans. I hope he has a smile on his face every morning. There might be crimson blood spilling onto the streets of this world, but I hope he is impervious to the strife and is grinning at the rise of the sun each morning.

I hope he has found happiness. Even if his happiness stems from a woman who can never be me. I hope there is warmth in his heart that only the companionship of human interaction can provide. Mostly, I hope he survives in this desolate world just long enough for me to save it.

I have mourned him twice now, but as I stare into the night sky, I still carry a fragment of him.

A fragment I can stare at until the end of time.

I carefully peel myself out of the bed, so I do not rouse Hattie. Her mouth agape, arms theatrically spread out and legs tangled in bedsheets. She does not wake as I stand beside the bed, staring in disbelief that she's alive again. Her heart beats. She's here. Despite everything else, there's happiness in her return.

With a final wayward glance towards the night sky, I slip out of the bedroom.

In this new, distorted version of the world, there is never a moment of silence. It's quiet, almost imperceptible to human ears, but I can hear them all. The cries of victims to others' sinister blades, falling to their permanent doom. Pleads from desperate souls who want to avoid death a little while longer, even when it looms ever closer.

I try to avoid the sounds I cannot silence. I wander

through my home, which reminds me more and more of the prisons that held me captive almost a hundred years prior. My gaze continually veers towards the windows. Towards those screams and pleads. Zeus's order is a whisper against my ears, against the cacophony of their anguish.

There's no room in this home that can stop the sounds, but I search. I hear them in my kitchen, trembling the wine glasses. They follow me to the dining room, the spare rooms, and even the bathrooms. I flee until I swing open a door, rush inside, and see someone who silences it all with their presence.

Gauze wraps around Ares's hands, but the gold blood peaks out of the white fabric as he pounds against the black punching bag. Sweat drips off him in rivulets as he punches the bag again and again and again. He hasn't noticed me yet, standing in the doorway, and I have lost the ability to speak. I have not hidden my despair well these past few days, but Ares has managed to conceal until now. His brow furrows with consternation as he releases all his frustration against the last remaining punching bag. Six others lay on the floor, tattered beyond repair.

Ares does not realize I'm here until I stand in front of the punching bag, holding it still for him. Our gazes lock. His hand stills in the air moments before it connects with the punching bag. While his are blue and mine are brown, I see myself in his eyes. We share the same frustration brewing until it threatens to boil over. We share the same helplessness, even though we are two of the strongest gods in existence.

Carefully and ever so slowly, I move the punching bag to the side and step forward. His hand lowers, but it hesitates to return to his side. It itches for more, and whether it's fatigue or apprehension, I do not question what *more* he wants. I stand a breath away from his heaving chest, craning my neck to stare at him. He's already staring back.

"Am I intruding?"

"Never." His voice comes out raspy. Guttural.

I run my tongue along my suddenly dry bottom lip, and I feel him, rather than see him, track the motion. Being around him always feels like the heart of a thunderstorm. A thousand bolts overwhelm my body.

"Do you want to spar?" I ask, unsure of his response.

"With you?" he asks. Before a witty rebuttal like *who else?* can leave my lips, he responds. "Always."

Yet, neither of us moves. We stand too close for a while after he speaks the last word, our stare unbreaking. There's more he wants to say and more the hand twitching near his side wants to do, but after an eternity of suspending in this moment, he's the one who breaks away. He walks towards the rack of weapons, hovering a hand over the spears, swords, arrows, and staffs.

"Choose your poison," he says without turning back to look at me.

Swords are my poison, but they are designed to cut and inflict harm. They are blades of mortality, and there might have once been a time when I wanted Ares to suffer more than anyone else. That time, however, has long since passed. I walk towards the rack of weapons, and I pick up a staff.

When I whirl around to face him, he strikes.

We spar until the accumulation of our sweat creates puddles on the ground, and I can no longer hear anything but my racing heartbeat. Ares is quick and efficient, but I'm resilient. Our staffs clang together with such ferocity that every half hour, they shatter under the weight of our unleashing frustrations. The fragmented weapons lay haphazardly around the corners of the room, thrown in rushed movements between two lost souls trying to find themselves through overexertion.

We are nose to nose, breathing each other's scents as we smash our staffs together and they simultaneously shatter. We drop our seventh staff onto the ground at the same time, but we do not move. Once more, the storm has claimed us. Lightning bolts and all.

"Saffron," he murmurs my name as silently as the winter air claims a gust of wind.

He lifts his hand, and there's a moment of hesitation written on his face before he claims a tuft of my hair from my quickly made ponytail. He twirls the hair around his fingers, enamored with the sight, and my breathing quickens. His touch and proximity quiet the world when nothing else can, and I take the next step. Our chests press against each other as he tucks the piece of hair behind my ear.

"You are more radiant than every battlefield and every sunrise." Again, his admission is almost too quiet to hear, but I hear it all the same. "You are more radiant than any sight this world offers."

"Ares." His name comes out as a gasp from my lips.

His hand cups my cheek. "If you want to disobey Zeus and go outside these walls. If you want to save every person in a twenty-mile radius and destroy everyone who chose Styx's side, I'll join you. I'll join you anywhere."

There's more he wants to say. An admission coating his lips. I forget everything else at this exact moment, waiting for those words.

But our illusion shatters as the training room's door opens with a clamorous creak. He drops his hand from my cheek and takes a retreating step. The electricity brewing between us has extinguished, and all that remains are unfulfilled possibilities. We both turn to the source of our interruption, and Hart stands in the doorway.

She's not alone.

Beside her, Zeus stands.

He glowers at Ares, undoubtedly hearing his words of betrayal moments earlier, but there's more than rage on his face. Fatigue wears a heavy shade of bruises underneath his eyes. Even the lightning bolt in his hand, which normally glows an inhumanely bright shade, is dim. Nearly extinguished.

Hart does not look any better.

While it may be Atlas who holds the world forever on his shoulders, Hart holds every inhabitant on shoulders too dainty for all the pressure. She slouches against the doorway, and only now, as she hugs her robe-clad body, I notice how much weight she's lost in such a short period of time. When was the last time she ate? When was the last time she thought of her health instead of war and prophecies?

"What did we intrude on?" Zeus asks with an air of accusation.

I glower at him. "Why are you here? You never leave your gilded palace."

My words deflate him, and a terrible sense of doom filters through the room like thick fog.

"They are gone," Hart says.

Her voice holds an eerie tune, not wholly belonging to her. Like at the beginning of the Underworld's deterioration, she sounds like a mesh of voices coalescing into one ominous, imposing sound.

"The queen lost her diadem, and the wine lost his vines." Her golden eyes find mine, and they brim with sympathy. They shine with tears that will never shed. "The dead lost their monarch, and they are only the beginning. It started with three, but it will end with a hundred. Rivers of gold and red will create a war the world will never be scrubbed clean of. The war begins on Mt. Olympus, and the river of gold comes swiftly and brutally."

I take a step towards Hart and Zeus, who wear the same shade of regret and determination. "When will this battle begin?"

I can see the backdrop of the morning from the window behind them.It rises to start a new morning in shades of all reds and oranges. A beautiful, gruesome sunrise.

"It already has," Zeus says, but he makes no move to transport us to Mt. Olympus.

He says the words that send chills down all gods' spines, the overthrowing of Mt. Olympus, but he isn't looking for reinforcement. Zeus stands here, already a broken god, because he let Styx have his throne.

He let Styx win.

# TWELVE

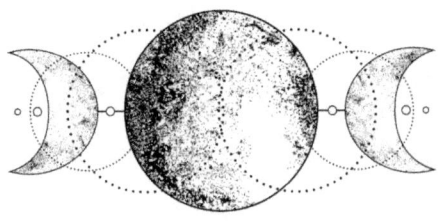

## HECATE

Styx does not choose our time of attack when the night sky can best blanket our arrival. We materialize at Mt. Olympus' pearly gates as dawn breaks through in hopeful rays of reds and pinks. She wants our enemies to believe their day will begin as the previous one, unscathed. She wants to expunge their dreams and expectations the moment they open their eyes. Styx marches our army of monsters, gods, and titans; obsidian green weapons ablaze at the start of the new day so she can see her enemies' slacken expressions.

We bring upon a day anew that delivers their downfall in slashes of gold.

And we start with the goddess of the hearth herself.

Hestia.

# THIRTEEN

HERMES

We revel in the darkness, surrounded by a roaring fire. Three of the huntresses sing, as Maressa sits beside them strumming a Kithara. I didn't think anyone in the modern world knew how to strum an ancient, professional version of a lyre, but Maressa creates life anew with this instrument. Vee and Shikari harmonize beautifully alongside Maressa's instrument, while Dýnami's voice makes dying cats sound pleasant in comparison.

There is laughter in the rubble of war. Peace where there should only be strife. Everyone eats, swaps stories, and wears smiles like armor. Maressa lays her head on my shoulder near the middle of the night, when the music fades. She falls asleep swiftly, and that is the moment I realize I am over Saffron. Because this brave, beautiful woman stole my smiles, and what an arduous task, to steal from the god of thievery.

I fall asleep with Maressa's head laying on my shoulder,

content for the first time in a long while. The stars guard us for the night, but unbeknownst to them, is what morning brings.

Soft, yet persistent hands shake me awake.

I open my eyes, expecting Maressa to still be beside me. Yet, it isn't Maressa who looms over me with terror. It is Iris, and behind her are Athena and Artemis. In all their hands, they hold their signature weapons. Iris's staff, which blooms every shade of the rainbow, turns into startling dark shades of blue as fear settles home in her heart.

Maressa's head still rests on my shoulder, serving as her pillow, and I'm careful to lay her head on the floor before I sit up. "What happened?"

Iris's hand curls tighter around her staff. "We need to go to Mt. Olympus. I can't feel Hera anymore." She shakes her head, and her multi-colored, curly tendrils quiver with fright. "The last time I couldn't feel Hera's presence, she was in the Dagger of Chains."

Iris is a messenger of the gods, just like I am. We deliver messages for all the gods, but she and I each have one god we follow most dutifully. Mine is my father, Zeus, and I can always sense where he always is except those few weeks when he lived within the Dagger of Chains. Iris's chief god, to whom she is most loyal, is Hera. Iris may love Artemis, and she may choose to ride alongside the huntresses, but her fealty is to Hera.

And if she can't feel her on Earth or Mt. Olympus…

I lurch to my feet, the wings on my sandals bristling awake. "We need to leave, but…" I look back at Maressa. "There's been more attacks on this hideout as the week has progressed. If we all leave, I don't know if they'll survive the next attack alone."

"We will guard the camp until you return," an almost whispery voice says. Lamb stands a few feet away from the goddesses, so easily hidden in the shadows I did not realize she wasn't asleep like the rest of the huntresses. "She will be fine, Lord Hermes. I will ensure it."

*She* will be fine. Not *they*.

How quickly Maressa Holliday has wrapped me around her finger.

"Thank you," I say to Lamb.

The quiet huntress only nods her head, but her hand lays casually on her god-bestowed sword. It's impressive how easily she can hide in the shadows, even with a four-foot-tall, shimmering, lime-colored sword holstered to her side.

Athena takes my hand, while Iris grabs onto Artemis, and we travel to Mt. Olympus. I fly at the speed of light, Athena wrapped around me. I fly for only a few seconds, traveling between Earth and Mt. Olympus, but my mind is a battlefield. Within my storm of thoughts, I picture the last battle I fought on Mt. Olympus. I see the cage Kronos kept me inside and hear my ear-piercing screams that Typhon laughed at, and I see him.

Epiales, boiling with rage as he watched my torment.

Why have I let him live?

The golden gates inviting us into Mt. Olympus have fallen. They lay upon the clouds in disarray. Scorch marks desecrate the gates' doors, warping the gate's walls. Screams bounce from every direction, along with the clanking of swords and the laughter of a few demented souls from Styx's side. The sun has barely risen, and blood-shed already covers the clouds in rivulets of gold.

I unsheathe Caduceus while Athena materializes her

sword and her signature shield, Aegis. Medusa's carved face glowers at the first monster, a cyclops, who barrels towards us with a spiked cudgel and a gnarled bellow. Athena rushes towards him first, and before I can move, she leaps into the air and uses the sharp edge of her shield, slamming it into the cyclopes' throat. The monster can only gurgle, then fall with a cacophonous thud as Athena's shield decapitates him.

Athena whips her head back, her platinum ponytail slices through the air as she faces me. "Thanks for the assist, dear brother." Iris and Artemis materialize in between us, both already holding their weapons. Athena rises once more, wiping the monster's mottled blood from her cheek with the back of her hand.

Crumbled buildings decorate the floor, alongside streams of ichor and discarded weapons. There are no words we can share to ease the disparity of our surroundings. We can only run, hoping to find the other gods not yet imprisoned within the Dagger of Chains.

Athena's arm reaches out, crashing into my chest. I slam to a stop just as a circlet of fire clashes against green-misted smoke directly in front of us. On the left stands Hestia, grim and determined with a gauntlet of fire, dutifully obeying her requests. Her gold-and-brown, curly hair fans across her face, but around her head like a crown is the pyre. It sings to her commands, rushing towards the goddess on the right, who foolishly joined a fight against Hestia.

Hecate stands there, her green magic raging against Hestia, her face strewn in concentration. Yet, almost imperceptibly, I can see Hecate's hands trembling as she struggles to hold her own against the indomitable force that is the goddess of the hearth.

Hestia has not raised a weapon since the Titanomachy

Wars. She has not historically chosen violence; only when it is the only viable option. Hestia is the best of us, but those who do not know the goddess well assume she is weak because she is not an Olympian. Foolish opposers forget that Hestia willingly gave up her spot as an Olympian because of her love for Dionysus and her refusal to support a war. They forget she is one of the most powerful immortals in existence, with the most devoted followers.

Hecate will not forget Hestia's power again.

The flames, once calm, mimic Hestia's ire, and they rush towards the witch goddess they have condemned. Hestia pulls out two throwing knives from under her modest, blood-splattered white gown. She raises them in the air, and fire laps at the metal. They spin around the blades, dance alongside the handle, and kiss the tip of the knife as it soars through the air towards her target.

But there is one thing that can always extinguish a flame.

Water.

A gust of black river water strikes the air between the knife and Hecate. It claims the fiery dagger, stopping its assault just as the tip grazes Hecate's forehead. Iris, Artemis, Athena, and I rush towards Hestia as Styx calmly walks into the space between her and Hecate. Hestia screams a battle cry as she rushes more fire and daggers towards Styx. Hestia and Hecate are towering goddesses, both nearly six feet tall, while Styx is petite. Barely over five feet.

Yet, as a horde of a dozen flaming knives rushes towards Styx, she holds up one hand and her blackened river obeys. It steals all the knives, extinguishing their flames, and she turns every dagger in Hestia and our direction. There is no pride or happiness igniting Styx's face.

She remains stoic, pale as death itself, as the daggers multiply and fly towards us. The original twelve daggers have morphed into over a hundred, and I duck as the blades threaten to skewer me.

I collapse to the ground on my chest, but I hear the screams of those who didn't drop in time. Hestia rolls on the floor, with at least eight daggers imbedded in her body. One of the strongest goddesses convulses; screams of true agony escape her trembling lips. These are not mundane knives. Styx imbued the blades with her black river, destined to curse whoever touches the water with never ending anguish.

Iris has one dagger in her shoulder, and she's twitching on the ground, spit dribbling from her mouth. Artemis quickly wretches the dagger out of Iris's shoulder, but it does not alleviate the pain. Torture takes a new form with Styx's magic, designed only to inflict unbearable torment.

Styx strolls towards Hestia, who grabs the dagger closest to her heart with unsteady hands. She tries, in vain, to free the blade from her chest. I stand to my feet, ready to move towards her, but Styx gets there first. The cruelest goddess to ever exist crouches down beside the kindest goddess and cups her face. I run towards them, but a wall of green smoke stops me.

Hecate stands there, grim determination on her face. Two swords materialize in her hands. "You should get off Mt. Olympus, Hermes. Go back to Earth and hide."

I do not deign my former lover with a response; instead, I attack. Caduceus slams into her swords, which she brings together in an x-formation to block my strike. Her green magic is like a sandstorm, surrounding us both in an impenetrable tornado. Nobody else may enter. Curses leave my lips as I strike again and again, only for one of her swords to block my attack.

Yet, even with the storm around us brewing and my curses spitting vengefully at my opponent, I can still hear Hestia's screams from where she lies beside Styx. I can still make out Hestia's words before I know, without being able to see her, that they will be her last.

"Men are foolish. That much is true, but that does not mean that all women are wise. You believe you are the smartest deity to exist, Lady Styx, but you are just another greedy soul looking for more without realizing everything you will lose along the way. It is only a pity that I do not get to witness the moment you will die penniless, with your last moments blinding you with regret, because it will be a glorious sight."

One last whimpered scream leaves Hestia's lips, but then I no longer hear her. Hestia does not deserve to be entombed in the Dagger of Chains or imprisoned in Styx's games, but the Fates had crueler plans for the most benevolent goddess. Her demise fuels me, and I scream louder as I strike Hecate's blades again. Yet, this time, I use every morsel of power in my body, and I break the blades in half.

Hecate stumbles back. Just one step, but it's enough. I race towards her, and I slam Caduceus into the side of her head. She crumbles to the ground, and her sandstorm of green smoke begins to dissipate. She is nearly unconscious, but her wide eyes still fight to stay open. I sit on top of her hips and raise my caduceus high into the air.

I strike down on her skull, hearing the sickening crack of bone giving way, but I'm not done. Hecate cannot die, but I can harm her enough that she doesn't get up for a long, long while. I strike down on her skull again and again and again and again. There's only mushed up brains and powdered dust where her skull used to be, but I do not stop. I strike down on her chest when there's nothing left of her head to obliterate. I hit her throat and her arms and her shoulders. My rage assumes a new, almost unrecogniz-able form, until a crash of black river slams into my chest, and I fly across the battlegrounds.

My back slams onto the ground, and if the floor was not made of clouds, I am certain the distance and force would have broken my back. Styx barely glances down at Hecate's body, unmoving for the next few hours, as it heals from the injuries I inflicted. Her heartless, black eyes bore into me and the goddess who helps me to my feet. Athena stands shoulder-to-shoulder with me, glowering at the goddess who started all this strife. In the distance, I see Artemis and Iris running towards a horde of titans, leaving Athena and I alone to face Styx herself.

At any moment, I expect to see my father. For King Zeus to come out of his hiding spot with a lightning bolt in his hand and authority brewing in those electric blue eyes, but as I look around the battlefield, I do not see lightning bolts crashing through the skies. Styx is the leader of the opposing side, and she should fight against our king, but she's strolling towards Athena and me. From where I stand, I can see Poseidon dueling against Uranus. I see Nike's wings as she smacks a titan and sends him soaring through the air.

I can see Aphrodite and Hephaestus back-to-back, fighting against a horde of Empusae. The Empusae are shape-shifting female monsters, with a single leg of copper under Hecate's command. They slither, hobble, and leap around the battlegrounds. As the sun reaches the top of the sky, the rays glint off their copper, sharp nails as they slash across Hephaestus's neck.

But I do not see Zeus.

Is Zeus already a victim of the Dagger? Has the crown already fallen from his white head, ready for Styx to place on her own? Some answers come readily, through either omission or observation, but I fear I will not learn this answer until the Dagger plunges into my gut and steals me away.

I grip tightly onto Caduceus and fight an instinctual need to tremble under the weight of Styx's gaze. She stands only a foot away from Athena and me. She glances at our weapons, both stained with her allies' blood, but her stoicism stays firm across her sharp features. I fear Styx does not care about anything except this crown on her head, and how frightful of a sight that is; a woman who cares about nothing except power.

"I have long since hoped that we'd meet again, Lord Hermes, away from my river and your secrets. So that you'd see that despite your thinly veiled efforts to keep her away from me and to keep my prophesied war from beginning, failure was your destiny."

Styx takes a step forward, and Athena places the tip of her sword against Styx's jugular. "Not another step," Athena snarls.

Styx does not smile. I do not believe she is capable of true happiness, but her lips twist up as she glances down at the sword. "Why do you hesitate in attempting to strike me down?" As Styx speaks, black river water drips from her perpetually wet, chin-length hair.

The water forms into two rivers upon her shoulders, then merges atop Athena's sword. We all know the power of Styx's river and the hatred with which it infests its victims, and Athena quickly drops her sword. She steps away from a battle because she is a pragmatist. Athena knows she will lose against the river. It is why we all swore oaths to Styx and her river, because deep down, we all feared this inevitability. We all feared that one day Styx would decide to leave her home in the depths of the

Underworld, and only a few could defeat her fathomless strength.

Styx locks her obsidian eyes on me once more. "I was told that you hid Epiales away from Saffron and me." In a slow monotone voice devoid of any emotions, she quips. "How rude."

She lifts her hands in a sharp motion, and black river pours out of her palms quicker than I can react. It wraps around Athena, and the hatred that streams out of the river infects her veins. Athena has always been one of the greatest warriors, who knows the right decisions in the face of war, but now all she has the strength to do is scream. A terrible, raucous sound escapes from Athena, tearing its way through her throat, as the black river floods her mouth. She drowns in Styx's power, on her hatred, and everything toxic originates from it.

I can't run to Athena and pull the water away. Water is untamable to almost all, and I cannot save her. Not unless I give Styx what she wants, which is Epiales's whereabouts.

Styx takes another step towards me, mocking Athena's previous threat. Her stare is unnerving and unblinking. "You hate her heart. If you tell me where you hid him, I will make sure he dies for you. You needn't bloody your hands." She stands over a foot shorter than me, yet still imposes the larger shadow. Styx places a frigid hand in the center of my chest. Athena still screams while drowning on the river water, as pain unlike no other racks through her body, but Styx's voice remains calm. "I will free Athena if you provide one small location. You are two of the wiser gods, I must admit, so look around. See the desecrated colosseums and realize that your best plan of action is to help me and escape before the Dagger of Chains takes you whole."

Only then does she look away from me to glance at

Athena. I follow her line of vision, and I wish I hadn't. The black river takes over the entirety of Athena's body. I see her face, tears streaming down, as the river continues to drown her, plunging into her mouth. Stabbing through her veins. Only her eyes are not victims of the river's torture, and they stare at me with unparalleled fear.

We have fought back-to-back for eons. We have faced Kronos twice, fought in the Trojan War as allies, and faced lieges of monsters. Yet, here and now, Athena shows fear. True, unadulterated terror.

A tear slips down my cheek, and Styx's cold, wretched fingers wipe it away. "There are worse fates for you both than the Dagger of Chains." She whispers. "If you do not answer my question, then she will stay that way forever. Captured by hatred's touch."

I only realize after she's done talking that she's still touching me, caressing the cheek where my tear fell, like the feel of sadness is foreign to her. Our bodies are so close, I must crane my neck down so I can stare at her. Unsurprisingly, she's already looking back at me with those bottomless, pure villainous eyes.

"Kronos once made me a prisoner on this mountain," I confess, and for a moment, Styx almost resembles someone with sympathy in her eyes. Almost. "He asked for a similar favor from me. He, just like you, wanted me to betray Saffron." She only stares at me, waiting for me to finish my thought. I lean so we meet at eye-level, and I spit out. "I won't be able to see it, but I can't wait until she rips every bone out of your body and ends your pathetic, immortal life."

Styx grabs a tuft of her black gown and wipes the spit off her face. Athena's screams grow louder, and I know it is because of my actions. Yet, I cannot change it. I have debated whether or not Epiales should die, but I know Styx can never have him. If she takes Epiales, who we all believe is Saffron's prophesied heart, then we lose the war. I may be selfish in my desire to ponder the possibility of killing Epiales and shattering Saffron's hope, but I'm not selfish enough to save myself and doom everyone else.

And where Epiales is, so is Maressa. I do not have time as war beats its steady drum, questioning what is happening between us. It is too new, and the world is too confusing to focus on her and me, but Styx wouldn't let her live. She'd kill everyone sitting at that bonfire with Epiales. The other human survivors, Maressa, Lamb, Dýnami…. my daughter, Jamila. They would all perish.

I wait for whatever comes next.

# FOURTEEN

HERMES

B ut what comes next, coincidentally, is a crash of seawater slamming into Styx.

She becomes a buoy in the water, colliding twenty feet away from me and into a crumbling building. As Styx's head slams against the edifice, she momentarily drops her black river from Athena's body. Athena crumbles, free and gasping for breath.

"Gross, it was you I saved, owl face?"

Athena, still gagging, glares at Poseidon from her kneeling position on the floor. He stands there, with the muses Thalia and Clio on either side of him, holding an ichor-stained trident.

"Screw…." Athena coughs and bits of Styx's black river spill from her lips. "You."

Poseidon grimaces. "Not even if you were the last woman on Earth." He turns to me. "Styx is getting up. It's time we go."

Clio and Thalia go to Athena, helping her up to her feet. Athena, still gagging, re-materializes her sword and shield. Styx stands, drenched in water, and glowering at the three goddesses separating her and I.

Poseidon grabs my arm. "They'll hold her off so we can run."

I rip my arm from his touch. "I'm not leaving Athena."

Athena has already been a victim to Styx's powers, and if Styx deems Athena responsible for my escape, then I know she will become a victim to it once again.

Poseidon grabs my arm again, whipping me around to face him. "She's after Epiales and she thinks you are the only way to get to him. She needs you, so that means you need to leave, and I'm the only one with water magic left to fight her off. So, let's go."

"The only one left?"

Poseidon glowers at me, any sense of humor gone. "Yes, they're all in the Dagger of Chains now. So, let's go before we join them."

Amphitrite, Triton, Asopus, and so many river and water deities are all gone. How many more join them in that prison? I turn to run, but before we flee from Styx, Clio screams out. "When you get back to Earth, save her!"

I don't know who *she* is that Clio is referring to, maybe Saffron, but I do not have time to ask questions. Poseidon, with his hand still grabbing a handful of my shirt sleeve, pulls me away from the goddesses fighting Styx. They will lose, that much is certain, but this isn't a battle we are meant to win. This is a battle where I only need to live.

Poseidon and I sprint towards the edge of Mt. Olympus nearest us. There is half a mile between us and our escape. Stymphalian birds soar above our heads, swooping down to take pieces of our flesh. Poseidon stabs a few with his trident, skewering their bodies, while I swat at them with Caduceus. We are so focused on our exit and these birds, so we do not see the other danger blocking our path.

Uranus, a deity I have only met in the pits of Tartarus, stands a few feet away holding the Dagger of Chains in his hands.

In the formative years of my existence, Uranus was the nightmare that goddesses told tales about to their demi-god children. Kronos was vile, but no immortal was as spine-chilling as the original king of the skies. Uranus, with eyes where souls go to burn and wither, was an immortal that swallowed the universe and every inhabitant in a world of despair.

And now he will help destroy the world it took eons to build.

An army of screaming furies and vengeful monsters flock around him. There is a cruel smirk upon Uranus's face as his electric blue eyes meet mine from across the battlefield that was once Mt. Olympus.

He is the origin of frightening bedtime stories, but he is not the source of my greatest fears. That belongs to the father of the monsters, who causes the clouds to tremble upon his arrival. He is taller than all the clouds in the sky and Earth itself, and he rises to his imposing height directly behind Uranus. This is the first time I have seen my torturer in almost a hundred years, and my blood chills at the sight.

I can hear my screams from decades ago, like I am suffering his torment right now. My muscles no longer know how to move, and my bones no longer know how to hold up the weight of my body. The gruesome creature responds to my fear, smelling it with a pleasant scent, wearing a cruel grin on his hideous face.

"Little god," his voice is equally treacherous and grotesque, and it slithers like the many snakes upon his body, threatening me with its poisonous bite. "It has been so long since we last saw one another."

That voice, the one that caused countless nightmares for decades after the last war, sends a familiar, fearful chill down my spine. The Father of Monsters, whose hands are only instruments for chaos, speaks to me, and I am suddenly back in that cage; his hands showing me just how cruel the world can be.

I stumble backwards, slamming into Poseidon's chest. He would normally tease me for my fear, but not today. Today, he tucks me behind him, and in a whisper, he commands. "The second I run towards them, you head in the opposite direction. Get out of here."

Uranus takes a step towards us, his grin growing at the sight of my visible fear, but that is as close as he gets to me. Gold glints from the rising sun as three knives slam into Uranus. He stumbles backwards, with three knives imbedding deep into his chest, and he glowers at the same goddess who arrives.

Gilded wings fly above me before Nike, the goddess of victory, lands in the space between Uranus and me. She does not arrive on the battlefield alone. With mechanical wings he designed, Hephaestus lands beside her, with Aphrodite carried honeymoon style in his arms. Eros lands a moment later, his white wings disappearing the moment he unsheathes his bow and one arrow.

Aphrodite, with her ever-changing forms, glances back at me with a smile. Sometimes, the smile has a dimple, but other times in different bodies, she has no dimple. Regardless, the smile is always gorgeously sad. Eros and Nike run towards Uranus and Typhon with a battle cry, knowing they will lose, but Aphrodite and Hephaestus stay put. Aphrodite places a tender hand over Hephaestus's cheek, and I only notice when she wipes it away, that he cries.

"In another life, I would deserve you." She leans forward, presses a kiss to his cheek, and runs into the battle alongside Eros and Nike.

Hephaestus glowers at me, like I am the source of all his heartache, and then he runs towards me. He pushes Poseidon out of the way, grabs both my arms, and transports us away. I have winged sandals and can fly by myself, but when I hear Typhon roar with rage because of my escape, my wings hide themselves in my sandals. The moment I hear *him*, I freeze. He is the monster responsible for everything broken within me.

I glance towards where Typhon barrels towards me, only to see a fifty-foot-tall wave. Poseidon is already looking at me with a wild grin on his face. "I never liked you much!"

He crashes the wall of water onto Typhon, and while I'm certain Poseidon will lose this battle, it's a nice last sight to see Typhon drowning. Hephaestus catapults us off the edge of Mt. Olympus, and his mechanical wings create whirling sounds as they descend back to Earth. From the top of the mountain, until we land back on Earth's soil, I can hear the battle cries. I swear my ears burn the moment we lose Mt. Olympus for a second time.

When we land on the ground, Hephaestus pushes me off him, brushing off his blood-soaked shirt like I'm the one who dirtied it instead of a battlefield. "Gods-damn you," he seethes.

"What did I do?" I snap, pointing up at the sky and all we lost. "Those were my loved ones too! It's not like I told Styx to go up there and take them all out!"

My voice cracks at the end, as I think of Athena wrapped in Styx's noxious river and Poseidon's last grin, before Typhon undoubtedly tears him apart limb by limb. I am at fault for innumerable errors. I should have told

Saffron about Styx from the beginning, so we could have been a united force against her plans. Instead of lying and tricking everyone around me, I should have tried honesty for a change.

But this battle is not my fault.

Hephaestus points his meaty finger at me. "She finally told me she loved me, and then I had to let her go." Spit flies from his mouth, showing just how broken this war is making him. "And now I must fight with you, the god she sacrificed herself for. A god she once cheated on me with. Now, I must work with you and not her. Never her."

"Had to? It was your choice to leave her behind!"

"No!" He rages, face bright red. He storms towards me, grabs a tuft of my shirt, and yanks me towards him. "It was that damn oracle's choice! She told Aphrodite that she had to be left behind. She told me I had to save you and not her, so curse you! If you weren't on that mountain, I could have maybe…" He drops my shirt, steps back, and runs a hand through his red locks. "Maybe I could have defied the oracle and saved Aphrodite."

Hart Sommers knew what was going to happen on Mt. Olympus. Just how much does she know?

"Why you?" I ask after a long lapse of silence.

"What?" he glares at me.

"Why were you the one who had to get me off the mountain? Why not Poseidon or Athena?"

"Sorry that you got the defective god to be your hero."

"That's not what I meant, and you know it."

Hephaestus says nothing. Maybe he doesn't know that I wasn't trying to insult him. After all, Hephaestus has been the source of many gods' mockery over the eons. He is the only god who hasn't been able to heal himself from every wound. Even Hecate, whose face I just smashed into oblivion, is going to regenerate and look the same as she did yesterday. But Hephaestus will always have a limp because Hera threw him off the mountain when he was a baby. No number of godly abilities will stop the pain or the need for a cane. No number of godly abilities stops him from being the only unattractive god, forced to be in love with the most attractive goddess.

Most attractive other than Saffron, anyway.

"I promise," I say, softer this time. "I wasn't trying to mock you or assume you couldn't help me. Thank you for what you did back there. I couldn't…" the words clog in my throat, unable to climb to the surface.

I couldn't have escaped without Hephaestus's help. While I can fly and move at the speed of light, I am a god deteriorating because of fear. Typhon steals away any godliness I possess until I am a puddle of anxiety and ineptness. If Hephaestus was not there to shuttle me away, I would be a prisoner to Typhon's cruel touch again.

Or, perhaps I would have known worse suffering under Styx's cold caress.

"I just meant that Hart said only you could save me and escape with me from Mt. Olympus. That's really specific. Do you know why she chose you?"

Hephaestus limps away, his back towards me. With seemingly no other option, I follow him. He doesn't initially respond, and there is an odd, lapsed silence.

Then, as we pass through the woods and see a crumbling city, he grunts. "She said my part in the prophecy isn't complete. I tried to convince her to let Aphrodite save you instead, but the oracle said nothing could happen to me before I found the former traitor and made her the perfect hammer. Whatever the hell that means."

But I know what that means.

Not the former traitor part, not completely, but I know why he needs to make a hammer. There are eight roles in this prophecy, and one role is the hammer. They will swing a mighty weapon that will start the ultimate battle between Styx and us. When I first heard the prophecy, I assumed Hephaestus would be the prophesied hammer, but he is only the blacksmith for the weapon.

The prophesied hammer is a woman who once betrayed us.

And it's Hephaestus's fate to find her before Styx.

# FIFTEEN

## HART

From my bedroom, the argument between Zeus, Ares, and Saffron rages on. The walls attempt to flee from their bellows, frightful of an escalated encounter between the three formidable gods. They scarcely noticed when I left the room, grounded in their rage and grief, but Apollo is ever observant.

For, I am the sun around which his world orbits, and every movement I make enraptures him. Apollo leans against the wall beside our ajar door, half listening to their argument but keeping his eyes locked on where I sit on our bed. There's a sketchbook resting on my lap, where faint outlines of figures upon a barred battlefield rest on the parchment. His eyes of vibrant green attempt to discern the faces beneath the blank spaces, hoping to glean knowledge I've purposely hidden from him.

Because if he knows the full truth…

I close my sketchbook and smile at my fiancé. "Close the door and come here."

I set my sketchbook to the side and lift the covers off

my body, and he gravitates towards me. A part of him wants to stay at the door, listening but not intruding, but he crawls into the bed as the morning light streams through the curtains. He lays his head on my lap and exhales a soft sigh of contentment when my hands gingerly run through his golden locks.

No matter how much time passes, and no matter how often I stare at his face, the sight of him still leaves me breathless. In awe that I met him, then somehow convinced him I was worth loving. He is too perfect, but he somehow sees me and mirrors that same sense of awe. Of perfection. From me. How baffling.

His eyes flutter shut, and a gentle ease filters back into his body. My nails gently scratch his head as we lay like this until the screams halt downstairs. A door slams shut with finality, and the house resumes its previous silence. Only when the room bathes in muteness, when the only sounds are our soft breaths, does he speak.

"All the gods are gone?"

"Not all of them," I say. "But Mt. Olympus is truly gone."

I can still see the sketch I made of this fateful day weeks earlier. The colosseums crumble into debris that the wind sweeps away. The ichor dries on the cloudy floor, serving as proof that a battle occurred, as there are no corpses. All the defeated souls are within the Dagger of Chains, which rests in Uranus's hand as he stands to Styx's right. Hecate is to her left, and Styx sits on the throne that belonged to Zeus.

A diadem rests on top of her short, perpetually wet hair. The black strands cling to his sharp, pale cheekbones, but she raises her jutted chin in the air like the diadem isn't too big for her head. Like the crown she fought so valiantly to covet, looks like it belongs. But everything with Styx is a façade. The diadem lays tilted, hanging on through stubbornness rather than belonging on the wicked goddess's head.

I remember the drawings of the first of many battles. Future historians hail it as the Battle of the Gold, for the river that will immortally stream through the grounds of Mt. Olympus. I sketched every individual feather in Nike's wings as she soared towards Uranus. Her small face strewn with determination, even as her eyes held the fear that came with a grim understanding of her fate. I drew the moment Uranus dug the Dagger of Chains in between Nike's rib cage, twisting it as she disappeared from existence.

Without leaving this home of bones, I have laid witness to all the macabre this war offers. I saw Poseidon's valiant fight against Uranus and Typhon. I bear witness to the moment the latter immobilizes the king of the seas. He ripped out his vocal cords and held down the thrashing, wounded god until Uranus pierced him with the blade. Everyone, from Artemis to Athena, from Hera to Demeter, has fallen victim to the Dagger of Chains and Hatred herself.

All immortals who remain are in this house or wandering towards the prophesied hero, hammer, and muse.

"Artemis?" I hate the fragmented hope in Apollo's voice as he asks about his twin sister, and my hand stalls in its descent down his long hair.

"I'm sorry, but she's gone for now."

Hesitation lines my next words. The future is tentative, and it plays a fickle game with me. I'm not fully certain fate has stringent rules. If I say the wrong words now, the fate of the world can disintegrate around me. Everything must be precise. Everything must go according to plan because if I make one mistake. If I say one sentence that isn't meant to be revealed yet, then Styx wins.

There is love, and then there is the emotion racking through my body, possessing me with Apollo. His mere existence threatens to unravel every bit of composure inside of me. I want to give him the world. To tell him everything I know. But I can't.

Hopefully, I can tell him one sliver of honesty without the world dying as a result.

"When you see Artemis again outside the Dagger," I say slowly, frightened that one word too many will ruin it all. "She will need you more than ever. Be there for her. No matter how much she pushes you away, be there like a shadow, no matter how dark it gets."

Apollo reaches his hand out, and it caresses the side of my face. "I wish you would talk to me," he murmurs. "There is so much you want to say, but so little you actually let out."

I tilt my head to the side and kiss the thumb that creates smooth patterns across my cheek. "One day I'll get to tell you everything." I kiss his thumb again, then stare down at him in all his resplendent beauty. "But until that day, I need you to promise me two things."

"I'll promise you a million."

"The first promise is that you will always love me, even when you don't agree with my actions."

His smile is the greatest sight in this world, and it threatens to incinerate me. "That, my dear love, is the easiest request of all. What is the next thing I must promise, μέλι?"

"I can't tell you that one just yet, but soon. Soon, you must promise me something that you won't like."

The soft smile he always wears in my company wavers.

"Talk to me. What is going on in that beautiful head of yours?"

I lean down and press my lips against his, which perpetually taste like the sun and everything that glows. He wraps a hand around the back of my head, and he furthers the kiss. He wants to talk, but I want to forget. For just an hour, I want to forget about all the images that paint a somber picture in my head, waiting to be released into the world. For just an hour, I want his touch. I want his kisses. I want his passion.

He obliges as he murmurs his love against my flesh.

My desire for an hour of momentary reprieve morphs into six hours of bliss. Nobody disturbs us as we finally join after weeks of stress and unspoken conversations bubbling to the surface. Now, as the sun sets, Apollo lays his head on the pillow next to me, wearing his soft smile of content even in his sleep.

I wrap the covers around my nude body, and I carefully slip out of bed. As I put on a tube top and a pair of my overused overalls, I periodically glance back at Apollo, careful to make sure he stays asleep for what comes next.

He doesn't stir as I slip on a pair of shoes and sneak out of our bedroom with my sketchbook hidden underneath my arm.

As soon as I enter the hallway, Hattie's loud voice carries across the house. She jubilantly tells a story about the past. I hear snippets of the story that are constantly interrupted by Saffron's rare laughter and Hattie's recognizable wheeze-laugh.

"You were convinced you were dying! Bleeding to death."

"I didn't know what menstrual cycles were, Hattie!" Saffron exclaims, but she has the widest grin on her face.

"And you were the jerk who let me freak out for longer than I needed to."

The two friends lounge in the living room, telling stories to Phobos and Deimos, who listen with visible confusion written across their brow. The four do not notice when I knock three times on the bedroom door designated for Zeus. Hattie playfully kicks Saffron, her grin consuming her sharp features.

Zeus opens the door and shuffles me inside. Their laughter dies with the gentle shut of the door.

There's a substantial burden with secrets such as ours. Zeus is the commander of his physical appearance. He can easily transform into a swan, a male in his early twenties, or an elderly woman. He can become anything he wants to be, but his emotions have warped him. The former king of Mt. Olympus still has hair as white as snow, with a matching beard, but his eyes no longer glow their signature electric shade of blue. The shine is gone, replaced by a haggard man with nightmares living inside of him.

"Do you have it?" Zeus extends his hand, deviating his attention from me to the sketchbook under my armpit.

I pull out the book, then the untethered piece of paper sticking out. I extend it to him, and only when he reaches for it do I realize that both of our hands tremble. This is it. The stepping stone towards the next battle. In the Battle of the Gold, nobody died; those we care for simply lay imprisoned. In Styx's destruction of the Underworld, many faceless humans were casualties, but we gained back some friends. Again, those we loved have shackles holding them down instead of death's frigid embrace.

But as Zeus takes the parchment paper, he knows this battle will embrace death. The next battle will begin in a few short days, and death will have his fill. It is a necessary sacrifice. All those who will perish in the days leading towards the next battle must die, but that does not mean their sacrifice is not worth mourning.

I see all their faces, past and future, as their lives fall, claimed by the father of all monsters. Fire cloys my lungs as Zeus rolls up the parchment into a scroll, wraps it tight, and grimly asks. "Does it matter who I give it to?"

"It must be Lamb."

His face scrunches. "Who?"

"One of your greatest weaknesses is your inability to pay attention to those you do not wish to seduce."

"I paid attention to you," Zeus quickly retorts. I simply glare at him as he relives the first interaction we had, where he tried to seduce me. "Okay, I see your point. Remind me who Lamb is, and I will be on my way."

"Lamb is one of the greatest huntresses this world has ever, and will ever, see. She deserves your respect, but if you cannot provide that, then she at least deserves to be remembered by you." I take an advancing step towards Zeus, who has quickly morphed into someone I feel comfortable enough to snap at. "She's the tall, mousy blonde you have seen for hundreds of years but ignored every time, but just in case that doesn't jog your memory, like it should." I produce a folded paper in my overall pocket, hoping I didn't have to give this to him, and I extend the drawing. "Here's a drawing of her. Do *not* forget her face again."

He, just like me, knows what happens next. Taking the folded paper, he opens it to reveal Lamb's stature. She stands in the prison cells, accompanied by her four-foot long, light green sword. Her Iris-gifted weapon glimmers in the photo, even without enhancements. She stands beside her huntresses against Typhon. Blood splatters her long face, smattering her intricately braided blonde hair. Fear contorts her face, but her enormous eyes narrow with determination.

There are others in the drawing, but I purposely crossed out their faces. I want Lamb to shine in this picture because even a mouse can appear valiant against a cat. Realization dawns on Zeus's face as he stares down at Lamb's, but he says nothing. There are no apologies he can make that I will believe or forgive. Lamb is nearly six hundred years old, but Zeus only remembers her name near the end of her heroic journey.

"When you see her, tell her to wait for Hephaestus. He must go with her."

"I wish you never told me our fate," he admits.

I open my mouth to respond, but he moves quicker than me. A lightning bolt materializes in his hand, and he strikes it in the ground between us. The action rattles the entire house, but when the light dims, Zeus is gone.

When I step out of Zeus's room, I do not go unnoticed. Hattie, Saffron, Phobos, and Deimos are all staring at the doorway I stand in, questions written on their faces. Saffron stands from the couch, hands on her hips.

"Where did he go?" she asks.

"We no longer have Iris," I say. "But the huntresses still need their sketches."

Or, in this case, a single sketch.

I walk away with the burn of four pairs of eyes searing into my back, demanding more answers than I am able to provide. Surprisingly, when I get back into my bedroom, Apollo still lies there, sleeping. He still wears that little smile, with no idea of what is next. Only Zeus and I do, and the truth keeps crashing towards me like waves in the ocean.

Visions splash against my face, and my fingers follow their rueful commands. I scarcely feel the pen in my hand or the paper beneath my palms. All I can sensationalize are the deaths and last screams surrounding me in a circle of flames. I can vaguely feel blood trickling down my fingers as I create one macabre art piece after another, but I am a woman possessed. Each battle I draw is with a combination of my blood and the threads of the future.

First, there was the Battle of the Gold, and ichor now decorates the white clouds of Mt. Olympus. The screams of Asclepius, Apollo's only son, burn my ears as the Dagger of Chains claims him. The muses' blood splatters across my face as if I were on the battlefield and fighting Typhon, Hecate, Styx, and Uranus beside them. As if I, too, fell victim to their smite. Two male bodies plunge off the edge of Mt. Olympus, avoiding a promised imprisonment from a battle only a rare few knew was coming.

Next, there will be the Battle of the Huntresses.

It starts with the piece of parchment Zeus delivers to Lamb, but it ends in the prison where Lamb's story began nearly six hundred years before. Hecate brought the original prison back from the rubble, and it's where they will find the prisoners from the Underworld. Typhon wields his mighty power in the prisons, believing he will destroy the huntresses as easily as he almost did in the Battle of the Labyrinth ninety years prior. Arrows fly in all directions as battle cries ricochet off the walls. I watch each sacrifice, each scream, and each thrashing body before the ceiling collapses and fire consumes the prison once more.

All colors of blood will splatter upon the ground, but only a few will survive to tell the tale of female bravery and an unvanquishable monster's ultimate defeat.

My body burns and recoils with pain, but I do not stop drawing because there are more battles underway. There will be the Battle of the Reds, where Saffron's Heart will die twice. This fate has been etched in stone for so long;

yet, no one will be prepared for the scream Saffron will emit. Blood slides down my ears as I draw Saffron's unmeasurable anguish, slicing through the ozone. Her scream forever becomes a part of the wind, repeating her devastation for all of eternity.

The prophesied Heart's blood will never leave this world. Where they die, a puddle of red will always remain etched on the ground.

Lastly, in the aftermath of immeasurable grief, the ultimate battle will begin.

The Battle of the Oracle.

My hand trembles as the pieces of the war intrudes my mind with vivid, brutal strokes. I can see each death, each sacrifice, each cut of skin before the world obliterates everything else. My eyes burn with smoke and blood and too many tears.

Death and sacrifice are a necessary part of winning this war. For the lives of trillions, the Fates require sacrifices. Magma must rise so that Styx may crumble. Throats must be slit so that the blood can rejuvenate the desire for necessary victory. Skulls must fly, so that monsters of epic proportions may fall. Each death I draw with bloodied fingers must occur so that all others may live.

"Hartika!"

Hands shake my shoulder and force me out of the future battles. Tears scream down my face, but I can still identify the terrified expression on Apollo's face. He kneels on the floor in front of me. I didn't realize I was lying there with a dozen covered pages laying haphazardly across me until now. He quickly grabs both sides of my face, but there are too many tears for him to wipe away. He only stares at me, his green eyes wide, as I collapse into him.

I sob with my whole body, and Apollo cradles me. He lays me on his lap, and I soak his shirt with my anguish.

There is no avoiding what I have seen. Because if I change the course of bloodshed and lost lives, then Styx will win. That poorly placed diadem on her head will be a permanent fixture, and Apollo will die.

So will everyone else I love.

When the tears finally subside, I reach for the papers. I expect to see the battles in brutal detail and see the faces of those within the prophecy. Instead, I only see three letters written over and over again on every single page. It mingles with my blood, and it's the scratchiest handwriting. Some letters are bulkier than others, but I can read those words perfectly.

Crumble like Pompeii.

Crumble like Pompeii.

CRUMBLE LIKE POMPEII.

# SIXTEEN

LAMB

War is where hope digs its own grave, lays itself in the six-foot hole, and waits to wither into nothingness. Long before Artemis had huntresses, and humans had nothing more than a weak fire to keep them warm, the first human woman named Pandora opened a box. This box unleashed the worst aspects of the world. It is Pandora, and the god who created the box full of strife, who I blame for the violence clamoring through the world. It is Pandora, who I blame for the turmoil I face in the deteriorated remains of a formerly vivacious bar, but I blame Pandora most of all for the hope she gave the world.

As the morning dips into the afternoon, and I am surrounded by humans and huntresses waiting for the gods' return. I know I should let the withering hope inside of me finally die. They have been gone too long, and in a time of war, when someone does not return, it means they won't. Yet Pandora left a festering wound when she allowed hope to enter the world. It is that torturous hope that has me staring at the sunset, expecting to see a rainbow manifest with my goddess in tow.

Instead of Artemis and rainbows, a crash of lightning jolts the few sleeping survivors awake. Epiales, or Erik as he calls himself now, still slumbers. A jacket conceals his face, which he has slung over his head. The rest of his body is curled into a fetal position. I do not stare at the former traitor for long. Zeus stands a hundred feet away, with a piece of rolled parchment in the hand not clasping his signature lightning bolt.

Zeus's eyes have always been the first indication he is not human. They blaze an unnaturally bright shade of blue, like lightning bolts thrash within his irises, never wanting an escape but desiring to be seen. Those shocking electric eyes lock onto me for the first time.

I rise to my feet.

I recognize the type of parchment paper in his hand. It is the same parchment that Iris received from Hart every day this past week. Now, it rests with the King of the Gods. A god who stares somberly forward and solely on me. He does not glance at the prettier humans, as he normally does, but he watches every advancing step I make. The recognition, nearly six hundred years after first meeting him, is an anchor, sinking into the pit of my stomach. He does not focus on me with adoration or appreciation.

When I reach Zeus and crane my neck to stare at the mountainous god, he stares down at me like I am already destined for death. He holds out the rolled-up piece of parchment, but when I wrap my hand around it, he doesn't immediately pull away. We both hold on to the paper, just one instead of the typical three, and he opens his mouth to speak. To me.

"I'm sorry." He lets go of the parchment and takes a

step back. The king of the gods, who no longer wears a crown on his white head, bows to me. He lowers himself in adoration of...me. An ordinary human. When he lifts his head up again, I'm surprised to see tears swimming in his eyes. "I am so very sorry."

Immediately, I see his sadness, and I think of Artemis. "Is she gone?" My voice turns shrill with worry. "Where is she?"

Confusion momentarily stuns him.

"Artemis!" I yell, stepping towards him again. "Where is she?"

A fresh wave of sadness slams into Zeus. For so long, I thought him incapable of any feelings other than pride and lust, but I am wrong. Tears slide down his face, slipping into his thick white beard.

"She is a prisoner of the Dagger, but that is not why I cry for you."

Suddenly, the parchment in my hand burns like a thousand suns. He doesn't leave, but he watches as I remove the ribbon around the parchment and unravel it. Like I thought, there is only one piece of paper instead of the typical three, and a human face does not stare back at me. A whorl of snakes on a massive, snarling face envelops me with mind-numbing realization. Fear isn't the correct emotion to describe how I feel when I see Typhon's face and the coordinates listed underneath.

I always knew I would die in the last battle against Typhon, but that doesn't mean I think I'm the prophesied huntress. I only know death awaits me beneath this monstrosities' grasp. My mind whirls back to that day in the arena, where I sat beside Hart Sommers. I asked her if I was going to die in this war, and she became so silent; I heard the *yes* in the whispered winds. My life has always had an expiration date, but now it stares at me with such finality.

My veins become ice beneath my skin, and I do not realize I am crying until the King of the Gods himself wraps me in a hug. He smells of dew and something sweet, and I nestle my face into his chest. War is gluttonous for unexpected turns, but being wrapped up in Zeus's arms and crying on him still surprises me. Artemis should be here, consoling me as the Fates near my life string with sharpened shears.

But it isn't.

Because I will never see her again.

"You must find Hephaestus," Zeus says into my hair. "I don't know why, but he must join you."

I pull away from Zeus's arms, and my voice croaks as I ask. "Can you bestow me one favor?"

"Anything."

"And a question. A question and a favor before I go."

Again, he says. "Anything."

"My favor." I choke back more sobs as I see Artemis's mournful face in the back of my mind.

I hear her wails from our time on Ogygia, when she thought I was going to die. My death will wreck her, and that's the real reason I cry. I have never feared death, but I fear what my death will do to my dearest friend.

"Tell Artemis that it isn't her fault. Tell her I said that she must forgive me for leaving her." I hiccup as more tears fall. "Tell her I will miss her, but I'll always be there when the sun rises and there's an apple in her hand."

Zeus does not understand the gravity of my words, but Artemis will. I just wish I was the one to deliver those goodbyes. Fate didn't wish me to live long enough to say it, so Zeus must carry the message for me. He nods his head, still mourning me. A woman, who he didn't deign a glance at, when life was vibrant and thriving. There's sadness in his expression, but regret lays in the undercurrents of his emotions. Regret for me, perhaps, but it is a question I will never have answered.

I wipe away my tears as I hear footsteps hurrying towards Zeus and me.

"And your question?" Zeus asks.

Dýnami stands beside me, ripping the parchment from my hand. I hear her gasp, and her own realization of where we must journey and subsequently die. I look only at Zeus, though. "Why do you care enough to cry for me?"

"Because a wise woman recently told me I fail to notice those whom I do not wish to seduce. With a touch of her hand on mine, this wise woman showed me everything you have done in your lifespan, and it is a shame you must die. You are one of the greatest huntresses this world has ever, and will ever, see." Zeus's eyes, bloodshot now with tears, burn into mine. "You deserve my respect, and I will remember you for the rest of eternity."

"What do you mean she's going to die?" Dýnami snaps, anger rolling through her. Anger is the easiest emotion to express when mortality rears its ominous head. "You don't know that!"

"Thank you for your respect, even if it is a little late," I say. I do not deny his claim that death will come for me. It is a sinking feeling I have harbored for a few years now, but I wish Artemis was here to say goodbye.

Zeus bows to me a second time. "It is, indeed, very late."

I hear more footsteps and familiar huntresses yelling around me. Yet, I only stare at Zeus. "One of my huntresses once said we are your shields, but that you forget we are shields who bleed. You chose today to never forget me again, but do not forget the other huntresses, either. Whether that is just me or us all, remember those who fall against Typhon. Remember the shields who bleed for you."

He opens his mouth to speak, but the typically cowardice king of the gods has shown too much courage for one day. Zeus disappears in a crash of lightning, but I know he heard my last words to him. Shikari and Hound hold the parchment now, the latter's hands shaking as she sees who we must face next. I hold out my hand for the paper, declaring Typhon's demise, and Shikari places it in my hand. All the huntresses stand around me, waiting for my final call, but I just stare at the paper bearing Typhon's image and location.

I do not know who else will die with me on this battlefield, but I know this is where my story ends. This is where the ink dries and the book closes. I have been so fortunate to have lived as long as I have, but staring at my finale is still daunting. I almost do not notice the clue Hart leaves on the corner of the parchment. It is the size of my thumbnail, but I see it. A pair of deer antlers.

I know who the prophesied huntress is.

I roll up the parchment, knot the ribbon tight around it, and face the horde of huntresses standing around me. Maressa, Epiales, and all the other humans remain at the bar, but they all watch our exchange. They see Shikari shake her head, tears streaming down her scarred cheek as she whispers one word. "No."

I nod. "Yes."

Jamila raises her chin, valiantly trying to camouflage her fright. "When do we leave?"

I look back at the humans, who Hermes begged me to stay and protect until he returns. I'm not sure if he will return, but despite my hope falling into a self-made grave, it still fights to climb to the surface. Zeus confirmed

Artemis is gone, but there's a nagging beast inside of me telling me to wait. Maybe it is my fear of death or the Fates' divine intervention, but I think Hermes is coming back.

"We will wait for Hermes until morning," I say to the women. "If he doesn't return, then we arm the humans and leave to search for Hephaestus and, finally, Typhon."

"One last monologue of the day," Reaper says.

Tears blur my vision, but I refuse to cry. "One last sunrise."

When we return to the bar's back porch, where we've set up a camp, some stare quizzically in our direction. They have all borne witness to Zeus bowing to me, a simple huntress, and questions brighten their eyes. Yet, I avoid them all. I start a fire, ignore some huntress' sobs, and focus on the crackling of the wood that I will miss so much. I roast what could be my last meal.

The humans fall asleep at nighttime, but all the huntresses stay awake. We pass around food and drinks, and trade our sobs for stories. Dýnami grins her gaped-tooth grin as she regales the time we broke into Dionysus's house and stole barrels of his wine. Vee sings an upbeat tune as an inebriated Shikari grabs a grumpy Hound's hands, hoisting them to their feet, merrily dancing around the campfire. Jamila admits the pranks she has pulled on Saffron and Hermes growing up, and we all laugh until our stomachs ache.

We all know that we march towards Typhon tomorrow morning. We all know that facing the Father of Monsters, who has been unvanquishable, is a feat that will steal many lives. Yet we choose to honor our last peaceful night together as a family. Because that is who we all are to one another. We are sisters in arms, and while we may bleed and fall in the coming days, we will laugh while we are still able.

June, with her only hand, points towards the start of the sunrise. The shades of orange peek out of the dark night, reminding us of where we must journey next. "It is time."

"Not yet." Shikari reaches into her sack and passes out three apples. I catch one, Hound the other, and Jamila smiles as a red one plops into her awaiting palms. "We still have a final monologue to share." Shikari's scarred, yet beautiful, face turns to me. "Our gracious leader, send us off."

I stare down at the greenish yellow apple in my hand. In my periphery, I see the sunrise growing brighter. In only a few minutes, the other humans at the campsite will rouse from their sleep, and our last hours alone will vanish. I might never have another sunrise, apple, and monologue, and I caress the side of the apple with the pad of my thumb.

"Many people's fears centralize on objects or creatures. They fear heights or spiders or, gods forbid, butterflies," I say.

"Hey!" Dýnami yells. "I told you that in confidence!"

I smile, but still don't look away from the apple in my hand. "But I do not fear the materialistic or colorfully winged bugs that have not killed anybody before."

"You are the absolute worst," Dýnami grumbles.

"What I fear most of all is that we will be the last group of huntresses in this world. That if we die." I choke back so many emotions as I croak out. "When I die, Artemis will come back to piles of corpses and quit. Before I became a huntress, I was nothing. Just a mute human prisoner in a cell that felt two inches big. I never thought I would be anything but a nameless girl in a pit full of other decomposing, nameless girls. Being a huntress gave me the greatest purpose in the world. Being a huntress has been the best gift the Fates could have ever given me. I found my voice here, as well as my courage and my freedom to be my unapologetic self. Honesty is a frightening weapon, but that's what it is. A weapon. Being a huntress helped me hone it, and without riding alongside Artemis and all of you women, I would have never found that voice that told me I was enough. I would have never found my authenticity."

My eyes rove over the huntresses surrounding me. I look at the youngest of us, Jamila, who sits proud and unafraid, even as death looms nearer. I find June, with one missing arm but a surplus of bravery. Dýnami, who is my longest ally amongst these women. She no longer smiles. Her joy wilts, but she extends a hand to me. She allows me to wrap my hand in hers and squeeze it tight. She lets me siphon a bit of her brazenness.

I see Shikari and Hound, arms slung over each other's shoulders, and I see Vee. Fearless, brilliant Vee, who is the only reason we defeated the Sphinx. Books poke out of her satchel, and knowledge swims in her bottomless brown eyes. She is a newer huntress, but she is one of the best.

Finally, I lock my gaze on Reaper, one of the first to start this journey with me. "I have grown so much over these centuries," I admit. "And I know I am going to die with a smile on my face because I have accomplished so much because of all of you. I do not know who will live to tell my tale, but I pray that however many of you make it out alive, that you make sure there are more huntresses riding from dusk till dawn. I would have never become who I am without being a huntress, and every woman who doesn't know where she belongs deserves to find themselves as a huntress too."

Everyone grows silent as my last words echo in the wind. Nobody responds to my monologue, but they savor the words. Let them enter their bloodstreams, where my plea and I will never die.

There's a crunch of leaves behind me, and when I turn around, there is Hermes. Beside him stands Hephaestus, with mechanical wings strapped to his back, snapping shut upon his proximity. I do not know how Hart has become a puppeteer, easily pulling the strings of gods, but she brings Hephaestus to me. Her plans click into place, one horrific battle at a time. Both gods wear gilded blood like coats of armor and solemn frowns that speak of the hardships that landed them here.

"Lamb, Artemis is-" Hermes begins.

"I know," I say softly, interrupting my friend. When I stand up, so do all the huntresses. We turn to face Hephaestus and Hermes, and I force a smile. "We heard about Artemis. Your humans are safe, but it's time we go now." I face Hephaestus. "And Zeus said you must join us."

Understanding lines the gruff god's face. "Then let's get on our way."

We walk towards death holding our heads held high.

# SEVENTEEN

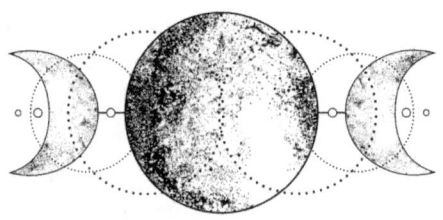

## HECATE

I am a soldier whose steps lead the way to Styx sitting upon the throne of the gods, but it is an unnatural sight. She wears the crown declaring her queen, but her chipped fingernails dig into the armchairs, fighting to keep her leveled in a place she does not wholly belong. There's an awkwardness to the image. I have worked alongside Styx for decades, and I have imagined this moment a thousand times, but visualizing it and witnessing it are two different experiences.

Titans, monsters, and gods alike fall to their knees in fealty to Styx. I join them, collapsing onto a knee and declaring her my queen, but my tongue feels like sandpaper as I repeat the words I have rehearsed a million times. My stomach recoils, filling with acid, like my fealty is noxious.

"My reign is here, but our work is not yet complete."

Styx faces her loyal subjects, but she has not declared victory yet. She is a daunting beast because even with a crown on her head; she does not speak with overconfidence. Styx does not leave pages unturned. Either the entire world is at her feet or only the few who kneel remain alive; to Styx, there is no alternative. There is no outcome where she fails, either through loyalty or bloodshed.

This is where Kronos failed.

He believed that because he was handsome and charming and said all the right words, everything else would fall into place. A perfect puzzle he pieced together without seeing the full picture. He assumed that because he sat on the throne of Mt. Olympus and had the god of nightmares in Saffron's ear, that he would wear the wreath of victory; males are foolish and brash. They do not think several steps ahead, not like Styx.

And I fear, not like Hartika Sommers.

"Hecate." Styx says my name, and only then do I look up at the queen oddly fitted into her throne. She does not smile when she speaks, she only exudes raw determination in destroying everything, not bending to her will. "Take Typhon and Uranus with you back to the prisons. Check on my pet and our prisoners."

Hope swells fast within my chest, rising like a flame I cannot extinguish. "And Mastiff, your highness? May I see him?"

"Yes," she hisses the word like a snake coiling around its victim, and I realize too late that I am the latter. "As long as you either deliver a name of one member of the prophecy or one of the prisoners' heads. Then, you may bring Mastiff here and choose a home."

*I may bring Mastiff home.*

The cursed promise of death or betrayal has an acrid stench, but all I smell are the roses of hope. I entwine Uranus, Typhon, and myself in my magic, and I transport us back to Earth. Back to the prisoners standing in between my greatest hope and me. While the immortals and I fought on Mt. Olympus and claimed it as our own, the prisoners wail as we cleave off their flesh.

"I will stay on the ground floor," Typhon announces. His voice is so deep, it is almost intelligible. It booms loud enough to rattle the walls and make the floors tremble, so I do not argue with him. He does as he pleases, killing anyone in his path, despite their allegiances. Wherever Typhon goes, screams follow.

Uranus grins at me. "Sounds like someone is having fun without us."

I open the door to the prisons.

Gareth French stands in front of Thanatos, holding onto his scythe, dripping with ichor, but he is not the only tormentor in the cell. Three former huntresses, who joined our side, stand in the cell with him. Raven, an elder huntress who killed Willow during the war with Kronos, leans against the only bare wall in the prison. She barely glances at me as she focuses on the two other former huntresses in the room.

Akita's curly, blonde hair cakes with red blood as she holds a knife precariously close to Sika's face. Sika glowers back at Akita, who betrayed and killed her mere weeks ago. Freshly made cuts, thick and still dripping with blood, decorate Sika's light brown complexion wherever her scant clothing doesn't cover. Akita's blade shines crimson, the instrument behind the many wounds across Sika's shoulders, neck, legs, hands, feet, ankles, and face. One of her eyes bleeds red from a cut across her eyebrow, but Sika does not stop glowering at the huntress who murdered her.

"Copperhead would be ashamed of you." Sika spits a blood-filled glob onto Akita's cheek, and the blonde huntress wails with rage.

"She wouldn't have died if it wasn't for you!"

Akita attempts to thrust the blade into Sika's flesh, but I hold out my hand and freeze the motion. Impossibly dark green smoke coils around the handle, stopping Akita a mere inch from Sika's shoulder. Akita whirls around to face me, eyes wide with rage and a hint of delirium, but I focus my attention on the third traitorous huntress.

Frigate stands in front of Willow with a set of pliers capturing one of Willow's fingernails. From the amount of blood spilling down Willow's hand, this isn't the first nail Frigate has ripped off, but Willow's face is hard as stone. She glowers at Frigate, who stoically stares back. They rode together for decades, but Frigate stares at her like one would a stranger.

Everyone betrays the ones they love for certain reasons.

Raven fell in love with Kronos and the lies he so expertly spun; she, similarly to me, betrayed family for romance. However, my love is a true soulmate, and hers was a façade. She didn't realize his deceitful nature before Lamb struck a dagger in the back of her head.

Akita betrayed her family for revenge, mixed with a dabble of insanity. Akita's closest friend's death spun her out of the realm of sanity, and in her spiral of grief and rage, she chose the wrong person to blame. Her vengeance focuses on Sika instead of Raven, a huntress who actually killed Copperhead, because of one small decision that put Copperhead in Saffron's room during an ambush.

Frigate, however, has no reason. She did not fall in love with a con man's tricks, and she did not lose her ability to think rationally over her dearest friend's death. Frigate is simply a bred killer, and she moved to where she would inflict the most harm. Styx prefers Frigate because they are both devoid of empathy and a thirst for inciting others' hatred.

I glance over at Raven, who picks her fingernails with a dagger. "How long have you three been here?"

"Give or take six or seven hours. No one is talking." Raven says without looking up from her dainty dagger as she files her nails with it.

"Because we don't bloody know anything!" Diam roars, rattling his chains with the movement.

*As long as you either deliver a name of one member of the prophecy or one of the prisoners' heads.*

Styx's command rings through my head with morbid finality, and I realize I am no better than the traitorous huntresses torturing their former sisters. I may not have fallen for Kronos's tricks like Raven or lost a close friend like Akita, but I let Styx's hatred worm itself through my veins. Slowly, the green mist stopping Akita from plunging a blade into Sika's flesh brims black with Styx's acrid magic.

I lock eyes with Persephone from across the room, and I ask. "Which one?"

Dried ichor covers every space of her pale flesh not concealed by her tattered, plum-colored gown. She has never looked weaker than in this moment, standing only because of the cuffs around her wrists; still, she glowers at me. Still, she fights against the chains.

"One what?"

The sound of my heels clinking against the cold, hard floor reverberates across the too-quiet cell. I walk until my hand reaches Persephone's chin. I dig my blood-red nails into her flesh until she bites back a hiss of pain. Leaning my face intimately close to Persephone's, I embrace the hatred Styx has infected me with, multiplying into blinding heights.

I no longer see a former friend; instead, I seethe with rage. "Which human dies tonight?"

A glob lands on my cheek. It's a mixture of saliva and ichor, but I do not wipe it away. I do not focus on anyone but Persephone, and I dig my nails deeper into her flesh. Blood blooms on my fingertips, but Persephone remains silent.

Without moving, I crane my neck until I see Gareth. "Kill them all."

Gareth has long lost the ability to blink or react. He simply raises his scythe high enough to cast a shadow over a red-headed human girl. Panda, I believe her name is, weeps at the sight. Her small body thrashes in the chains, but there is no escape from her fate. Gareth takes a step forward, and urine trickles down the length of her pants.

"When did you turn so cruel?" Persephone speaks through clenched teeth, and I can hear the rage and sorrow she bears. Rage for my current actions, but sorrow for the loss of the goddess I once was, someone who loved Persephone dearly.

Gareth's scythe kisses the underbelly of Panda's chin, and she cries out. "Please, gods, no!"

Her lover thrashes in his chains. I remember the human boy well. Pyro. His eyes fascinated me enough, those bright orange orbs, that I wanted to covet him. It is rare for humans to have wiccan abilities, but I thought he might have. So, I fought against Hermes during the days of human enslavement to possess Pyro, and I almost won, too. Yet, Hermes bested me, and now Pyro screams for Panda's life.

Gareth raises the scythe, ready to slice off Panda's head, but I stare at Pyro and order Gareth to freeze with a single "no." He does not respond or look in my direction, but he pauses his swing. I stare back at Persephone. "Who should go? You have twelve seconds to either speak the name of a member of the prophecy or name a prisoner who should die as payment."

Twelve. The number of Olympians who fell from their celestial home this morning. Twelve. The number of Olympians who denied me my happy ending. Twelve. The number of Olympians who found an eternal home in the pits of the Dagger of Chains, coiling in agony.

"Twelve," I say.

"I have loved Panda since the moment I saw her." Pyro stares pleadingly at Persephone, fear painting his eyes like twin flames.

"Eleven."

Tears roll down Pyro's oddly colored eyes. "And in our first tryst at life, I failed her." He hiccups through a wave of anguish.

"Ten."

"I didn't save her from another human, China, as she killed the love of my life."

"Nine."

Pyro's sobs join Panda's, which grow louder with each passing second. "All I could do was kill myself and join her in the Underworld."

"Eight."

Snot joins the tears trailing down Pyro's cheeks. "Now is my chance, Queen Persephone-"

"She is no longer a queen," Frigate interrupts.

"Seven."

"To save the love of my life," Pyro finishes as if he never heard Frigate and me.

"Six," I say.

Pyro flinches, but his voice does not wobble with uncertainty. Assuredness levels his cadence as he says. "Say my name, Queen Persephone."

"She's not a queen any longer," Frigate says once more.

Pyro glowers at Frigate. "She will always be my queen." He focuses his ire on me. "Even if others forget."

"Five," I say to him more than Persephone.

"Let me save her in this lifetime."

"Four."

Tears build in Persephone's purple-rimmed eyes. "You are a hero, who I will make sure the world does not forget about twice."

"Three."

Persephone levels her gaze with me. "There is something rotten within you, Hecate, something I no longer recognize. You did all of this for love, but you betrayed everyone you loved. Killed innocent humans as you destroyed their afterlife. You will kill a soulmate in front of the other. You said you did all of this for love, but I think you can no longer can tell the difference between love and pain."

"Two." The sound is guttural.

"I choose for you to kill Pyro. Kill an innocent boy in front of his soulmate and try to tell me again that you betrayed us all for love."

"You heard the former queen." Tears obstruct my vision as I sharply order Gareth. "Kill Pyro. The boy with orange eyes."

I do not turn to face the bloodshed, but I know when it happens. I stare solely at Persephone as the swipe of the scythe breaks the air with a *swish*. A loud thunk hits the cell wall, accompanied by a solid *thump* on the ground. I hear the unmistakable collapse of a decapitated head, followed by the worst scream. It threatens to break Panda's throat apart, but she does not stop screaming for the love of her life who died in her place.

His soul swarms into me as a pure white orb. It slithers into the center of my throat, right where his life ended, and I feel it burrow into my flesh. The pain of his soul entering my body is worse than all the millions that flooded into me throughout the week. It is this pain, not the action of killing Pyro, that causes tears to stream down my face.

Right?

I materialize a bag in my hand, and I thrust it towards Gareth. "Put his head inside."

The scythe drips with Pyro's blood, and I must look away. But it's only because his soul hurt entering my body, nothing else. It can't be anything close to mournfulness. Because if I mourn his loss, then guilt is quick on my heels. And if I feel guilty for this death, then I truly am the worst version of myself.

I hurriedly wipe away my tears before Gareth mutely passes me a bag dripping with blood from the bottom. I grab it and turn on my heels, walking out of the room as fast as I can. My hand wraps around the door, and as I swing it open, a broken voice screeches my name.

I shouldn't, but I turn around.

Bloodshot green eyes stare back at me with such vibrant hatred that even Styx, the personification of hatred herself, would flinch at the sight. Panda's body lays collapsed, solely supported by the surrounding chains cinching her arms. She only has the strength to keep her head up and skewer me with her abhorrence.

"He loved me, and you took him from me."

Panda has much more to say, but I cowardly walk out of the room and slam the door behind me. I do not care what the traitorous huntresses, Uranus, Typhon, and Gareth do to those who remain, but I can no longer be in the room. Ignoring the bag I grip tightly in my hand, I teleport myself from the prisons and onto Mt. Olympus.

Styx waits for me, black eyes zeroing in on the bloody bag in my hand. I throw Pyro's decapitated head between her feet, wanting to distance myself from him and Persephone's last words.

"Where's Mastiff?" I try to grunt out the words, but my voice sounds broken instead. Tattered like the broken-hearted woman I just left.

"Your new home is formerly Hera's. He's there waiting for you." Styx snaps her fingers, and one of the traitorous muses rushes to retrieve the bag and set it on her lap. Styx peeks into the bag, shakes her head with a tsk sound, and closes it. "Next time, when I ask for a head, I want it to be someone I know. Some hapless boy does nothing for my cause, dead or alive." She drops Pyro's head in the bag like discarded trash. "Next time, I want a huntress's head."

It takes every ounce of willpower to bow before my queen and grit out. "Yes, your highness."

Styx waves me off, and I hurry my steps towards my new home. She's already talking to the remaining immortals about eradicating the human camps scattered throughout the world. To start humankind a new with only devote followers, but I block out the direct order.

I try to ignore the memories of my last time in this room with Hera. The mistresses of Zeus's past circling around Hera as she realized her fate was within the Dagger of Chains. I know Styx placed me in Hera's former room because of those memories, which will surge back every time I see the newly cleaned walls.

But it is all worth it.

Right?

Mastiff waits in bed for me, yet when I enter, he looks at my arms first. They're painted with black veins now, baring a stark contrast to my pale flesh. His Adam's apple bobs at the sight, but he smiles when I walk towards him. I collapse into his arms, and I try to ignore how he stills, ever so slightly, at the contact. I try to ignore how often his eyes roam to my black veins or the blood staining the hem of my dress. Mostly, I ignore the flinch he makes when I press my lips to his.

"I missed you so much." My lips caress his face, his neck, his collarbone, as I wait for his response.

"I missed you too," he says, but it's delayed.

I ignore that too.

# EIGHTEEN

## SAFFRON

I secure a mask of enjoyment upon my face, hoping it hides the overwhelming guilt seizing my bones and slowly, torturously strangling me. I laugh at Hattie's jokes, swap stories of my own with her and our small audience, but internally I only hear the screams coming from outside. Since Mt. Olympus fell this morning, those bellows of helplessness have grown louder. Styx has laid siege on the world, destroying everyone who calls the mortal realm their home.

Zeus has ordered me to stay put.

Put on a cheerful face.

Pretend everything is fine.

Nothing is fine.

We are at war, where those who bleed red are on the front lines while we hide in our corners. Hattie and I tease each other, while Phobos and Deimos laugh on, and I scheme. I wait until Zeus leaves to deliver the huntresses with a new message and Hart slips back into her bedroom.

I wait until Hattie is on her sixth or seventh drink, eyes barely open, and I help her to our bedroom. Impatience thrums in my veins as I wait for Hattie to fall asleep.

Then, I rush out of the bedroom.

Phobos and Deimos stand on either side of my door, but before they can ask where I'm going, I stammer. "Where's your father?"

They share a look, and Deimos clears his throat. "I'd assume the training room again."

Neither god stops me as I jog down the staircase. I can feel their eyes burning the back of my skull, watching my every step, as I veer a corner and all but jog to the training room. Just as Phobos and Deimos predicated, Ares stands in the training room, drenched in sweat. He discarded his shirt across the room, and I stall at the doorway.

I am not unaccustomed to the sight of a shirtless male, but Ares is a rare god. His muscles display proof he's bred for the battlefield. He mercilessly trains every day for inevitable combat. His muscular physique is evidence of his determination in every gym and training room, and every word I planned to say clogs in my throat. Ares notices me the moment I swing the door open, and he lowers the training sword, chest heaving with exertion.

Every molecule of my body hums with awareness of him. Shirtless, sinfully muscular, him. I should look at his face, and those navy eyes are boring into mine. It is the proper thing to do, to stare at the person's face you speak with, but propriety has never been my strength. I cannot look away from him, even as he takes a step forward. Then another.

Electricity scours my spine, heating every square inch of me, and I can't look away. I came down here for a reason, and it wasn't to ogle at him. Yet, he advances until we are only a step apart, and I forget why I came to search for him.

"Saffron." He says my name like it is the last word he will ever utter, like I am his ruination.

I finally draw my eyes to his, and gods, there has never been a more handsome face. I should feel guilty for this internal confession because Epiales is still out there, but I have always been the foolish moth to Ares's flame. Ever since I was a young human girl, chosen by a god who thirsted for my demise, I couldn't stop staring at the beauty beneath all the monstrosities.

A smile, small yet very present, curls over his lips. The same lips I didn't realize vexed me until words tumble out of them. "Are you alright?"

Am I?

I finally draw my gaze up to his navy eyes, and they darken to an almost onyx hue. He cautiously raises his hand, the movement contradictory to his normally smooth and deliberate actions. His hand stumbles as it reaches for me, uncertainty lined across his forehead. For a moment, I think he will drop his hand and try to pretend like he never searched out my touch, but he doesn't.

Ares curls a piece of my dark hair around his finger, eyes fixated solely on the way the curl feels against his callous touch. It's almost too much, this simple act of twirling a piece of my hair. The only piece of hair not tucked into a braided ponytail. He takes one last step, ensuring he consumes every sense of smell, touch, sight, and sound. All because of one piece of stubborn hair that refused to go into the ponytail.

"You have always had the prettiest hair. The pretti-est…." He hesitates, but then grunts out. "Everything."

Despite how sweaty he is, he still smells like sandalwood. He still smells so gods-damned inviting. His other hand rests delicately on my hip, but he doesn't take the irrevocable step. He waits for me to press our bodies together.

I don't know how to move forward, how to speak when there's too much to say and too much hesitation to let them escape. I just stand here, letting his touch electrocute me and wanting...I don't know what I want, but I want something. Something I shouldn't crave from a god who tried to kill me and killed Hattie's sister. Something I shouldn't desperately wish from a god who stares at me like I am the weakness that could strike him down at any moment.

I take the last step forward. "Ares."

He closes his eyes, and a shudder racks down his body. Like, for all his life, he has wanted me to say his name just like that. With reverence. With want. He drops his grip on that single piece of hair and moves his hand to the back of my head. He grabs that braided ponytail tightly, and there is an absence of his former hesitance.

Ares is going to kiss me, he is going to unravel me, and I don't know if there's a way back.

I don't know if I want to go back to a world where I do not feel him pressed against me.

Using his grip on my ponytail, he cranes my neck back, and I exhale on a gasp. He stares at my lips, drinking in that little sound, and leans down. I can taste his desperation in the small, contended sigh against my mouth. We are closer than we've ever been before, and just like in the moments before one's death, our past replays itself in my mind.

First, I relive the day he almost killed me when I stared at Medusa's decapitated head, her eyes covered by a cloth. Ares held a dagger to my chest, his hands brushing against my bare flesh, as he told me I was more beautiful than

Helen of Troy. He said that he had to kill me because if I lived another day, I would be his ruination.

Then, when we met again at Dionysus's party. I didn't know the strength of my powers yet, and Ares could have killed me. We stood alone in Dionysus's backyard, with only an unconscious Apollo and a fountain for company. He could have killed me, and he said he wanted to, but he hesitated. He warned me I was dangerous to him, while also praising my appearance. Like I was the god, and he was the human who shrouded me with prayers. And on that fateful night, despite wanting to kill me, he was the only one who gifted me honesty in a room full of deceit.

In flashes, as his lips near mine, I see our time together in Poseidon's castle.

I had a nightmare, one that Epiales didn't create, and I couldn't stop screaming. Hattie and Hermes tried to stay beside me to stop the anguished sound, but I kept calling out one name in my sleep. Ares. He stayed with me all night, despite barely talking to me prior, and made sure I could sleep without the screams accompanying me. Even when Hermes rested, Ares did not.

Mostly, I see the night in Poseidon's prison cells. When Kronos manipulated me with a shot from Eros's arrow into my arm and I fell under Kronos's spell, only Ares could free me of the compulsion. He let me rip his bones out as he told me a tale that tethered me to my sanity. Bone after bone flew from his body, causing him unimaginable pain, and he did it just to protect me. To keep me safe as he told the horrifying story behind his actions during the time of human enslavement.

Every action, big and little, over ninety years, surges back into my mind as his lips are closer than ever before. I have known for a long time that Hermes was my second love, a familiar one, but with minimal passion. Recently, I accepted Epiales as my first love, which roots itself in passion and the greatest heartbreak, instead of my soul-mate. Yet, how did I not notice who has stood in front of me this whole time?

How could I not notice that it's him?

"Ares." His lips are so close to mine, a breath apart, as I stare up at him. "Are you my third-"

"Sorry to interrupt," a soft, feminine voice says.

Ares drops his hands from my waist and ponytail, and he takes a step back. He glowers at Hart in the doorway, while I cannot look away from him. The god who feared what we could become from the first moment he saw me. The god who I recognized when Circe turned him into a dog, even though I couldn't recognize Hermes. Ares, who stares at me with such reverence and fright, who joins me on every battlefield, and who creates a thunderstorm within me every time he is near.

He is my soulmate.

My destined third love.

How have I not noticed before today? Hart talks to us, but I can't hear a single word she says. I can only stare at him and wonder if he knows, and if he does, then why he hasn't told me? He has watched me fall in love with two other males, but he has remained on the sidelines. He even helped me see Epiales before Hermes took his memory away forever, but why?

"Saffron?" a feminine voice says.

I spin to face Hart, who stares back at me with red-rimmed eyes like she has been crying endless tears. Band-aids cover her fingers, which she picks despite the red blooming on top. She looks between Ares and me, under-standing settling on her face, but she doesn't give us a moment alone. She walks into the training room and pulls a piece of paper from her paint-splattered overall pocket.

Hart gives the paper to Ares. "Your boys and Cerberus are waiting to join you at this location."

Ares doesn't immediately take the rolled-up piece of parchment; instead, he glances at me. There are a million questions and emotions raging war across his face in the three seconds we stare at one another, but with Hart here as an unwanted observer, Ares looks away and snatches the parchment. He unrolls it, and I can only make out a few numbers, and the word **NOT** in all capital letters.

His jaw clenches so tight that I think all his teeth will fall out, and he curls the parchment tight in his grasp. Without a word, he storms out of the room. A few minutes later, and the unmistakable slam of the front door echoes down the hall and into the training room, where I still stand in disbelief.

"Where did you send him?" I ask Hart. She turns around and walks out of the room, but I follow her. This time, I yell. "Where did you send him?!"

Hart ignores me, and I jog forward. I grab her shoulder, and I spin her around to face me. "When I first met you, I was terrified of you," Hart whispers, like she doesn't want the others in this house to hear this declaration. "Soon after I met you, I found you levitating a god in the air and torturing him with your magic, and I thought you a monster."

I drop my hand on her shoulder.

"So easily, Styx could have made you the monster I thought you were in those first thirty seconds. You have that darkness in you, writhing inside and begging for a release, and she could have played you like one of her dolls. It would have been so easy for her if it wasn't for how well Ares hid your *secret* and how much she underestimates the humans in your life. You will have a lifetime with Ares after Styx is dead, but you damn the world if you try a moment earlier. She doesn't know who he is to you because of your past with Epiales. Keep it that way, or you will be exactly what I thought you were when we first met. A monster."

I stand there, frozen, as she turns around and leaves.

# NINETEEN

## HERMES

I see the world through red and gold-colored glasses. Hear the rustling trees like they are swords clashing together. I complete tasks, like traveling in search of food for humans, hoping I can escape the feeling of bars closing in around me. Suffocating me. Brutalizing me. I do not sit down from the moment I return to the campsite at sunrise. There is not much to do, but I find remedial tasks, like checking bandages and refilling water bottles. I valiantly attempt to ignore the howling winds, which haunt my memories and remind me too much of Typhon's serpentine, guttural laugh.

Nighttime descends upon the campsite, and I cook the food I have secured. I place each meal on a plate, and I pass it around. I provide second servings to those who ask, or even if they don't, I keep moving. Keep trying to forget how sticky Mt. Olympus's cloudy ground was when coated with gilded blood. As soon as someone finishes their plate, I either give them seconds or collect the trash. I move, move, move until someone touches me.

*Epiales touches me.*

Startled, I almost drop the trash in my hand as swarms of images return. Styx's prideful glean. Hecate's magic surrounding the battlefield. Kronos's taunting nickname for me. Typhon's gargantuan hand wrapping around my throat. Epiales grinning at my suffering. The screams, they personify into a version of myself that's broken beyond repair. Cracked like marble, unable to fully repair.

The most recent battle where I lost my family blurs with the days of my torture eighty-eight years prior. I lock gazes with Epiales right now, and he throws me into the past. He's presently here, but all I see is the version of him who stood on Mt. Olympus and stoically watched as my bones and sense of security shattered repeatedly. This silver-eyed monster forgot everything he did to me. Epiales, or Erik, or whatever in the gods' names he calls himself, grins at me. It's a pathetic one, brimmed with sympathy, but it consumes half his face. The same face that used to torture me. The same face of the god who personifies nightmares, and ensures I suffer with them for the rest of my life.

I stumble away from him, snarling as his hand drops back to his side. "Get the hell away from me."

The pile of paper plates mutely falls to the floor, but it seems the loudest in the world, the way I flinch. I dare to jump out of my flesh, and it's because of him. The monster who took my wife, but most of all, took my sense of safety. It died on Mt. Olympus almost ninety years ago, and now past and present meld together into this conglomerate of terror.

"I'm sorry," he says. "I was just trying to help."

Epiales's voice is so calm, so sickeningly sweet that the grating sound of his voice is nails dragging themselves down my spine. He drops on his knees in front of me and picks up the plates and fallen trash. Every so often, he glances up at me, and I hate the sight of him. Hate everything he has done to me and hate how he doesn't remember a single bit of it. I resent my decision to gift him with memory loss because he now has inner peace while I continue to suffer in the past.

I took away his memory, and now that loss tortures me.

Gods, why didn't I kill him before my conscience could talk me out of it?

Suddenly, as I see him beneath me, there are two wishes I want the Fates to grant me. First, I wish I had never taken away his memories. I want him to look at me and remember every moment he let Typhon torture me. Every time I screamed for mercy, screamed for *his* mercy, and he pretended not to hear me. I want him to look at me and realize that taking my wife from me was the least of my many reasons to abhor him.

Second, I wish I could pull Caduceus out and slam it into his skull. It'd break so easily now that he's human. Brain matter would puddle around him on the floor, and he'd never get back up. I wrap my hand around the handle of my sheathed Caduceus, but then a storm of inky black hair and sinfully plush lips stands beside Epiales.

Maressa places a hand on his shoulder, and he smiles at her. Together, they tidy my mess, and I just stand there dumbfounded. I do not need my heart to beat to live, but it thumps so loudly it threatens to burst free. My hand stays on my weapon, waiting for the inevitable moment Epiales reminds me he is a malevolent tumor and needs to be removed from this world. I hear his jeering taunts from ninety years ago in my head, playing the most evocative tune, as I wait for him to try to harm Maressa.

Tears blur my vision as I wait and wait.

And wait and wait.

But nothing happens.

They stand up, plates filling both of their hands, and only then does Maressa face me. I wonder how I look through her lens. Am I a hapless god who trembles like a leaf on a windy day? Or do I appear like a selfish god, staring down at two perceived humans as they clean up my mess? What wrong, distorted version of myself does Maressa see as she cranes her head up to face me now?

I turn around and walk away before I get an answer. A fire roars and broken people laugh in an effort to stitch themselves back together. I walk far enough away that I can still view the building, but I no longer hear the voices. Most importantly, I sit on the ground covered in debris and dried blood far enough away from Epiales, ensuring I do not see his face. Willing myself not to cave into my carnal desire to murder him in front of everyone he deceives with his false kindness.

Why does my heart beat so fast?

I place my hand on my chest, willing it to slow down, but it palpitates as soon as I acknowledge it. I do not need oxygen to breathe, but suddenly there's a heavy force sitting atop my chest. It obstructs my breathing, and I can't…I can't breathe.

A wheezing, unnaturally human sound escapes me in irregular breaths. I clamp my eyes shut; all I see are streaks of gold against fallen, white columns. I hear Poseidon's last words to me. Picture Hecate's crushed skull. Then, the image switches. At first, I see Hecate on the opposing side of a war atop Mt. Olympus's gilded home; the next, she's sitting in a cage with me. Her anguish matches mine, mirror images of one another, as we both weep with pain and anguish and helplessness.

I feel Typhon ripping apart my body, using my bones as toothpicks, and watching me stitch myself back together with a rueful laugh and a promise for more strife in the morning. I can't breathe as memories flood through me. They reach my throat, and the water of past trauma drowns me.

I can't breathe, I can't breathe, I can't-

"Hermes." A soft, melodic voice breaks through the wheezing and the memories.

I don't open my eyes because I'm not sure I have the strength, but I know it is Maressa who sits on the ground next to me. We have only known each other a few short days, but I would recognize her voice anywhere. She places a gentle hand atop mine, which sits on my pulsating heart, while she wraps the other around my side. She rests her head against my shoulder. The moment I feel her against me, I finally allow the tears to fall.

I finally breathe.

I hid this version of me from Saffron. Not because I didn't think she'd understand. Saffron would understand all too well what it means to suffer with nightmares and monsters of our past, but I couldn't do it. I couldn't break through my dignity to confess what I needed to breathe life into. I couldn't admit to Saffron, who fell in love with a happy version of me, that I was irrevocably broken. The pain was too raw to admit aloud because I never needed anyone to save me from my mind before, and it's terrifying. To admit you are imperfect, especially to a woman like Saffron, who I thought was impeccable in every way.

Maressa doesn't ask me why I sob and heave in a desolate part of the crumbled world; she just holds me. Her thumb gingerly grazes the top, then bottom, of my hand in a smoothing motion. Eventually, I match my breathing to the slow rise and fall of her thumb.

When the anvil lifts from my chest and the waves of anxiety lessen, I whisper through a croaked voice. "I am the god of thievery and mischief. I am the god of travelers and messages. Every story ever written about me is in jest. I am the comedic relief. I am the troublesome god no one takes seriously. That is what the world wants me to be. It placed me in a box, and it demanded I stay within those four walls."

"Even during the Titanomachy Wars, I was exactly that god. The one who teased and almost always smiled. The one who stole trinkets from the titans and still managed to complete my work as the messenger of the gods. I would have breaks from fighting a war to take human souls to the Underworld, and my resolve never faltered. I was impenetrable to anything but mischief, trickery, and fun. Gods, I used to find fun. It's why we were so perfect in the beginning."

Maressa remains silent. She doesn't fill in the spaces when I falter, and she doesn't correct me when my words come out in ragged breaths. She keeps her head on my shoulder and keeps trailing her thumb up and down the length of my hand. It has only been a little over a week, but her company brings me peace the way nobody else has before.

How odd.

I let the tears fall, landing on our conjoined hands. "Then Kronos decided *not* to put me in the Dagger of Chains. He decided I was to be one of his pets on Mt. Olympus, along with Hephaestus, Hecate, and Ares."

There is a detached tone of my voice; even my cadence slows as I try to separate myself from the truth of my past. Yet, the tears streaming down my face are the cemented proof that I cannot escape. A jagged part of me started on that fateful day. If I had known Kronos would send me to Mt. Olympus in a dog-size cage, break me bit by bit, then I would have had time to say goodbye to those I love. To let them mourn the version of myself that dutifully stayed in his box of expectations.

That jovial, teasing side of me withered in that cage, and there's no sign he will ever come back. Never fully.

"I can't get those dark days out of my head, no matter how hard I try to smile it away. No matter how hard I try to be mischievous and make jokes, I still thrash and scream when night comes. I still feel Typhon and Kronos and *Epiales* tearing apart my flesh to find nothing of value inside." I spit out the last name, with a repulsion rivaling the former two.

*Epiales.*

He hurt me the least during my captivity on Mt. Olympus, but he is everywhere I turn. He is the epicenter of all my anguish. Both in my marriage and within the cage.

"I am supposed to be a master trickster, who welcomes all weary travelers with a witty remark on my tongue, but they stole my trust in strangers. Stole my ability to do anything but work. I avoid sleep and communication and…anything that makes me feel."

I look down at Maressa, and after a second of feeling my eyes burrowing into her skull, she lifts her head, and her gaze locks with mine. For a moment, I'm so spellbound by how bottomless her brown eyes are that I pause, but I must eventually speak.

To finally say the words I should have said before ninety years of anguish drowned me whole. It should have been Saffron who heard these words, or any of my brothers. Hephaestus was there with me. He would have understood that while he coped with what happened to us, I couldn't. My mind spun back to the place of my worst suffering, and I couldn't jump off the ride of whirling thoughts and endless nightmares.

"Do you know how agonizing a world is where you are too afraid to speak? To be your complete self?"

For the first time, she answers one of my hypothetical questions. "Yes, more than you know."

I wait in silence for her to elaborate, but Maressa Holliday wishes to remain an enigma, and my brain holds too many secrets needing an escape. One day, I will learn the secrets Maressa Holliday wishes to keep, but for now, it is time I expel my truth. To finally be honest.

"I lost everything because I couldn't admit that I never truly left that cage on Mt. Olympus, but I want to stop living there in my mind. Stop hating those involved, even if they don't deserve forgiveness. I want to stop living my life ninety years in the past. Every day, I live in the past. It's why I can't let go of things, and people, who no longer fit in this version of myself. Because I haven't left that cage."

Saying the truth is frightening, but hearing myself admit my self-isolation is heart shattering. Maressa knows what I need without the words to express them. She climbs into my lap and wraps her arms around the back of my neck. She holds me tight as every bit of my truth pours out in the loudest breakdown of my immortal life. I do not know how long we sit here, cradled in each other's embrace, but she doesn't let go when I stop crying. She stays rooted on top of me, squeezing me, until I can speak again.

"I'm sorry," I say. "I shouldn't have-"

She pulls back and places both of her hands on either side of my face. "No, I don't accept your apology because you have nothing to apologize for." She runs her fingers over my cheeks, wiping away my tears as she murmurs. "There's strength when honesty trumps mischief. I commend you for being strong enough to be truthful because it's easier to hide with your secrets because I haven't yet learned that skill. I always want to hide from my truths. To put them in that same box you conform yourself in, but we do not have to be in a box of others' creations."

She hesitates for a moment, then leans down and presses her lips against mine. They're smooth and perfect. Pure nirvana.

When she pulls away, she whispers against my mouth. "You do not have to be in that cage any longer. Even if I must drag you out every single day."

Powerful goddesses have surrounded me all my life; gods, I was married to the single most powerful goddess in existence. Yet, I am guilty of hubris, because when I look at Maressa brushing away my tears and declaring she will fight my nightmares with me; I have never seen a woman more fearsome.

"Epiales," Maressa says the name so softly and hesitantly. She looks at me, waiting to hear if I will shut down her inquisition, but I stay silent. I wait for the question I know comes next. "Why does that name sound familiar?"

I almost decide to play my role as the trickster and evade the question, but I am done molding myself to others' expectations. Not around her, at least.

"He is a god wiped from history," I say. "He is one of the Oneiroi; a personification of nightmares."

I almost admit I'm surprised the name sounds familiar to her. Even younger immortals, like Phobos and Deimos, did not know who Epiales was prior to his imprisonment in Tartarus. But I bite my tongue.

Maressa mulls over my words, then asks. "Why was he wiped from existence?" Her wide, inquisitive eyes meet mine again, and a thousand lightning bolts find a home within my veins. "Was it because Saffron killed him at the end of the final Titanomachy War, or because he is human and sharing a campsite with us?" I do not know how to respond because my ability to speak leaves the moment a confident smirk curls over her full lips. "It may have taken a few days to discover who you were, Lord Hermes," she says tauntingly. "But when a man of unnatural beauty lands in the middle of nowhere without an idea of who he is, I get curious. Curious enough to put all but one piece together."

Realization dawns on me. "The last piece was knowing his name."

Her smirk turns into a triumphant grin. "I'm right, aren't I? Erik isn't a human with amnesia." I glint of gold sparks to life in the distance. "He is a former-"

I shove her down onto the ground, catching a spear-shaped icicle in my hand as a raucous horde of traitorous immortals rush towards our campsite.

Gold blood oozes from the tip of the spear, splitting apart my flesh, but I barely feel it. I stand to my full height and throw the weapon across the ruins of a former town. Arrows forged from ice fly towards Maressa's fallen body. I jump on top of her and accept the blades as my penance for not getting her and the others to safety faster. I let my daily nightmares of the past blind me to the present dangers, and they could die for my mistake. Arrows pierce my back, decorating me in the shame of my mistakes, but I cradle Maressa's head in my arms. Refusing to let a single blade touch her.

I lift my head enough to stare down at her in all her brilliance, and I whisper. "Get back to the campsite. Take Er..." I almost say the blasphemous name, but I'm done lying to those I care about. I have made that mistake one too many times throughout my life. "Take Epiales," I correct. "And anybody else who can run. You go south, and you pray to Saffron. Every second of every step, you pray to her. She will hear, and she will come for you all."

More arrows slam into my back, robbing thoughts from my lungs. I can only lean down, kiss the center of her forehead, and whisper once more. "Run and pray. I'll be right behind you."

I stand and whirl to face the nearing crowd of traitors. Khione, the goddess of snow, stands in the middle of a court of cyclops. The few who did not die by Poseidon's hands in his underwater castle stride towards me with spiked clubs; flesh sticking to their razor-sharp, grinning teeth. Caduceus materializes in my hand, and my winged sandals stir awake. I fly a few feet above the ground, icicle-shaped weapons decorating my body, and I move faster than the speed of light towards Khione and a horde of cyclops.

They do not understand the gravity of their mistake.

They tried to harm Maressa, and for that, they will suffer unimaginable terror.

# TWENTY

HERMES

Caduceus smashes into the skull of the cyclops to Khione's right. There is a glimmer of recognition across the goddess's face before I throw my gilded weapon towards the cyclops on her left. It slides through the cyclops' eye, spilling out the other side. Both monsters collapse to their knees, then fall face first into the dirt.

Khione covers her fist in the form of a black of ice, and it slams into the side of my face. I stumble a few steps back, but I extend my hand and beckon Caduceus forward. Before she can punch me again, I swing my weapon, and it strikes her with such force I hear the unmistaken crack of her cheekbone.

She wipes a slew of ichor from the corner of her mouth with the back of her hand, and two ice katanas materialize in each hand. Two more cyclops rush at me. Speed is my sole advantage in this battle. I deflect one of Khione's blades, then swirl towards a cyclops and shatter every bone in his hand as it strikes against Caduceus instead of my face.

I jump to the side before Khione's katana can collide with my stomach, then duck beneath another cyclops' fist. Another cyclops slams his spiked club down towards my skull, and I move directly into the next act of deflection. I'm only delaying the inevitable, but eventually, I cannot avoid their blades. Four cyclops surround me now, and my speed isn't enough.

I side-step another blade, but a cyclops' fist slams into my cheek in preparation. I stumble backwards, and that's all it takes. Khione slices across the side of my face, and the exposed flesh sings with frigid agony. A spiked club pierces the back of my neck, burrowing into my flesh, and I can barely scream as I fly above them.

I extract the spiked club from the back of my neck, and I soar back down. My body stitches itself together quickly enough to accept more pain. I hit Khione with Caduceus, but only on the shoulder. I notice my movements getting slower, and sadly, so do my opponents. One cyclops crashes his fist against into my nose. My gilded blood decorates my face, ensuring that it and my opponents are all that I can see.

Two cyclops grab both of my arms, and they slam me onto the ground. Before I can thrash and fight through the restraints, two more cyclops pin down my legs. The floor trembles with dreadful anticipation as Khione stands above me, eyes glinting with malice.

"Styx will be most pleased with our new toy." She lifts her head, locking her gaze with one cyclops holding me down. "Let us take him to-"

An arrow pierces her forehead. She stumbles back one step, rips the arrow from her head, and looks back at her assailant. I wiggle under the cyclops' hold, vying to see who foolishly tried to interfere in a battle between gods and monsters, but I cannot see through the wall of beasts around me.

I can see Khione, though, and she grins with unadulterated glee.

Which only means one person.

"Epiales," she sings his name. Dropping the arrow onto the ground, she ignores me entirely on the floor. I scream and pull and try to bite one of the cyclops' fingers, but my attempts remain futile. Khione strolls past me and reaches Epiales. "It has been so long since I have seen your handsome face. Where have you been hiding, sweet nightmare? And who are your human companions? Treats for me?"

She purrs adoringly at Epiales, and I forget his kind acts throughout the week. I forget every word Saffron and Maressa have spoken in his defense. I hear a villain coo after him, and I loathe myself for believing, even for a second, he could be better than his past-

A scream fractures my thoughts. Khione's head falls a few feet beside me. She's still alive, screaming as her head attempts to return to its rightful place atop her neck. Her frosty gaze narrows on the former personification of nightmares himself, brandishing a sword bloodied gold.

Arrows decorate the sky, and while most of them do not land anywhere near the battlefield, a few inexperienced archers get lucky. They rain down on the cyclops and me, and while three hit my shoulder, waist, and thigh, I barely register a pinch of discomfort. The cyclops surrounding me suffer the most. They wear more arrows than clothing, and as they thrash in discomfort, their grip on my arms and legs lessening enough that I rip myself free, soar towards the sky, and land several feet away.

My feet slam on the ground directly next to Epiales. A few of the stronger humans stand beside him, but there is only one woman who captures my attention. Maressa stands to Epiales's right, holding a sword in her hand that is almost taller than her. Behind her, about a hundred yards away, are the rest of the humans with arrows notched on their bows, firing another round against the cyclops as they rip the other arrows out of their flesh.

"I told you to take them and run." I loom over Maressa. There's a foot and a half height difference between us, but she grins like she is seven feet tall.

"And I didn't listen. You're welcome."

"What did the ice goddess call me?" Epiales asks.

I do not have time to argue with Maressa about running towards danger, or answering the questions Epiales tries to pry out of me with his burning gaze. I whirl to face the cyclops again.

"If you get hurt, yell for me," I tell Maressa. "Scream as loud as you can, and I'll run for you."

"Awe, thank you, Lord Hermes." A voice that is not Maressa's responds.

I glower at the source of the voice. A middle-aged man with a receding hairline and a goofy grin, stares at me with such reverence. "Reginald, I wasn't talking to-"

"You are too good to Reginald, Lord Hermes," Maressa mocks beside me.

I run towards the remaining six cyclops. One died from a perfectly aimed arrow to his eye, but too many remain for our small horde of humans and me to fight. Khione screams instructions to all the cyclops to reattach her head to her body, so she may join the fight, but I get there first. I grab her head of white hair, and I race back to Epiales.

I place Khione's head in his hands. "Keep this as far away from her body as we can. We might have a shot at helping the humans survive if she stays immobile."

"Okay." Epiales takes the head, places one hand over

Khione's screaming mouth, but then he turns to face me and hesitantly says. "Lord Hermes?"

I flinch at the sound of my name from his lips, but I crane my neck back. "What?"

"I can't be what you say I am."

I don't have time for his existential crisis, and I fly away. A cyclops has his hand wrapped around Reginald's throat, and I slam Caduceus into the cyclops' skull. It splinters in half, and he collapses onto the ground. I catch Reginald before he plummets twenty feet from the sky and set him on his feet.

He cries while grinning. "I knew you'd save me!"

"Okay, Reginald." I sprint away before he can declare his unending love for me.

I face two cyclops as the rest of the humans face off against the remaining three. Time eludes me, but I spare a second to look back at the humans. Reginald is dead, now a pile of broken limbs on the blood-soaked ground, but the rest of the humans survived. Those who stayed back to fire arrows now join the others. There are almost ninety humans facing the five monsters.

Standing at the helm is Maressa. She wields her weapon with quick accuracy. It is she who causes the cyclops nearest her to scream. It is she who makes the bastards bleed. No one else has even nicked her flesh. She spins and thrusts and parries away, and I take a punch to the face because I cannot tear my eyes away from her.

She's incredible.

But it is because I look at her in enthrallment that I see the moment one cyclops swings his spiked club towards her face. She ducks in enough time to save her life, but a blade slices across her forehead.

Blood blooms at the crown of her head. Two droplets trickle down the expanse of her round face. One is red, brightly contrasting her dark complexion. The other is a shimmering, inhuman shade of gold. Maressa wipes the blood away with the back of her head, barely reacting to the discolored hues, and she rushes back towards her opponent.

I pause at the revelation.

The law prohibiting the birth of demi-gods ended with the final Titanomachy War. While most gods avoid having children with humans, fearing of the repercussions new heroes bring, their existence isn't unfounded like when Saffron was a mortal. Still, the news jars me.

I missed the obvious.

She looks just like Clio, the muse of historical poetry, with the same pouty lips, round cheeks, and impossibly dark eyes that take over half her face. Foolishly, I forgot the quick exchange between Clio and me during the battle. Her last words to me were a plea to save *her*. I didn't know who *her* was, but now I see all too clearly.

But how could I have not known until I saw her blood?

She plays an ancient instrument like her mother and aunts, too. Gods, I should have known she was a child of a muse, the way her sinful, velvety voice demands the attention of everyone within hearing range. I have not heard her sing yet, but I'm sure once I do, the last thread of me she hasn't stolen will unravel for her.

She stumbles backward, and the same cyclopes advances. Terror drags its claws down my spine, and I try to run towards her, but one cyclops grabs the back of my neck. He yanks me back, and I scream louder than I ever have before. She wobbles to her feet, but the cyclops she faces swings the spiked club again while she's still disoriented.

Epiales screams her name, too.

I swing Caduceus blindly behind me, hoping to hit the

cyclopes who has a hold of me, but he pins me to the ground. I lose sight of her, and that's it. There is no way she survived a club to the face, demi-god or otherwise. Except, I don't hear her scream. That means there's a chance, right? I spin out of the cyclops' hold, smash Caduceus into his jaw, and run away from the second cyclops nearing me.

I must get to her.

Please, don't make me lose her when I've barely gotten the chance to know her.

I take one step before the two cyclops I face grab my shoulders, and they yank me back. But I catch a glimpse of her, still bleeding gold and red, yet alive. Alive because a familiar three-headed dog feasts on the dying cyclops who tried to end her life. I must be hallucinating because Cerberus saves Maressa's life, while Ares, Phobos, and Deimos destroy all the other cyclops facing the humans.

I try to swing Caduceus, but one cyclops catches it with their free fist.

Cerberus comes to my rescue next.

He leaps over one cyclops, pinning him to the ground and all three mouths sink into his neck. The cyclops twitches, fighting his fate for a moment, before succumbing to the razor-sharp teeth of a very good boy. The last cyclops smashes his spiked club against Caduceus, but it's the last act he makes.

A sword plunges through his chest, and the cyclops falls.

Covered in the blood of the monsters, Ares stands in full armor. His chest heaves and rage paints a brutal picture across his face. He points towards where Epiales stands with Khione's decapitated head in his hand. "Care to explain yourself?"

I run from my brother, and I collapse to my knees

where Phobos and Maressa sit. Phobos materializes gauze, but I swat him away. "Go take care of a different human." I lock eyes with Maressa. "This one is mine."

I do not get to speak a word to Maressa before Ares barrels back towards me. "You have been hiding him all this time?!" Ares grabs onto my arm, and I cannot fight him. He yanks me up to my feet and his fist slams into my face. "Saffron has been in ruins, wondering if he died!" He punches me again; there is no god who inflicts as much pain as him. "You are the messenger of the gods, and you've known for over a week that he is alive. Still, you don't tell her?!"

He punches me again, and again, and I crumble onto the floor.

It takes both Phobos and Deimos to pull Ares off me, and I heal from my wounds the moment Ares walks away. It doesn't discount the fact that I deserved those hits. He's right. Saffron did not argue Epiales's fate when I decreed that he'd lose his memory, but that was before Styx destroyed the world. Eighty percent of humans have died, and I know Saffron thought of him.

I could have gone to her and told her he's alive, but I didn't. I couldn't face her and admit that she was right about everything. She was right. Epiales changed when she brought him back to life in Ogygia. She was right when she divorced me and told me we weren't each other's destined soulmates. Those two truths would become so real if I went and talked to her.

But this is a conversation I expected from another god. Persephone, Apollo, or even Aphrodite could have yelled at me like this, and I'd agree with their statement. Those gods care about Saffron enough to speak on her behalf, but Ares has tried to kill her for eighty-eight years. I jump to my feet, my rage blinding me from saying anything rational.

"Why do you care? You have never cared about Saffron!" I yell the last part, and both Maressa and Ares flinch.

Because it sounds like I still love her romantically.

I didn't realize until I see Maressa flinch that I no longer am trying to get her back. The love I had for Saffron was beautiful, but it was safe. It was based on love, but not passion. Comfortability and friendship molded our marriage, and until this moment, I thought I wanted that version of love forever. When Maressa recoils when I defend Saffron, my viewpoint changes irrevocably.

I want the passion of true love. I want to smile and feel a thousand bolts of electricity every time I am near her. Not Saffron, but Maressa. I turn to face Maressa, opening my mouth to explain myself, but Ares cuts me off.

"The oracle ordered us to bring you all to safety." Ares faces the crowd of humans more than me, frowning the entire time. "So let's go."

"Where are we going?" Maressa asks, and Ares's sharp gaze lands on Epiales.

Epiales is the reason Ares's jaw hardens, and a storm brews within him. Ares rips Khione's decapitated head from Epiales's hand, and he throws it at me. Khione screams. The moment she lands face-first in my hands, she bites my palm.

"Ow!" I drop her, only to pick her up by the hair a moment later.

"I'll kill you for this!" Khione seethes.

Ares grumbles. "We're going to the only safe place on Earth. Saffron's mansion. Hermes, you know the way. Join us after you dispose of Khione's head."

Ares leads the humans away while I reacquaint Khione with the bottom of the Black Sea.

# TWENTY-ONE

SAFFRON

I wait until I think Hart is asleep to enter her art room. The room is next to the one she shares with Apollo, so I'm careful as I creak open the door and enter. There is a truth hidden in these brush strokes I need. Somewhere in this room, beneath the blurs of paint and scribbles, there are answers behind the prophecy that will kill my prophesied heart, destined to either grant us freedom or imprisonment under Styx's eternal reign.

I cautiously walk into the room, where handprints covered in red and gold paint every square inch of the walls. Torn up parchment lays like sand upon the ground, and every corner is full of canvases. A sense of foreboding crawls up my spine the longer I stand here, walking around a battlefield unlike any I have seen before.

Crouching down in the far-right corner, I pick up the first art piece. The canvas is a blur of rushed brushstrokes and slashes of unidentifiable blobs. There are no people in this image that I can discern or clues that lead towards our future. The only part of this art piece I can understand are the words painted in black with a shaky finger.

CRUMBLE LIKE POMPEII.

I pick up the art beneath it, and it is almost identical to the first piece. Gold paint slashes brutally across the page, with a white circle under it. The gold almost creates a river, careening around the nondescript canvas. In the center, the same three words are written quickly and in black ink.

CRUMBLE LIKE POMPEII.

Another canvas is only red. The art splatters the center like spilled paint, with whitish gray across the perimeter, like walls, a floor, and a ceiling. There's nothing else but slashes of red, whitish gray borders, and the black ink that saying the same three foreboding words.

CRUMBLE LIKE POMPEII.

I gather another and another and another. Still, the same. They all look identical and nonsensical until I pick up the last one in the pile.

Brown starts at the bottom of the canvas and rises almost to the top. Red and small splashes of orange spill throughout the canvas, with a splatter of gold on the far edge opposite the brown paint. This one still makes little sense, but those damning words cover every square inch of the canvas. Sometimes, Hart writes the words so small they almost look like tiny specks of soot. Other times, the words bleed across the canvas from one side to the other. They vary in penmanship. Some, she writes in perfect calligraphy. Others are scratchy messes, like Hart used her nails to draw them instead of a brush.

The door creaks open behind me. I turn to face Hart. She has a gold robe draped over her, tied at the waist. Her endless waves of curly black hair fall untethered by ribbons or bows. She leans against the doorway, clasping her gold feather necklace like she always does when nervous, while the other hand wraps around her waist.

I lift the canvas in my hand, asking. "Is this the last battle?" When she doesn't immediately answer, I add. "You wrote those words the most on this canvas. Why? What does it mean?"

"You should get dressed for the day, Saffron. It will be a busy one."

I stand with the canvas in my hand. "Don't deflect," I snap. "Answer my questions."

"In two days' time, you may meet me here again and ask. Until then, you have an hour to get ready. Wear something dark, yet nice." Hart turns around, and she leaves.

I almost run after her, demanding that she tell me everything now. It is my life that this prophecy toys with, like I am a puppet, and the prophecies is the puppeteer. Yet, for reasons I don't fully understand, I listen to her. I return to my room and I sit in front of my mirror.

When Hattie wakes up in my bed, she sees me applying mascara. Silently, she walks towards me. I have never had the talent of shielding my emotions; rather, they play across my face like they're written across my forehead. Weariness and anger coalesce, and I know Hattie can see it upon my pinched brow.

But instead of asking me what is wrong, knowing she can find the answers in every crevice of this world, she asks. "Do you want your hair curled?"

We spend the morning together, choosing each other's gowns and giving advice on makeup. We fall into a sense of peace, slipping into old routines. When we were both so young, we used to conjure up endless excuses to spend our mornings just like this. We would go through my closet, choosing the grandest gowns, and prim each other. She'd curl my hair, I'd straighten hers. She would hum absentmindedly, and I would find the perfect pair of earrings for her.

I choose to materialize a silver gown for her. It has off-the-shoulder sleeves and spills down to the floor with the same ease as a waterfall. We pair her gown with silver, rain droplet earrings and a diamond encrusted necklace. She described the gown she wanted me to materialize for myself- a strapless red gown with Grecian-style gold embroidery down the length of the train- and it slips onto me like a second sheath of skin. She places gold flower pins throughout my curls, then clasps a golden necklace tight around my neck. A ruby, almost shaped like a heart, sits in the center of my chest.

"When it is all over, let's make every day an occasion to look this hot," Hattie says, when we stand face-to-face.

"When this is all over," I say with a growing grin. "Let us have a party every night. Even if it is just a party of two. Let's celebrate every day we are young together."

Hattie holds out a pinky, and I wrap mine around hers. We kiss the ends, grinning the whole time.

Linking our arms together, we walk down the staircase, but halfway down, the front door swings open. Ares steps through the doorway, and our eyes immediately lock. I see no one else but him, resplendent in armor unscathed from battle, and a million strikes of lightning scatter between us. His eyes, dark as midnight blue, search my face first. Then, slowly and torturously, they careen down my gown, leveling on my waist.

When his eyes meet mine again, my name enters the room.

"Saffron," a desperate, broken voice says.

It isn't Ares's.

A second later, that broken voice adds, "My queen."

Ares's face crumbles, then smooths into impassiveness a

second later. But I saw the glimpse of disappointment and heartbreak, and it creates a fissure in my chest. Ares walks away without even saying a word. He moves toward the training room, where he spends most of his day, and now I can see the others who fill up the door frame space.

Cerberus bounds up the steps, two of his heads laying in Hattie's hands the moment he reaches us, while the third licks at me. I scratch behind his ear the way he likes it, as my gaze roams through a sea of familiar and unfamiliar faces. Phobos and Deimos awkwardly wave before walking in the direction their father stormed off towards, while Epiales and Hermes stand side-by-side.

I never thought I would see the day when these two males could stand so close without attempting to kill one another. Hermes steps through first. His eyes roam over my face, but the usual expression of blanketed want is gone. Instead, remorse burns in those sparkling green eyes. He takes another step, then another.

But then I drag my gaze back to him.

To Epiales.

He stays ramrod straight in the doorway, but I can still hear the echo of my name, followed by my nickname, on his lips. I take a step down, and Hattie removes her arm from mine.

"You remember me?" I ask in more of a gasp than anything articulate.

Epiales shakes his head. "No. A-At least, I don't think so." He stammers, more anxious than I have ever seen him. He rummages a hand through his curly, inky locks. "I just heard your name in my head." He looks away, stammering. "I'm sorry. I'm not making much sense."

Hermes always stares at me when I look back at him with questions in my eyes. He looks a mess. Patches of dirt and a mixture of human, monster, and godly blood cover his skin. His normally shaggy hair is slick with sweat, sticking haphazardly around his face. He searches my face for injuries, like I am the one covered in blood, sweat, and grime.

When I look back at the doorway, where Epiales and a horde of humans stand with uncertainty, I say. "We have plenty of rooms. Come inside, shower, and then we will talk."

A pretty, dainty woman with short-cropped black hair steps through the doorway first. She bows the moment she enters my household. "Thank you, Lady Saffron."

Hattie scrambles down the stairs. "No need to bow. Saffron isn't *that* special." She looks back at me and winks, then turns back to face the woman. "Come on. Cerberus and I will show you to your room."

I stand in paralyzed disbelief, looking between Hermes and Epiales, as Apollo and Hart bound down the stairs. Just as Hart told me to look nice today, she also dresses in an elegant gown. It's strange, seeing Hart in anything but her tattered, paint-splattered overalls, but today she wears a white gown with yellow flowers across the corseted top. It has puffy, see-through sleeves and a visible corset; she is gorgeous. Her long hair spans down to her waist, and it bounces with each step she takes.

Hart takes Epiales's hand in the doorway and says. "I have been wanting to meet you for a long while. Come, let's get you acquainted with the place."

She leads Epiales away to a room on the ground floor, so our paths don't yet collide, while Apollo grabs two other humans. There are a dozen total, and eventually, Hattie, Hart, and Apollo find rooms for them all.

Then it is just Hermes and me standing in the foyer.

I take a few hesitant steps down the staircase. "You look a mess."

A rogue grin quirks up his lips. "And you look magnificent in the face of war. I don't know why I'm surprised."

He strides up the staircase until we stand one step apart. Despite him being on the lower step, he still looms over me. In just a few steps, the smile is gone, while the actions of our past thicken the space between us.

"He doesn't think he remembers anything, but he does." Hermes whispers, careful no one but us shares this conversation. "He remembers there is a woman worth waiting for, and I think he remembers that he once did terrible acts. I think he tries to be the hero because, deep down, I think he remembers he was once the villain."

Hermes's words bring forth hope, but confusion wades in the undercurrents. "Why are you telling me this?"

He reaches forward and cups my face in his hand, and I let him. I let him stare down at me, his past, and realize I'm not in his future. He realizes this now. I don't know if it is the drums of war or someone else entirely, but he doesn't stare at me with want anymore. He smiles down at me as sadness builds in his gaze.

"Because it took the world to end for me to realize you were right. He changed just like you and I did. You were once all I wanted, and I let myself hide so much to keep you in a box packaged just how I wanted you. For that and so many more reasons, I'm sorry. I'm sorry I took him away from you. I'm sorry I lied to you so many times. And I'm sorry-"

I silence him by enveloping him in a hug. He wraps his arms around me, and we fall to our knees at the staircase. He cries in my arms, and I hold my first husband tight. Through sobs, he attempts to clean the mistake of his mischief with honesty. He tells me a story about a god who once thought himself unflappable, who still lives with invisible scars from his time as Typhon and Kronos's prisoner.

He tells me how this once unflappable god fell from grace, and how every action in the ninety years since has rooted in fear he tries to smother.

The tears stop near the end as he whispers finally. "My feelings about the past don't change how I betrayed you." He lifts his head from my shoulder and tears roll down his cheeks. "I don't know how you will ever forgive me."

"I forgave you the moment you walked through those doors. You will always have a piece of my heart, Hermes, and I will always thank you for stealing me." We both smile at that. "Thank you for being my first date, my first kiss, my first home that felt safe, and hopefully my forever friend."

"Thank you for being the best first wife a lowly, thieving god could ask for."

I wipe away the last tear he sheds. "Can I confess something?" I don't wait for his response. "You smell putrid, and I refuse to let my friends suffer smelling this bad."

We unscramble from each other's arms and walk together towards his new room, where the sounds of his laughter stitch something together in my heart, something I didn't realize had torn.

# TWENTY-TWO

## HART

The moment I drop off the last human into their current bedroom, I use the few minutes that a human distracts Apollo to sneak into Zeus's room. Unsurprisingly, he sits on the edge of his bed, waiting for me.

"He's here," Zeus says, his tone gravelly and revealing too many secrets. He does not have to say his name because we have both waited for two people to enter the war, and they each walked through the doors this morning.

I close the door behind me. "And so is she."

"Five members of the prophecy finally rest under this roof. Finally." Zeus breathes a sigh of relief, but we both know our work is far from over.

"The rest will arrive at midnight, but prepare yourself. The end is near, and with the end comes more bloodshed. In these next two nights, the last pieces must fall together if we expect to win this war."

"The huntress will clip the monster's life strings," Zeus whispers the words.

"And the heart must die twice. One will take place tonight, and the other will occur the following night. Prepare yourself, for the screams start soon." I walk out of the room, then sneak back into my own. By the time Apollo is back inside our bedroom, I lay in a tub full of bubbles with the bathroom door ajar. "Come join me!"

I force happiness into my voice as Apollo runs inside the bathroom, discarding every scrap of clothing. He slips into the tub with me, and I cement this moment into my mind. Despite the war's screams echoing in my ears, I find true peace for potentially the second to last time within his arms.

For tonight, the Battle of the Huntress begins.

And tomorrow night, the Battle of the Reds destroys Saffron's heart.

# TWENTY-THREE

LAMB

In fact, it was not our last sunrise together.

Hephaestus uses one of his inventions to create a roadmap with the quickest destination to Hart's coordinates. On the first day, Hephaestus tried expediting the trip by using his mechanical wings to fly each of us individually to the site. However, the Fates had a unique plan in store. Hephaestus and Jamila flew for one mile before the wings crashed. They came back with soot on their face, and Hephaestus wore the deepest frown.

We walk through deteriorated pathways and decimated towns for three days.

Once, we slept.

Or, correction, Hephaestus and a few huntresses slept.

Yet death sings a somber tune, growing louder with each mile I pass. I do not want to spend my last few hours within this world falling into oblivion. I want to see each speckled star in the sky and the faces of those I love for as long as the Fates will allow.

Their scissors hover over my thread of life, but they

have not yet broken it. I still have time to see all my friends for a few minutes, hours, or days longer. There is no laughter as many of us walk the trail towards our demise, and we rarely speak. Still, I treasure these moments with my sisters. I only wish Artemis were here to say her good-byes as well.

On the third day of our travels, when my shoes fill with blood and my eyelids weigh three tons, I see it. The destination we have walked towards for three days looms atop a hill many of us have trekked before. It shouldn't exist anymore. It is cruel that I must die in the same wretched place that raised me.

But I will be damned if I don't burn this place down for the last time as I go.

Dýnami stumbles to a stop, her jaw slackening at the sight. "How?"

We all stop with Dýnami, mirroring her disbelief at the sight in front of us. One of the former prisons during humanity's time of enslavement has risen from its ashes. Almost ninety years ago, many of us burned it to ash after finding a home full of young corpses inside. I suffered such anguish in those monochrome walls; the cell feeling smaller and smaller with each year as I neared adulthood.

After the final Titanomachy war against Kronos, the Olympians voted and destroyed all remnants of the prisons. They didn't want historians to stumble upon the gods' greatest mistake. Yet, here one stands. It looks the same as it did five hundred years ago when I lived within it. There isn't a single charred corner or crumbling brick to show its wear and tear. Hecate is the goddess of necromancy, and it is like she brought her malevolent child back to life to cause more strife.

"Our sisters are in there?" Shikari's voice wobbles.

It's a subtle, an almost imperceptible sound. Almost. Yet, it's still there. That tremor of fear.

Shikari grew up in a prison halfway across the world on an Eastern continent. She understands too well the terrors that take place between these brick walls. Ninety years ago, during Kronos's resurgence, Shikari was also one of the huntresses, with Dýnami and me, who helped us cut down hundreds of bodies from this prison's ceilings. Hundreds of children, who were too young to suffer such grisly fates.

Hephaestus's bushy eyebrows scrunch together in confusion, but he is the first to move forward. He doesn't glance back at us to make sure we're following. Perhaps it is because he knows our fates have intertwined with this prison and all who thrash within it.

I reach my hands out for the two huntresses- Dýnami and Jamila- nearest me. Dýnami takes mine and squeezes tight.

"When we get out of here." Dýnami's voice breaks as the lie spills from her lips. "I'm going to demand that Athena get me more of that rocky road ice cream, and I don't want any of that off brand nonsense. I want some real, chocolatey good rocky road ice cream."

Jamila takes my hand next. "And I want a cheeseburger that's so greasy it spills down my fingers. As soon as we get out of here, that's what I'm eating."

Out of the corner of my eye, I see June stumble backwards. As the sun sets behind her, it creates a backdrop for her missing arm. She still holds the cyan-colored axe Iris gave her in her right hand, but the left is gone forever. She stares forward, fear widening her already impossibly gigantic eyes. Memories of our last battle and all she lost cause her to take another step back.

She shakes her short hair. Her bangs partially conceal the tears forming in her eyes. "We will not live if we join him." Anger laces her tongue to hide her fear. Or to try to hide her fear. It is clear to all of us she trembles with fright that threatens to turn a brave huntress into a deserter. "There is no point in talking about stupid ice cream flavors or cheeseburgers. We need to turn around and let him handle this. We shouldn't have to do this! It is a suicide mission!"

Vee places her hand on June's shoulder and whispers. "No, it is a rescue mission. We have sisters inside those walls who will die if we do not get them. You fear death, but until a beast rips my head clean from my neck and my heart ceases to beat, I will believe I will survive. And *when* I get of here with my sisters, I will demand that King Zeus himself gift me the best mozzarella sticks this world has ever eaten. And, I want a library in my name. The biggest library in all the world."

Vee holds out her other hand, one not atop June's shoulder, and Shikari grabs it. She grins wildly, a sliver of her former rebelliousness shining freely. "Careful, smarty pants. It almost sounds like you're committing hubris."

"Some call it hubris. I call it the truth." Vee grins now, and in the face of fearless death, she has never looked more radiant.

"Praise be Artemis, but I love her sacred deer when he's nice and crispy." Shikari slaps her free hand with Hound's, who mirthlessly glowers back at her dearest friend. "What about you? Want to chomp some deer meat together?"

Hound's lips snarl in disgust. "How am I friends with you?" There's a slight pause, then Hound squeezes Shikari's hand and adds. "I want a cupcake with frosting and sprinkles."

"I want a robotic arm." We all look at June, who still trembles, but she no longer retreats from battle. She glowers at the prison looming ahead of us, and she seethes. "When I get out of that gods-forsaken prison, I want Hephaestus to mold the greatest robotic arm this world has ever seen. Imagine the stories that would they write about me, the one-armed huntress."

I could see it.

June, with an arm that morphs into a sword. Our enemies would fear her, but more than that, women would hear her story and gain hope that they could be more than housewives and mothers. They would look upon June, this fearsome one-armed woman, and see that anything could happen. The children who have one arm will look upon June, hear her stories, and know they can do anything too.

I smile at the thought.

Hound grumbles as Reaper jumps forward and takes her free hand. Her crooked teeth gleam against the colors of the sunset. Hound tries to rip herself free, but it is a weak attempt. Hound is the brawniest of us all, and she could easily distance herself. Reaper squeezes Hound's hand tight.

"I don't want any fancy food. What I want is a dress. A bright yellow dress with the biggest *poof* you've ever seen!" She makes a motion with her free hand like she's lifting the skirts of this obnoxiously enormous dress she wants to wear, and she looks at me with such joy. Like she's wearing the gown now instead of her everyday garb. "Won't I look beautiful?!"

"The prettiest."

"What about you, Lamb?" Jamila asks. "What do you want when we get out of there?"

All my sisters wait for my answer, but I can smell the cold, inviting roses of death. It comes for me, and I will not run from its frigid touch. Between Hart's silence at the arena, and how Zeus cried for me as he delivered the coordinates to my execution, my death has been a fiery-laden promise. I do not want to dampen their hope, which rises from the depths of their watery sorrows, but I know my fate.

It ends here.

"I do not hope for life," I admit. "For I have been fortunate to live for over half a millennium. I have fought so many battles, and I have enough stories written about me. My hope for when I enter this prison is that I save as many of you as I can, so you may have your greasy cheese-burgers, robotic arms, mozzarella sticks delivered by Zeus himself, and the prettiest yellow dresses the world has ever seen." I stare forward at my burial ground, and I smile despite Thanatos's scythe nearing my neck. "To die is not a frightening endeavor when you have lived as freely as me."

I walk with my hands clasped between Dýnami and Jamila's, and those behind me follow my lead. It is time we etch our names into history. It is time for the Battle of the Huntresses. Eventually, we let go of each other, but only once we reach the top of the hill and all that surrounds us are wilting trees, an impatient god, and a monstrous prison.

Hephaestus stands behind a tree, and we follow suit. We slip into the shadows I have long admired, and Hephaestus whispers. "I see the most movement from that barred window on the second floor." He points to the dimly lit room and adds. "That's where I think our pris-oners are located."

Along the perimeter of the prison, guards stand stationed and armed. From the distance, none of them look familiar, so they must be human. There are three posted on each wall, except where the front doors are located. They have doubled their security beside the door, and we all unsheathe our weapons.

Jamila, Hound, and Reaper are our archers, and the guards do not see them until arrows lodge in the middle of their foreheads. All the security on the wall below the dimly lit window collapse. Hephaestus, June, and I run first. We crouch so that the darkening sky shadows our movements, but two men approach our wall.

Our archers shoot them down with the same efficiency. June momentarily sheathes her axe and rummages through her satchel. She produces a rope with a grapple hook attached. She swings her arm several times in a counter-clockwise motion, then flings the rope towards our intended window. Distantly, my ears perk to arrows thumping into chests, followed by low grunts from fallen traitors. This prison is a beacon for bloodshed, but for the first time in my life, the arrows reach the guilty. For once, the innocent remains unscathed.

I grin as the grapple hook snags one of the window bars, and June matches my enthusiasm. Hephaestus merely grunts, then climbs the rope first. Quickly, he reaches the top, and with one hand wrapped around the rope, he uses his other to grab one of the window bars. He rips it from its place and throws it to the ground in between June and my feet. He continues this motion until every bar lay discarded on the surrounding ground.

Only then does June start her ascension up the rope, and I turn to face the thicket of trees the rest of the huntresses hide behind. I silently call them over with a wave and help every huntress as they shimmy up the rope. Hephaestus stays at the windowsill and pulls the few women needing help over the rim.

Soon, it's just Dýnami and me.

"Are you sure?" Dýnami asks with the slightest waver in her voice. "Are you sure this is the end for you?"

"I could be wrong."

But I'm not, and those are the unspoken words we both hear.

Dýnami wraps me into a tight embrace. She's the second longest surviving huntress, and she threatens to break my spine in half by how hard she yanks me towards her. I wrap my arms around the back of her neck and hug back.

"I love you, sister," she throatily says.

"And I, you."

We pull away and smile through the tears building to the surface. Dýnami nods towards the rope. "You first. Age before beauty and all that."

I smile despite myself, then climb the rope. Hephaestus holds out a helping hand and hoists me over the windowsill. Just as he predicted, we have fallen into a prison cell filled with familiar faces. Except these faces no longer belong to living souls. They swim in their own blood, with unblinking eyes staring up at nothingness.

Akita and Frigate lay side-by-side with matching slit throats. Their blood creates a pool around them, and even in death, they wear a mask of disbelief. They trusted whoever killed them, just like Sika trusted Akita before dying by her hand. Just like I trusted Frigate before I woke with her pressing a pillow against my face, trying to smother the life out of me.

"Holy Underworld." Dýnami stands beside me now, grinning wider than before as her focus narrows on Akita. "Who beat me to it?"

Another body hangs amongst the ruin, but this time, I do not know who the corpse is. I might know them; except they do not have a head to identify their body. A decapitated body hangs limply from chains hanging around their wrists. It is clear the body belongs to a male, and from the stench radiating from him, he has been deceased for a few days.

I turn to Hephaestus. "Can you rip the chains clean?"

He grunts. "Why?"

But he doesn't wait for a response. Hephaestus limps towards the corpse, and with the same ease as he dismantled the window bars, he crushes the chains. He delicately lowers the body onto the ground, laying his back to the floor. I take a step towards the corpse with a drachma burning a hole in my satchel. But Hephaestus is there first. He materializes a single gold drachma and lays it atop the body's chest.

Hephaestus whispers a prayer in the ancient tongue, then stands. He wears annoyance on his brow, but the god of blacksmithing holds more compassion than he wishes to admit. "Let's go."

He pushes open the ajar prison door, and we follow him. As soon as I walk through the threshold, raucous screams penetrate my ears. Vee stands beside me, and her jaw slackens as she murmurs. "I don't believe it."

"There's…" Jamila smiles widely. "My grandma."

Persephone is one of many fighters on the ground floor of the prison. She spins twin daggers in her hands, deflecting every blow. Uranus tries to strike her with the Dagger of Chains tight in his grasp. Rage paints the prettiest shade of red across the Queen of the Underworld's face, but she is not the one I am most excited to see on the battlefield.

Willow and Sika stand back-to-back, as they sling arrow after arrow at their opponents. Dozens of traitorous Stymphalian birds lay scattered in a circle around them. I have always said that Willow and Sika are the greatest huntresses of all time, and as another daunting, bone chilling sight looms higher than the clouds on the other side of the prison, I know which one of them must kill him. Hypnos and Thanatos fight side-by-side, along with Zig and Diam against Typhon. The herculean sized monster roars so loud that the ground splinters, but they will not slay the undefeated Typhon.

Sika will wield the final blow.

I have never been more certain of a truth than this one.

On the piece of parchment Zeus gave me, with the coordinates to this prison attached, Hart created a drawing on the top corner. I have stared at this scarification mark across the expanse of Sika's arm for centuries. The moment I saw the deer antlers, with a thicket of trees in between them, I knew the message Hart spoke without written confirmation. Sika, whose scarification mark bled onto the parchment, is the prophesied huntress.

This is why Hart sent Zeus to deliver the coordinates to the prison. None of the surrounding huntresses are the prophesied huntress. It was always my job to find her, drag her back to the land of the living, and complete her destiny. It was always my job to have the other huntresses and I join her in her heroic journey, and die if I must.

Hart sent me to my destiny, and to a battle of victory none of us will ever forget.

I unsheathe my sword once again, the lime green blade glinting against the dimmed lights of the prison, and I grin wider and scream louder than ever before. "FIGHT!"

We run to our destiny, weapons ablaze.

# TWENTY-FOUR

## RAVEN

Long ago, I broke the cardinal rule as one of Artemis's devoted huntresses by falling in love. I met him within my dreams. He was a resplendent sight of golden hair, eyes as electric as lightning striking against an ocean blue, and a smile capable of convincing anyone that the world was better in his proximity.

I rarely associated with men, given my fealty to Artemis. There were rare exceptions, like Hermes and his male slaves, who I trained. Sometimes, I would see Apollo, but he didn't look me in the eye, fearful of his beloved twin's anger.

But I wasn't like the other huntresses.

Willow stared at Artemis like she held the sun, moon, and stars within her eyes. Lamb did not understand lust and desire, and she never wanted to open its book to find that knowledge within its pages. Reaper cared more for stories and fairytales than reality, and when other huntresses filtered in over the centuries, they all fell into one of those three categories. They either loved women more ardently than men, enjoyed fairytales and adventure more than romance, or they did not find interest in anything romantic.

I always wanted to find love with a man, though.

I would gaze out at the forest green, hoping a young man would stumble through. While Reaper dreamed of fighting dragons and cyclopes, I dreamed Artemis would see the yearning across my face and grant me a chance at love. Then, I would finally know how it felt like to have a man's arms wrap around me as I fell into a deep sleep, and those arms would remain coiled around me when I woke.

So, when I saw him in a dreamworld of his creation, how could I not fall in love with the titan of time?

He said the prettiest words, promised me the prettiest futures, and he became everything I desired within this world. Suddenly, the chafing on my inner thighs from riding horseback too long grated my nerves. The endless nights of eating charred rabbit made me yearn for the candlelight dinners Kronos treated me to in my dreams. Soon, the waking world was the veritable nightmare, while my dreams were my escape.

I would do anything for Kronos, and I realized too late that his aspirations were always to manipulate me. He started asking for small favors, like where the huntresses and I were journeying towards. In between peppered kisses that felt like Elysium itself had entered my bloodstream, Kronos would ask me if any of the other huntresses did not love the ride as much as others. They were questions I knew I should not answer, but I wanted to make him proud of me. I wanted him to love me.

I spoke only a few names, like a new slave named Diamond, and Kronos was so proud of me. I wanted to always have an answer to his questions. Never have I felt love before, so I didn't realize my feelings for him were not reciprocated. Kronos's arms around me were a coil of manipulation, and I didn't realize. It felt exactly like how I had imagined love would feel.

Kronos's manipulation bled through me until all I wanted was him.

His words.

His touch.

His orders.

When I killed Willow, I didn't realize I was one of thousands of soldiers marching to his drum. I didn't realize that I wasn't special to Kronos until Lamb killed me, and my soul floated through the living room where I had died. Hermes saw my soul, and instead of sending me to the Underworld like every other human who has recently died, he told me to watch.

Watch as Kronos spun the same stories of false love to others.

Watch as Kronos did not ask where I was because he didn't care I had died for him. Hermes stood beside my spectral form, and he saw the moment I realized I was nothing but a pawn to Kronos. Only when realization dawned on me did he take my soul to the Underworld.

He gave me a golden drachma, despite killing one of his friends. "Why?" I asked.

Hermes looked out at the dark sight of the Underworld and said. "Because I think if you could reverse your actions, you would."

He was right.

If I could go back in time and replay my first dream with Kronos, I would not accept the pretty lies and deceitful promises. I would stay loyal to Artemis, and I would not take the journeys with her for granted again. I always wanted love, but I didn't realize until that very moment that I had already experienced love.

Lamb, Reaper, Artemis…Willow. They were my sisters. Oh gods, I killed my sister.

"I would," I whisper to Hermes. "I would go back and change everything if I could."

His winged sandals lifted him off the floor, and he left me at the gates of the Underworld.

King Hades and Queen Persephone sent me to the Fields of Punishment, and my torture did not involve pushing a boulder up a hill or endless starvation. Instead, I sat chained in front of a mirage that played Willow's murder on endless repeat. There was no sleep in the Fields of Punishment. No chance to escape my harrowing decision. I had to watch my arrow sink into Willow's forehead again and again and again and again. I regretted killing my sister the moment Kronos's power over me slipped away, and for eighty-eight years, I watched my greatest shame.

Hermes was right. I would change the past if I could, but I didn't think I would get the opportunity to right my wrongs until the Underworld fell beneath Hecate's dark magic. She freed us all from the Fields of Punishment, and she asked each of us if we wanted to join Styx's side.

*We would get retribution against the gods who hurt us,* Hecate said.

But the gods never hurt me. It was me who hurt them. Not all of them were perfect, but Artemis and Hermes granted me kindness at every turn. I did not need retribution from them. They needed retribution from me.

When I walked into the prison cell where Willow stood chained to a wall, my chance at fixing my mistake became clear. I pretended to hate Willow, and I grinned when she screamed in torment, even when I wanted to run to her aid. I agreed to join Styx's side if I could watch over the prisoners.

*To torture them,* I added, and Hecate accepted.

For over a week, I have bided my time. I stood watch as Styx, Hecate, Uranus, and their mutilated Gareth tortured, killed, and maimed countless humans and gods. I feigned amusement when blood splattered across my face, and acted like I lived for the huntresses' demise, like the other traitorous huntresses, Akita and Frigate.

For over a week, I waited until Styx trusted me enough to allow the other huntresses, Gareth, and me to interrogate the prisoners instead of Hecate. The witch goddess and Uranus still visit the cells, so I patiently learned their routine.

Hecate materializes within the cell around noon every day and inspects the torture I let Gareth, Akita, and Frigate inflict. I lean against the wall, pretending not to care how Willow has lost every single fingernail or that Akita skins Sika's arms, creating a heap of blood on the floor.

Hecate only stays for five minutes, then leaves.

Uranus stations himself at the prison, but he whistles every time he comes near the cells. Roughly every two hours, I hear his whistle. I think he whistles to frighten the prisoners, and he is successful with humans like Panda, but he gifts me with the warning of his arrival.

On the third day of this new routine, when I'm positive neither Uranus nor Hecate will deviate from their plan, I lay out an escape. I smirk as maliciously as I can when Hecate visits up. I give her a report, and without glancing at the prisoners, she leaves. Uranus shows up twice, whistling both times, and I giggle to sound like I enjoy his flirtatious remarks. I force a laugh as he teases the tip of the Dagger of Chains across Persephone's cheek and Thanatos's eye. I compliment him when he gets Hypnos to flinch as he pretends to stab him in the stomach with the Dagger.

Before he leaves, Uranus places a kiss on my cheek and whispers in my ear. "Come to my chambers tonight." He drags the Dagger of Chains down the expanse of my arm; I think it's his way of caressing me.

I hold back the bile building in my throat as I purr. "Of course, my liege."

He leaves, whistling as he goes. Once he is far enough away that I can no longer hear the haunting tune, I unsheathe my miniature axe. I use it to feign disinterest, picking out gunk from my fingernails as I muse. "Gareth, what were your wife and child's names again?"

Sympathy nestles into my veins when I look at the formidable human. There was once a time when Gareth French was a simple human male, with a family and kindness in his heart. He was not a murderer or a torturer. He had his own thoughts unpolluted by Styx's magic and experimentation. The version of him that his wife and child loved is gone, leaving behind an apathetic machine.

But his hand holding Thanatos's scythe twitches at my inquisition.

He doesn't answer.

There's a beat of silence, and he walks towards a new prisoner. He drags the scythe behind him. A dreadful screech bounces off the walls before he makes an abrupt stop directly in front of Hypnos. Gareth's movements are robotic as he lifts the scythe and rests it under Hypnos's chin. Hypnos trembles within his chains, but his face remains stoically on Gareth.

"Griselda and Trinity, right?" Gareth stands ramrod straight, and ever so slowly turns his neck to face me. I attempt nonchalance as I pick my fingernails with my axe.

"That's what you told me their names were when you brought them to Styx on the first day, right, Akita?"

Gareth faces Akita now. She drops her knife, and it clatters to the floor, landing on top of Sika's blood. Akita takes a few steps away from Gareth. "I-I-I don't know what you're talking about." She glowers at me and mouths. *'Shut up'.*

I pretend I don't see her lips moving in silent protest. "Those were the names of his wife and child, right Akita? I could have sworn you said those were their names when you grabbed them from the horde of newly reanimated humans and brought them to Styx." I force a fake laugh, but who can truly find joy with what I'm about to say next? "You even said that the little girl, Trinity, screamed so loud when you held her down for Styx. You were so grateful when little Trinity got her throat slit by-"

Akita slams me against the wall. I let her think she is stronger than me as she presses her forearm against my throat, but her arm trembles. Fear plagues her startling bright eyes, which threaten to pop out of their socket.

"Shut up!" She screams.

Gareth takes a step towards Akita and me.

"Trinity." It's the first word he has said since Styx experimented on him, turning her into his warped lap dog. The single word comes out so broken and hollow I almost regret my next words.

Almost.

I grab Akita's wrist, twisting it until I hear an unmistakable pop, and I spin her around. Akita's back slams into my front, and I hold both of her arms against her chest in an x-formation.

She tries to wiggle free, and when her attempts prove futile, she screams. "Frigate!"

"Right, Frigate was there too," I say to Gareth. "Akita held your little girl down on the ground as Styx slit her throat, but Frigate asked that your sweet, sweet wife, Griselda, suffer a bit more."

Frigate steps away from Willow, and she turns her bloodied blade towards Gareth. She waits for him to attack her; it is a wise move because Gareth's entire body trembles. His robotic movement sharply turns from Akita and me to Frigate, then back at us. He cannot discern what is true given the falsities Styx polluted his mind with, and a pang of sympathy hits me once more.

"Frigate bragged for three days straight about how Styx let her dismember your wife. I can give you the gory details if it will give you some peace." I have one hand on top of both of Akita's in the x-formation on her chest, but I weave my other hand into her curly blonde hair. Yanking her head back, I let Gareth see the expanse of her long neck. "Or I can help you kill the two women who helped Styx murder your family."

Gareth shakes his head, short-circuiting with the onslaught of news, but my plan depends on him. On the sliver of humanity Styx could not expunge from within him. I rely on his need to avenge his family because that gnawing need is why Gareth's path collided with Saffron's. It is why Styx told me she targeted Gareth. Because she wanted a loyal lapdog with a face Saffron could easily recognize in a game of manipulation Saffron will be ill-prepared for.

I say to Gareth, who is still in this robotic body somewhere. "I know what Styx did to you. It was terrible. It has changed your entire viewpoint on the world, but these women helped kill your wife and child. If you don't believe me, both bragged about where they buried the bodies. I can tell you exactly how they killed your family, then show you the corpses as proof."

"You traitorous bitch!" Frigate runs towards me with her blade raised high, but she only makes it two steps.

Gareth grabs her by the back of the neck, and he lifts her in the air. She makes a terrible squeaking sound as Gareth's free hand grabs her knife-clad wrist and brings it close to her neck. Frigate kicks and twitches in his grasp, but she is no match for his inhuman strength as he drags her own blade against her throat.

Blood spills an endless stream down Frigate's neck as Gareth drops her. Frigate falls on her knees with a clatter, and she grasps her neck with both hands. Her attempts to staunch the blood are futile, and with eyes brimming with disbelief, she stares at me until she collapses onto her back. She does not rise again, and Akita knows her fate.

Akita screams and thrashes in my arms, but I do not lessen my hold. I stare up at Gareth as he advances towards us, one rigid step at a time. "Trinity." He pushes out the word like it is his sole tether to sanity.

Gareth wraps his hand around Akita's throat, and she sobs and wiggles in our grasps.

I tell him. "They're buried outside near the dead tree where there is no grass." He doesn't look at me as he pulls Akita from my arms and drags her towards Frigate's corpse, but I whisper. "I'm sorry for your loss."

Gareth lays Akita on the floor next to Frigate's bloodied corpse. She sobs and tries to apologize, but he silences her platitudes by slitting her throat down to the bone. He doesn't wait to watch her die. He storms out of the room to dig up the corpses of his family. There was nothing silent about Frigate and Akita's screams or Gareth's abrupt exit, which means I only have a few minutes before Uranus and possibly the terrifyingly tall Typhon enter the room.

I grab my keys and unlock the prisoner's chains nearest the door first. Hypnos collapses onto his knees the moment his chains come free, but as I run past Pyro's corpse and towards Willow, I yell to him. "Hurry! Grab the keys from Frigate's pocket and free as many as we can!"

I catch Willow before she falls, and she instinctually wraps her hands around my biceps for stability. Then, a split second later, she remembers who she holds onto and lets go. She collapses to her knees, and I rush to unchain the next prisoner. Angel, Saffron's childhood friend, latches onto my shoulder the moment he's free, and I drag him with me to free Persephone.

The queen is the first to ask. "Why are you helping us?"

Persephone does not fall when I free her, and she takes the burden of holding Angel for me. Hypnos has freed everyone else. Still, I don't answer the question. A fist flies towards me, but I do not deflect it. I let Sika's knuckles slam into my cheek, even as pain blooms across my face.

"Because if I could reverse my actions, I would." I turn to face Willow. "Willow, I am so sorry."

Willow does not respond, but I expected her fist to create twin bruises on my cheeks. Instead, she pretends I am not in front of her, staring at her with such remorse. She deserves to ignore my existence, but it hurts more than Sika's punch.

Willow faces Persephone. "We will need weapons if we expect to leave here alive."

Thanatos, Hypnos, and Persephone materialize weapons for everyone but me. Willow and Sika have matching bows and arrows, except the bow, the quiver, and arrows are all white with gold etchings on the side. Panda gets a sword, which she holds with shaking hands, while Angel has two small axes. Diam mirrors Heracles with a club in one hand and a spear in the other.

Thanatos picks up Gareth's scythe, while Hypnos let his light blue magic materialize into a matching, curved weapon as his twin. Queen Persephone manifests twin daggers for herself, then looks at me. "Do you need any more weapons?"

Once again, I unsheathe my axe, but it is not the only weapon I hold dear. My left hand holds my axe, but my right removes my favorite weapon. My golden hammer shines dimmest amongst all the god-gifted weapons, but I have always battled with my sacred weapon. I grip onto the brown and gold-embroidered handle, and I shake my head.

"Lead the way, traitor." Sika sneers.

Gareth left the door open for us, and we slip out of the cell easily because the army waited for us on the first floor of the two-story prison. Humans, gods, and monsters litter the prisons since the first day; except the humans are not prisoners. No, they spend countless nights sleeping in cages with pleasant smiles on their faces.

There are hundreds of cells in this prison, and they are all filled with people ready to live and die for a goddess as twisted as Styx. They stand on the ground floor with green, almost black, misted swords and spears, wearing grim looks of determination on their faces. Beside them is every monster I can think of, ranging from the Lamia to the Minotaur to the Empusa. Giants of staggering heights stand beside Arachne, while Stymphalian birds circle around their heads.

And there is Uranus.

And Typhon.

They all stand there, armed for a battle, outnumbering

us in both numbers and strength. Persephone, Hypnos, Thanatos, Willow, Sika, Panda, Angel, Zig, Diam, and I stand atop the staircase and stare down at our grim destiny. I wrap my hand tighter around my hammer. Uranus takes a few steps forward and cranes his neck to glare at me.

"I had hoped Queen Styx was wrong about you. That you were loyal to us." Uranus pauses, then almost sounds hurt when he adds. "To me."

"I already made the greatest mistake in the world by bedding a god with silk-laden promises. It will not be a mistake I make twice." As I say this, Willow's bright blue eyes bore into the side of my head, and I grip my weapons tighter. "Queen Persephone, can I ask a favor?"

"Depends." Her voice is calm in the face of adversity, but still unwaveringly firm. "What is it, child?"

"Is there a way we can spare the humans who stand on this battlefield? I don't think they understand how convincing lies can be. That most lies are prettier than every truth. They saw a way free of a world they felt shackled to, so they believed every lie, not realizing how monstrous they would become."

I see the horde of humans on the ground, with weapons other gods created for them, and I see a glimpse of my former self. I was so certain Kronos led me down the correct path and that I was not a villain for my actions. It wasn't until Lamb ended my life, and Hermes spent a few minutes allowing me to observe the error of my ways, to understand that I was just another piece on a god's chess board. He didn't care about me, and Styx does not care about any of them.

They just don't know it yet.

"Please, don't let them make a mistake that changes who they are forever," I say. Maybe if I can save them, it will lessen the guilt gnawing inside me. "Don't make them victims of their own vulnerability. So far, their only crime is believing pretty lies. I hope we can keep it that way."

Queen Persephone wraps her hands around the staircase railing, and she whispers without looking away from Uranus. "Hypnos, you heard the girl's request. Put them to sleep and get them all out of here. Don't let them die because one foolish mistake stockpiled into a dozen equally foolish mistakes." Her purple-rimmed eyes finally land on mine, and she says. "Hermes was right about you."

She doesn't elaborate.

Persephone jumps off the railing, crashing gracefully onto the ground floor first, followed swiftly by Hypnos and Thanatos. The latter joins Persephone and rushes towards Typhon, who cracks his neck, then grins with jagged teeth as he rises to his full height. The prison ceiling breaks upon the mightiness of his height, and the ground splinters as he laughs at the fear etched on all our faces.

Typhon takes the first step towards the invisible line separating our two sides.

And a battle I'm not entirely sure I will survive erupts.

Hypnos runs towards the humans, swinging his scythe as his magic of sleep creates a rainbow of dazzling, powder blue rain on the unsuspecting humans. They drop onto the floor, and Hypnos materializes his wings. They fan across a mile expanse, and he picks up two fallen humans. He leaves and returns within a blink of an eye and repeats the same action.

Two by two, saving humans from their own gullible nature.

The rest of us spring down the staircase, where Uranus waits for me. His lip snarls with displeasure, and he sneers. "You just made the worst decision of your life."

I place myself in a fighting stance, my axe and hammer lie across my chest in an x-formation, and I grin unabashedly at my adversary. "Actually, Lord Uranus, I believe I just made the first right decision in my life."

Uranus bellows as he clangs his sword against my hammer.

Our dance begins.

# TWENTY-FIVE

LAMB

"Let's go kick some monster a-" Dýnami begins to say.

"Not yet." Dýnami pouts, but I continue. "We can't go down there without a plan. Even with four gods on our side, we are grossly outnumbered. With him on the opposing side," I point at Typhon, who swats Thanatos and Hypnos aside like pesky gnats. "We need a plan if we want to survive long enough to kill him."

"She's right." Vee then asks. "You once said you burned down a prison, right?"

"This very one," Dýnami interjects.

Vee then faces June. "Do you still smoke?"

"Smoke?" I glare at June, who is the brightest shade of red. "You told me you quit."

June's bottom lip juts out as she pouts. "I was hoping to take that secret with me to my potential grave, but thanks, Vee. Yeah, I do smoke."

"That's so bad for your lungs," I admonish.

"When's the last time you heard of a huntress dying of cancer?" June quickly retorts.

Vee ignores our bantering and holds out her hand. "Give me your lighter."

"Why?" June goes into the pocket of her pants, gripping her lighter into a fist.

But it is clear why Vee wants a lighter.

"You're going to burn this place down," I say, almost in disbelief.

"Again," Dýnami adds.

June places the lighter on top of Vee's awaiting palm, and the latter focuses her attention on Reaper. "Is your jacket cotton?"

Reaper flips the jacket, looking inside like it will hold her answer. Uncertainly, she says. "Think so."

"Then give it to me."

Reaper does not argue. She quickly sheds her jacket and throws it at Vee, who catches it with her free hand. We all watch as Vee goes to the ground, lays Reaper's jacket on the floor beside the lighter, and pulls out her satchel. She retrieves an orange, quickly peels it, then places the peel in the center of the jacket.

Shikari and Hound eat the orange, clinking the two halves together like celebratory drinks.

Jamila stares on with confusion. "What are you doing?"

"I was hungry," Shikari quips, but we all ignore her.

Vee explains. "Orange peels are natural fire starters, and cotton is one of the most flammable fabrics. If I can start a fire big enough on the top level, all we must do is keep every monster and traitorous human inside this building, and they will die with the flames."

Hephaestus grunts and turns to the open door of the prison cell we just left. He snaps his fingers and fills every inch of the cell with kindling. "The only way you can keep every monster in this building is if you all stay and fight them. To keep them distracted long enough not to notice the flames covering all the exits," Hephaestus says.

But I don't miss the way he says we need to, not him. The journey Hart placed him on has a different destination than ours. While mine ends at the pyre where I grew up, Hephaestus's does not.

"All of us?" Jamila asks, and I hate how soft, how youthful, her voice sounds.

I knew I would not leave this place alive, but the reality of our mortality weighs like a heavy anvil against the others' chests. "Most likely," Hephaestus says. "I'm sorry."

Dýnami exhales a soft whistle. "I guess no rocky road ice cream for me."

She wipes away the one traitorous tear, and we all pretend not to see it.

June, who was the first to try to run at the sight of the looming prison, smiles sadly at all of us. "I wouldn't want to die with anybody else." Yet, her voice shakes in her futile attempt to seem strong while staring down death.

Vee ignites the orange peel, then loosely places the jacket around the quickly blazing orange. She looks at all of us with such determination written across her face, and she tosses the flames behind her. The flames land in between a stack of Hephaestus's kindling, and it isn't long before the pyre shines bright enough to illuminate the fighting grounds beneath us.

"I love you all," Vee says.

We move to run down the steps, certain our death paints itself in the flames, but before we embrace our imminent demise, I say. "Sika is the huntress. We protect her at all costs, so she can deliver the final blow."

*Even if we die in the crossfire,* I almost say.

"How do you know with certainty?" Vee asks, staring at

me like my harrowing expression will unlock an answer to her riddle.

"Hart told me."

And there is nothing more to say.

Any of our self-proclaimed guesses about the huntress's identity evaporate, and there is only certainty behind the oracle's premonition. We say goodbyes using only our eyes, and then we run. We let adrenaline guide our every step towards our adversaries and allies, while a hidden melody no one else can hear graces my ears. I have never heard this woman's voice before, but her velvety song carries through my ears. It is a tale about bravery and underestimating a lamb before her slaughter.

Before now, there has been a sliver of fear with the revelation that I will die, but it burns with the embers. My death will not be in vain. For eons to come, people will sing about me. No one will place me in the shadows again.

Smoke covers the ceiling of the prison, creating an ominous mist over our funeral pyre. Most importantly, it blinds Typhon. He is a creature of staggering height, whose head is as tall as the clouds and wings are as long as the prison hall, but with the smoke coiling and hissing around his shoulder, he cannot see the doom about to smite down on him.

This is our chance to kill Typhon.

His feet are the size of twenty combined boulders, and they clamor against the floor in a blind attempt to kill his adversaries. Above me, the second story railing collapses, but the war rages on. Just as Vee predicted, every opponent is more preoccupied with winning this battle rather than fleeing from the flames.

The temperature in the room rises to a sweltering heat, and the fire licks up Typhon's arms. He momentarily pauses in his fight against Thanatos as his hands slam against his arms, extinguishing the flames. For a few seconds, he stops stomping his feet into the ground, breaking the floor and surrounding humans' bones, and the huntress and I capitalize on his distraction to climb him.

I climb onto his foot as I thank the Fates for aligning my life with Artemis's. My war cry bellows from my lips, scratching up my throat, as I thank Iris for gifting me with a sword more powerful than any human-made weapon. I slam the blade down into Typhon's foot as my sisters rise higher. His bellows are loud enough to reach Mt. Olympus, but above the screams in battle, I see them. The sisters I have missed so dearly, who took a portion of my soul when they died.

Willow and Sika stand below me on the ground floor. Their arrows mark each Stymphalian bird with perfect accuracy. The birds plummet from the sky like raindrops, clattering against the soot-covered ground.

"We'll get the birds!" Shikari screams, referring to her and Hound. "Get Typhon's smelly ass!"

Shikari and Hound trade places with Willow and Sika. Now, the two bickering best friends stand back-to-back, point their weapons towards the ceiling, and continue to shoot down Stymphalian bird after Stymphalian bird. Shikari's red crossbow glints, the fire growing larger, as each arrow lands directly in the bird's skull.

Sika takes two steps away from the Stymphalian birds before Dýnami rushes to her. Enough of us fight against Typhon that the two soulmates have enough time to wrap their arms around each other in a bone-crushing, heart shattering embrace. Sika covers her face in the crook of Dýnami's neck, inhaling her scent, but that isn't enough for Dýnami. She grabs both sides of Sika's face and raises it, so they lock eyes.

Dýnami grins her gaped-tooth grin and even with a cacophonous war around us, I can hear Dýnami say. "Hey, sunshine. I've missed you terribly."

Sika slams her lips against Dýnami's. Their moment isn't long, only a few seconds before a Stymphalian bird swoops down and tries to kill them. Shikari shoots down the bird a breath away from Sika's neck, and it sobers the reunited soulmates.

Dýnami climbs on Sika's shoulders, her weapon pointed towards our opponent. "Now, let's go kick some monster ass!" Dýnami screams louder than the air can contain, leaping from Sika's shoulders and slamming her godly-gifted magenta spear through Typhon's kneecap.

The monster bellows with rage, and because her weapon is also a gift from a goddess, it does not break from the weight of Typhon's bones. Instead, she rips it out and plunges it back inside his leg, twisting the blade as his blood splatters across her face and neck. He swats at Dýnami, and as she and her spear fly off him, they crash onto the ground a few feet away.

I use his distraction to my advantage. I raise my sword high into the air, and I yell as I strike it down onto two of his toes. The digits sever from his flesh and bone, distorting his sense of balance.

Two hands push at my shoulder, and I fall off Typhon's foot. My back hits the concrete ground, stealing the air from my lungs, and *something* rips at the skin on my back. I bite back a moan as I see the atrocity before me. Zig lies atop me, and where I once stood, Lamia hisses and growls. I didn't even see Lamia coming, and if Zig didn't push me away, then she would have ripped my back in half. I would have died before I had the chance to see Typhon perish.

Before I could witness Sika make history by vanquishing him once and for all.

Zig smiles down at me, his rakish expression always the warmest part of the coldest pits of the Underworld. "Fancy seeing you here."

Zig rolls off me, then throws both hands to swing an axe towards Lamia. The monster dodges the blade, but it boomerangs back to Zig. He catches it, jumps to his feet, and takes one step towards Lamia. That is when Typhon lifts his foot and stomps the ground.

Killing Zig on impact.

"No!" The scream rips out of me, and I rush towards anyone I can hurt. Anyone I can blame for taking the life of a man who already survived countless battles. He never stopped smiling, never stopped fighting for his right to exist in a cruel world, and now he is gone. Just like that.

A white orb escapes from the pile of blood and guts that lays where he once stood, and it flies out of the room. His soul is gone forever.

I refuse for his death to go in vain. Every vessel of my body steers me towards him. To mourn him as he deserves, but my eyes bleed red. That vengeful side of me, which bleeds a warrior red, rushes towards Lamia. She isn't fast enough to face my ire. My sword becomes an extension of my arm, and she only deflects once before I sink my blade deep into her chest. She whimpers as I yank my sword free, kicking her to the ground.

The monster never rises again.

My rage for Zig serves as ammunition.

I turn to run back towards Typhon, but then I see the impossible. The great, unstoppable Typhon wobbles where he stands and begins his descension to his knees. There are at least a hundred arrows in each thigh, with blood oozing down his kneecaps. The room trembles as the mighty monster tumbles. His knees smack against the ground and splinters form in the ground, like an earthquake has taken place below the prison. The arrows break upon his fall, and they tumble on the surrounding floor.

The fissures in the earth created from Typhon's fall stretch across the entire prison. It starts at the front door, but weaves throughout the floor in the shape of a snake. I balance myself enough to stop from tumbling forward, but curiosity has me looking at the nearest crevasse. It is at least a mile deep, so when a monster falls, it plummets to its death.

A redhead I immediately recognize as Panda, a former slave of Hermes, falls into the chasm with six monsters. Her scream is deafening until she is silent forever.

Queen Persephone tries to catch herself, but she tumbles into the cracks along with Panda and monsters like the Minotaur. Neither the monsters nor Panda could have survived the landing, and if they had, then the Fates secured them a long, torturous death. Rationality tells me to run back to my sisters and Typhon, but instinct over-rules reason.

I rush towards the splinter in the ground, where Perse-phone fell. Stomach-down, I lay upon the battle floor. I see Persephone surrounded by mangled corpses. A few unfor-tunate humans whimper from their Typhon-made coffin, but Persephone stands amongst their oddly angled necks. I see Panda's corpse, eyes still open in fright, and I glance away.

I am about to extend my hand for the goddess until a female voice screams. "Lamb! Behind you!"

# TWENTY-SIX

LAMB

I whirl onto my back fast enough to see Arachne, a creature that is a lethal combination of a spider and a woman, who is now a monster of fire, brimstone, and murder. Flames consume her body as she leaps on top of me. My head bounces on the ground, decorating my vision with spots, but nothing is as excruciating as the pain that accompanies the flames. Her legs, completely colored with the reds and oranges of the fire, pierce my flesh.

Fire explodes within me, and I don't have the strength to do anything. My sword clatters to the ground next to me, and my blood ignites, exploding inside of me. My scream tears every vestige of strength I have. She has my torso pinned to the ground, and with her legs penetrating my shoulders, I cannot move.

I can only accept my death as the flames multiply from her body onto a part of mine. The flames greedily engulf my shoulders and neck. I choke on the scent of my burning flesh, while my vision becomes spotty, but then I see it. A blur of lime green glints above me, and then a sword- *my sword*- swings for Arachne's neck. Sickly colored blood splatters across my face, then Arachne's snarling head plops on the ground next to my hip.

The same woman who decapitated Arachne rips her corpse off me, then jumps on top of my body. There is so much pain, but she extinguishes the flames with her body and hands, patting at the few parts of my skin still ignited with the flames. I sob as the pain overwhelms me, but then I stare at the woman who saved my life.

Willow smiles through her own pain. "Hi."

The tears burn as they slip down my unscathed face, landing on my mottled shoulders. I can't stop as I croak out "hi" to my closest friend. The sound is barely recognizable because of the burns on my throat, but tears build up in Willow's eyes, too.

She stands, and she holds out her hand for me. Mine intertwines with hers, and she helps me to my feet. The stench of my burning flesh has taken up residence in my nostrils, and I cannot escape it, yet I still smile.

"I didn't think I would see you again," I admit.

"There's no stretch of this world where we wouldn't collide again." Willow tugs at my arm. "Come on, we need to help her."

I drag my gaze towards Typhon.

And it is Sika in the middle of the battle.

Hephaestus and Hattie's husband stand close by them and fight the few monsters, like the Empusa, who are still alive. Hypnos continues to fly in and out of the prison, carrying a different slumbering human each trip. He spares no time to focus on anything else but his one task of saving the humans from joining and dying in a fight where they do not belong. Thanatos faces all the remaining Stymphalian birds, but he quickly strikes down each one.

Despite his victory, Thanatos keeps whipping his head

around to find Jamila, as she fires arrow after arrow at Typhon. All the remaining huntresses- Shikari, Hound, Reaper, Jamila, Vee, June, and Dýnami- follow Sika's command. Sika's hair creates a halo of flames around her, and everything about her tells me how foolish I was to think anybody else could be the prophesied huntress.

In blurry fragments, I remember the last conversation I had with Sika, when I was bedbound, and she was telling me her monologue of the day. *"I was back in the prisons. The same one we burned down during the fight against Kronos. I was alone, but at the same time, I wasn't. There was a monster there, with a laugh so loud it splintered the ground."*

She thought it was a nightmare, but it was a premonition. In the nightmare, she lost against him, but it was a warning of what she needed to avoid. Sika is destined to kill Typhon, and it is our destiny to help her complete this mission.

"We will need Thanatos or Hypos to get Queen Persephone out of the fissure because of their wings," a distinct female voice says, one I recognize instantly. A voice that brings dreadful memories to the surface. A voice I never thought I would hear again.

I slowly turn around and face Raven. The same Raven who stole centuries with Willow away from me. The same Raven I murdered in retribution. She looks the same. Same naturally tanned complexion. Same long, obsidian locks with a scarification mark covering the expanse of her chest. But the hidden smirk she always used to wear is gone. Now, she stares at us with nothing but regret.

Good.

I take a step towards her, but Willow squeezes my hand and stops me from advancing closer. "Why would I trust anything you say?" I snarl.

"She's the one who freed us from the prison cell,"

Willow whispers the words, and I almost do not hear them over the roar of the flames. Willow stands beside me, and her gaze locks on Raven. "But I will never forgive you for killing me."

Raven flinches like Willow slapped her across the face, and by the growing bruise on Raven's cheek, I hope she did. "I'll get Thanatos to free her while you both return to Sika. She needs help to kill him, and I'll just be an unwanted distraction." There's a pause, and then Raven says. "And just because you won't forgive me does not mean I won't be eternally sorry for what I have done."

"From now until I die again, I will hate you for killing me." Willow spats. "I loved you like a sister, and you betrayed me. So, I hope you survive this battle. I want the rest of your eternally miserable life to be filled with regret, knowing that nothing you can do will ever garner my forgiveness."

Tears build in Raven's eyes, but before we can see the tears cascade down her face, we turn and quickly move towards Sika. Towards the battle we know will end our lives. True to her word, I see Raven run in the opposite direction towards Thanatos.

The ceiling crumbles around us, sizes varying. Some are the size of a small rock, but other parts of the ceiling are as long as my body. As we sprint hand in hand, we zig-zag through the fiery remains. My throat burns a pain worse than I have ever experienced, but I force myself to move faster. I will be by Willow's side until the very end, and I will make sure Sika's nightmare does not become a reality. Sika will defeat him, even if it kills me.

I run, not paying attention to anything except Typhon, as he slams his fists against the ground to kill my sisters. I run, noticing nothing but Typhon, Dýnami, and Sika.

Until a burning figure stands in my way.

258

Uranus.

His face will heal when he escapes, but right now, the right-side spills down his neck like burning rubber. Burn holes pepper the expanse of his clothes, making the object in his hand even more visible. The Dagger of Chains curls tight in his right hand. He tries to grin victoriously at Willow and me, but he can barely lift the right side of his mouth.

He steps towards us, and we charge.

I have rarely faced immortals on the battlefield, but I fight most efficiently with Willow. She throws my sword at me, and the light green sword glows the moment it lands in my palm. Willow produces her bow and an arrow, and together we create a masterpiece.

As she shoots, I dive and slice at his heels.

He screams, and she silences him with an arrow in the center of his open mouth. Uranus swipes at me with the Dagger of Chains, but Willow strikes an arrow through the center of his wrist, and I chop off his hand. I have always heard harrowing stories about Uranus, the first immortal king, but now I understand why he was so easily overthrown.

Now, I understand why the stories say each child is stronger than their parent. Unapologetically, I commit hubris as I remove the Dagger of Chains from his dismembered hand, sheathe it to my waist, and conquer a battle against a god. Uranus thrashes on the ground, holding his dismembered arm, and we run towards Typhon with certainty he won't follow.

I spare a final glance at where we left Uranus, and he is gone. He fled like I knew he would, leaving behind only his stump of a hand.

Sika smiles when I stand beside her, my green sword glinting against the flames. Cinder falls like raindrops atop her halo of hair, and she has never looked more fearless. "I've missed you."

"Missed you too, and I've come with presents."

I produce the Dagger of Chains from my belt, and Sika's hands tremble on her bow. She has been fearless since the moment I entered this battlefield until now. She stares at the Dagger of Chains, and the color leeches from her face. Tears build up in her wide eyes as they lock with mine.

"Give the Dagger of Chains to someone who needs to survive, and make sure they take her out of here with them," Sika says. I don't have to ask who she wants taken away from the battlefield. There is only one human Sika would ask me to drag away from certain death. "I don't care if they need to drag her away, kicking and screaming. She can't be here when I die. I can't watch her die if I'm to succeed."

Sika's voice holds the magnitude of a thousand broken love stories, because once again, she must break her soul-mate's heart. Shatter it into a thousand irreparable pieces. The war rages around them as ash falls from the sky like snow. Sika can't look at the woman who stole her heart years ago, one joke at a time. She can't look at her favorite person just yet, because she knows it will be her last time. In the heart of this fight, Sika only stares at me, the recipient of her request.

Dýnami wears a roughish grin as she tightly grips her Iris-bestowed weapon. She fights beside Reaper, oblivious to the hidden conversation on the other side of the battlefield. She swings her weapon, spearing through the Empusa's eye, and she does not know Sika has finally turned her attention onto her, tears brandishing her too-wide eyes.

I never asked if they had time for goodbyes the last

time Sika died, but I know they won't receive that gift tonight. Dýnami is willing to die for Sika, rather than lose her again, but Sika needs Dýnami to live. Needs her far from Death's reach so she can destroy the unconquerable. I wonder if her love for Dýnami is why she failed in the nightmare weeks ago, because she cared more about saving the love of her life than completing her destiny.

Killing Typhon.

"Promise me," Sika says, choking on the words. "That you will do everything to get Dýnami out of here. She must live. I can't do this if she doesn't live."

Tears fall down Sika's cheeks, but she is not fearful of her own life. Sika has embraced her fate tonight, just as I have. No, Sika cries for the unspoken words between her and Dýnami. She cries for the fear that Dýnami will join her in the unknown void, where the newly died have gone. There's no Underworld for us to venture towards. We may be heroes for dying tonight, but Elysium Fields is not our future.

"I promise," I whisper, almost too quietly for anyone to hear, but the weight of my vow thunders around the floor. Our hearts are heavy with the finality of our decisions.

Sika reaches forward and presses a kiss to my forehead. "Run with her."

I shake my head. "It's not my fate to leave you here. I wasn't there when you needed me the first time you died, but I will be here now."

"You will not ask me to leave you both." Willow slings arrow after arrow, sweat lines her brow as she focuses solely on Typhon. "I will die with you both."

It is befitting that Artemis's favored three are who stay until the end.

There is no huntress in this room who wishes to leave the battlefield. There is no time to argue in the face of war, so I run towards the one person who has a loved one waiting for them outside this battlefield. The one human in the prison who has the strength to pull Dýnami away and also has the motivation to survive. Hattie's husband, Diam, slashes a slew of Stymphalian birds' bronzed feathers with quick efficiency beside Hephaestus.

"What do you want, girl?" Hephaestus grumbles. "We're busy here."

I hold out the Dagger of Chains for Diam. He lowers his spiked club, and he turns to face me, confusion written on his brow. "Sika is the prophesied huntress, and she will lose if Dýnami stays on the battlefield. You need to lead her away to safety and deliver the Dagger of Chains to Saffron."

Diam takes the Dagger without hesitation, only to throw it at an opponent behind me. I turn just in time to see the blade sink into a low-level god's chest, sucking him into the eternal prism. The Dagger, as if knowing it belongs with Diam, boomerangs back to him. Any question he might have about why I chose him evaporates when the Dagger chooses him.

It eliminates any question I had about choosing the right person to lead Dýnami away, too, because the Dagger of Chains has never chosen a host before today.

Diam grips the handle until his knuckles whiten. "When do you want me to take her away?" The Dagger glows within his grasp, and I know there is something more that awaits Diam other than this battlefield.

"As soon as possible." I run back to the battle, back to where I'm needed, but I only take two steps before another part of the ceiling collapses.

Hephaestus kills the final Stymphalian bird, and he gruffly adds. "I'll help you take her away the moment there is a distraction."

The distraction comes obediently and swiftly. The part of the ceiling directly above Jamila and Vee, who fight on the farthest left of Typhon, collapses.

"No!" Thanatos's scream is louder than any strike of lightning, and he rushes towards them.

Towards her.

Thanatos stares only at Jamila, and he catches the crumbling exterior moments before it crashes on Jamila and Vee's head. Yet, he doesn't look away from her. In the thicket of battle, Thanatos carries part of the ceiling on his back. The Personification of Death delays Jamila's demise, suffering the painful consequences.

Flames surround him, but Thanatos doesn't lower the roof, because if he does, then the rest falls with it. He groans, "Go".

Vee and Jamila run to the other side of the battle while flames collect around Thanatos's body. He screams in agony, but he doesn't drop the ceiling.

Not yet.

Diam and Hephaestus use the distraction to their advantage. They both grab onto Dýnami, lifting her off the ground, yanking her away from the battlefield. I watch as Dýnami's face first scrunches with confusion, and then she looks at Sika with terrible realization. She fights and kicks and claws at the two men who lead her away from the battlefield, but her attempts are futile.

They restrain each arm.

They drag her away from Sika, from her sisters, and from her certain death.

# TWENTY-SEVEN

LAMB

Hephaestus releases Dýnami.

He lets Diam take an elbow to the face by Dýnami, before Diam wrestles both arms and throws her over his shoulder. Hephaestus runs towards where Raven stands with Queen Persephone and Angel, as they fight against three giants. Raven spins, slicing one of the giant's shins with her axe, before Hephaestus grabs her. He grips her waist, slings her over his shoulder, and runs towards the exit.

She stabs his bad leg with her axe, but for a god who forever suffers with pain, he doesn't slow down. Hephaestus limps towards the exit, where Dýnami equally thrashes around in Diam's arms. Both women scream, trying to escape their captor's hold, but the Fates need them to survive this battle. Both women can vanquish men and monsters, but not today. I do not know why Hephaestus needs Raven until I see her drop her hammer onto the ground.

There's no way she's in the prophecy…right? Fire comes from every direction, and I no longer have a moment to ponder Raven's role.

I run back to Typhon to watch as he rears a fist towards the closest huntress: Sika.

I'm not close enough, but June is.

June sees the fist flying forward, and she leaps in front of Sika and shoves her onto the ground. Typhon aimed for Sika, but he gleefully takes June's life instead. He slams his fist into her face, and she dies on impact. Her decapitated head falls to the opposite side of the prison, while he discards what remains of her corpse a few feet away.

The ceiling trembles with wicked force, killing both foes and allies, and yet none of us stop fighting. Reaper, with burn marks decorating her arms, wields her sword beside me without a molecule of fear that today might be her last day on Earth.

But then the flames grow hungrier, demanding more sustenance.

A banister falls where we stand, from the weight of the flames. I jump out of the way, followed shortly behind Reaper. A part of the railing, heated by the fire, falls on the top of my foot. Flames lick upon the skin, but I hurriedly pull away.

Reaper is not as fortunate.

The banister falls upon her throat, and the once strong huntress can only scream as she wraps her hands around the piece, trying to lift it off her throat. Skin from her hands and throat leave with the railing, but she isn't strong enough to lift it.

"Persephone!" I whip my head around, screaming for the only god who can move. Other than her, Thanatos is the last remaining god on the battlefield. He cannot run to lift the fiery object off Reaper's throat, and it is too large and heavy for me to lift.

But I see why she can't come to save Reaper's life.

Two giants slam her body to the ground, pinning her, while a third wraps its hand around Angel's throat. Saffron's childhood friend from the prisons, who I met a few times in Nike's mansion, only kicks once in protest before the giant crushes his windpipe.

The same moment Angel stops twitching underneath the giant's grip, Reaper spits out blood and goes eerily still. Just like all the others who have died, a white orb escapes their chests and flies somewhere the Underworld cannot reach.

I have no choice but to run back to Typhon.

Back to my coffin.

Huntresses of both the present and the past surround Typhon as he kneels upon the ground. Arrows decorate his skin like jewelry, but he still has his strength rivaling any other monster. Counting myself, seven huntresses surround Typhon. Queen Persephone fights the remaining giants, and Thanatos still holds the crumbling ceiling, so we do not die by fire before we can end Typhon's life.

So, it is just a horde of huntresses against Typhon.

Typhon on his knees; yet, he is still a mightier enemy than anything that we have faced before.

Luckily for us, the flames left crater-sized holes in his wings. He cannot run, and he can barely move them as a weapon, but the rest of him is still merciless. His hands are as powerful as a building as they crash upon the ground, hoping to eliminate another huntress with a fatal fist. Snakes live like a crown atop his head and cascade down his back. While some are dying from the flames, most shoot out like the speed of an arrow. Their fangs pierce nearby huntresses wherever they can reach.

"Lamb!" Sika yells. In one hand, she now holds Dýnami's god-gifted spear. She deflects Typhon's slamming fists, while striking him with brutal efficiency. Without looking at me, she orders. "Grab two huntresses and kill those damn snakes on his back and head!"

"Jamila! Vee!" They both follow my lead as we run to Typhon's back.

I run towards the snakes until one of them is foolish enough to leap for me. Bite marks decorate all the huntresses', but I will not be one of them. Just as the snake's mouth opens, ready to bite into my flesh, I jump up into the air.

I am faster than the snake as I slice my sword downwards, decapitating one of the hundreds that live on Typhon's back. Behind me, the other huntresses scream, but I cannot afford to look back at them. Snakes jump at me in all directions.

My sword and I ready ourselves for them.

Jamila and Vee fight with the same ferocity.

Yet, the latter is so focused on the snakes that she does not see the gigantic hand reaching out for her. I leap into the air, and I strike my sword down on the bone connecting Typhon's hand to his wrist. My scream comes out strangled because of my burns, but I place my feet on his forearm, and I yank down.

The strength coursing through my veins is not wholly my own, and I thank every god who uses me as a vessel right now. I am a mighty warrior for Artemis, but I am not as strong as a god. I should not be able to saw through his flesh and bones, but I have a strength I've never experienced before, and I don't stop.

Typhon's sickly blood splatters my face, my neck, my shoulders, but I continue dragging my sword through his muscles and tissues. He screams, but Jamila distracts him with arrow after arrow on his exposed forearm. Meanwhile, Vee uses her throwing knives to cut any tendons I miss as I saw through his flesh.

Eventually, his hand falls dismembered onto the floor.

Just as I cut off Uranus's hand.

We dispose of every single snake next. One by one until there is nothing left on his back and head. Vee and I slice every snake on his back, but Jamila shot every single snake atop his head with perfect accuracy. Even if Thanatos continues to look at Jamila, like she holds the stars and the moons for him, she is a huntress through and through.

The room is now consumed with fire, and we are all that remains. The prison reeks of the stench of burning corpses, and not even one of us is unscathed from the pyre. Yet, all of us who remain move together until we are a united force against a fiery, deformed version of Typhon.

We rise beside Sika again, but it is a small army. Sika, Willow, Shikari, Hound, Vee, Jamila, and I face the most formidable monster in history. A group of injured huntresses stand as his prophesied doom.

"You cannot defeat me!" Typhon yells, his voice causing the floor to tremble with fright, but we all look at each other with resolve.

We all have injuries, whether they are burn marks, snake bites, cuts, or arrows protruding from our body, but we are a fearless group. We look at one another with prideful realization, knowing we will die tonight, but not before taking down the most powerful monster in all of existence, a feat not even the gods could accomplish.

Sika takes a step forward, her blood drenched spear swinging in her hand. She slowly drags her gaze from the floor to the ferocious Father of Monsters, wearing a grin that exudes confidence. It is the face of a huntress in front of her greatest victory.

"Watch us do just that." Sika raises Dýnami's spear in the air, and we race towards Typhon, and the flames, to die just as all heroes should.

We are a blur of moving bodies and pure determination, but I see the moment Typhon grabs Shikari and squeezes the life out of her. The moment her body collapses to the ground, Hound screams in rage. In Hound's desperate act of avenging her friend, she dies the same fate. I climb up the expanse of Typhon's body with Willow, Vee, and Sika, as Typhon swats Jamila off his arm.

She falls into a vat of flames, and Thanatos screams her name. In his desperate attempt to save her once more, Typhon releases the ceiling. He runs to her, covering himself further in the fire, and grabs her mottled body. He cradles her in his arms and flies away with what remains of her.

The ceiling falls as Vee, brilliant, fearless Vee, reaches Typhon's neck first. She uses her throwing knives to slice through his throat. She doesn't reach an artery before he uses his last remaining hand to swat her away. This time, there isn't a god to catch her when she falls prisoner to the sea of fire beneath.

Only three of us remain.

Willow, the first huntress to join Artemis's regime during the time of human enslavement.

Sika, the prophesied huntress destined to kill Typhon.

And me, the shadow who helped them achieve so many heroic plights. But I'm more than that.

I'm the huntress who killed Typhon's wife, the Echidna, time and time again. I'm the huntress who united the rest of our clan after death momentarily seized us. While no one will remember me with the same fervor as

Sika, I know Artemis will remember me. Her longest living huntress, who was her comfort when she thought she had no one else.

After centuries, I learned I am more than a shadow, and tonight I finally step into the sun.

I leap off Typhon's chest, my sword raised high toward his last hand. I know it is my death, but I distract Typhon from his true fate. He focuses on me long enough for Sika to use Vee's throwing knives, which lay embedded in his neck, as stepping stools. As I plunge my sword into his palm, Willow fires arrows into his mouth. He slams my body into the fiery wall beside him, and I hear an audible crack. It's my back, and I lose all sensation in my legs, but I live long enough to see it.

Flames consume me, but they don't conceal my vision.

Typhon focuses on Willow's assault after mine. He screams when he opens his mouth and reaches for her. His teeth crunch into her abdomen, and Willow dies as she's bitten in half. I do not mourn my friend because wherever we go, we will go together this time. Willow's death also serves as the perfect distraction.

Typhon does not see it, but I do. Sika leaps, her lover's weapon the same color as the flames, and imbeds the god-gifted spear through Typhon's eye.

It pops out of the back of his skull.

Typhon drops me as the life leaves his body. I use every vestige of strength I have left to smile at Sika, who smiles back as the flames take us whole.

# TWENTY-EIGHT

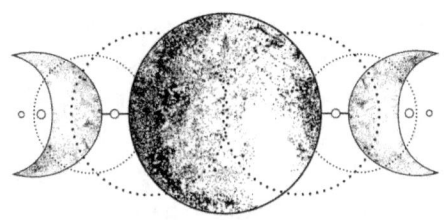

## HECATE

Dawn arises, and with it, cruelty ruptures my chest.

I awake with a gasp, clutching between my breast as pure malice wiggles its way through my skin and heart. All the souls who have nestled into my body are white as snow, except this one. The largest soul, etched in black, burrows its way inside me, and the pain is unlike any other.

It is Typhon's.

I know it the moment the soul consumes me. Typhon is dead, and his soul joins the other monsters and humans who have no Underworld. A part of the prophecy has come true. The prophesied huntress has killed the mighty Typhon, and with that unquestionable truth, the war's outcome tilts out of our favor.

I'm careful as I extract myself from the covers and Mastiff's arm draped over my abdomen. Quickly, I throw a robe over my body, and I exit my new home. The smell of burned flesh permeates across Mt. Olympus. I follow the smoke billowing around one immortal near the Olympian pantheon. I arrive at the steps, where Uranus kneels before a frighteningly infuriated Styx. She raises her arms, and a swarm of her black river water thrashes from her hands, dousing the burning, writhing body of Uranus.

The fire extinguishes, but her rage swells. She brings her river water back towards her, but it doesn't slither back into her veins. She wraps the black water like cobras coiling around her arms. Her eyes, Stygian black and full of devious intent, match the color of her river as she glowers down at Uranus. Her upper lip curls into a sneer, and it is the most expression I have seen on Styx's face across the eons I have known her.

"What. Did. You. Say?" Each of her words come out slow, deliberate, and full of sharpened blades.

Uranus trembles, his body soaked and his skin slowly regrowing over the burned patches. He doesn't look up at Styx; instead, the former king of the world stares down at his knees. Fear emits a putrid stench from him, more potent than the odor of burned flesh, which still surrounds us. Despite how many traitorous gods find a new home within our version of Mt. Olympus, I am the only one who steps out to witness this exchange.

The others cower behind their pantheon, fearful of the magic swirling and expanding around Styx.

"Raven, one huntress you recruited to your side betrayed us. She killed the other huntresses we allied with, and she freed all the prisoners." His Adam's apple bobs painfully as he pushes out his next words. "That's when Hephaestus and a horde of huntresses arrived at the prison site. They started a fire, and it grew too big, too fast to extinguish. I promise, your highness, I tried."

"No, you did not." Styx stands on the highest step of the Olympian pantheon. She remains rigid to the spot where she doused Uranus with her river and extinguished the flames, but now she takes one step down. The single movement creates an ominous echo, and Uranus flinches. "It is a foolish task you embark on."

"What task is that, my lady?" His voice wobbles, his fear reaching new heights.

"Lying to me when I can smell deceit like poison on your tongue." She takes another step down, and he flinches again. "This is your sole warning not to spin blasphemy into your story of failure."

"I knew what it meant when I saw all the huntresses there with Typhon." Uranus's entire body shakes as he relays a story that slowly weaves together in my mind. A story not of our success, but of our failure. His failure. "I went after the huntress who we thought was the prophesied one to kill Typhon."

Lamb.

I was the first one to call out her name amongst our predictions. She survived Ogygia; she has Artemis's unwavering trust, and she is a lamb I foolishly saw as prey for many centuries. Lamb could be the huntress because she is the last one anyone would assume to take the mantle of slaying the un-slayable.

Amongst those in the living world, Dýnami was the most obvious guess, or Jamila. Many immortals like myself see Lamb as nothing but a meek animal, ready for the slaughter, much like her moniker. That is why I thought it had to be her. Because our inclination towards underestimating humans has been the downfall of immortality for centuries. It is why Kronos lost the war, because he underestimated Saffron and her human friends.

"What happened next?" I ask, speaking for the first time.

Neither Uranus nor Styx glance in my direction, but

Uranus answers through clenched teeth. "The bitch cut off my hand."

"Were we correct in presuming Lamb as the huntress in the prophecy?" Styx's voice is eerily calm, but I know the falsity of her tone. Rage pools deep within her, waiting to rise like a tide and consume Uranus whole. "Did the meek little human kill Typhon?"

The longest silence stretches as sweat trickles down the side of Uranus's face. He doesn't answer right away, but his hands tremble. He can barely keep himself upright on his knees, which means his answer will be the catalyst to Styx's barely contained rage.

"I am not sure, your highness. She took the Dagger of Chains from me, and I." He audibly gulps. "…ran."

Styx takes two last steps down the pantheon stairs, landing directly in front of Uranus. She reaches out a hand, and he whimpers when her filthy, jagged nails dig into his chin. She lifts his face, and while hers remains as stoic as marble, his fractures with fear. His eyes threaten to pop from their sockets, and his bottom lip trembles. How could he have once been a mighty king when he cowers like this? When he flees the moment, one woman bests him?

"You ran." Ichor dribbles down his chin where her nails dig deeper, and she sneers. "You ran from a human girl."

"She is not just some human girl." Finally, Uranus locks eyes with Styx. "That is why we failed at the prison site, your highness, because we all look at those huntresses the same way, as inconsequential human women. I ran because I finally saw she was more than that, and I wanted to make it out of there without becoming a prisoner to the Dagger of Chains. That was my fate when I looked into her eyes. Imprisonment and humiliation."

Styx's black river shoots out of her arms, sinking into both sides of Uranus's neck like snakes. The fangs, made of her sinful water, pierce his skin. He collapses to the ground on his back, screaming and trying to pull the snake-shaped river off his neck. Yet, his fingers slide through his serpentine assailant's midsection without being able to grab anything solid. He thrashes and screams, but there isn't any reprieve.

Styx turns to face me, and her face of marble has a single crack cascading down the corner. "Go to the prison site and report back what you see."

I let my green smoke envelop me, and I transport myself to a place of ash and death. The Fates play a spiteful game because what I find is their creation. The prison itself has burned to cinder, but the battle plays out in front of me with eerie detail. Smoke preserves Typhon's body, along with the weapon that ended his life. The surrounding ash that fell on him formed a protective shell that calcified instantaneously, defying the laws of science.

Only the work of the Fates.

A spear ended Typhon's life. It juts out on either side of his skull, directly through an eye. His body lies on the ground, but he is not the only one preserved in such a fashion. All the huntresses who died killing him lie around him in a circle. It is impossible to identify the women. They are nothing but human-shaped, calcified ash.

Yet, impossibly, a single piece of parchment paper lies beside one huntress as the sole survivor of the pyre.

Careful not to step on any corpse and destroy the image of this war, I walk towards the piece of paper and carefully extract it. In the center of the paper is a set of coordinates, undoubtedly giving the un-imprisoned huntresses the prisoners' whereabouts, but in the only corner that is not smeared by soot, is an image.

A perfect drawing of Sika's scarification mark.

I recognize the mark right away. I saw it every single day she was a prisoner in our cells, thrashing to escape. She died weeks ago in Poseidon's castle. She was dead. If I didn't release the Underworld and its occupants, and if Styx didn't insist on keeping Sika alive for information, then Typhon would not have died. Sika was the prophesied huntress. A huntress that was already killed, who we unknowingly gave a second chance at life, only to defeat us.

I curl the parchment around my hand, and with only the dead to hear, I scream with rage.

Hubris is the act of believing one is better than the gods, but in this rare case, Hartika Sommers is better than Styx and me. I thought it was odd how unprepared the Underworld was to our attack, considering they had an oracle on their side. But that was Hartika's goal. She let us destroy the Underworld and steal away all the members of the dead as prisoners because she knew they needed to be alive again.

We fell into a human's trap, and now I stand in the rubble of our mistakes.

When I return to Mt. Olympus, the words die upon my tongue. I can only place the parchment paper in Styx's hand and wait for the realization to dawn on her face. It takes two seconds. Two seconds to open the folded paper, see the scarification mark once etched in Sika's flesh, and to understand. The oracle played us for fools by letting us destroy the Underworld.

How many other members of the prophecy did we resurrect, and hand deliver back to Hartika and Saffron?

Styx folds the paper four times, carefully tucks it into the sleeve of her black gown, and opens her palms. The black river slithers like snakes back to her awaiting arms.

Uranus still screams on the floor; twitching, as the aftereffects of her sinister magic courses through his gilded veins.

She waits until he stops moving, stops bellowing in pain, then says ever so softly. "Get up."

It takes him four tries, but he finally rises. Uranus's head remains bowed, but he clenches and unclenches his fists in silent frustration. Styx undoubtedly sees this but ignores it.

"Tonight, Hecate and you will take the Furies, the Harpies, and three humans who have long missed their chance to see Saffron again. You will go to her castle of bones, and you will kill *every single human* who slipped through the Underworld gates. Kill more, if you would like, but all who died once must die again. Except Epiales. Her heart cannot die twice with our hands. We played into Hart's games by destroying the Underworld, and it is now time we remedy our mistake." She takes one step towards Uranus, and he jumps back. The smallest smile dances across Styx's lips. "Fail me again, Uranus. I dare you."

"Never again, your highness."

Styx turns around and walks back up the steps of the Olympian pantheon, with her dress creating a train of obsidian water behind her. It consumes the steps of the pantheon, swallowing them whole. Neither Uranus nor I move until she closes the pantheon door with a cacophonous finality.

Only then do we prepare for a battle where red blood will spill.

# TWENTY-NINE

HART

Nighttime sprinkles through the windows, encapsulating the house of bones in darkness. Laughter replaces itself with soft snores. Words falter as silence reigns supreme. Apollo rests beside me with a contemplative smile on his face. I immortalize this image in my head, of his face when slackened with peace, as I slide out of bed.

The rest of the home hears the soft whirl of fans as they fall asleep, or the gracefulness of nothing at all, but as I stroll towards my art room, I hear the crackling of rising flames. The warmth caresses my cheeks, promising mass bloodshed and finite screams. I slip through the slightly ajar door, pick up a handful of paintbrushes, and drop three colors onto my palette.

The reds and oranges of flames and the black of a life snuffed out.

I draw the moment Gareth French kills Akita and Frigate, then stumbles down the stairs past the soldiers waiting for the prisoners to leave their opened cell, and towards his family's freshly dug graves. Pain etches itself around every jagged corner of my easel as Gareth bends over the dirt and digs through the material with his bare hands until he finds the worst possible truth.

The level of decomposition decorating his wife and daughter erodes what makes them appear human, but their faces are still recognizable. I hear his wail of anguish as if he were right beside me, and then I paint the moment he uses his mechanical arm to rip into his own chest and remove his heart. Before life extinguishes his heartbroken eyes, he lays his heart between his daughter and wife and collapses beside them.

Behind Gareth's tragic tale, a flame begins.

It starts small, only covering a single prison cell. The gods and fates work together to create a symphony of martyrdom for the spatter of huntresses and heroes who choose to die on this pyre-spun battlefield. I spare a single tear for each life stolen by the flames and one goddess's greed for a throne that doesn't belong to her.

I mourn the loss of Zig, who once again chooses another's life over his own. My fingers tremble as I hear the crunch of his body breaking into a thousand irreparable pieces beneath the weight of a monster's foot.

The moment Panda's head cracks against the unforgiving ground, I shed another tear. Flames take most, like Reaper and Vee. Crushed windpipes steal the life of Angel, Shikari, and Hound. I paint each undistinguished line, immortalizing their deaths forevermore. The canvas is a timeline, starting the moment Gareth leaves the prison cell, and ending when Sika slams Dýnami's magenta spear through Typhon's skull.

Lamb and Sika succumb to the flames, smiling at one another as death steals two brave souls, but I do not paint their demise. I let them live on in this one image, grinning until the end. The moment I paint the last detail; the brush drops from my quivering fingers. Daylight streams through the crack in the door, and with that comes more bloodshed.

Sleeplessness has been a sordid friend of mine. Instead of freedom in slumber, I walk hand-in-hand with insomnia. There are too many stories left untold. Too many instances, where I must ensure the war goes exactly as planned.

I exit the room with the canvas in my hand. It is still wet, but I set the painting on an awaiting hook next to my door. Those who died in the Battle of the Huntresses will be eternally remembered. They shape the future of the many heroes who will come after them, fueled by the late huntresses' bravery.

Vibrant colors exude past the art piece, creating a silhouette of each lost life. Typhon is still the soot black, but Lamb shines the brightest shade of green. Sika is a blur of magenta, just like the spear she used to kill Typhon. Vee exudes a stunning yellow, while Shikari bleeds a vibrant red. Their auras tell their stories, and we are even more magnificent because of the stories our lives tell.

There are only a few precious minutes between the quiet of the sunrise and the cacophony of more death, and I spend those last moments crawling back into bed with Apollo. I wake him with kisses along his cheeks and jawline, laying in between his eyes as they flutter awake. He smiles at me, still sleepy yet encompassed with joy.

"μέλι." Apollo leans up and rests his lips so delicately against mine, they feel akin to clouds. "Oh, how I've missed you."

A laugh escapes. "You saw me before you fell asleep, you silly god."

"And that was too long not to see you." He reaches up

and wraps a tendril of my curly black hair on his finger. "Haven't you learned I'm forever enraptured by you?"

I lean down, hoping I can have one last kiss before the world implodes once more, but I hear the drums of war against my ears again. So soon after the Battle of the Huntress, which no one in this home knows about, but me. Our lips are a breath apart when a scream ruptures at the front of the house.

"Let me go!" Dýnami screams, her throat raw with rage and pain so acute it can only be understood as true heartbreak. "I will kill you!"

Apollo scrambles out of the bed, and I race beside him for a sight I already expect. Diam has Dýnami slung over his shoulder, and bruises cover his dark complexion. He has a welt growing on the side of his head, pairing brutally with a swollen eye, scratch marks across his neck, and a purple bruise beside his jawline. He drops Dýnami to her feet, and he doesn't duck as she swings her fist towards his face.

It crashes against his cheek, but he doesn't back down. He lifts his head, meeting her furious gaze with his own admonished one. "I had to, Dye."

"You didn't have to do anything, you piece of shit! I thought you were my friend!" Dýnami crumbles to her knees and a sob wrenches from her lungs. It isn't long until there is a full audience at the second-floor railing staring down at Dýnami. "She was my world, and you took me from her! You stole my breath when I just got her back."

Saffron and Hattie are the first to run down the staircase. Hattie jumps into Diam's arms, crying with relief that she's reunited with her husband, while Dýnami glowers at their happy ending when hers is gone forever. Saffron wraps Dýnami in a hug. At first, the huntress tries to push Saffron away, but grief swiftly tires her. She places her burly arms around Saffron, and she sobs. Her cries are not filled with relief; rather, it is knowing that her worst nightmare has become reality once again.

Another two figures walk into the house.

Raven is not slung over Hephaestus's back, although it is clear by the scowl on her lips that her arrival is not by choice. The former traitor wished to die on the battlefield to atone for her sins. But Hephaestus and I had other plans. She stands in the doorway, with soot coating her tanned cheeks and anger bright in her onyx eyes.

Hephaestus glowers at me from where he stands on the main floor, but Apollo doesn't notice his brother's ire. Apollo runs down the stairs, eyes assessing each person. "What happened? Are you all alright?"

The moment the question leaves his lips, Thanatos soars into the room. Hypnos flies into the room shortly behind him, holding Queen Persephone in his arms. Normally, the sight of so many immortals returning unscathed would incite a level of excitement. Except, today is not a typical day. Today, Thanatos holds a delicate, burn-covered woman in his arms, fighting with every vestige of strength to survive the day.

His black wings tuck into themselves as he slams his feet on the ground. In his arms rests the huntress's unconscious body. Flames lick up her once smooth, dark complexion. Her curly hair hangs in singed layers, while her chest barely rises and falls.

Thanatos focuses on Apollo, his arms holding Jamila tight, as he grits through clenched teeth. "Save her."

Hermes jumps off the railing, slamming onto the floor, and races towards his daughter. Saffron glances away from Dynami to see Hermes rip Jamila from Thanatos's arms and rush her to the infirmary room. She pulls herself from Dynami's embrace, and a croaked sound escapes her.

Saffron's only daughter, not by blood but by love, barely looks alive. She hurries into the infirmary after Hermes and Thanatos, with Apollo close on their heels.

The humans, including Epiales, who Hermes saved, stand at the railing. Their confusion is apparent, but they cannot look away at the carnage on the ground floor. Zeus moves to stand beside me, hands curling around the railing, as we wait. Hephaestus shuttles Raven into the infirmary for the burns decorating her arms and neck, but she continually swats him away.

Beneath the screams and sobs and raucous, confused voices, I can just barely hear Raven saying, "I don't deserve it. I don't deserve to be alive instead of Willow-"

"I won't repeat myself for a hundredth time," Hephaestus grumbles. A second passes, and before they slip completely into a room where I cannot hear them, he says. "The Fates decide who lives, dies, and thrives. It was her time, and unless you want to speak Hubris, you will accept that it is your destiny to be alive and hers to perish."

Raven glowers at him before they fully enter the infirmary, not understanding Hephaestus's words are meant to comfort rather than annoy.

Phobos and Deimos rush down the stairs and into the infirmary after the others, who have all sprinted there, but Ares stumbles at the top step. He looks back at me. "I want to go help her," he says through gritted teeth.

"Comfort her tomorrow," I say.

Every fragment of Ares's self-control tells him to listen to my command, but it is not in the god of war's nature to obey others' commands. His jaw locks, and his eyes burn a fiery shade of blue as they bounce between Zeus and me.

"Listen to her. Go train or wallow," Zeus commands. "But leave Saffron alone."

"And what if you're wrong?" Ares takes a step towards

me, but Zeus stands between us. Ares would never hurt me, but Zeus stands in between just in case. "What if you're telling us nonsense because you don't actually know the future?"

Lightning crackles in the space between Zeus and Ares. "I've witnessed the visions myself. Do you wish to brand me a liar too, son?"

Ares glowers at his father, defiance bringing a snarl to his lips, but he doesn't say more. He spins on his heels and storms away. Zeus doesn't move from where he stands, but he turns his head to meet my gaze from the corner of his eye. "Should we go?"

"Not yet."

I need to wait until despair reaches its peak, when any idea is better than death. Only then will Zeus and I enter the room with our proposal. Only when Apollo has tried everything to save Jamila, except my one suggestion.

Much at the behest of my heart, the prophecy I have contorted is going according to plan.

My eyes burn with the tears I should not shed, as the screams from the infirmary escape from the walls and seep into my guilt-ridden body. I know that this is necessary for the safety of the rest of the world, but the knowledge of the deaths that must occur doesn't sit well in the pit of my soul. As I lean forward on the railing, I can hear the soft sobs from Saffron as she sits beside her adopted child. My stomach churns with nausea.

I listen to the helplessness in Hermes's demands, and I wait for my moment to stride into the infirmary. The wheels move the course towards victory against Styx, but there is still so much I must do.

There are still more deaths I must guide…

"No!" Saffron outcries, and the sound is loud enough to rattle the walls. "Po, she will not die!"

It's time.

When Zeus and I walk into the infirmary, Jamila lies on a bed deathly still. The stench of blood and burned flesh permeates the air with the reminder of death, and Jamila is the cause. The three others who lay on infirmary beds-Diam, Raven, and Dýnami- have minor wounds in comparison.

I try to ignore Diam's screams as Phobos peels the burned flesh from his body, and Hattie cries next to him as she holds his hand. I try to ignore the groans that leave Raven's lips as she sits in an infirmary bed as Hephaestus stitches a wound on her shoulder. Dýnami thrashes in her spot as Queen Persephone tries to give her a sleeping potion, crying out for Sika nonstop. Everyone else who joined them in battle is dead, and Jamila's soul marches towards the afterlife, too.

Jamila hasn't opened her eyes since Thanatos brought her inside. She will not recover on her own. As long as she is mortal, she will die. Thanatos stands at the foot of Jamila's bed as Apollo cleans the blood surrounding Jamila like a stream. Apollo's lips furrow in a deep frown; the knowledge that Jamila will die weighs upon his chest. He has told them that Jamila's death is a certainty, but Saffron still stares at him with hope. Hope that her daughter will not perish because of a war she blames herself for enacting.

I look at Thanatos once more.

With Jamila's death looming in the air like a stench, not a single person has noticed how Thanatos stares at the burned remains of Jamila. I am the only one who looks at Thanatos as he watches the huntress with a cruel mixture of love and heartache. He might not even know the truth, but I know with certainty that he is watching his soulmate die an excruciating death. A soulmate who never wanted love but an immortal life in the wild with Lady Artemis.

The Fates have other plans for Jamila Pyro, and they start today.

I walk over to Apollo, and I wrap my hand around his. I squeeze just once before he lets go and faces Saffron and Hermes. "It is a miracle that she has stayed alive this long. Eighty percent of her body is burned, and she has multiple stab wounds." They both shake their heads at Apollo, but he continues. "Hermes, Saffy, she-"

"No," Saffron silences him with the sternness of a leader; sharp, brown eyes glare at Apollo as the tears spill down her cheeks. "Do not say it."

Apollo flinches, but he says. "I will make her as comfortable as possible, but it is best you say your goodbyes."

"There has to be something that we can do," Thanatos's voice is weak, heartbroken, and trembling at the thought of losing his soulmate. "We are gods." He stabs his finger hard into the center of his chest. "I am the god of death. I can keep her alive, ensure the Clotho doesn't clip her life string."

"That will not be a life, Thanatos," Apollo says gently, but sternly. "It will only be a prolonged sentence. I'm sorry, but she won't wake up. She won't be the same person again, even if you refuse to give her death."

"We are gods," Thanatos seethes, body trembling with a surplus of emotions. "There has to be more we can do."

Apollo opens his mouth to interject, but I speak first. "There is something you can do, Lord Thanatos."

All of us, Hermes and Saffron included, look at Thanatos. Hope blossoms over his appearance, enlivening his eyes that are as dark as night, and he nods his head. "What can I do? I'll do anything."

"Marry her," I respond.

At the same second, three voices speak.

"What?" Hermes demands.

"Marriage?!" Saffron outcries.

"She won't want to marry me," Thanatos states with all the sadness in the world. He stares down only at Jamila. "She doesn't want love, and she certainly doesn't want marriage. All she's ever wanted was to be a huntress. She would never forgive me if I take that away from her."

A tear slips from Thanatos's eye and lands on Jamila's chest.

"But you are her third love. Her destined soulmate. If there is a chance to save her, then take it." I step towards Thanatos, but he doesn't register my nearness. His only focus is the woman he loves who wants nothing to do with him.

"Does she know?" Saffron asks. "Does she know what you are to her?"

"I've known for two years now. It was one night when you tried to go to the Underworld, and Hypnos and I came to stop you. Jamila offered me a cup of tea, and I just knew. From one interaction, I knew."

He falls into the chair beside Jamila's bed, de-materializing his wings so he can fit. He reaches out to touch her but stops himself because of her wounds. Yet, he doesn't look away. Despite the burns covering her entire body, he stares at her with such adoration.

"A few days later," he says. "She begged you to let her move out. She stopped talking to me and would leave the room anytime I entered. So yes, I think she knew what I was to her, and she has avoided me ever since. That is why there must be another way. Not for my sake, but for hers. She decided against falling in love with me. She wants Artemis and the huntresses, not me. I don't want to take that from her."

"Fate already took all but two huntresses from her," I say.

Dýnami sobs again. A new rack of anguish terrorizes her body, and I try to ignore it. Even Raven cries in her bed, though no one has sympathy for her. I focus all my attention on Thanatos.

"If you marry Jamila, she becomes a goddess. She will live long enough to heal from these injuries and wake. You are giving her the choice to live when no one else in this room can," I say. "She will be grateful that she gets to wake and see her family again, even if she doesn't get to go back to Artemis and the remaining huntresses."

"Jamila doesn't have long," Apollo says so quietly, so mournfully. "You need to decide now what to do."

"Tell me what to do." Thanatos stares imploringly at Saffron and Hermes. Tears brim the god of death's eyes. "Tell me what to do, and I'll do it."

Hermes and Saffron don't hesitate. They say. "Do it."

I glance behind me to where Zeus stands. "Marry them."

Zeus walks towards Jamila's bedside, but each movement he makes is rigid because he knows the trajectory of this decision. He stands in front of her bed and whispers. "Take her hand as gently as you can and repeat after me."

Death wraps his hand around Jamila's mostly unscathed one, but before Zeus can begin, another voice breaks through the silence. "Marry Hart and me, too."

I feign shock as I spin to face Apollo. He smiles down at me with a mixture of sadness and determination. He reaches forward and cups my face with his hand. "I love you, Hartika Sommers, more than the moon loves its stars. Marry me so that I do not have to worry if you won't come back to me on that last battlefield. Marry me, so I wake with certainty that you are my forever, regardless of the decades and eons that pass. Love me forever, my μέλι, and let me call you my wife."

I caress the side of his face with my hand, treasuring every part of my soulmate. "I will love you forever as your wife."

Despite the macabre state of the room, Apollo grins wider than ever before.

In a room of burned flesh, endless screams, and a comatose huntress, the joining of four soulmates occurs. Above Diam's bellows, Raven's muffled grunts, and Dýnami's sobs, Zeus asks Thanatos, Apollo, and me to conjoin our love forever. As Diam's burned flesh is being peeled off his body and Raven's leg worsens by the second, Zeus tells the gods to kiss their brides.

I wrap my arms around Apollo's neck and press my lips against his. Beside us, Thanatos leans down and kisses Jamila's forehead.

Just as the prophecy needs.

# THIRTY

## SAFFRON

I never thought I would sit, once again, under the roof of my house and see Diam and Hattie as more than corporeal forms. In the deepest recess of my mind, I would dream of this moment. That my friends, including Zig, would come back to me. Yet, wishes have a cruel way of twisting one's words until that very dream becomes a nightmare.

We are together again, minus Zig, beneath my roof of bones. My hand curls around the blanket beside Jamila's scorched, slowly healing hand, while Hattie lays her head against an unconscious Diam's chest. He rests, covered with bandages from where Phobos slowly removed the burned flesh, but he is mostly unscathed.

Raven refused to stay in the infirmary, despite Apollo's request, and Hephaestus helped her to a room next to his after he stitched her wounds. Dýnami does not have the strength for more than sleep. Her external wounds are minimal, just a few bruises, scratches, and one sprained ankle, but inwardly she suffers.

Even in sleep, Dýnami cries.

Hermes sits on the other side of Jamila's bed. His head lies beside her bandaged shoulder, careful not to touch her, as he restlessly sleeps. Between the snores, he murmurs our daughter's name. As if even in sleep, he begs her to return to us. My mom pulled Thanatos out of the room; otherwise, he'd be here too.

This isn't how I imagined a reunion with my closest family, but it is what the Fates have cruelly spun. Only Hattie and I are awake, even as the midday sun breeches the windows and shines auspiciously brightly.

"Did Diam say what happened to Zig?" I can barely push the words out, my throat jagged with grief.

Hattie shakes her head. "Not details. Just that Zig pushed Lamb out of the way and took the killing blow himself."

"I wouldn't expect him to die on a battlefield any other way. He has always cared more about those around him than himself."

Hattie's eyes wander towards Jamila's bed, and she winces. "She looks so much like her mother."

"She looks so much like you," I say almost immediately.

Hattie scoffs, but the chiding tone doesn't hold the same mirth as usual. "I wish."

Yet, their similarities are unmistakable. While Jamila's complexion is darker than Hattie's, nearing Diam's umber skin more than Hattie's ochre one, Jamila is a reincarnation of my best friend. They both wear the same crooked smile, and their eyes both glint a mischievous shade of brown a shade away from obsidian. When Jamila laughs, it is the only glimmer of Hattie on my darkest days. Generations may separate Hattie and Jamila, but there is no denying their familiar relations.

I carefully reach for my daughter, pushing a curly strand of hair off her forehead. I ignore just how singed that one piece of hair is; instead, I focus on her face. It is mostly unscathed, especially on the right side, and that's where my attention fixates. "She reminds me of you, too."

"How so?" Hattie asks.

"She is stubborn like you. There was one time when she was fourteen or fifteen, she decided she wanted to face Argus in a fight. She said that Athena trained her enough so that she could face any opponent, even a giant with a hundred eyes." Even now, I exhale a puff of air, almost resembling a laugh. Years have passed, yet the image is still so fresh in my mind. "Argus went easy on her, but he pushed her down a hundred times. Knocked her weapon out of her hand an additional fifty, but each time, she'd jump back up. Each time she'd fall, she'd grin, grab her fallen weapon, and stand back up. They sparred for over three hours until I finally lied and told Jamila that Argus was too tired to continue. To this day, Jamila says that because Argus was tired of pushing her to the ground, she was the winner. She would have gone days, losing time and time again against him, just on the off chance she could beat him once."

When one story begins, another flows out.

"She's fearless like you, too," I say. "Jamila has wanted to be a huntress since she was a little girl sword fighting with Athena. Once, against my permission, Athena commissioned Hephaestus to build a mechanical monster for Jamila to face."

"Which one?" Hattie asks, intrigue hitching up her voice an octave.

I suppress an eye roll. "The Minotaur. Athena didn't tell Jamila either. She just told Jamila to show up to their usual spot, and instead of Athena being there with wooden swords, it was a twenty-foot-tall mechanical bull."

"Oh gods, what happened?"

"What do you think? A mechanical bull whopped her ass. She came home with a broken arm, a few broken ribs, and a fractured cheekbone." Yet, I grin. "I was so mad. Jamila was only sixteen years old, and Athena had no right setting this up without my permission. Yet, as soon as I healed all her bones, Jamila asked me if she could fight the mechanical Minotaur again. We grounded her for a week the moment the question left her lips."

"And did you let her?" Hattie asks.

A soft male voice scoffs. "Gods no we didn't." Hermes lifts his head up, and while fatigue still paints a pale shade across his face, he answers Hattie. "We told Athena and Hephaestus to burn that mechanical bull to the ground or we'd bury it in the middle of a desert."

"But they didn't burn it," I say. "A few days later, Jamila came bouncing into the house."

"Covered in a dozen bruises," Hermes adds. "But grinning like a fool."

"Athena let her fight the bull again," Hattie says, but there's a humorous edge to her voice like she is suppressing a laugh.

"Athena let her fight the mechanical Minotaur again." I confirm. "But this time she won. She used every day of her grounding studying the Minotaur and learn all its weaknesses. She started learning how to fight with both arms in case the Minotaur broke her sword arm again, and she trained relentlessly."

"You're forgetting the best part." Hermes laughs softly. "A few days later, Jamila admitted she thinks she broke her other arm in the fight. Sure enough, she broke the other arm and fractured her ankle."

"Almost lost a tooth, too." I say.

Hermes looks at me, his boyish grin shining through, and I smile back. "We really have an incredible kid," he says.

Despite everything else, Hermes is right. We raised a perfect, fearless, stubborn daughter. We both look down on our daughter, who may look more like Diam and Hattie, but we get the joy of calling her ours. I lean down and press a kiss on an unscathed part of her forehead. Hermes' gaze meets mine the moment I lift my head.

"The perfect kid," I concur.

"Perfect because she looks like me, right?" Hattie teases from across the room.

"Or perfect despite her relation to you," Hermes kids right back.

Hattie rips the pillow from underneath Diam's head, causing the back of his skull to smack against the headboard, and chucks it at Hermes. He catches it, grinning from ear-to-ear, while Diam groans.

"Was that necessary?" he asks.

Hattie leans down and kisses him. "Yes, darling. Very necessary."

He groans as he sits in his bed, either from the growing lump on the back of his head or from his previous injuries.

"How are you feeling?" Hermes asks.

Diam narrows his eyes at my former husband. "Like I just fought titans, Typhon, and a dozen other monsters as a fiery building threatened to collapse on me. How in the gods do you think I feel? I feel like that stupid mechanical bull you kept yapping about ran me over, backed up, and ran me over seven more times."

There were only a few moments where simple conversation slipped through the cracks of disparity, but Diam's words obliterate anything but the somber truth of our situation. Silence drapes over us, nestling us in the reminder that one friend does not sit in this room with us. Zig isn't here. He died, along with almost every huntress, in the prison where I grew up. That place of sorrow and helplessness eternally claims Zig, who lies on that unforgiving ground, without a burial right or a chance to enter the Underworld once again.

"He wouldn't want us sad," Diam grumbles, but he reaches for Hattie's hand for comfort. She squeezes him tight. "We all know Zig hated when we had a funeral for him the first time. Complained it was too sad."

I remember too well the first time Zig died. He was the first person in my life who died without a war waging and titans inflicting harm wherever they went. It was a heart attack. One second, he was alive and grinning at me. The next? He was a corpse. Gone forever as his soul went to join the trillions in the Underworld.

But this time, I do not have the peace that comes with knowing Zig's final destination. His death the first time shredded a bit of my innocence. I've never been able to stitch it back together, but at least then I knew he was safe in my parent's domain. But now? Now, I don't know where his soul landed. I only know one truth: that his second death was more brutal and painful than the first.

"No," I say, shaking my head. "Screw Zig's plight about not making us sad because death is sad. It's heart wrenching and devastating and a part of the cycle of life that we all know is coming, yet hate when it arrives. We should be sad he's dead, more this time than the last. When the war settles, and we survive together, we should have that funeral. We will cry and mourn, even if that's the last thing Zig wants, because it's what we need."

We do not have the time for a proper burial, and Hart suggested we wait until we can free Artemis from the

Dagger of Chains before having a massive funeral for those we have lost. But in this quickly assembled infirmary, the four of us mourn our friend. We share stories about Zig's life, crying and laughing interchangeably. We spend hours in this room together, remembering Zig and everything he meant to all of us.

Hattie and I find a spot on the floor to sit, hip to hip. Her arm wraps around me, and my head lies on her shoulder. Hermes never moves away from Jamila's unconscious form, and he only moves to swipe a stubborn tendril of her hair off her face. Diam tells the most stories. He regales us with tales of their time in the Underworld together, and eventually he tells us the harrowing details of Zig's death.

"I'll miss him every day, for however long the Fates want to keep me alive," Diam ends with, and we all silently agree.

One part of his story snags at me. "Wait, you have the Dagger of Chains?"

"I do." Diam grunts as he turns his body to face the side table nearest his bed. He rustles through the drawers, then digs into his pockets. His face falls with dismay. "I *did* have it."

I turn to Hermes, and he holds his hands up. "Don't look at me. I did not steal it!"

Despite myself, I grin. "That wasn't why I was looking at you. I was wondering if you saw anybody take it out of this room?"

Hermes's gaze wanders back to our daughter and he murmurs. "I was too preoccupied to care about anything else but her."

"Is she alright?" A deep voice asks.

Three figures stand in the doorway, fighting to be the first one to break through. Thanatos wins, and he rushes back into the room, smelling of soap. He crumbles into the seat I once occupied, but he doesn't grab Jamila's hands. He itches to touch her, to make sure she's okay, but he doesn't. Instead, he looks between Hermes and me, expecting the worst, yet hoping for the best news.

"Nothing has changed," Hermes says. "But did you see anyone holding the Dagger of Chains? Diam had it, but now it's missing."

Thanatos focuses all his attention on Jamila and shakes his head. "Wasn't really focused on the others, sorry."

"I can look around for it," Persephone says. She stands side-by-side with a ghost in the doorway, but when she leaves, all I can do is stare at him.

Epiales.

He stands there, so unsure of himself as his hands move in and out of his pockets, and he can't fully look at me. He bounces his gaze from Hattie to Hermes to Thanatos, but he mainly focuses on the floor nearest me. I rise to my feet.

"Did you want to talk?" I ask.

Epiales finally looks at me, and those sparkling silver eyes brim with hesitance. "If that's alright with you."

"Let me know if anything changes, alright?" I ask Hermes, and he nods.

"And I'll check on you in a bit, too." I say to Diam, who only grunts in response.

I lean forward again and press a kiss to Hattie's head. "Try not to steal anymore of Diam's pillows."

She grins up at me, eyes twinkling with mirth. "Can't make any promises."

I slip out of the room with Epiales, and we silently walk towards my bedroom. I try to stay focused solely on Epiales, who stands close enough to me to reignite a thousand bolts of electricity, but my eyes continue to wander in search of *him*. My third destined love. Ares is somewhere in his house, and I search for him from across the room.

Yet, he's nowhere in sight.

Briefly, I wonder if Hart had the same conversation with Ares as she did with me. Did she tell him to stay away? My eyes drag back up towards Epiales, and I wonder, is it because of Epiales that we must distance ourselves a little while longer? There are a thousand questions, but the one person with the answers refuses to speak.

I open my bedroom door, and Epiales walks inside. There are two chairs in the far corner of my bedroom, and Epiales takes one of them. Hesitantly, I take the other. We sit a foot apart, with our bodies angled towards one another, but we have never felt farther from one another.

He lifts his gaze, and I did not know how much I had missed the sight of his silver eyes until right now. I see him in the stars sometimes; or, more accurately, I see his eyes in them. If two stars are close, then I think of these silver irises as if they were gazing down at me, but the stars are nothing compared to the real thing.

And he's right in front of me.

"Hi," I whisper.

# THIRTY-ONE

## SAFFRON

E piales' boy is too stiff and full of anxiousness. He digs his hands further into his pockets, like I'm a stranger, rather than his one constant in almost a hundred years. He drags his gaze back down to his lap, and he stammers. "My favorite color is brown."

"What?"

Our time on the island swarms back to me. This same revelation left his lips, but it came with such reverence. This time, he speaks with hesitance, like any word he says could be a fuse, igniting something wicked within me.

"Asking a person their favorite color is common, especially when you work at a bar full of drunk girls that talk a lot. Each time someone asked, the answer came immediately. I'd say brown, with no idea why. There are more common answers out there, and more colorful options, but I'd always say brown. I didn't understand why until now." Epiales lifts his head, and his eyes snag on my hair. My long, wavy brown hair always seems impossible to tame, but he smiles ever so slightly at the sight. "I used to have dreams about a girl with brown hair, and while I never saw her face, I always felt entranced. Her hair spanned out across a sandy beach. I always wanted to meet her, but I'm thinking I met her a long time ago."

"You met me a long time ago," I confirm. "And that's how I already knew brown was your favorite color."

"You did?" He shakes his head in disbelief. "Of course you knew that already. It's only me who forgot you and not…"

His sentence drifts, but I finish where he left off. "I didn't forget a single thing about you, Epiales." He winces at the name. "Or Erik. Hermes said that was your new name. Do you prefer that?"

"I don't know anymore."

"You once told me that brown was your favorite color because of my eyes," I say.

Epiales focuses on my eyes almost inquisitively, like he is trying to determine if he stills feels my eyes are the most beautiful color he's ever seen. He decides as he grins. "They are beautiful. Your eyes."

"Thank you. Is there anything else you remember?"

His smile vanishes.

In its place, sorrow creates a shadow around him, reminding me of his former powers when he was a god. The shadows circle around his body, shielding him from the memories fighting to the surface. I don't even think he realizes shadows surround him, cocooning him in their frigid comfort. It is the first time I have seen a glimpse of his powers since I brought him back to life. Have they always been there, waiting to reappear when he needed them the most?

I say nothing, but I watch them spin and coil around him.

"I learned who Epiales was." He clears his throat and

amends. "*Who I was.* I was a god of nightmares, and that makes perfect sense because all I see are nightmares. We live in a world without dreams, but I am afflicted by them. Tortured the moment I close my eyes of what I'm quickly learning are sordid decisions of my past, rather than horrific figments of my imagination."

"What do you see?" My voice wavers with uncertainty and a surplus of fear, but there is a glimmer of hope. I implore the Fates to gift him with some recollection. Anything that will bring back the former version of him, who used to love to bake and spin stories so eloquently.

"I barely remembered the nightmares until the day I met Hermes again. Then, all I could see was a place of clouds and alabaster columns, and I was torturing him." He shivers at the memories, but he doesn't hide from them. He continues. "I was peeling apart his skin, and I felt such joy despite this terrible act. I fought laughter as a monster of staggering height broke his limbs, and I relished his pain. Yet, each morning when I woke after those nightmares, it was me who felt the suffering."

I realize it now, Epiales does not want a reconciliation between him and me. He scarcely remembers me. Only wisps of my hair and a beach filled with joy remain of our love story. He is not here out of love for me, but out of guilt for what he has done to Hermes. It is why he flinches every time he hears his real name.

"Then, the nightmares changed," Epiales says with disgust on his tongue. "And we were on a battlefield. I continued to hurt him, but I wanted to pretend it wasn't me who hurt Hermes. Just a monster with a face identical to mine. I knew I had hurt him in more ways than I ever harmed a man before. But for as long as I can remember, I only survived those nightmares because I convinced myself they were fake. Now I know them to be true, and I cannot live with myself. I'm a monster with only one wonderful memory in a sea of anguish."

"My brown hair on the beach," I conclude, is his only wonderful memory.

He nods his head. "All I see are travesties, except for you. Sometimes, I'll get a rush of joy when I smell strawberries. Or a woman will ask me out at the bar, and I'll think of the most radiant smile. I'll reject every woman because I'll endlessly search for that one perfect smile. For that exact shade of brown hair. For the smell of strawberries that always reminds me of the one who made me crave the scent."

"Is that." I lick my lips, trying to find the strength to finish the sentence. "Is that all you remember of me? Strawberries, my hair, and a smile?"

He doesn't immediately answer, which is all the answer I need. It is all he remembers of me. Even as he sits in front of me now, he knows nothing else about us.

"I know you knew me well," he says, but his tone is uncertain. Hesitant. "And you didn't just see me as a villain. As a beast who tormented others for enjoyment."

I reach forward and clasp his hands in mine. I squeeze them until he finally looks up at me. There is so much pain in those silver eyes. When will the world finally gift him some respite?

"You are not a monster," I say. I hope I push through enough sincerity in my voice that he believes me. "You are the entire reason I am here now, alive and sane. If it were not for you, then I would not have understood love enough to experience it not once, but three times." A tear falls down his face, and I wipe it away with the back of my thumb. "Once upon a time, your body had more than a hundred scars, and you thought yourself hideous for them, but I have always and will always find you beautiful because of the broken parts. Not despite them."

"I tortured him, and I enjoyed doing it," Epiales's voice cracks.

"You also liked to bake and tell me stories. You enjoyed living on a beach with me, and you liked the man you were becoming when desperation and revenge didn't fuel you. I won't pretend that you have always been good, but I can say you've always wanted to be happy, even if you once went searching for that happiness the wrong way."

There is a long pause before Epiales croaks out. "I like to bake?"

I grin at my first love, even if he does not remember me the way I fondly cherish him. "When we first met, you didn't tell me your name. You only introduced yourself as my storyteller. It does not matter if you choose to go by Epiales or Erik because I will always call you my storyteller, even if I'm the one who must play that role from now on."

"What stories did I tell?" he asks, curiousness clearing away the sorrow.

"You told me stories about monsters like the Minotaur and heroes like Odysseus, and now it is my turn to tell you stories about a misunderstood god named Epiales. I will start with two stories, our first one and my favorite. Are you ready to hear them, my storyteller?"

He looks down at our conjoined hands and nods his head.

And I teach him about how a misunderstood god became a villain, then a hero.

All for one girl.

# THIRTY-TWO

HART

Apollo reminds me of his love with every ginger caress of his lips against my back. I lay face down on our bed, blankets laying across my waist, as Apollo peppers kisses along every freckle on my back. Every kiss accompanies two words he continually says in disbelief.

"My wife." He creates a hymn just from those two words as his hand splays across my exposed flesh. As he kisses every piece of bare skin with reverence, as if he is the lowly human and I the god. I slide my hands underneath the pillow I lay on as Apollo gifts me another kiss and another awestricken. "My wife."

"I'm sorry we had to get married like that. I know you wanted a big wedding."

"Marrying you, my μέλι, is the grandest gift the Fates have ever given upon me. I would marry you in an infirmary a thousand times over, if it was the only way I could call you my wife." He presses another kiss, and my heart shatters a little more.

Gods, I love him.

There is no one on this earth, between now and eons later, who is a better fit for me than Apollo. His open communication is one of his greatest qualities, but his willingness to protect those he loves before his wellbeing is a detriment to his future. I curl my hand around the dagger's hilt that is hidden underneath my pillow and I turn my face so I can stare at him. Memorize every detail, burn it into memory.

With the hand not holding the dagger, I reach for him. I cup my hand around his cheek, and I suppress a sob as he smiles innocently down at me. "I always wondered why I received this power," I say. "Why was I, over anybody else in this world, given the power to see the future? This ability has been gone for eons, and for the longest time, I thought I was undeserving. It should have gone to someone strong like Jamila, or fearless like Dýnami. But it is because of this war that it must be me. The one who loves you enough to destroy everything else to keep you safe."

Apollo tries to laugh, but it's a confused and forced sound. "This conversation has gotten far too morbid on our wedding night. Let's talk about this tomorrow."

But there is no tomorrow for us.

Tears well in my eyes, blurring my husband's perfect face from view. "I have seen every scenario of this war through nightmarish dreams, scratchy drawings, and my blood on a canvas. Millions of truths have shone in my eyes, and only one instance shows the Olympians winning against Styx. I must follow this one scenario perfectly because if I don't…"

I can't finish my sentence.

Through visions, I have borne witness to Apollo's death a thousand times over. I have watched as Saffron ripped out his bones or Hecate slammed the Dagger of Chains into his chest, then threw the Dagger into Charybdis' whirlpool. The only solace to those visions is the knowledge I am able to stop Apollo's death from becoming a reality.

"And we will do it together. You and me against everything and everyone." He leans in and presses a kiss to my lips. It is the sweetest goodbye.

I pull away slowly, torturously. Because that's what this moment is: pure torture. I should be happy tonight. I should have one night with just him and an absence of responsibility. It's my wedding night, for gods' sake, but the world does not stop just because I politely ask it to.

"You are the greatest love of my life, Apollo." I say the words against his lips, and I taste his smile. "And I will miss you most of all."

He never sees the Dagger of Chains coming until it slides into his forearm. He pulls away from the kiss, and his eyes widen in disbelieving betrayal. His gaze snags on the Dagger of Chains, but before he can say anything more or ask any further questions, he's gone. Where he once lay in bed beside me, there is only a trickle of ichor and the Dagger.

I talk to the Dagger of Chains like he can hear me. "If I do not follow this scenario exactly, then Styx wins. I've tried to find another way. Trust me, I wanted to find another way, but there isn't one. The only way Styx is defeated, and I save the world, is if I do everything exactly the way the prophecy foretold it. I'm so sorry. I love you so much."

My betrayal leaks acid through my esophagus and down to my stomach, and I run to the bathroom. I retch everything inside my stomach, hoping to expunge my guilt, but even as the nausea settles, there is still the burning residue of my decisions. Hopefully, one day Apollo will understand why I had to do this, but I fear the moment will not come soon.

I brush my teeth, put on a shirt and overalls, and pick up the Dagger of Chains. Carefully, I hide it in one of my overall pockets, and I slip out of the bedroom. Most of the occupants of the house, like Hattie and Hermes, are in the infirmary while others, like Ares, are avoiding Saffron. None of them pay me any attention as I knock on Zeus's bedroom door.

He opens almost immediately. His eyes rim red, whether from tears or alcohol, I'm uncertain. My decision to bring Zeus into the fold has left the king of the skies haggard and distraught, but it was a necessary decision. Unfortunately, everything I have done since I first learned of my role in this prophecy has been harrowing, yet necessary.

I remove the Dagger of Chains and place it in Zeus's palm. "Remember, Diam must receive this before he leads the humans to safety, but he cannot let Apollo or Artemis out. Not yet. Apollo cannot be in the last battle or we will lose everything."

Zeus takes the weapon from me, glowering at the blade as though he could smite it by sight alone. "My children are inside this blade, living in agony, and you want me to wait." His rage slips off easily as fatigued realization takes the reins. "How long until the last battle?"

"In two days' time, and it will all be over. Either we win, or we lose everything. Regardless of how these final two battles end, everyone currently imprisoned in the Dagger will find freedom again. We just have to wait just a little while longer."

I spin to walk away and go to my next destination, but Zeus's words stop me. "Are you sure this is the only way? Hart, you-"

I cut him off, unwilling to hear the truth of what comes next, even if I know it with unwavering certainty. "Tonight, come out of your room only when you hear the last scream. The heart dies tonight as the home runs red, then Saffron will know everything, and the final battle plans will lock into place. It's too late to change anything, and even if there was a way to change our course, it would end in our ruination. So no, your majesty, there is no other way."

"You are brave for a human so young," he says.

I force a smile on my face, but it isn't for me. It is for Zeus, who has somehow morphed into my closest friend in a time of harrowing choices. "I'm no longer human, remember?" I hold up my wedding band for him to see. "No matter what happens, I get to be Apollo's wife. I get to be a goddess with stories I always hoped I would experience as a little girl. That is enough for me. I'll see you in the morning."

He doesn't respond, but I feel the burn of his stare as I walk across the second floor towards Hephaestus's room. After I knock, he takes nearly five minutes to answer the door, and when it swings open, he scrunches his face with annoyance. He looks behind me at first, expecting Apollo or another god, then frowns in confusion when he finally focuses on me.

"What do you want?" Hephaestus grunts.

I remove a sketch from the pocket of my overalls, and I hold it out for Hephaestus. "Thank you for saving the Hammer. Now, I need you to make her a weapon." He takes the piece of paper, and I say. "You have only two days, and you will start in the morning. Tonight, I need you to ignore a tornado and go to the kitchen at exactly eleven o' seven. Bring Raven with you. Both of you need to be armed."

Curiosity moves his hands, and he opens the folded

parchment. He raises his bushy brows as surprise writes a reddening picture on his face, but there's a note of appreciation, too. He folds the parchment, tucks it into his pocket, and then crosses his arms over his chest.

He leans against the doorway and says. "Fine, I'll do it on one condition."

"Which is?"

"Answer two questions."

"Ask them," I say. "I have little time."

"Why do I need to be in the kitchen at some random time?"

I don't hesitate. "Because tonight will be the Battle of the Reds. Around ten tonight, an army will attack this house, and the prophesied heart will die. The heart must die if we want to win this war, which means I need as few immortals around as possible, but someone important will die if you don't go into the kitchen at that exact time. We cannot afford to have any heroes tonight, except for you saving a girl in the cupboard at eleven o' seven tonight."

"Why this girl?" he asks.

"She is the prophesied muse. She must live for the ultimate battle, and you need to ensure it."

Hephaestus's room is near Saffron's, only two doors down, and he glances in the direction. Right now, she sits in there with Epiales regaling stories of their past. She's paving their own story from the unfortunate fate of their past, but she does not know what will happen tonight. She cannot know because she will risk everything to stop the Fates from snipping the most important life thread.

"Who is it?" Hephaestus asks. "The heart?"

"You had your two questions answered." I spin on my heels. "Goodnight, Hephaestus. I'll check on your work midday tomorrow."

Regret brings my gaze bouncing between the infirmary

and Saffron's room. A terrible scream will soon fracture the ozone layer and permeate the air forevermore, but the spawn of such a terrible death will bring the dawn of victory.

I slip into my room, close my eyes, and pray to all the gods that Apollo will forgive me for the decisions I had to make.

# THIRTY-THREE

HERMES

Saffron walks out of the room with Epiales, and I wait for the sensation of jealousy to infest me. I ruefully expect the acidic taste of envy to slide down my throat, burning in its descent to the pit of my stomach. It's how I always feel when I see Saffron beside Epiales. Burning, coiling jealousy, except today.

I watch them go, and even as an hour passes, I don't hear the rushing beat of my heart threatening to hammer out of its chest. All I hear are the cacophonous snores coming from Dýnami and the soft whispers Hattie and Diam share. The surge of rage that comes from Saffron & Epiales's proximity never arrives.

Saffron has enamored me since the moment I met her almost a hundred years ago, and even as she dissolved our marriage because of my lies, I still adored her. But now, I realize everything we were and everything we were meant to be instead. Friends, that is our true destiny. Friends who face wars together, rather than husband and wife who merely exist side-by-side.

Hattie waits an entire hour before she glances between the empty doorway where Epiales and Saffron once stood, then to me. She raises a dark brow. "How do-"

"Darling," Diam interjects. "Don't be nosy."

Hattie crosses her arms over her chest and pouts. Actually, sticks out her bottom lip and sullenly whines. "Fine. You're no fun."

Diam only smiles. "I love you too."

Thanatos silently sits on the other side of Jamila's bed and stares only at the invisible line around her ring finger tethering them together.

"You did the right thing," I remind him.

"If I'm not in the room when she wakes for the first time and learns what I've done to her, please remind her she can divorce me." Thanatos runs his thumb across the top of her hand.

"What you've done to her? You saved her life," Diam says.

"I made her break her oath to Artemis." Finally, Thanatos's gaze roams towards Jamila's face, and the normally stoic god crumbles at the sight of my daughter. He wipes the traitorous tear before any of us can see it slide down his cheek. "My fear made me forget I stole her choice, and now she lost what she coveted most."

Being a huntress is all Jamila has ever wanted in life. I want to tell Thanatos he is overreacting, and Jamila will be grateful he saved her life, but the lie never leaves my lips. The truth is, Thanatos is right. She wished to be a huntress until her last breath, and we forced her life to steer in a different direction. We changed the Fates' plan of a premature death on a battlefield to immortality with the god of death.

This isn't what Jamila wanted, but it is what Saffron and I needed.

"Saffron and I begged you to save her, so if there is anyone who gets her ire, it will be us. Not you," I truthfully admit. "Thank you for saving our daughter, even if she doesn't forgive any of us for it."

Thanatos remains silent for several long minutes until he whispers. "Did you just…" He looks up at me with disbelief. "Tell me the truth?"

Hattie theatrically gasps, and I glower at her.

"I am capable of honesty," I say.

Hattie snorts while Diam interjects. "Let's change the subject."

Hattie grins up at her husband, then turns to face Thanatos and me. "Do you all want to hear a story?"

Diam groans. "Dear gods, Hattie, don't."

Hattie continues. "Odysseus told me a story that involves a donkey, a cantaloupe, and two furious farmers in Elysium. Do you want to hear it?" I have known Odysseus for two eons, and I unfortunately know this disgusting story. I am about to interject that I do not, in fact, want to hear this story, but Hattie begins. "So, one day, a farmer wanted to know if a cantaloupe could-"

A soft knock on the infirmary door interrupts Hattie's traumatizing story, and spell-binding brown eyes find mine in the doorway. Maressa stands in a pale pink pajama set, with white lace around the shorts' hem. There has never been a more radiant sight. She smiles as a blush creeps across her high risen cheekbones.

"Is this a bad time?" Maressa glances at Jamila's comatose form, and her smile wilts. "Should I go?"

"No!" I say it too fast, as I scramble to my feet.

I can feel Diam and Hattie's eyes bore into me, questions writing an odd expression upon their faces, and my cheeks suddenly grow hot. Was I too quick to respond? Did I sound desperate?

I clear my throat, smile, and say slower. "No, you don't have to go, but I think I need a break. Maybe something to eat, if you'd like to join me?"

"I'd love that," she says.

We walk together into the kitchen with only subtle glances and unspoken words in between us. Our eyes meet once, but quickly, we both look away. My cheeks burn as we step into the kitchen.

I finally break our silence. "What are you in the mood for?"

I open the pantry to find only saltine crackers just as Maressa responds. "Mac n' cheese sounds amazing."

I close the pantry and turn to find Maressa trying to sit on the counter. She has her hands placed on the counter, with her back pressed against it, and she tries to jump high enough to land on the countertop. I watch her attempt twice, but her petite body only gets halfway there before her feet land on the solid floor again.

Has there ever been a more adorable sight?

I stride towards her, murmuring, "Let me help."

Placing my hands on her hips, a thousand bolts of electricity jolt through my bloodstream. I lift her up with ease, feeling the silk of her pajama shorts with the movement. A waft of vanilla floats through the space between us as I place her on the countertop, but I don't immediately move my hands away. She's a magnetic pull I cannot free myself from, and as I stare at her plush lips, I move closer.

She slowly opens her legs, and I nestle into the space between them. Her hand hesitantly reaches forward and cups the side of my face. I have reached Elysium within her gaze. She is the most exquisite creature I have ever seen, and with her this close, I gorge on her. The vanilla scent coils around her, the blush tinging her cheeks, and the way she stares at me with the same fervent hunger.

"Tell me to stop." One of my hands trails up, feeling her subtle curves, skimming the side of her breast, before capturing the back of her neck. I move closer and use my grip on her neck to angle her face closer to mine. Our lips are a breath apart when I whisper again. "If you want me to stop, tell me now before I unravel. Save me from my destruction and tell me to stop."

Her impossibly long eyelashes flutter, and her mouth parts. I expect her to listen to my plea, but she murmurs in a huskier tone. "Kiss me, Hermes."

My lips slam against hers without hesitation, and I become hers in one moment. I have survived eons on this Earth, and I have loved and lost many. Yet, no kiss has ever felt like this one. The rest of the world fades into nothingness as her mouth molds with mine, and I've reached Elysium's gates. There is no grander moment of peace than this right here, enveloped in her warmth and scent.

I squeeze her waist, bunching those small shorts in my hand. My fingers graze exposed flesh, and there is nothing in this world I want more than every scrap of fabric taken away. I breathe in the moan she releases as I slide my hand underneath the short fabric, feeling for everything she's willing to gift me.

I live suspended in jubilation, floating in the air of peace, but I forget Styx thrusts us into war. Solace is not readily given, no matter how temporary, because that is when we are the weakest against her attacks. I drown myself in Maressa until my desire dissolves into pain. A sword juts out of my stomach, the tip a mere centimeter away from Maressa's abdomen. I whirl around fast, smashing the assailant's cheek with the back of my hand.

A gray-haired figure flies across the room, crumbling onto the ground ten feet away. I turn my back to Maressa. "Rip the sword out."

Her hands shake on the handle of the blade. "I-I don't know if I-"

The gray-haired figure slowly rises, and I yell. "Now, Maressa!"

She pulls it free, and I bite back a scream. I face her once more, and I cradle her face in my hands, cementing every bit of her into my mind. More rushed feet reach my ears. "Hide in the cabinets with that sword, and if anyone but me opens, you ram that blade into their gut." I lean forward and press a quick, chaste kiss on her lips. "Okay?"

Tears well in her eyes, but she refuses to let them fall. She nods her head, and I help her off the counter before facing my opponent. Caduceus materializes in my hand, but I am not prepared to match the gaze of the person across the room. I never thought I would see her again, but when our eyes lock, it feels like the past one hundred years never transpired. The betrayal still bleeds fresh wounds.

"China?"

She looks exactly how she did on the day she died. Her black hair still has streaks of gray, but now she does not hide the fury she feels towards me. A hundred years ago, China worked with Kronos because she felt like I failed her soulmate, Falcon. She killed Panda because she learned too much about her deceit, then Hattie killed China before she could poison Saffron and deliver her to Kronos.

China pretended to be my friend for so long that I didn't even see the signs of her betrayal until it stole the lives of Panda, then Pyro, by default. China holds a blade in each hand, and she snarls at me. But she's no longer alone.

Another familiar face stands beside her, holding a crossbow. He, too, looks exactly like he did on the day he died. Not even thirty years old, Falcon stands beside China, with rage painting a clear picture on his face.

He deserves to hate me.

I let Poseidon and Athena into my home, and they created a battlefield within it. Falcon was one of many victims of Poseidon and Athena's longstanding rivalry, and because of his death, China morphed into the traitor she is today. Both, despite appearing more like mother and son than soulmates, stand united against me.

They stand united for Styx.

Uranus and the Harpies stroll into the room beside China and Falcon. Suddenly, my Caduceus doesn't feel like enough to save the brave woman hiding in the cupboard behind me. The momentary peace I found withers as the Harpies extend their wings, levitate in the air, and fly towards me.

Smacking one harpy on the jaw, I watch the moment the bone juts out of the skin. But as I whirl around to face the second, the third Harpy digs her talons into my shoulders. I muffle my scream as the second one jumps on top of my face. I fall to the ground, the back of my skull bouncing, as claws and pain rupture every other sense.

Except China's words. I hear those words with bone chilling clarity. "He had a girl with him. She's hiding here somewhere."

I punch the harpy that's perched on my face, and she stumbles back, but the third creature reaches for my throat. It rips apart the skin and ichor spills down my body onto the kitchen floor. One of the three Harpies thwarts every step I make towards Uranus, who prowls towards the cupboards. Even the one with the broken jaw flies towards me, clawing at every scrap of exposed flesh.

I can only watch through limited vision, while my blood covers my eyes, as Uranus opens the first pantry. He slams his sword into the space, then rips his blade free, closes the pantry door, and tries for another. Helplessness claims me once again, and I can't break free. As I fight the Harpies to little avail, China and Falcon stand over my body. China slams one sword through my calf, pinning me to the ground, while Falcon repeats the assault on the opposite side.

I do not care about my pain; it is Maressa who I fear for most. Despite the agony their claws and my former friends' blades inflict, I will not die from these wounds. Maressa is a daughter of a muse, but she is only a half-blood. She cannot sustain injuries against an immortal of Uranus's magnitude.

I scream for her, not myself, but China and Falcon still grin like they won.

Until a hammer smashes Falcon's skull in, and he crumbles onto the ground. Brain matter decorates the floor, and China's fury replaces my screams. She spins around, facing Raven. Hephaestus, who once stood beside Raven, runs towards me. He rips one of the Harpies off my face by the back of its neck, then uses his other hand to grab a tuft of its hair.

He rips the harpy's head clean off her neck, but I scream at my brother. "Save her!"

I will sustain a million injuries if it means Maressa is alright. Hephaestus barrels towards Uranus, slamming him into the doorframe until it splinters, while Raven uses a floor-length, plain hammer to knock away China's remaining weapon.

I wrench one of my hands free, and I slam it into the nearest harpy's stomach. I reach for intestines, then grasp and tug. The harpy bellows, but I do not stop, even as the final harpy scratches at my face, eyes, and neck. I paint my body in one harpy's intestines until it collapses on the ground beside me.

The last harpy screeches, but she doesn't attack.

Raven's hammer slams into the center of its skull. The impact is so hard that both creatures' eyes pop from their sockets. I roll my body to the side just as the harpy collapses beside her sister. Only then, I see China's fate before my eyes in shades of only red.

China's face is nearly nonexistent. Her brain matter and blood coalesce with Falcon's as they lie side-by-side, as corpses. White orbs escape their bodies, and they fly towards the front of the house.

That is when I hear it.

The most ear piercing sound to ever exist.

Hephaestus wrestles with Uranus on the ground, but when the sound reaches all our ears, even they stop fighting. A scream so brutal and heartbroken punctures the air and becomes a fixture of the wind. Saffron bellows loud enough to cause parts of the ceiling to collapse. Some of it falls where Raven stands, and I leap over the space and fall on top of her. I take the brunt of the ceiling's rage, but I cannot avoid the sound.

It is the sound of Saffron's heart dying.

It is the sound of the war drums.

# THIRTY-FOUR

## SAFFRON

I weave the beginnings of our story the same way he first introduced my world with his. I begin with the story of Theseus and the Minotaur, but through my eyes. Instead of just teaching him about Theseus and the Minotaur, I explain how he first spoke the tale to me. My words are less about Theseus facing the Minotaur and more about how Epiales first appeared to me when I was in my most hopeless state, and he spun himself into swirls of shadows that I could not unwind.

I tell him about how, despite the eeriness of the shadows, his arrival in my dreams brought me comfort. His melodic voice soothed away the hunger and feelings of disillusionment within my depressing, comfortless world. My story spins towards our happier moments within the dream world. I tell him he used to call me his queen, and how I would wish to sleep solely so I could return to him.

My storyteller.

Sometimes, there is a flicker of recognition across Epiales's face, like when I tell him about how I thought the stars were white cookies, so he later baked some for me. Most of the time, though, he listens like a rapt audience member without a glimmer of memories. It is disheartening, watching the man who stole my heart stare back at me like a stranger, but I endure his lack of recognition and continue our tale.

I do not solely tell him the good, but I explain why he committed the atrocious acts plaguing his nightmares. My voice wobbles with the smallest fragment of guilt when I talk about how I killed Morpheus, the god of dreams. I take Epiales's shaking hand when I explain how Morpheus fell in love with a human slave, with hair as white as snow, and he risked everything to help her escape her dismal fate within Heracles' mansion.

I run my thumb over one of the tattoos on top of his hand, where a multitude of scars used to thrash beneath, and I tell him about his part in helping Morpheus defy Zeus for the betterment of a few human girls. Epiales asks me to point to where his scars used to be, but there were so many. I hold back tears as I regale the story of how he first revealed himself in our dream world, convinced that I would view him as a hideous monster.

"I told you that scars are a story written upon the skin, and you were more beautiful for the stories you told." My finger continues to trace the tattoo of the crow, its mouth open wide with rage, and I smile despite knowing he doesn't remember any of our conversations. "It was the beginning and end of us. That dream."

I do not shy away from discussing his desperation, and every act he committed with Kronos, hoping to escape from Tartarus. He listens astutely, but when I mention Glasswing, his hand within mine flinches.

I look up at him. "Do you remember her?"

"Does she have a butterfly on top of her eye?" I nod

my head, and he shudders. "When it is not Hermes who screams in my dreams, I see her fall into a river, and I just know it's my fault. Somehow, knowing nothing else, I know I am to blame for her death. I just...cannot remember why."

I tell him, and I pause while he weeps.

Time is an unknown entity as he and I sit in my room, and I play out the story of his life with only words. He occasionally asks questions, hoping it will reignite something within him, but it almost never works. Those memories, and the man I loved within them, are gone.

"And we loved each other," he says at the end of my story.

Both of our hands are now intertwined, and while the touch is familiar, the way he looks at me isn't. He stares at me like he is hoping I hold the key to unlock everything forgotten within him. His stare brims with disappointment because I cannot unlock the mysteries of him.

"Our love was complicated, but yes. We loved each other very much."

"Were we soulmates?" he asks in the past tense.

Tears build in my eyes as I shake my head. "I think you know the answer to that."

He runs a thumb over the top of my hand. "Maybe in another lifetime, we could have been."

"We had glorious moments, you and I. Destiny just wasn't on our side." He looks up at me, and I fall in love once more with the depth of his silver eyes. "But I will always love you. From today until our last, even if we are nothing but the past."

"Hopefully one day I remember some of those stories," he whispers. Almost wistfully. "It sounds like I was truly happy."

"We were," I smile at him, and he smiles sadly back.

He is the first to pull away. His hand slips out of mine, and he moves from my space. His smile still paints a sad picture, but his eyes twinkle with something. A glimmer of recognition. "I'm suddenly famished. Would you like to join me in the kitchen? We can bake something together."

I stand up. "I would love that."

We walk down the staircase as Epiales regales stories of the life he remembers. He tells me about his friend, Maressa, and the bar they worked at together. He explains that he only got the job because he stumbled into the bar one day. Maressa took one look at him and said. "Finally."

From then on, they were best friends.

An infectious smile grows on his lips as he explains some of his favorite customers, crazy stories that took place days before the world's demise, and his ideas about how to serve more customers on Wednesday nights. There is unbridled joy as he talks about his job. This side of Epiales, unburdened by the weight of mistakes, is a side I have never witnessed before.

And fewer views have ever been more soothing.

It always seems like the most beautiful sights fall into ruin the quickest. I stare at my past in his resplendent beauty, and out of the corner of my eye, I see the front door to the house. Green smoke slithers underneath and slides up the length of the door. The smoke surrounds the lock on the door, and the click of it reverberates for miles.

"Erik," I say the name he prefers, but the smile growing over his lips at the sound quickly dissolves when he catches my expression. "We are closest to the infirmary. Run inside and tell Thanatos and Hermes we're under attack."

Epiales runs while I walk towards the danger that's pushing the front door open. Hecate strolls inside, as I expected, but she is not alone. I open my hand, feeling for my sword *Οστά*. Hephaestus crafted the sword made entirely out of bones, so I could summon my weapon no matter how far I am from it. The bones rattle to my silent call, and before Hecate and her small army can take an advancing step, I clench my newly arrived sword in my hand.

Hecate glances at my weapon. "That's a neat trick." She drags her gaze back to me and smirks. "Too bad you can't use your magic on us."

Long ago, when I was a foolish demi-god girl, I jumped into the River Styx. My only goal was saving Hattie from the hordes of monsters and titans breaking into the Underworld castle's gates. I made a deal with Styx, protecting her and her army from my magic. It was naïve of me to enter an oath with Styx, but I thought it was the only way to save Hattie's life.

Now, I reap the consequence.

Even as battle whirls, I try to summon my magic. I can feel every bone in Hecate's body, and all the surrounding traitors, but every time I try to propel them towards me, nothing happens. An oath sworn to the River Styx is the most binding, and I foolishly fell into Styx's trap before I understood the gravity of oaths.

The furies stand around Hecate, a small army of humans behind them. One girl, nearest the back of the army, covers most of her face with curly black ringlets, and something familiar ignites within me at the sight of her. Yet, before I can stare longer, examine her until I learn the truth, the Furies attack.

Each Fury holds a cudgel in their hands, and they each screech an abominable sound. They soar through the air, only to crash around me. I swing my sword, slicing one's arm clean off while elbowing another. The small human army runs into the house, but Hecate strolls towards me and becomes my principal focus. Her magic, which was once only green, seeps onto the floor with black veins.

I duck, narrowly avoiding one of the Fury's cudgel from slamming into my skull, and I slide onto the floor. The growing smoke makes it nearly impossible to see, but I spin my sword into a circle around where the Furies surround me. Two are fast enough to fly in the air, avoiding the blade's brutal kiss, but I hear the sickening crack of the third Fury's heel meeting my sword. I slice through the tendons, and the Fury bellows with rage.

I sever both feet from her body, and she tumbles onto the floor. The smoke rises higher, covering Hecate, the Furies, and me in a tornado of contaminated green. Hecate steps into the tornado, and our eyes lock. The remaining two Furies fly away, leaving the one bleeding out on the floor with Hecate and me.

I glance at the smoke surrounding us and the inky black infestation seeping into her magic. "What happened to you?"

Hecate grins, but I don't miss the gloves covering her arms. I see a peek of black veins crawling up the hem of the gloves, betraying the truth she poorly attempts to hide. White orbs crash through the tornado Hecate has created, and they worm their way through her flesh. She momentarily winces as these souls enter her body, and instead of her typical blue or green eyes, they flash black.

Hecate looks down at me and snarls. "I am becoming omnipotent. That is what is happening to me."

I smirk and take an advancing step. "Is that what Styx told you? That you were becoming all powerful?" I produce a bitter laugh and stand toe-to-toe with Hecate. I must crane my neck to stare at her. She towers over me with five-inch heels, making her over six feet tall. "Styx knows how to tell the most convincing lies, doesn't she?"

Hecate grabs my face, her nails digging into the flesh, but I barely balk.

My grin grows tenfold. "She's poisoned you in front of your face, and you thanked her." Gold blood blooms atop her gloved fingernails as she nicks my flesh. "I always found you cruel, but as the years pass, you grow foolish in your malice. Hatred has turned your veins black, and the rot will only continue to grow."

She pushes me away, and I stumble back a few feet as she screeches. The sound scratches at her throat, sounding hoarse and so broken. The version of Hecate I once knew has vanished, and in her place is a malignant invention from the darkest recesses of Styx's mind. Hecate manifests a sword of all green and black magic, but I see more black than green. More darkness than light.

I grin. "Finally."

I have ached to fight Hecate for decades, and our swords collide as we both yell. We match each attack with a perfect deflection. The tornado of magic swirls and builds around us, but we do not stop. My sword hits hers the same moment she attempts to knee me. We elbow and kick and once; she tries to bite me. This is nearly a century of building abhorrence, and as the butt of my sword smacks against her lip, I laugh as gold and black blood dribbles down the side of her face.

"SAFFRON!"

My laugh dies because it is Diam's voice. The anguish breaks through the tornado Hecate created around us. I run out of the swirl of magic, and I follow his voice. He hasn't stopped screaming my name. Repeatedly, I hear my name, so broken on his lips.

No.

No, no, no, no, no, no, no, NO!

Anyone but her.

I crash into the infirmary, and every nightmare has accumulated itself into this moment.

There isn't a vestige of life left within her. Crimson blood creates a halo around her head, and I can only fall to the ground and beckon the murderer's bones towards me. She's too limp. Too…dead. I scream loud enough to shatter every piece of glass. The sound, which comes from unfathomable anguish, breaks through the wind. My scream becomes a part of the world forevermore, but she is gone.

I crawl through the blood and bones and tissue to get to her. I cradle her in my arms, but she's too limp. There's nothing I can do to save her, and so with my screams as a haunted symphony around me, I hold her close and I sob.

For my heart is dead.

# THIRTY-FIVE

## GLASSWING

For eighty-eight years, from the moment Saffron wrapped her arms around me and thrust us both into the depths of the River Styx, I have lived on a repetitive loop of suffering. The river peeled off my skin, imbued the remnants of my body with a thousand pinpricks, then watched with rueful anticipation as I slowly stitched myself back together. Then, it started all over again. Pain, more pain, a momentary reprieve, then an onslaught of further agony.

Moans of surrounding sufferers within the river broke my eardrums. We all lived in eternal punishment for crimes unbefitting this torment. My screams became my only friends, and every torturous second, I prayed Epiales would finally save me. When he visited me in my dreams, he promised he would save me from those who hurt me. Because every other god only knows how to hurt.

And oh, how I hurt.

Lady Styx held the instrument to my suffering for eighty-eight years until all I knew were my screams, others' moans of anguish and hatred. Hatred at Saffron for throwing me into this eternal torture. Hatred for Epiales for never coming for me like he promised. There is only hatred left, and this little kernel of hope that I can finally be free from this river.

It is Lady Styx who pulls me out of her blackened water. The day she frees herself from the Underworld, Styx kills the other occupants of the river and takes me safely to Earth. She heals my wounds, even if the scars disappear. They cover every square inch of my body, mangling my once beautiful face until no one who once knew me would recognize my new beastly exterior.

Lady Styx places me in a new silk gown, feeds me, and heals parts of me. I can still hear my screams and the other victims' moans in my ears. They play a somber tune I can never escape from, but the physical pain does not return. It is because of Saffron that the pain began, but it is Lady Styx who saved me from the anguish.

Once I am able to do more than shake and cry and beg for death, Lady Styx tells me a story. It is about Epiales, the god of sinful beauty, who promised to save me from a world of enslavement and suffering. Lady Styx tells me Epiales could not reach me because Saffron stole him from me. She killed Epiales, just like how she killed me, but Lady Styx helped bring Epiales back to life.

And Epiales needs me to save him now.

"Your Epiales has suffered so much," Lady Styx has told me every day for the past two months. "He needs you to find him and save him. As you have been a prisoner with chains brandished by the cruelest gods, your lord is now wearing the cuffs around his wrists. He is now the one in danger, and he is now desperate for you to save him. Be his savior, as he tried to be for you, sweet girl."

That is Lady Styx's nickname for me. Sweet Girl. She

does not curse me with the name Psyche gave me, Glasswing. I like Sweet Girl better. Anything is better than being named after the butterfly sitting on my eye, stealing away its vision and my former beauty.

"Is that why Epiales did not save me from the river?" I asked Lady Styx many times. "Because Saffron killed him?"

"Yes," Styx always responded. "And she has him again. You must save him from the woman who killed you both once, and you must bring him to me. *To us,* who wish to keep him safe."

Lady Styx makes me wait two months to save Epiales from the vile Saffron, but on the night with no moon, she sends me with Lady Hecate, Lord Uranus, the Harpies, the Furies, and a small group of like-minded humans. I almost faint when I see Saffron for the first time since she thrust me into eternal torture.

I have become an accumulation of all the hatred within the River Styx, mangled with scars and horrific memories, but Saffron has never looked prettier. She is resplendent in a gown of silken red. Her hair, which flows effortlessly down to her breasts, appears to glow a vibrant chestnut shade. She is a goddess now, for no human could be as glorious to behold as Saffron is now, and my hatred grows tenfold.

I am now a monstrosity, while she is everything I wish I could be.

Lady Hecate distracts Saffron with a tornado of growing magic, and I rush towards where Epiales ran. The other humans follow me, our green-misted weapons raised high in the air. As we run inside, I almost stumble when I see the additional few people with Epiales. Hattie, Saffron's closest friend, sits on a bed with a dark-skinned male wearing a bandage around his head. Thanatos, the personification of death, stands beside an infirmary bed where a heavily burned woman slumbers.

The other humans scream and run towards the others in the infirmary, but I focus solely on Epiales. His silver eyes, so wholly god-like, crash into me, and my heart skips a beat. Suddenly, all the pain that thrashed inside me for eighty-eight years vanishes, and all I see is him. He was my everything, and the dreams we shared suddenly feel as if they had transpired yesterday.

"You're really here," I take a step towards him, unmistakable awe in my voice.

Two Furies fly over my head, one landing on Thanatos, while the other reaches for Hattie. The darker-skinned male lurches from his bed, and he jumps on top of the Fury. He crashes onto the floor with the monster, and he yells behind him. "Wake up, Dýnami!"

Hattie whirls to face the sleeping huntress in the far corner of the room, then yells. "How in the Gods has she not woken up yet?!"

A battle unleashes around the room, but I only stare at Epiales. My Epiales. I grin. "I'm here to save you."

Epiales should smile at me. He should be grateful. I'm here to save his life. I'm here to whisk him far, far away from Saffron, who murdered us both. He should smile, but as I continue to step towards him, his forehead creases and his lips draw into a frown. I reach for him, my hands trembling as they grab both sides of his face, and I whisper his name like a hymn. "Epiales."

But he flinches.

Why does he flinch?

Lady Styx told me he wanted me to save him. We shared something special in those dreams, and Lady Styx told me that Epiales felt the same way. Yet, I hold his face in my hands, and he doesn't smile.

He…doesn't…care.

"Do you not remember me?" My voice cracks and crumbles, threatening to deteriorate the thread of sanity I've held onto for him.

For my Epiales.

"Ma'am, I'm sorry, but-"

"MA'AM?!"

He doesn't remember me.

We shared laughter and stories and he just doesn't… remember. Tears build in my one eye, streaming plentifully down my cheek, and I shake my head. I try to ignore the impersonal tone of his voice. I try to forget the way he stares at me with little to no recognition.

"How did you forget me? You're my world, and you forgot me?! I came to save you." I don't realize that I unsheathe my dagger until I press the hilt against his throat. His Adam's apple bobs, and I nick a bit of flesh. Red blood trickles down the blade, and I stare at it, trans-fixed. "You're not Epiales. Epiales is a god. He bleeds red. You don't bleed red. You're not real. It's the river. The river makes you see things." I use my free hand to smack my skull once, twice, ten times as I grit out. "The river makes you see things. The river isn't truthful. It. Shows. Imposters." I glower at the falsity that stands before me. "You. Are. An. IMPOSTER!"

I raise my dagger in the air, and I hope the real Epiales sees everything I do for him. I'm willing to kill someone who pretends to be him, who Saffron created to trick me, all for him. My mind plays so many tricks because the river destroyed too much of my sanity, but I have enough sense to save Epiales now.

To kill the imposter once and for all.

I strike the dagger down, my blurry vision from of all my tears. I do not see someone push the Imposter Epiales away. My dagger makes its descent, but it hits the wrong target. The false Epiales is on the floor, with only the smallest trickle of red blood from where I nicked his throat; however, the one with the dagger thrust into their chest is real.

Hattie stares back at me with tears building in her eyes.

*Oh no, oh no, oh no.*

I rip the dagger free, and there is so much blood. It creates a waterfall down Hattie's chest and she falls backwards. Her back and skull crash onto the ground, and I'm covered in her blood. The wrong blood. This is supposed to be the fake Epiales's blood. I was supposed to come here to save Epiales, but his imposter lives and Hattie…

*Oh no, oh no, oh no.*

Hattie was always nice. Or, as nice as someone could be as a prisoner of King Hades and Queen Persephone. We suffered in the Underworld together. Styx reminded me that Hattie is a victim of Saffron's torture, just like me. I wasn't supposed to kill Hattie.

I was supposed to save Hattie next.

Imposter Epiales crawls towards Hattie. He places his hands on top of her wound, and he screams. "DIAM!"

The dark-skinned man, who must be Diam, decapitates one Fury, then turns to face what I've done. His entire face falls when he sees a blood-soaked Hattie, and he runs towards us. I stumble back, my dagger clattering onto the ground, as Diam lies on the ground opposite the Imposter Epiales. He replaces Imposter Epiales's hands on top of Hattie's wound with his own, and he sobs. Then, he screams one name repeatedly.

"SAFFRON!"

"SAFFRON!"

"GODS! SAFFRON, COME NOW!"

Hattie reaches her hand up to cradle Diam's face, and

she gives a sad smile. "You are my moon and my stars. My entire galaxy." She coughs up blood, and Diam weeps. Hattie tries to wipe away his tears, but as she reaches for his tears, her hand falls. Her chest stops its natural rise and fall.

Hattie dies.

"You're an imposter," I whisper to Epiales.

He turns to face me, and there is so much hatred in his silver eyes. Those silver eyes I loved on the real Epiales. I open my mouth to say more, to explain why I mistakenly killed Hattie instead of the one deserving my wrath, but nobody has ever cared to hear my side of the story. Saffron runs into the room, collapses beside Hattie's corpse, and then there is only pain.

I feel the moment she rips every bone from my body, and then there is nothing.

Blissful.

Peaceful.

Nothingness.

# THIRTY-SIX

## SAFFRON

R ed blurs my vision, and it is all that I can see. All that I can breathe. My hands move to a beat I cannot hear, but I obey. Bones rush towards me, and I don't know whose bones I summon, but I know they deserve my smite. Diam tries to reach for me, but I pull away and stumble away from the infirmary.

I latch onto Hecate, who stands in the center of the living room. The bones of those I murdered spin around my head like a crown, but they also shatter the oath I had with Styx. Glasswing was part of her army, so when she killed Hattie, she decimated the promise I made. Hecate sees the bones, and faster than I can react, she disappears in a plume of black-and-green smoke.

I follow a crashing sound from the kitchen, and the moment I step into the room, I raise my hand in the air. Three Harpies, China, and an unfamiliar human lay dead on the floor. But when I raise my hand, Uranus stops his punch towards Hephaestus's face. His eyes widen with unmistakable fear, but I do not care. I slam his back against the nearest wall, pinning his arms and legs, as his bones quiver underneath his flesh. Eager to follow my every command.

Hermes runs to a cupboard, pulling it open to free a trembling Maressa. He wraps his arms around her, while Raven runs to Hephaestus. He checks her for wounds, then all four of them focus on me. We can all hear my screams, which are now embedded in the wind that whistles through my home of bones. Tears never stop streaming down my face as I'm covered in Hattie's blood and all those who I killed in retribution for her death.

Crimson blood creates a river starting in the kitchen, spilling out of the infirmary, and it cuts my home in half. It's all I can see. Hattie's blood. My sister's death. I stare at the blood, and I collapse onto my knees. I still hold Uranus against the wall, but I barely focus on him.

A pair of arms grab me, and by the thousands of electrical bolts shooting through my bloodstream, I know who comforts me. Finally, I feel like I can let go. Dropping the bones that spiral above my head, I spin my body and I wrap my arms around Ares. I sob into the crook of his neck, and he holds me tight.

"Chain Uranus up," Ares growls at someone. "Now."

I don't care to see who imprisons Uranus. My only focus is the soft kisses Ares places on top of my head, and the way his hand runs up and down my back in a gentle motion. My body trembles within his touch; it is the only thing tethering me to any sense of comfort.

"Hattie's dead," I whimper into his shirt.

He scoops me up honeymoon style, and he whispers. "You can drop Uranus now, beautiful. You don't have to do anything but mourn now."

I lay my head on his chest, and again I whimper. "Hattie is dead."

Ares presses a kiss to my forehead, and he silently walks me up the staircase. He doesn't take me to my bedroom, where a thousand memories between Hattie and me try to survive without her. He leads me towards the room he occupies. Snot and tears and blood coalesce in his shirt, but he doesn't complain.

He holds me closer and quietly asks. "Do you want me to clean you, or do you just want to lie down?"

I sob harder. The only reason I need to be cleaned is because I'm coated in Hattie's blood.

"Hattie is dead," I whimper again.

Ares decides for me. He continues to cradle me in his arms as he turns on a bath and sprinkles in my favorite strawberry-scented salts. Every so often, he places a kiss on my blood-soaked head, unperturbed by the carnage draping over me.

Once the bath is full, he whispers. "I'm going to set you down now, sweetheart."

He places my feet on the cold bathroom floor, and I cry the moment his hands aren't on my body. "Hattie...is... dead."

There was no peace in a death like this.

Blood covered her entire body, and there was so much pain in a jagged wound like hers. Ares's hands return to me, one on the strap of my gown and the other tenderly on my waist. He slips the dress off, then quietly sets me into the bathtub.

I grab his hand before he could pull away, and I can barely see him through my tears. But gods, I can feel him. He always feels like the heart of a storm, thunderous and full of electricity, and I need him more than I need air to breathe. Ares sits on the ground next to my tub, and he uses his free hand to reach for a cloth that he lathers with soap.

"Tell me if you want me to stop." He wipes Hattie's blood off my shoulder first, and I stare only at him. I can't look down because the clear water fills with her death, creating a pink shade I can never unsee.

"Hattie," I whimper her name. It's all I can do. All I can think about. "She is dead."

"I know, sweetheart." He runs the cloth over my shoulder blades so gently, I can barely feel it.

Loud footsteps clamber near, and Persephone rushes through the bathroom door. She sees me, covered in my friend's death, and her entire face crumbles. "Oh, my sweet daughter." Persephone falls to her knees next to Ares, and she whispers. "I got this." She plucks the cloth out of Ares's hand, and his jaw clenches.

But he nods his head.

He stands, his hand slipping from mine.

And I scream.

I scream and I scream and I scream for Hattie, for him, for everything I don't get to have.

My throat is raw from how loud I am, from how broken I have become. I only stop screaming when I feel him again, warm and full of everything that centers me. I don't realize that I'm tugging him, pulling him closer, until he slips into the bathtub fully clothed.

He wraps his arms around me, and I lay my face on his chest. I sob until my eyes finally take pity, and they close with reprieve.

When I open my eyes again, it is with one unwavering realization. Warmth surrounds me. Cerberus curls up in front of me, and Ares is against my backside with his arms wrapped around my waist. I wake with tears already in my eyes. I wake with images that I cannot unsee.

Hattie, laying on the ground with a halo of blood

around her. Diam, screeching my name like I can reanimate the dead.

She has died before, but not like this.

Before, her breathing was shallow, her eyes rimmed with pain and wrinkles, and she begged for her long human life to be ended swiftly. Before, I had killed my dearest friend, knowing she was better off in the Underworld with her husband than the slow, painful death of old age. She had died before, and I almost did not survive the loss.

But I did.

I do not think the same could be said the second time around.

She was young this time. Her smile was wide, her eyes still twinkled with a desire to live, and her heart tethered itself to the living world. A single blade ripping through the air stole her before I could say goodbye. Before I could save her.

Before, those who had died went to the Underworld. Before, I could visit her and Diam in the Elysium Fields, but the messiness of the present replaces the safety of the past. Now, I live in a world where Hattie's soul hides, and only the monsters know the whereabouts.

Like everyone else here, I thought Epiales was my prophesied heart. I expected his death, not hers. Now, I sit upon my bed and know I was fooling myself into thinking he was my heart. I can survive without romance, but I cannot wholly breathe without the person who helped shape me into who I am.

It was because of Hattie that I grew a backbone in Hermes's mansion.

It was because of Hattie that China did not kidnap me and take me to Kronos.

It was because of Hattie that I discovered Epiales's plan was wrong.

It was because of Hattie that I sided with the Olympians all those decades ago.

It was because of Hattie that I found the ability to use my powers and kill Coeus, who dared to hurt her in the Underworld.

It was because of Hattie that I did not see myself and my powers as monstrous.

It is because of Hattie that I embraced my role as the savior.

It is because of Hattie that I became the mother of Jamila.

It is because of Hattie that I am alive today.

And yet, all I brought her was death.

I was a nuisance, a complicated mess, and I ruined her. I wish the Fates could turn back time so that I could never speak to Hattie in Hermes's mansion. Maybe if I had never been a part of her life, she would have lived a life of peace because all I brought her was strife.

Ares squeezes me tighter as I sob out the same three words, the only words I can muster. "Hattie is dead."

Cerberus whimpers beside me, joining me in my grief, while Ares silently holds me as I sob. Sleep claims me frequently and unpredictably. Sometimes I think I am asleep, but my eyes remain open, and I stare at the wall, hoping for a dream where she is alive again. Other times, I swear I'm awake, laughing with her, smiling like nothing horrific happened, but with her presence is the agonizing realization that this must be a dream.

Because Hattie is…dead.

They are the only words I can push out of my lips and grief claws its way through my rib cage, digging into what little remains of my beating heart. Ares never leaves, not even when I yell to replace my scream, now a part of the wind, with something new. Something angrier. He doesn't leave me even as I whimper for the seventieth or hundredth time, the same three words that encompass everything I'm feeling right now.

Hattie is dead.

Some visit me, like my mom. Persephone sits down on the edge of the bed, and she tries to reach for me. Yet, when her hand touches mine, I picture her corpse where Hattie's was, and I scream and thrash in Ares's arms. Time is merely an illusion that I haven't delved deeper into. There is only this bed, the gnashing feeling of a torn heart struggling to still beat, Cerberus, and Ares.

Tears never stop spilling down my cheeks, and I whimper. "Hattie…"

This time, I cannot let the other two words escape. Ares wraps his arms tighter around me, and he whispers in my ear. "Death claims all heroes' lives because bravery like hers is a dangerous weapon to wield. That level of bravery is contagious, too. Hattie Pyro is a gods' damn hero, and her death just sprung to life a hundred more heroes who witnessed her bravery or heard her story."

"But…" I say, the first word that isn't the gnawing truth tearing me up.

He knows my next words and says them first. "Yes, beautiful. Hattie is dead, but she's always going to be here if her hero's tale continues to be told. She will continue to live in our orbit, immortalized like Heracles and Odysseus." He pauses, then adds. "Like Sika the Typhon Slayer and Lamb, too." It takes every shred of my strength to turn my body, so my back now faces Cerberus, and I can stare at Ares. He watches the tears track down my face, and he opens his mouth. "I'm sorry for your loss," he says.

I hiccup back another sob and whisper. "Hattie…"

"I know, sweetheart."

"Is a hero?" I end my statement with a question.

But the smile that peels over Ares's lips, a smile designated for my eyes only, confirms it. "Yes, Hattie is a hero the world will never forget. She saved everyone in the infirmary, and she broke the curse that stopped you from killing Styx once and for all." My tears slow down enough so I can see the honest, adoring way he looks at me. I am covered in my own tears and snot, but he stares at me like there is no grander sight in all the world, across every eon. "She may have hated me until the end, but I will revere her for all of eternity. When I speak of the greatest heroes, her name will be the first on my lips."

I wrap my arms around him, and I hug him. He quickly hugs me back while I nestle my face in the crook of his neck. As I find peace within him amidst the tragedies.

"Hattie is a hero," I squeak out.

He kisses the top of my head and repeats. "Hattie is a hero."

I fall asleep in his arms with a new sentence repeating itself in my head, the tune less haunting than the one before.

# THIRTY-SEVEN

HERMES

Dýnami and I help Diam bury his wife.

He stops digging every few minutes because he will look at his wife, his soulmate, and sob again. Each time he sobs, Dýnami rushes for him. She wraps him in her arms. Each time, he tries to fight her off, but eventually, he crumbles into her arms. These two astutely understand the pain the other is suffering through. In less than twenty-four hours, they both witnessed the other lose their soulmates.

I dig a six-foot hole, but when I reach for Hattie, Diam tackles me to the ground. I do not deflect as he punches me once, twice, three times in the face. Dýnami wraps an arm around his shoulders, pulling him off me, but I do not reach for Hattie again. Someone switched her outfit after she died. She no longer wears the blood-stained clothes she died in; rather, she almost appears peaceful in a light green sundress.

If it was not for the gaping wound in the center of her chest, she almost appears like she's sleeping. It has only

351

been a day since she died, and we could not get Saffron out of bed for this moment. Diam thrashes in Dýnami's arms before he crumbles into sobs again.

Periodically, through the sobs, Diam croaks out to me, or maybe Hattie. "I'm sorry."

But he has nothing to apologize for.

I already healed from those punches, but he has yet to heal after the anguish of losing his soulmate. He deserves to punch the one nearby entity who will heal instantaneously. He suffers because his wife could not heal from a wound meant for a former god. Dýnami holds Diam until his sobs relent for a few minutes.

He crawls towards his wife and bites back more tears as he tucks a piece of her straight, black hair behind her ear. "I love you more than the stars and the moon and all that comes after. You are my soul, Hattie Pyro. My absolute soul." He lays his head on top of her chest, and he sobs some more. "My absolute soul," he repeats.

Eventually, Diam musters the strength to lift his head from his wife's chest, and he looks at me. "Help me," he says.

Dýnami gingerly pulls Diam free, and I pick Hattie's corpse bridal style. She falls too limply in my arms, but I fly down to her burial ground and lay her gently. I arrange her arms, so they're crossed over one another atop her chest. I fix that one hair Diam tucked behind her ear. Then, I too shed a tear for my dear friend.

I fly back up to the ground floor, then pass everyone a shovel. Diam only has the strength to hold his shovel, staring at the hole stealing his wife from him forever, but Dýnami helps me. We continue, even as Diam falls to the ground again, heaving and begging for his wife to come back to him. We place the last patch of dirt on her grave.

"What was her favorite flower?" I ask Diam.

He doesn't answer me. He uses his grip on the shovel to stand up, then he storms into the house. Dýnami glances at the burial spot and whispers. "A saffron flower. Cover this grave in a thousand and one saffron flowers."

So, I do just that.

Then, I go in search of the goddess whose screams remain forever a part of the wind and air. It's a terrifying, grief-stricken sound, her scream, and it is everywhere I go. Every step I take, I hear the moment of Saffron's greatest anguish. When the wind gets louder, smacking against the glass windows to get inside, I hear her scream like the night replays itself.

I knock on her bedroom door, and when there is no answer, I quietly peel it open. Cerberus lies on one side of Saffron, curling in the crook of her legs, but Ares encapsulates most of her body. Her head lies on his chest while his arm drapes over her. Almost a hundred years ago, I stole Saffron from Ares, but at this moment, everything between them clicks into place.

"Holy gods," I say. "You're her soulmate. Not Epiales. You."

Ares doesn't deny my claim; instead, he asks. "Can you lower your voice? She's finally sleeping without screaming for the first time since it all happened."

I stumble into the lounge chair closest to the bed. "But you tried to kill her. That night I stole her away."

"Worst day of my life." Ares finally looks up at me and says words I never thought were in his vocabulary. "Thank you for stopping me. Thank you for saving her from me."

Ares is my brother, and I have known him for eons. Argued with him, fought alongside him, and yet never have I seen him so open. So vulnerable. He lived with Aphrodite for eons, baring children with her, but it was never like this between them. He never realized his mistakes and tried to change himself to be better for Aphrodite.

For Saffron, though, he apologizes. For Saffron, he makes active efforts to change.

"Does she know?" I whisper my question.

"I think she just figured it out a few days ago." Ares looks down at Saffron, and I don't think I ever looked at her that way. He stares down at her as if she is the answer to every question he has ever asked in his lifetime. "She deserves more than war and bloodshed, and I tried to make sure she was happier with someone more deserving. I tried to hide my feelings for so long, because I'm too... tainted for her. You, and even Epiales, are less horrific than me. More deserving for someone like her than me."

He reaches for her, gingerly caressing the side of her face. Even in her sleep, she smiles at the touch.

"How could someone as brutal as me deserve something this perfect?" he whispers the words more to himself than me.

"How long have you known?" The moment I ask, I learn the answer. His face falls, and he drops his hand from her face. Still, I ask again. "How long, Ares?"

But I know.

Ares recognized her as his third love, his soulmate, since the moment he laid eyes on her. He knew on the arena floor when he fought, like his life depended on it, against Persephone and Hades. He knew when he tried to kill her in his mansion before I kidnapped her. When I married her, he knew she belonged with him instead. When she was stranded on an island with Epiales, he knew that Saffron was an extension of his soul.

It all clicks into place.

"Kronos knew," I realize aloud. "It's why he captured you with Hecate, Hephaestus, and me on Mt. Olympus.

It's why Kronos never questioned you or tried to convince you to join his side of the war."

More moments and memories between Ares and Saffron surge in my mind, and gods, how could I have not noticed? I am the god of mischief, who sees all with unparalleled clarity, but I didn't notice the way Ares always stared at her from across the room. Or how in Poseidon's castle, when her nightmares caused her to scream so loud the glass walls almost broke, Ares was the only one capable of stopping the nightmares.

It is why when Kronos struck Saffron with Eros's arrow, Ares was the only one capable of distracting her from killing us all. She might not have known why they've connected across a century, but Ares has known his heart only beats for her since the moment they met.

"It's why you didn't come to our wedding," I say solemnly.

"You deserved her more than me," is all he says.

I scoff. "No, I didn't, you utter fool."

"Careful, brother," Ares snarls, but he still whispers.

All for Saffron.

"I will not be careful because you are a fool, Ares. I thought she was my soulmate, but all along, you've known. You knew she was the one thing you wanted in this world more than war and bloodshed and death, but you tormented yourself. You would have lived in regret for all of eternity, instead of accepting the one shred of happiness everyone deserves."

"I tried to kill her the day we met," Ares whispers angrily. "I killed her best friend's sister."

"Because you went insane, not because you are a ruthless, apathetic god. Morpheus wormed himself in your brain, and he made you see things that weren't there."

"How do you know that? I only ever told-" He stops, and he looks down at Saffron.

"I was married to her for fifty years, and one night, she told me everything you said because she wanted me to know why she forgave you for everything. A part of me always wanted to hate you for trying to kill her, but then Saffron told me what happened to you. She defended you. She told me how Morpheus came into your dreams every single night for hundreds of years-"

He clamps his eyes shut. "Be quiet."

I continue. "She told me that Morpheus made you fall into a state of paranoia, where the month and years faded into an endless stream of sleepless nights and horrific hallucinations."

"Shut up, Hermes."

I don't stop talking. "She told me how Morpheus used his magic for the worst, and that for centuries you didn't realize how many people you killed, until Morpheus finally died. You realized the monster you became after you finally slept, after going hundreds of years without rest."

"Hermes, stop talking."

"No," I say. "Because I love Saffron, and she deserves to be happy. Because I love you, brother, and you deserve to be happy."

"You love her." Ares opens his eyes, and I hate the hurt that lives in them. "You want her back still?"

I shake my head. "Yes, I love her. I once thought love had to be romantic, but that wasn't my story with her. I will always be grateful for the time we had together, but our destiny is to be friends. We weren't soulmates, but you two are."

Ares stares down at Saffron's sleeping form and whispers. "It's weird, talking to you about her."

I let out a snort. "Yeah, maybe, but I'm the only other

god in this world who knows what happened to you with Morpheus."

"It was a long time ago."

I nod my head. "It was, but so was our captivity on Mt. Olympus, and I still have nightmares about that time." The words flow out, and it feels liberating to admit my fears aloud. Frightening, yet liberating. "We as males do not talk about our trauma because we must portray a specific image, but I'm done. I have never felt as free as I do now, being honest about who I am and what I've survived. It's time you realize that Morpheus's words still haunt you, and that a small part of you still believes you deserve to be tortured for the actions Morpheus guided you towards. You deserve to love, Ares, even if right now you can only confess it to your soulmate's ex-husband."

Ares says nothing, and I stand up to my feet. "When she wakes up, can you tell her I checked in? And that we buried Hattie in a garden surrounded by saffron flowers?"

He nods his head, and I walk away.

I open the door when he speaks. "I love her." Ares closes his eyes as he says the words, which come out fast, jumbled, yet truthful. "I love her more than I thought it was possible to love another soul, but I still hear him every night. I still hear his words repeatedly every time I fall asleep. There hasn't been a night when I close my eyes, where Morpheus doesn't follow me there. Unless I'm with her. I take away her nightmares, but she frees me from mine, too."

"Sounds like you two should have been together from the very beginning," I say.

"I'm sorry," Ares says. "You're right. I should have-"

I cut him off. "There isn't a single part of my life that I regret. Not anymore. I have an amazing daughter because I married Saffron. Because I lost her, I could see everything inside myself that needed to change. I'm happier because of the time I had and lost with her, but you should tell her in the morning how you feel."

"Hart said-"

"I'm sick of Hart telling everyone exactly how their lives should play out. She knew Hattie was going to die, and she let it happen. So, screw Hart. Tell Saffron how you feel in the morning and apologize after."

I head straight to Maressa's room. My hands shake as I knock on her door. When she pulls open the door, resplendent in another pajama set, I don't hesitate. I lean down to her, wrap my hand around the back of her neck, and I claim her mouth on mine.

Maressa wraps her arms around my neck, and she jumps up. I catch her, never moving my mouth from hers, and I walk us towards her bed. I lay her gingerly on top of the blanket, and only then do I pull away from the kiss.

She smiles up at me, lips red from our kiss. "This is a welcome surprise."

"I just told someone that they need to stop being afraid of saying how they feel, so I must tell you I don't want to be casual with you. I do not want these moments between us to just be a spontaneous excursion because of war and adrenaline. If you accept, I would like to make you my girlfriend. When this war ends, I want to take you on a date. I want to shower you with gifts and affection, and I want you, for however long you will allow. It's difficult to be in a relationship with a god, but-"

"Hermes," Maressa says, stopping my rant. Her cheeks tinge pink. "I would love to be in a relationship with you. Now, kiss me."

I fall into bed with her, feeling peace even as the war drums grow louder.

# THIRTY-EIGHT

## SAFFRON

"Your prophecies can kiss my ass; I'm not leaving her right now," Ares growls.

The gruff, furious tone of his voice jars me from sleep. My eyes crust together from the hours of tears and fatigue, but I force them open to take in my surroundings. My face still lies on Ares's chest. Soft fur tickles the back of my legs where Cerberus curls around me. Ares's hand rests on the small of my back, holding me to him, but I'm astutely aware of the additional presence in the room. The smell of honey wafts forward, identifying her far before I hear her voice.

"It has been two days since she left this room," Hart hymns admonishingly. "It is time she rises."

Ares spits venom at Hart. "She just lost a piece of her heart, so if she needs over two days to mourn that loss, I'm going to be here to help her repair what's left. So as kindly as I can right now, ask anyone else to do your dirty work. She's mourning and doesn't need to leave until she's ready."

"Saffron," Hart's voice is melodic, but also reveals that she knows I'm awake. Ares looks down at me, and our eyes lock. I stare at him as Hart says. "I am sorry about Hattie's death, but I need you to get up today. In the two days since her death, Hecate told Styx that you broke the oath and are able to kill them now. Styx and her army have collected every human across the globe. These scared humans are prisoners on Mt. Olympus, dangled like fruit for you to grab. Right now, Styx expects you to mourn a few more days so she can ensnare those humans, so we need to act first. Otherwise, Styx doesn't fall into our trap. We will fall into hers."

I sit up for the first time in two days. Ares follows my lead. Hart looks between Ares and me, evaluating the two of us, as if we are a math equation she must solve. She says nothing, but her gaze wanders beyond where we sit on the bed. Her gaze darkens, too. The normally bright honey-colored shade of her eyes turns onyx. I realize, with a chill careening down my spine, that she's seeing the future as she looks at us, determining if our proximity is a detriment to her plans or an unescapable fate.

When her eyes return to their shade of honey, Hart speaks again. "If you don't put my plan into motion today, then Styx will use the twenty-seven point nine million humans left alive on Earth, who she has already captured, as ammunition. Hattie." I flinch at her name, but Hart continues. "Was your prophesied heart for two reasons. One, because she is your truest sister, but the second reason is because she is the symbol of humanity for you. If we give Styx one more day to ruminate Hattie's death, she will realize Hattie was one of twenty-seven point nine million pieces of your heart. She will torture and kill the humans so brutally, you will shatter at the sight. With only twelve humans in this house, half of them past their child-bearing years, humanity will go extinct. You will be too broken to pick up and glue yourself back together in time for the ultimate battle."

That is when her gaze returns to Ares.

"If Styx gets one more day to think about Hattie's death and steer it to her own advantage, then Saffron won't be present for the last war. She will be in this bed, sobbing in your arms, as the rest of us return to the battlefield. We will all fall victim to the Dagger of Chains, including you and Saffron. So don't you see?" Hart stalks toward the bed and stands at the foot of it. Cerberus growls at Hart, but she ignores him, settling her attention on Ares and me. "Styx wins if Saffron stays in this bed, mourning when we cannot afford the time."

"Get. Out." Ares's voice drops to glacial temperatures, and Hart takes a step back.

Hart turns and reaches the door, but she doesn't leave.

She spins her body to face me. "You once made an oath in a river of black,

An oath that saved Hatred from your attack.

Then a butterfly of scars and insanity

Entered your home and desecrated your humanity.

Now, goddess of bones and deliverance.

Let Hatred pay for her ignorance.

Let the final battle wage."

Hart smiles without mirth. "And rip out that bitch's rib cage."

Hart repeats the promise Styx made to me eighty-eight years ago when I was a prisoner of the river. She focuses on me, face as eerily stoic as Styx's herself, as she speaks with the villain's monotone voice. *"I swear to you, young one, that if Hattie's blood spills by my hands, or one of my follower's hands, then I am at your mercy."*

With that, Hart leaves.

I wait until I no longer hear her retreating steps, and I turn to face Ares. He reaches for me, cupping the side of my face. I speak before Ares has a chance to, and I say. "If Hart is right and humanity dies, if I stay in bed one more day, then no one will remember Hattie. No one will be alive to remember her as a hero, and I need her to be a hero, rather than a corpse marked for death because of me. Please, help me get out of bed. I need to turn this sadness into rage."

Ares slides out of the bed, and he holds his hand out for me. His smile is cautious, but it's crafted solely for my eyes. "Then let's get out of this bed and fight."

It's safer to mourn. To sit in this bed and cry away every fragment of myself until all that remains is my grief. But I made a promise to Styx eighty-eight years ago that if she was responsible for Hattie's death, then she would die by my hands. It is time I uphold that promise. I take Ares's hand, and I let him materialize armor onto both of us.

He wears his typical garb of Ancient Greek warriors. It is bronze plating, accented in red, with a boar's head in the middle. A helmet with a red plume nestles underneath his arm, but I now match him. He materializes bronze armor for me, too. Mine is a modern interpretation of the Ancient Greek armor, with red leggings underneath the bronze-plated armor. Red accents the lines, hosting a rib cage emblem in the center of my chest plate.

I trace my finger along the emblem, reminding me I am the only one with the power to rip every bone from Styx's body and end her life. My eyes meet Ares's again, and he walks behind me with a red ribbon in his hand.

He pulls up all my hair, and as he braids the tresses, he whispers in my ear. "After this war is over, I will tell you I have been in love with you from the moment I first saw you on that arena floor. I will tell you I knew my heart would beat only for you for the rest of eternity. After we win, and you have the chance to process everything that has happened to you, I will finally kiss you and tell you that you are my soulmate, my exquisite Saffron." I don't realize he finishes the braid and ties it with a red ribbon until he presses a soft, promising kiss to my cheek. "I will tell you that you are my destined third love, and for as long as the sun rises and the moon sets, I will bend my world to fit yours."

He walks around to face me head-on again, and he holds out his hand. He smiles nervously, like he doesn't realize I feel the same way about him. That I have felt this unparalleled pull towards him since the first night I spent in his house.

I take his hand, and he whispers. "But until we win this war, I have been told by a pesky oracle that I'm not allowed to say a word. So, for now, we go down to the training room, and you properly kick my ass."

"Will I get to tell you I feel the same after the war?"

I do not mistake the shock reverberating off him or the way his eyes become misty. He clears his throat several times before responding, "Yeah, sweetheart. You can tell me you also love me after the war."

He cups my face in his hand, then leans down and presses the softest kiss to my lips. It only lasts a second, but almost a hundred years of pent-up feelings release with this kiss. With his lips against mine, it finally feels like I know how to breathe.

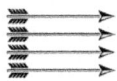

WHEN WE ENTER THE TRAINING ROOM, ALMOST EVERYONE is inside.

Dýnami throws a spear at a dummy precariously close to Phobos' head. Persephone spins daggers, which Hypnos deflects using a blue-accented scythe. Hermes trains with Maressa, using a xiphos; the two laugh almost the entire time their swords clash. Raven fights against a dummy because no one will duel with her. Deimos pushes Epiales to the ground. He has evidently forgotten most of his fighting skills, but Deimos helps him up a moment later.

Even the humans Hermes brought with Maressa train with another, although their form and technique are atrocious.

Only four people are missing from the training room: Hart, Zeus, Hephaestus, and Diam.

I can still hear Diam screaming my name, hoping for a miracle where there isn't one. "I need to do something before we train." My eyes roam back to Raven. "Will you spar with Raven until I get back?"

Ares snorts. "You want the two most hated people in here to fight? Alright."

But he places a kiss on top of my head, and he walks towards Raven.

I spin on my heels, and I walk towards Diam's room.

Diam lies on top of his bed, with one of Hattie's shirts cradled in his arms. He stares out the window at nothing and everything. I saunter into the room, closing the door behind me, but he doesn't react. He, like me, didn't expect to live a life without Hattie again. Especially so soon.

"I need you to get up." I wanted to sound confident, but my voice breaks as I look at one of my close friends. Diam doesn't stir. He doesn't react as I walk towards him and sit on the edge of his bed. Their bed. "Diam, please. Get up."

He doesn't react.

I shake his leg, only to realize it's coated with dried

blood. Unlike me, who had Ares helping me, Diam hasn't bathed in the two days since Hattie died. He hasn't even taken off the clothes. I shake him harder.

"Do you not hear me?! I said get up!" I shake harder and harder, but while his body jostles with the movement, he doesn't even look at me. His gaze stays fixated on the window, clutching her shirt. "Diam, I need you. Get up!"

I grab a pillow from his bed, and I throw it at him. It bounces off the top of his head, but he doesn't react. He doesn't even blink. Once again, tears stream down my face as I throw more things at him or in his vicinity. Every single stupid throw pillow. A pair of shoes.

Nothing works!

I shake the mattress, and I scream. "Get up!"

I flip the mattress, and he tumbles out. I'm careful not to have him hit his head, and I run over to him. He lies on the floor, still gripping that shirt, and I collapse at the spot nearest him. I grab the edge of the shirt, and his eyes fly up to meet mine. Endless pools of anguish live beneath those dark eyes, and I don't tug the shirt free.

I'll succeed, but at what cost?

"Hattie and Zig are dead. Our family is gone, and now there is only us." I openly sob now, my tears mingling with his, landing on the patch of floor separating us. His tears are the only indication that he hears me. "If you do not want to get up for the rest of the world, then that's fine. I don't care. But get up for me. You're all I have of them, so get up. Fight with me. We are family, and I need you."

Diam looks up at me, finally registering my presence, and his bottom lip trembles. "She's gone, Saff." He falls into my arms, and I hold him tight. "Hattie. Oh gods, my Hattie."

I hold him like this until the morning dips into the afternoon, and the sun begins its descension. Only then does he stop crying, lift his head, and notice the armor cooling his face. "Can you kill her?" Sorrow mingles with rage until all that encompasses him is ire. "Can you kill Styx?"

"Yeah, I can kill her, but I need my brother with me."

My brother locks hands with me, and we stand up together. When we turn to face the door, Hart leans against it. She looks between us with a frown on her face, but I know she stares at us and sees fury within our scowls.

"I will never forgive you for knowing she was going to die and letting it happen," I snap.

Hart solemnly nods her head. "I understand, but hate me after the war. Right now, I need you both to follow me."

We do not separate our locked hands the entire time. She takes us to her art space. I couldn't understand anything in the art room when I entered a few days ago. It was all undecipherable splashes and shapes. The only part of the art I could clearly see were the words written on every canvas.

*Crumble like Pompeii.*

Now, as Hart opens the door, I see every single art piece with harrowing clarity. She painted every moment. My time with Epiales on Ogygia. The Battle of the Huntresses, where Lamb falls to her fiery death with a smile on her lips. I avoid the art piece with a river of red, and I stop Diam from looking, too.

We stand in front of the final art piece, and those three words written on the canvas now make perfect sense.

Zeus stands beside the last art piece, and suddenly his haggard appearance makes sense. He has followed every order Hart's given him without argument, while the rest of us have asked a multitude of unanswered questions. Zeus has known everything for a while, and now Diam and I will learn the truth, too.

We look at Hart, and she says to me. "After you visit Hatred on Mt. Olympus, the plan will slide into motion. Soon, we either win this war or we are Styx's prisoners forevermore. It all lies on your shoulders now, Diam the Seeker and Saffron the Savior. Now, it is time you learn everything that needs to happen and everything we can't do."

We look at each other, mirrored expressions of shock on our faces. It has been no secret that I am the Savior, but Diam is the prophesied Seeker. Neither of us guessed his part in this war, but now his fate lay etched beside mine. He squeezes my hand harder.

Zeus produces the Dagger of Chains, which Diam *lost* amid the aftermath of the Battle of the Huntresses. He holds it in his palm, and it soars from Zeus's hand. The Dagger of Chains has claimed an owner, and it lands delicately on top of Diam's hand.

Zeus says. "It was always supposed to be yours, Seeker."

Hart adds. "When the time comes, when you lead all the humans in the world to safety, you will hear the call of the Dagger to release the gods within. Do not release anyone until after you return to the home of bones. No one can help you on your journey except those who fought at the Battle of Pompeii."

"Stop being cryptic and just tell us what we need to know," I add.

Hart holds out her hands for Diam and me. "I will show you both everything. When you touch my hand, you will witness every vision I have received since becoming the oracle. I must warn you, you will see the path of victory, but you will also see the thousands of ways we would lose this war if even one event strays from my plans. You will see why I had to let Hattie die."

Diam and I wince.

"You will see why Epiales had to lose his memory," Hart continues. "Why Jamila had to marry Thanatos, and why Raven had to be saved instead of the more benevolent huntresses. Everything has a meaning and a purpose, and now you must learn it all."

Diam and I keep our hands intertwined, but we place our free one on top of Hart's.

In a spiral of colors, we learn it all.

We finally learn how Styx crumbles like Pompeii.

# THIRTY-NINE

SAFFRON

We stay in the art room for hours, learning every detail of the final battle. By the time Diam and I stumble out of the room, it is night-time, and no one is still training. So, I wander down to the kitchen.

There, I find Epiales, and a stream of black smoke billows out of the oven. He opens the oven door, coughing and waving his hand in front of him, trying to hide his first attempt at post-memory-loss baking. I walk towards him, and I feel his eyes track my movements as I lean down, pick up the muffin tray with bare hands, then drop it on the stovetop. The burns heal instantaneously, but Epiales still stares at me with his mouth open in disbelief.

"Are you suddenly intrigued by baking, or are you trying to get your memories back?" I ask, leaning against the cabinets next to the stove.

His pale cheeks tinge red. "I was trying to make those white cookies you told me about a few nights ago. The ones you thought were stars from the sky." He rummages his hand through his curly black hair and mumbles, almost quiet enough for me to miss. "I was trying to apologize by making the cookies, and I can't even do that right."

"Apologize for what?"

I know why he feels like he needs to apologize, and her name is the one thing everyone thinks about, but no one says aloud. "She died to protect me, and I'm so sorry." He says.

"Someone wise told me that being a brave hero like her is contagious. When you witness something as courageous as her saving you, it creates more heroes than ever before. When I heard this, it reminded me of the Lernaean Hydra. Do you remember that monster?"

Epiales shakes his head.

I explain to him. "When you cut off a Hydra's head, two more grow back in its place. That's how I think of heroes now. When you watch one hero display an act of intense bravery, you wish to become a hero yourself, and in this time of war, I believe we need more heroes now than ever." My eyes roam back to the burned pastries in the muffin tin, then back at Epiales. "Maybe instead of a baker who tries to make cookies in a muffin tin, you can be a hero instead."

There's a stretch of silence, then Epiales asks. "You don't make cookies in a muffin tin?"

I turn off the oven, then hold out my hand for him. "I have to go for a few days, but before I do, I'd like us to share one more story."

He takes my hand, and a spark shoots between us. It is dim but ever present. He smiles down at our joined hands. "I think I would follow you anywhere."

There is currently nothing beautiful surrounding our world, only ruin decorates the scenery. So, I take him where we have always found comfort in the grotesque. I bring him to the front porch, far from everything except the sky. It is too early to see many stars, but a few stubborn ones peek through, demanding to join our story.

We lay our backs on the ground, just like we did on Ogygia when we gazed at the stars. Yet, our eyes find each other rather than the sky. He smiles at me, but I can't muster one back. "What is our story about today, my queen?"

That is what I miss most about our time together, the nicknames and stories we share. "You know that was the first name ever given to me?"

"Really?" he asks.

I nod, "Yeah. During the time of human enslavement, humans didn't get names until a god claimed them with a scarification mark, and that didn't happen until our eighteenth birthdays. For the first two years we spoke in my dreams, I wasn't Saffron, and you weren't Epiales or Erik. We were each other's queen and storyteller."

"Now, you are both of them," he says with reverence. "Is that our story today? About why I call you my queen?"

"Somewhat. It's the story of how I killed you."

Surprisingly, he doesn't pull his hand out of mine. He stares at me with those impossibly perfect silver eyes, and he waits for me to begin. So, I start with the day he showed me his face for the first time. The story evolves as I explain every argument we shared, when he showed me Tartarus, and how the prison withered him into near nothingness. My voice hitches when I talk about the Battle of the Labyrinth, because even eighty-eight years later, talking about killing Epiales tears apart pieces of my soul.

"Kronos devised a plan as a prisoner. He said that only he knew the incantation on the Dagger of Chains to release the gods from their prison, and he would only repeat it if you and I got to go on our first date."

"But it was a trick," Epiales says.

"You remember?" I ask, surprise lacing my tone.

Slowly, Epiales nods his head with his own surprised response. "He shot you, right?"

"Yeah." Despite the darker story, I can't stop the smile growing over my lips. He only remembers the worst, except for the moment he went from villain to hero to save my life. "He shot me with Eros's arrow. One side can make you fall in love with the first person you see, but the lead side-"

"Makes you hate the person."

My grin grows. "Yes. Kronos had Raven shoot me, and I fell under his spell, but he told you about his plans. You escaped from the prison to find help. To save me."

Tears of what I recognize immediately as relief fill in his eyes. "I remember," he says. "I turned into a crow to leave the cell."

"Yes!"

"And we got to you in time. Athena, Ares, and me. We shot you again with the lead side of the arrow, and you killed Kronos."

I squeeze his hand as relief bleeds through my grief-stricken heart. "That's exactly what happened. You knew if Kronos failed to trick me into killing everyone, then you would die, but you sacrificed yourself to protect me."

Epiales says. "It's why I betrayed him, because he was going to kill you. Right?"

I nod my head. "You become my hero that day."

"I'd rather die a thousand deaths than watch you suffer even one," he whispers, not realizing he said this very sentence to me a long time ago.

"You were my first love," I admit. "And gods, I wish

you remembered that, too. Our love was like a fire, burning and extinguishing so fast, but as long as you remember you are not a villain, but a hero, then that will suffice."

"You keep saying that word. Hero," he tests out the four-letter word on his tongue. "Why?"

I answer him by telling him a final story, one I pray he doesn't forget.

THERE ARE NO GOODBYES BETWEEN THOSE I KNOW WILL DIE on the last battlefield and those I will see again.

I saw the future through flashes of the color of death, and now I understand the power of silence. Through those visions, I understand every murky decision Hart had to make for the majority of the world to survive. I will miss Hattie and the others who will die with great fervor, but I bore witness to the travesty this world becomes if I don't make their sacrifice worthwhile.

I walk towards the room where we imprisoned Uranus without saying goodbye to anyone. Uranus thrashes in his chains the moment he sees me standing in the doorway, armed with my sword of bones and sheathed in armor made by Ares himself.

"Let's go on a journey, shall we?"

In one hand, I have my blade of bones. In my other hand, I hold the end of five chains. One chain leads towards the cuff sitting painfully around Uranus's left ankle; the second one encircles the right ankle. The third chain leads to his left wrist, while the fourth goes to the x-shaped spears, impaling Uranus's palms to immobilize his powers.

But the fifth chain is my favorite.

Hephaestus molded the chains to prevent any god from hoping to escape, but he designed the neck chain for torture. He took inspiration from the iron maiden and heretic's fork. The inner perimeter of the cold, bronze bar around his neck hosts long, sharp spikes. Hephaestus designed the weapon to be exactly three centimeters from Uranus's skin, so if he so much as talked, then Adam's apple would face brutal consequences. If Uranus tries to rest, let out a scream, or even breathe too loudly, then pain would ensue.

Yet, before I start my journey with Uranus, I ask him. "Do you remember the dream we once shared? It was on the night I killed Epiales."

He won't talk with the spikes precariously close to his throat, but I can see in his eyes that he remembers. He remembers how he frightened a young girl, who was too new to the world of gods and prophecies to understand anything but fear.

I walk towards him, coiling the chains around and around my hand until I stand face-to-face with the shackled deity. "After that dream, I convinced myself you were going to be the most terrifying creature I would ever face." My eyes peruse his ichor-covered flesh, and I make sure he sees the disgust on my face as I muse. "But you were just an enormous disappointment."

He opens his mouth to repute my statement, but the spikes dig into his jaw and chin. Instead of words, a stream of ichor spills out, and I ruefully grin. Each step Uranus takes elicits a grimace, one that brings me a surplus of joy.

While Maressa occupies Hermes's attention, I imitate my ex-husband and steal a pair of his winged sandals. I use them to fly Uranus and me towards Mt. Olympus. He screams the entire way up as the spikes slash through his skin, but I do not slow. He is part of the reason Hattie died, and while I understand every step of this war has a purpose, I still harbor the rage that my best friend perished to save the world.

And Uranus is one of many immortals to suffer my wrath.

The moment my winged sandals land atop the clouds of Mt. Olympus, the familiar warmth I associate with these golden gates fails to rush forward. Instead, corpses line the front gates. Mt. Olympus's gates are not meant to be in humans' reaches, but over a hundred of them lay across the perimeter with their bodies oddly bent. Most do not have eyes or all their limbs, and I hold back my bile of revulsion.

In Styx's version of eternal reign, this is the humans' fate.

They all will die by her hands or the hands she puppeteers. Humanity, as the world knows it, will cease to exist within the first one hundred years of her totalitarian dictatorship. People will quiver in the veil of darkness she sheaths the world within, praying to a god who will not listen, hoping they will not die today.

Blood drips from the newly made spiked tips of the golden gates, and it is a bright shade of red. The gates have closed, with a lock ensuring they remain this way. I glance down at Uranus, who swims in his own ichor. "Do you have a key?"

He shakes his head, then makes a strangled sound when the slight movement causes two spikes to slide into his flesh. I lean forward, pulling Uranus with me, and knock three times. Almost immediately, the lock dissolves in green smoke tainted with black tendrils, and the gate swings open. I tug his chain, and we advance towards Styx.

The homes are the same as the last time I was on Mt.

Olympus, all alabaster smooth and impervious to war's onslaught of pain, but too much has changed. In front of the homes, nestled between columns, lay poorly stitched tents. Inside these small, A-frame tents are human families of four or five. They cram together in these spaces, and there isn't a single soul unscathed. They all wear scrapes and bruises, slings over their arms, or shunts atop their legs.

Worse of all, these humans have twin necklaces around their throats.

One necklace is black and made entirely out of the River Styx. It doesn't touch their flesh, which would cause them immediate agony, followed by death. Instead, the black river water hovers over their flesh, teasing them with the promise of an excruciating death.

The other necklace is the darkest obsidian green, with tainted black veins throughout. This necklace squeezes their neck like a choker, and I understand why the twenty-seven million humans enslaved on Mt. Olympus wear these necklaces. Both Hecate and Styx expected my arrival, and the necklaces around the humans' throats are a warning of what will happen to all of humanity if I try to kill either of them.

All the humans on Mt. Olympus starve. Their clothes cling to boney skin, and as they see me, they reach their hands out in hope of…something. Anything, really. Loyalty does not shackle these humans atop Mt. Olympus. Rather, fear roots them to the spot.

"Savior," one croaks, then another and another. They all say my moniker, followed by one wish. "Save us."

I wonder if the mangled corpses at the front gates were the ones who asked for basic human decency, like food, water, or a blanket, or if those were the few humans who tried to escape Styx and failed.

This is her army of humans, frightened and helpless, reaching out and hoping I can free them. I tug Uranus's chains a little harder, finding little solace as he grunts with pain. With each tent I walk past, and with each empty stare from another human, I materialize a bag of bread. Yet, all the humans barely reach for them. Hunger laces their parched lips, speaking a language I can hear despite a lack of words, but they don't rush towards the bread.

They fear to even eat in Styx's proximity.

Many immortals and monsters are on Styx's side, with glittering gowns and a surplus of food. They stay far from the humans, but when they see me approach, they part with fright. The centaurs, traitorous muses, and many others create an open path between me and the throne, where the wrong goddess sits.

Even from Mt. Olympus, I can hear my screams that have now become a part of the wind. Humans and creatures alike hear my bellows for a friend who I could not save. One frightened, low-level god opens the throne room door for me, where Styx and Hecate wait inside.

Styx sits on Zeus's throne, pretending it belongs to her, but that is all it is. Make believe for a goddess with futile hopes. I will watch this world burn before I let her keep a crown on her head, and as my eyes clash with Hecate's, she stares back with a mouth agape. Styx sits confidently on my father's throne, and she bares a glint of confidence in her dark eyes because she still believes she can thwart me.

Then I focus back on Hecate, and there's a glimmer of doubt.

"Get on your knees," I snarl.

Uranus immediately obeys. As if he were my dog, the once vicious immortal collapses onto his knees and looks up at me with a plea to survive. Long ago, he came to me in a nightmare, and he promised to be my demise. Now, I know he is nothing but false bravado. Now, I know I am the one he should have feared in that nightmare, not the other way around.

"Do you remember our first conversation, Lady Styx?" I ask, focusing all my attention on the two formidable goddesses before me.

Her jaw ticks the tiniest bit to show her annoyance at my reference to her as a lady rather than a queen, but it is the only shred of emotion she deigns to show. "Yes, I remember our first interaction well. You bound yourself loyal to me."

"It's been eighty-eight years since we made our oath, and while you might not remember every word you said, I do, with painstaking clarity. When my heart died," I don't have to act like this one sentence wrecks me. My voice cracks of its own accord because I can still feel where Hattie's murder ripped my organ apart, leaving only the ruinous parts intact. "I've played our conversation on a repetitive loop inside my head."

I curl Uranus's chains completely around my hand, and I relish the sound he makes as he gurgles on his own blood. "You said '*Swear that you will come back to me when I call for you. When you're summoned, you must acquiesce, without question, to one demand. With this oath, you promise eternal loyalty to me. I will never die by your hands.*'"

My voice sounds eerily similar to Styx's, as I imbue no empathy in my words as I recall the first part of her oath. "I remember my words," Styx says. "Must we repeat the past? I much prefer we pave the future together."

Ignoring her, I continue. "*I swear to you, Lady Styx, and to your river, I will come back when you call for me. I will not deny or question the one favor you ask of me. Obediently, I will grant you that favor if it is in my power. I swear to be eternally loyal to you as long as my friend is safe.*"

Realization dawns on Hecate's face before Styx's. The latter remains eerily calm as I wrap Uranus's chains around my hand once again, and he screams beneath a flood of ichor filling his throat.

"Do you remember what I said next? Because I do. I told you in that river eighty-eight years ago that if your games lead to Hattie's death, then any oath I have sworn to you will be void. I said that if Hattie dies by your hands, or the hands you puppet, then I swear I will use whatever power I supposedly have to kill you."

Styx holds a glass of nectar in one hand, and ever so subtly, that hand begins to shake. "Remember, child, that I have Mt. Olympus filled with ninety-nine percent of humanity. If you try to kill me, Hecate will use the necklaces around their throats to decapitate them. One snap, and they'll be dead. Same if you kill Hecate. I will end your humans before you can end me. So, tread carefully with the rest of your story."

I drop Uranus's chains, and the foolish immortal emits the smallest sigh of relief. The goddesses, however, hold their collective breath. Uranus's bones sing to my call, and I raise his body in the air. He kicks and tries to scream, but the spikes dig into his flesh. Before I remove a single bone, his blood *drips, drips, drips* on top of me.

I happily bathe myself in his ichor, welcoming the honeyed color to decorate my new armor like an accessory, and I lock eyes with Styx. She attempts to hide her fear, but it's there. Ever present in the archaic, obsidian gaze of the worst monster across all the eons. Her fear mirrors a star blinking out in a black night sky.

"That day in the river, what did you say in return, Lady Styx?" I ask the question that finally makes her flinch.

Styx attempts to hide her flinch by sitting straighter on her throne, but I see her unease. I note how she sets down her glass of ambrosia to hide how her hand trembles. There is a long pause where Uranus continues to gift me droplets of his blood, which rains on my hair and shoulders, because I wait for Styx to repeat the oath she made to me all those years ago.

*"Styx's most fatal flaw is how she views humans," Hart told Diam and me after she showed us the visions of the final battle. "It was the same way Kronos fell. They know humans are physically weaker, so they find them inconsequential. Yet, it is humans who are most resilient. It is humans who became both of their downfalls. Styx did not realize when she made an oath to a naïve demi-god in the river that the one human girl she bartered with would be her ruin."*

Styx speaks slowly, like every syllable must be in the same infliction it was eighty-eight years prior. "I swear to you, young one, that if Hattie's blood spills by my hands, or one of my follower's hands, then I am at your mercy."

I rip out every bone out of Uranus's body, and I direct every one of them at Styx.

His rib cage falls upon her lap, while the others penetrate the wall directly behind her. A patella crashes into the glass of nectar Styx held in her hand a few seconds prior. A shattered collarbone impales Hecate's thigh, and she collapses with momentary pain. She glowers at me as she rips the collarbone from her thigh, her ichor joining Uranus's on the floor.

I walk towards where Styx sits until my feet wade in a puddle of nectar, broken glass, and Uranus's bones. I look down at Styx, sitting on a throne unbefitting a monster such as her, and I raise my hand with a silent command of her bones. Her femur thrashes within her body, pressing against her skin upon my command.

"I will kill all the humans. Hecate and I can destroy them with a snap of our fingers," Styx sneers, but fear causes her voice to wobble. She finally realizes she can lose this war. "You can kill one of us, but not before the other kills them all."

I lean forward until my mouth is a breath away from hers. "If I wanted to, I could kill you both right now before you even snapped your fingers to end the humans. For my entire life, I have restrained my powers. You do not understand the gravity of what I am capable of. I could paint your blood with Uranus's and Hecate's. I could destroy you without breaking a sweat." Reaching for her face, I snatch her jaw with one hand and relish the sound of her gasp.

But then I surprise the goddess of hatred.

I drop my hand around her jaw, and I collapse onto my knees. My tears are a show for her to believe, but they are real. I miss Hattie so much, and a wretched sob seeps from my lips as I place my hands on Styx's knees. I sob for my dead heart, whose death prophesied my role in the war. The prophecy stated that depending on how my heart died, her death would tilt me towards joining Styx's side or Hart's.

I can barely muster the words beneath my sobs.

Styx savors my anguish.

"I want to kill you so badly, but I want Hattie back more." My eyes drag towards Hecate's, and they swim with the tears I authentically shed for my dearest friend. My truest sister. "Hattie would have gone to the ends of the Earth and back for me, and now it is my turn to do anything for her. Those white orbs that enter your body, they are the souls of those who died since you destroyed the Underworld, right?"

Hecate answers, cautious of my reaction. "Yes, every dead soul lives in me now."

Styx reaches for me, grabbing my jaw similar to how I took hers in my hand a moment earlier. She seizes control from Hecate and me, and she forces me to look back at her face. To see the light of victory return in her onyx gaze.

"You want to see Hattie again?" Styx's voice drips with a false sense of sympathy.

I nod my head, and it isn't a lie.

There are a multitude of travesties I would commit to have Hattie back with me, alive and happy, but I cannot subject the world to Styx a moment longer. Hecate surrendered the world and all its occupants for one soul, and I bear witness to how it has destroyed her. Black veins now slither up her neck, dancing across her jawline. And that is the fate I would succumb to if I joined Styx's side to resurrect Hattie.

It is a temptation, but nothing more.

I lie through my teeth. "Bring Hattie back for me. I need my heart back, and if you spare Epiales in your reign, I will help you do anything else you wish."

"Will you kill the Olympians for me?" Styx runs her jagged thumb nail down my cheek, feigning a maternal gesture.

"As long as I get Hattie back, I will do anything."

"There is something so achingly beautiful about sadness," Styx says, but she doesn't understand any emotions other than hatred and greed.

Sadness is an anomaly to her because she has never suffered loss or mourned the space they leave behind. She doesn't find sadness beautiful; she finds it a mystery she has yet to solve. Still, I let the villain have her grand speech. I let her believe I am putty in her hands, groveling before her as another one of her frightened followers.

Styx continues. "Shattering hearts, yearning for unachievable desires, should be carved into statues to be admired until the ends of times. Crying away the world through burning tears; it is poetically gorgeous. Those who are perpetually happy see sadness as a grotesque creature, one they fear because they do not fully understand the purpose behind this emotion, but I understand."

No, she doesn't.

She doesn't know the gravity of killing one of your three great loves, then stitching him back together with your own humanity. She doesn't know the empty hollowness that Hattie's death created in my heart because she has never experienced the love of a sister who teaches her how to change the way she learns to see the world. Styx doesn't know what it is like to watch her daughter, whom she loves, lay in a hospital bed with no signs of waking, no matter how many times she prays for a better outcome.

Styx's black-rimmed, jagged fingernail knicks my cheek. "It is only when you're sad that a glimpse of your true self emerges, a part you try to lock away in a chest whilst swallowing the key. The happy might appear strongest, or even those like Ares who live in the depths of their rage, but every other emotion is just a shield sheltering the truth. It is only when a person cries, when their heart rips open and there is no certainty it can sew itself back together, that they show their true feelings to those nearest. I see your true self now, Saffron, and it is famished. You need the hunger that comes with a kill, and young one, I will give this to you."

I abhor this woman, but I croak out two blasphemous words that I pray to the gods she believes. "Thank you."

And just as Hart said it would happen.

Styx stupidly smiles.

# FORTY

HART

A rt is a story without ink, and it tells a tale without words. Saffron leaves with Uranus, cementing the last battle of the penultimate war, and I stand in front of a painting that tells its truth. My fingertips hold the stains of gold and red, which decorate a scene of five eventual deaths.

It all begins with Saffron and Hecate on the far right of the art piece. They walk side-by-side, and green magic tainted black with Styx's hatred oozes around the traitorous witch goddess. Millions of humans walk behind them, and while they do not wear chains, they bear the faces of prisoners forced onto a battleground.

On the far left of the art piece, another version of the battle begins.

The prophesied hammer, who once betrayed the goddess she loved most by killing Willow, stands with an eight-foot-tall hammer in her hands. It should be too magnanimous for a human woman, but Raven grips the black and blazing teal hammer in both hands, and she releases a battle cry. The sound that screeches out of her lips happens when she raises that monstrous hammer in the air. Lightning crashes into the heart of the hammer, and the startling teal accents blaze to life.

She slams the hammer down, and when she does, the war truly begins.

It begins with the savior and the hammer, but it ends with the seeker and the seer. It ends with me. With no other fates to string together to ensure victory, I finally let myself feel fear. Only a few months ago, which feels like eons now, I was a miserable girl spending my days in a loveless engagement. I wished I could live a life of importance, where I was a warrior marching onto a battlefield.

Now, that wish has come true, and along with it, is unbridled fright.

I clasp my hand around my gold feather necklace, a gift my father gave me so long ago. I run the pad of my thumb over the feather's ridges, and I close my eyes to shed a single tear. My father does not wait for me behind my eyelids, but it is Aashritha. My ancestor, who was the first oracle in our lineage and the first who spoke of the prophecy leading me on my path today.

She is not just a figment of my imagination, but Aashritha is here in the hidden coves of my mind. All the most prominent oracles of the past live within me now, having access to my mind for their knowledge. But the other oracles do not show themselves. Only Aashritha reveals herself in a shimmering, sleeveless yellow gown.

Beneath my closed eyes, there is no scenery or beauteous sight to distract me by. There is only darkness and Aashritha. She walks barefoot through the black ground, which has the same texture as sand. Her gown creates a train behind her, but the more she advances, the more the yellow gown's train mirrors spilled ichor careening through a crime scene.

"I've been waiting a long time for this moment, Hartika."

She repeats back the first sentence she ever said to me, and I only realize now that her words are intentional. When we first met, she was not waiting a long time to meet me. She was waiting for eons for this battle, so she could watch Styx- her murderer- die. Aashritha knew the fate of everyone in this war long before I did.

It makes my confession easier to release. "I'm scared."

Those were the first words I ever said to Aashritha, but they are truer now than ever before. Aashritha stands before me, and she gently pulls my hand away from fidgeting with my necklace. She places both her hands in mine, squeezing them reassuringly. I know that everything I have done, manipulating those around me to fall into the perfect line for the perfect outcome of the war, was a necessity. I know I am only an instrument for the Fates, and I play their lyre perfectly, but that doesn't change the fact that I'm new to this world.

That I'm young, and I'm scared.

"I was your age when I died," Aashritha tells me once more. We repeat the conversation we first had together because it was truly meant for now, to remind me why I must move forward with the final war. "Twenty-six is too young to receive the weight of the world. It was too young for me to die, but the Fates know the path we must take. They know the fear we have as we take the steps they meticulously planned, but we have to keep moving. We must accept that path one step at a time."

"I will not succumb to my fear," I promise her, even as the tears fall. "But will you stay with me? Will you promise to always speak with me?"

Aashritha's smile is kind, and it almost looks like my mother's. "Hartika, I live in your mind now. It is mine and the other oracles' afterlife, and there is nowhere I would want to be more than here with you. Open your eyes and know I will be here for it all." She pulls our joined hands towards her lips, and she presses a kiss atop my knuckles. "I will always be here."

I open my eyes and turn to see Zeus standing in the doorway. He holds his lightning bolt in his hand, which crackles to life, but his face holds the grim reminder of what comes next. The last step towards victory.

"Are you ready?" he asks gravely.

But I'll never be fully ready for what comes next.

I force a smile as the few tears I shed dry on my cheeks. "Let's go." We walk down the staircase from my art room and onto the ground floor, where everyone waits for us. "Hey, Zeus?"

We descend the staircase as he says, "Yes, Hart?"

"Thank you for not allowing me to suffer with this information alone. Thank you for letting me have a friend in the mayhem."

Zeus looks down at me, and the smallest smile blooms over his lips. "It is an honor to call you a friend."

Together, we move towards our army and the end of it all.

# FORTY-ONE

HERMES

Only an hour prior to our departure, Maressa learned she was the prophesied Muse. The one destined to lose her voice forevermore because of this battle. I am the god of mischief, and I intertwine myself with lies and deceit. Nobody can tell lies around me, not even a woman as captivating as Maressa.

She feigned surprise, and many believed her agape mouth and widening eyes.

But not me.

She wouldn't look at me as she asked Hart question after question. "Why me?", "What will I have to do?" but none of the answers stirred a look of genuine disbelief. Maressa anticipated every answer, like she already knew.

Like she knew all along that she was the prophesied muse.

We all wait at the front of the house for Zeus and Hart to come down the stairs for further orders. The battlefield is miles away, but it looms ever closer. I continually glance down at Maressa, who purposely avoids my stare, and in a rupture of words, I stumble out. "What are you? And don't lie to me. Please."

Persephone, who stands beside Cerberus next to us, looks down at Maressa. Before the latter can respond, she asks. "You have not told him yet?"

"Told me what?" I glance between Maressa and Persephone, who both have my answer written on their faces.

"This isn't the time." Maressa stares at the floor rather than me, and there's a slight tremble in her voice. "I can tell you after the battle is over."

"Now is the only time we have. We won't have time to talk on a battlefield, so before Hart and Zeus come downstairs and demand we start this war, I want the truth." I hesitate a second and add. "You taught me how important it is, to be honest."

My instinctual reaction is anger. I want to yell at her, to demand all the answers she has locked away in her mind. We have recently begun something which has spiraled so quickly into ardent feelings. It shouldn't happen this fast, but there is no way I can go back to a world without her in it. A single word for how I feel about her threatens to leave my lips, to dance around the air bristling with the tension of an upcoming battle. Because of that one word, which I know she feels too, I believe I deserve the answer to every question surrounding her.

But she keeps nervously cracking her knuckles and worrying her bottom lip with her teeth. She won't look at me, and Persephone places a sympathetic hand on her shoulder. My anger extinguishes like water upon a flame. I move towards her and gingerly clasp her chin in between my fingers.

Persephone steps away, while Maressa lets me tilt her face up towards mine. Her eyes swim with too many emotions to absorb. Sadness, regret, and even fear live within her bottomless brown eyes.

"I have made a million mistakes across my eons-long existence. I have lied and stolen and tried to trick my way into keeping people and things that do not belong to me. There are parts of myself that are hideous, and yet you only bring out the best of me. You have let me show you the scared and jagged pieces of myself, and you haven't walked away."

The next words that torment my mind, begging me to release them, frighten me. There have only been two women before her, who I have felt this way towards. One is now an enemy who betrays me at every turn. The other is Saffron, who I lied to so many times in a failed attempt to keep what never belonged to me.

Yet, the words come out with more truthfulness than ever before. "I love you, Maressa Holliday, and I won't walk away from you, no matter what you're hiding from me. I promise, whatever it is, I'll find as beautiful as every other part of you. Even your jagged parts are perfect to me."

There's a soft groan to my left, where Phobos stands. "Is this really necessary right now?" Cerberus nips at his foot. "Ow!"

"I'm not human, which you already know," she begins.

My mind goes back to the first battle we fought in together, where I watched her fight with an ease that only comes from familiarity on a battlefield. She fought with such grace, and when she bled both red and gold, her efficiency made sense. She was a demi-god, and any child of a god has an innate ability to wield a weapon at a speed and skill-set far above a typical human. But I have loved someone half-human, half-god before, and she knows this.

Yet, she cries, which tells me I have guessed wrong about her lineage.

She isn't a demi-god.

I wait, ever patient, for her next words.

"About three thousand years ago, I was a nymph. A daughter of Melpomene, one of the muses, and Demeter tasked me and my half-sisters with befriending and protecting a young goddess." Maressa's eyes drag from me to where Persephone stands beside Cerberus. While still looking at her, Maressa continues. "When Hades stole that young goddess in front of my own eyes, my sisters and I ran to Demeter and told her. Demeter said she was turning us into the perfect creations to find our young goddess, Persephone, but her gift felt more like a punishment."

I know where this story is going because I remember the day Demeter found out that Hades kidnapped her young daughter, Persephone. Persephone was only twenty years old, the youngest immortal at the time, when Hades opened the ground and swallowed Persephone whole. I know what Demeter did to those nymphs, who she tasked with protecting Persephone, before Maressa's wings unfurl from her back.

Maressa silently cries as she reveals herself, and why she is the prophesied muse clicks into place. I thought she was a daughter of Clio because Clio begged for me to protect her, but she wanted me to protect her niece, who has already suffered enough mutilation in her eons' long lifetime. Maressa's feet change into bird's feet, but the rest of her is the same. She still wears the most beautiful face the Fates could ever gift someone, with doe-shaped brown eyes and chin-length black hair. She still has round cheeks I've kissed a dozen times, and she still smells like vanilla.

Even if she is a siren, she's still my Maressa.

"Demeter said she turned us into these *monsters*."

Maressa stops, choking on her last word with disgust at what she's become, and angrily wipes away the few tears that fall. "So we could better find her daughter in the ocean, and she gave us wings, so if we found her in the ocean, we could fly her away."

"It wasn't the only reason we became sirens, though," Maressa continues. "It was a cruel punishment for losing her daughter. Because once we entered the water, magic compelled us to kill any sailors who passed us. We had to use our singing voices, which we once loved so much, to murder innocent men. Soon, we stopped looking for the young goddess altogether. I lost myself in those seas for decades, singing men to their deaths anytime they drew near. I can't tell you how many sailors I murdered, compelled by a magic within me I didn't want or understand."

"How did you get out?" I ask because I never heard of a siren who left the water. All her sisters still live within the ocean, luring sailors to their deaths with the prettiest songs.

"Aashritha and the other oracles who burned to death in the Delphi came to me in a dream. Or, at least, I think it was a dream. My time in the ocean is so fuzzy, but they were all there in my mind. They stood in front of me as burned, mutilated versions of themselves, but they were there with me. They told me I had a greater purpose with my singing voice than the waters, and they told me everything they knew about the prophecy with Styx."

"My dear friend, I am so sorry," Persephone says.

Maressa looks between Persephone and me, but she says to her former friend. "I tried to save my sisters, but they said that because I was the only one who wasn't fully a god but a demi-god, that I was the only one who could pull myself out of the water's compulsion. But I promise I tried to free my sister, your highness. But when I couldn't, as soon as I escaped the water, I went looking for you. I wanted to tell you everything, but I couldn't go to the Underworld without dying and whenever you weren't in the Underworld…"

Her words fade, but we know what she wants to say.

Whenever Persephone is not in the Underworld with Hades, she's with her mother, Demeter. The same Demeter who turned Maressa into a bloodthirsty monster, constantly luring men to their deaths with her singing voice, which she once loved but now hates.

"I was told I was the muse in a prophecy that would begin eighty-eight years after the savior's blood shifted from red to gold, and it was my job to search the world for the prophesied hero. I had to look for a male without a name, whose silver eyes were like a star in the sky," Maressa says, as her eyes roam to where Epiales stands. He is in a conversation with Diam, oblivious to his part in Maressa's eons' old story. "For thousands of years, I've wandered around the world, searching for Epiales and writing the perfect song for this exact moment."

Maressa's gait is different with bird claws for feet, but she's still Maressa. Wonderful, beautifully bright Maressa. She stands in front of me, over a foot shorter, and I lean down to kiss her. Her lips are so soft against mine, and the moment our mouths touch, a thousand bolts of lightning run down the length of my body.

When she pulls away, Maressa asks. "Are you sure you don't hate me now? I knew I was going to lose my voice, a voice Demeter made me hate, so I could help stop Styx forever, but I didn't expect you. The oracles never told me I would meet you, and that I would fall in love with a god who is so above me. I wouldn't blame you if you change your mind about me. You expected a Demi-god because of my blood, and technically, I am a demi-god. My mom,

Melpomene, fell in love with a mortal king, but I'm a monster who is about to become a mute. So, if you leave now, I understand-"

I slam my lips against hers again, and I stop the terrible words from leaving her lips. I don't care if the war starts now, and I'm a victim to a rainfall of terror, as long as I get to kiss away her insecurities. As long as I'm here to tell her what I should have said a thousand times over, regardless of how sudden and new we are.

My lips hover a breath away from hers, my hand curled into her hair. "I am in love with you, Maressa Holliday, and I will love every part of you. The beautiful, the jagged, and everything that comes in between."

"Zeus and Hart are coming downstairs now," Persephone says.

Maressa steps away from me, but she wears the biggest grin upon her face. "I love you too, Hermes."

She lets her last genuine words be a declaration of love.

We spin our attention to Hart and Zeus, who stand side-by-side at the bottom of the staircase. One of the humans who came to this house with Maressa, Epiales, and me cries out. "Why can't we go with you? We want to help!"

A few more humans join into the discourse, but Hart faces the one who first spoke out. He is a tall, gangly male with a patchy beard growing in and short auburn hair. "Everyone has their purpose in the last war, Marvin. Yours and a few select others have an important job, one which requires you to stay here."

His face pales. "H-How do you know my name?"

I didn't even know his name, and I lived with him at the bar for a week.

Hart ignores his question. "You and the others must get the infirmary ready for when the seeker returns here. He will come back with many malnourished and injured humans. It is imperative that you heal as many as you can because every soul who enters this mansion cements the future of the world that Styx tried to obliterate. Practice your skills with a needle and thread, and prepare yourselves for your own battle within these four walls."

Hart then turns to Thanatos. "There will be no death if you can avoid it."

Thanatos bows his head at her. "I will try," is all he says.

I look at who remains.

Ares stands in the front, flanked on either side by his twin sons Phobos and Deimos. They wear similarly designed armor, with spears locked tight in their grasps and swords sheathed close to their hips.

Queen Persephone stands regally in her fighting armor in the darkest shade of purple. She still swears a diadem atop her head, but her long, brown locks are braided and slung over one shoulder. Cerberus stands proudly to her left, wearing a helmet on two of his three heads. Hypnos, one of the few gods who does not sport armor, stands to Queen Persephone's right. He wears his typical gray robe, and the hood covers his scarred face. He holds two bags, both emitting a soft blue glow. Hypnos spins them by their strings.

I wear simple silver armor beneath a white shirt, but my Caduceus garners anyone's primary attention. I elongated it, so it stands almost ten feet tall. My snakes around my Caduceus have come alive and slither around Maressa's arms, hissing at anyone but me if they get too close. Maressa doesn't balk in fright at the snakes, but she smiles and pets the top of their heads.

She wears a light pink chest plate, with a simple outfit underneath, but her bird wings peek out of the sides. She holds a sword in both hands, with her short black hair pulled up into two twin buns. Seeing her in her true form is new, but it is still breathtaking.

Farthest from everyone else is Raven and Hephaestus. They are both garbed head to toe in matching obsidian armor. Her long, black hair is in a ponytail that falls out of her helmet and blends into the chest plate. He holds a magnificent hammer that gleams gold like the sun, but it is a decoy to the true hammer who stands beside him. Raven holds what appears as an ordinary hammer, slightly taller than two feet, with a glowing teal raven at the center of the handle. The moment she touches her monikered bird, the hammer transforms into the weapon required to begin the war.

The two unlikely friends and social pariahs glance at one another and bump fists.

Lastly, farthest from me, are Diam, Dýnami, and Epiales.

Diam still bears the visible marks of a man with his heart ripped out of his chest, but he stands with his chin held high. He understands now why he cannot wallow in the grief of his love lost, because it is his destiny to lead the human prisoners away from the bloodshed. It is his destiny to pave the future of the world.

Diam holds twin curved swords in his hands, with golden blades, and beside him is Dýnami. They look nothing alike, but they are mirrors of one another. They both understand the importance of what comes next, and a friendship forged by death and trauma bonds the two warriors together. She holds a spear as tall and monstrous as her former one, but it is not godly-gifted or magenta-colored. Her former spear lays deep in the skull of the slain Typhon.

Both wear armor, and both bear scowls of determination and revenge on their lips.

Partially hidden behind them is Epiales. He stands less sure of himself amongst natural warriors. He forgot a time when he fought as well as all of us, with shadows that beckoned to his every command. In his hand, he holds a Stygian blade, but my eyes focus on the sliver of smoke curling around his wrists. He hasn't noticed it, but I see the glimpses of his magic returning.

Zeus slams his lightning bolt into the ground, and we disappear from the home of bones.

Light surrounds me in all directions as the storm takes us away from security and towards our inevitability. When the light subsides, my boots sink into wet grass across a flat plain so barren that even trees do not greet us upon our arrival. It is the perfect location to end this bloody war, where nothing but damnations of our creation will disturb us.

Across this plain, our army separates into four quadrants: the north, south, east, and west. Maressa, the muse, will sing her story on the far north of the battlegrounds, with Zeus, Persephone, Cerberus, and me protecting her long enough for Saffron to remind every god why we should fear her.

Saffron will enter from the east side with Hecate and an army of over twenty million humans forced into Styx's service.

On the south, ready to lead the humans away to safety, is our seeker. Diam readies for his journey with Dýnami beside him. Epiales stands there too, but his destiny differs from Diam's. He will stay in the south, fighting amongst the final horde of monsters. Ares, Phobos, and Deimos will remain beside Epiales, but there will be a time when they fall and only Epiales remains.

That is when his destiny as the hero will emerge.

Last, Hart stands on the west side of the battlegrounds with Hypnos, Raven, and Hephaestus. Hypnos' purpose in this battle is to stop any gods or titans who do not fall victim to Maressa's song by sprinkling them with his magic. We will dispose of them all until the only immortal on the western side of the battlefield is Styx.

"The moment we see Saffron emerge in green smoke, we begin." Zeus lock eyes with Maressa. "Be ready."

And now we wait to kill Styx once and for all.

# FORTY-TWO

SAFFRON

It was my decision, paved with good intentions and naivety, to enter the River Styx eighty-eight years ago and accelerate us towards this bloody war. It is only befitting that it is me who begins its end.

One day, if I was truly on Styx's side in this war, she would betray me. She would make me watch as she extinguished humanity, one brutal demise at a time, but for now, she wishes to placate me. She wishes to use my skills to murder gods until they are all gone and no one can compete for her throne.

So, she agrees to use my idea of an open field for the final war.

Styx, believing she has me on her side, does not want the opposing army to hide behind buildings or trees. She wants an open field where her terror can strike uninterrupted. "They will see you and try to run," Styx says. "We don't give them an option to run."

"I found the perfect location. It's in the center of the United States and stretches about five miles in all directions without even a hill in sight," Hecate informs. I bite back my grin. The very location Hecate finds is the one where Hart and my army stand at, waiting for us to arrive.

"Which gods are still free from the Dagger of Chains?" Styx asks me.

I answer honestly. "Zeus, Persephone, Hypnos, Thanatos, Ares, Phobos, Deimos, Hephaestus, and Hermes. Epiales is there as well, although no longer a god."

She does not ask which humans are alive, which further proves to be her fatal flaw, because we have the seer, the hammer, the seeker, and the muse among our army. All of them bleed red, but she preoccupies herself only with those who do, or once, bled gold.

"Kill Zeus first." Styx's voice remains eerily calm, even as she commands me to murder my biological father.

"Alright." We have never been close, so my lie easily leaves my lips without Hecate or Styx questioning my fealty.

"The others will die after Zeus, but they all perish. When they do, you get Hattie's soul back."

I should agree with everything Styx commands. I want her to believe I am on her side. Correction: I need her to believe every word that leaves my lips is for her cause, so she may sit eternally on Mt. Olympus's throne.

But on instinct, I blurt out. "I can't kill Persephone or Hermes."

Even stranger, at the same time I speak, Hecate says. "Not Hermes."

We lock eyes.

Neither of us were destined to be with Hermes forever, but we both have shared great, heartbreaking love with the god of mischief. We look so different, Hecate and me. She is all long limbs, bright eyes, and a thin physique. My body is shorter and curvier. One of my thighs alone is the width of both of hers together. Yet, the same god fell in love with the both of us. Yet, we still protect the same god who will forever hold a place in our hearts.

Styx sighs in aggravation. "Fine. Don't kill them. Immobilize them. The rest die."

Ares's face blinds my vision for a moment, but I must pretend. They do not know who Ares is to me, and it is safest for him if it stays that way. I lift my chin in the air, and I lie through my teeth. "Anything to get Hattie back."

"Then it is time." Styx looks at Hecate. "Bring our army forward."

Wisps of green and black smoke emit from Hecate's veins. It encompasses the surrounding ground, floating up and caressing our arms, neck, and hair. Soon, I'm enraptured by the tainted magic, but I can see the other members of Styx's army within the mist. Polyphemus, the infamous and most brutal cyclopes, stands beside the Minotaur. Centaurs like Nessus raise spears and swords in the air, laughing as a battle draws near. The worst surviving creatures, gods, and titans thrive in this green and black mist. I loathe standing beside them, but as I carve each face into my mind, I vow to ensure they all die tonight.

Styx's army is twenty times our size, but it is mainly because of the humans given black-tainted green weapons. Their bones jut out of their skin, and their eyes are hollow as they prepare for battle. They are victims in this war, just like humans are always the casualties in fights amongst gods.

Hecate transports us away, moving every immortal, monster, and human to the pre-discussed location. Hecate, the army of over twenty million humans, and I stand stationed on the eastern border of this twenty-mile battlefield. Styx tasks us with finding Zeus and killing anyone who interferes with our crusade.

The monsters, like Nessus, Polyphemus, and the Minotaur, are on the southern border. Their goal is simple: kill anyone in sight. They do not have a particular target, but their job is to create as much bloodshed as humanely possible. There are a hundred centaurs with Nessus and a dozen remaining cyclopes with Polyphemus.

Styx takes two immortals, Priapus and Oizys, and an army of three hundred Stymphalian Birds to the Western front. They will find Hart, and they will aim to kill the oracle who attempts to thwart every one of Styx's plans. Hart will wait for her there, with Hephaestus, Raven, and Hypnos.

Lastly, on the Northern front, are the few titans never released from Tartarus during Kronos's reign. They chose neither the gods' nor Kronos's side in the last war, but they now stand with Styx. Besides those few titans, there are a handful of low-level gods and goddesses. All are ready to find the Muse, the Hammer, and the Seeker and extinguish them.

As my vision disintegrates as the green smoke envelops every sense, I smile with victory because Styx and this army are oblivious. They do not know that my veritable army, with Hart at the helm, is waiting for us at this location. The moment the green mist evaporates, they will see the battlefield for what it truly is.

A trap.

And it will be too late.

There are only a few seconds where I'm encompassed in Hecate's smoke, and I swear I see Hattie's face within it. Perhaps guilt has finally warped my sanity, causing me to hallucinate what isn't there, but I open my mouth to say something to her. Anything while I finally have the chance.

I want to tell her I miss her.

Although it has only been a few days without her in my life, I can already feel her absence wrapping invisible hands around my throat. Suffocating me. I want to tell her she was my heart because she was a sister, not by blood, but by love. She's my heart because she was ultimately the reason I fought with the Olympians against Kronos.

She was my pair of eyes every time I went blind with indecision, fear, and anger.

I am the goddess of humanity because I loved Hattie and her race more than I had loved anything else in this world. Before I knew the magnitude of loving a romantic partner, Hattie taught me how to love unapologetically. She taught me love exists as a family. Family, you would die for a thousand times over.

I want to tell Hattie she is the reason I mastered my powers and gained the confidence to become who I am today. I want to tell her these things as an imaginary version of her stands in the smoke with me, but the green dissipates too quickly. She's gone too fast, and only one word escapes.

"Goodbye."

Too quickly, Hecate's magic evaporates, and we stand on the plains field. Millions of humans follow behind Hecate and me, waiting for further instructions with fear written across their brows. Although we are at least five miles away from every other section of this war, almost immediately, Hecate and I hear the screams.

"Was it worth it, Hecate?" I ask. "Was betraying almost every person you love worth resurrecting one life? Was destroying the world and most of humanity worth one life?"

"He's alive and safe back on Mt. Olympus," Hecate

responds slowly, and she attempts to sound stoic, but sadness laces her tongue. "He won't die in this battle."

"That doesn't answer my question."

"Is Hattie worth it?" She counteracts my question.

The screams surround us now, and the humans take a terrified step backwards.

"It's strange to say, but you, Phobos, and Deimos have known me longer than anyone left alive. You and I interacted more than I did with Phobos and Deimos. It was you who gave me my scraps of food, even when you knew it wasn't enough to stop the gnawing hunger. It was you who heard me cry every night for a world where humans were finally free." I surprise myself with the calm, sympathetic tone in my voice. Hecate deserves my sneers and hatred; instead, pity lines my words. "I may hate you, Hecate, but I also think you know me better than anyone in this world because you saw the most vulnerable side of me. A side desperate for a world of freedom."

I turn my body to face her. To truly see her. The black veins from Styx's corruption encompass both arms and snake up her neck. Soon, there will not be a fragment of the version of Hecate who loves Mastiff inside this walking experiment. Soon, Hecate will only be a vestige of Styx's magic. She will kill with only hatred flooding her vision, permanently turning her blue eyes black.

"Tell me, Hecate, is Hattie worth me joining Styx's side?"

I move faster than Hecate.

Before she can disappear in a puff of green smoke, my power wraps around each bone in her body, and I pull, mustering all my strength. Unlike every other immortal I've murdered, Hecate fights back. She tries to pull her bones back into her body, but I collapse to my knees, and I command all of her bones towards me.

Hecate crumbles onto the floor across from me, screaming as half a dozen bones fly out of her pale skin, then another dozen shortly after. She tries to wrestle her bones back inside, but it is a futile effort. Her skull pushes against her scalp, fighting fate before eventually relenting. The moment her skull lands in my hand, sticky with ichor, the rest of her bones come easily.

The skin and muscle that remain of Hecate crumble.

My screams, which are a permanent fixture of the air, grow louder upon Hecate's death. Killing Hecate has ruined any chance I had to see Hattie again. Her soul, like all the others who have died since the Underworld's destruction, thrashed into Hecate's body. Hecate was the only deity in this world who knew how to free those souls. To bring them back from death once more.

But I killed her, damning all those souls who perished to disappear with her.

We have lost so many lives, and now they will never be found.

When I killed Hecate for the betterment of mankind, I sealed the fate of not just Hattie, but I ensured I would never see Zig again. I damned all the huntresses, from Lamb to Sika, to never go to Elysium's gates like they deserved. My friends from when I was human, like Angel and Panda, are gone forever. They will never be in the Underworld, sipping on wine in Elysium. All the fallen soldiers of this world, who I loved, will not live again in the Underworld; their lives ended the moment I ripped Hecate's bones out of her body.

But Hart showed me why this death had to happen, even at the sacrifice of Hattie and the others' souls.

If I killed Styx on Mt. Olympus like I desired, then Hecate would have escaped in a plume of green smoke. As the goddess of necromancy, she would have dedicated her immortality to bringing Styx back to life. It would have taken three hundred and seventy-eight years, but Hecate would have brought Styx back to life and the war would start anew.

Hart showed me we would not win this war twice.

I had asked Hecate if Hattie was worth betraying the world and humanity because we both know that Hattie signified so much more than herself. Hattie was the reason I became the savior, and while she is gone, the rest of humanity isn't, and they need me to be their ray of hope. If I let the world crumble so I could keep Hattie with me, then I'd shatter everything Hattie helped this world achieve.

I am dripping in Hecate's golden blood when I turn around to face the millions of humans standing behind us. Their green-and-black misted swords disintegrated with Hecate's death, and the millions of starving, frightened humans stand collapse to their knees.

They all had to choose between certain death or joining Styx's army, and they opted towards survival. I stare at the decrepit, dehydrated humans kneeling in front of me, and I am brought back to the days when I was in the prison cells. I see each of them, shivering from both fear and starvation, and their faces morph into those with whom I spent my first eighteen years of life.

Upon the shivering faces, I see Glasswing and Angel. All the little kids whose shared the prison cell with me. The boy who tried to kill himself in the prison by banging his head against the cement wall. All the humans who I grew up with, and who all died premature deaths, are alive again in these humans' eyes.

"I'll never kill a human again, not for as long as I exist." I look down at the future of humanity. "We have lost trillions of humans in this war, and we will not lose a single more." I point towards the southern side of the battlefield and wait until many of them raise their heads to follow my movement. "Eventually, a man with a battle axe will come from this side of the war, and he will lead you to safety. Until your seeker arrives, I'll make sure no one harms you."

I remove my sword from its sheath, and I stand guard in front of the humans. They did not deserve to be shields for the gods. I am tired of allowing the humans to be our shields who bleed.

A gentle hand, hard with calluses and hard work, touches my calf. I look below me, and an elderly man looks up at me with tears in his eyes. "Thank you, Savior."

Another hand touches my shoulder. She's a woman in her early twenties, and she, too, says. "Thank you, Savior."

Another hand, and another, "Thank you, Savior."

Twenty million souls surround me, uttering the same three words. "Thank you, Savior."

I cry silent tears as I wait for Diam to arrive, while I thank Hattie for granting me the divine gift of being the goddess of humanity.

# FORTY-THREE

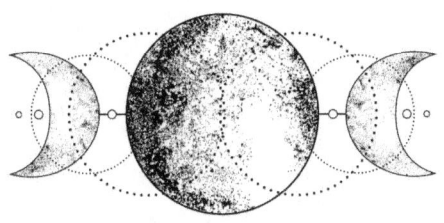

HECATE

G oodbye, Mastiff.
And thank you, Saffron.

# FORTY-FOUR

RAVEN

My first life was one of mistakes, where I had followed the wrong path and was rightfully gifted with death in return. My first life existed with the purpose of dying and riddled with mistakes, but as I stand beside a powerful god, clasping a weapon superior to the bows and arrows that never felt right, I know my purpose.

I am the hammer.

I'm here to change my story. No longer do I wish to the be an impatient woman with piles of mistakes. I wish to be the hammer ushering in an age of good.

I stand at the far west side of the battlefield and wait for the signal to attack. My hands tighten around the handle of the hammer as I search for a wisp of green smoke on the eastern front. Hephaestus stands beside me, holding a decoy hammer in case Styx's army attacks before I can strike.

He nudges me with his elbow. "Loosen up. You look ready to take a shat."

When Hephaestus pulled me away from the Battle of the Huntresses, where I was ready to die amongst my former sisters in retribution for my crimes, I expected to loathe him. I wanted my fate to be intertwined with the huntresses, even if it was only in death, but the prophecy had other plans for me. Hephaestus saved me, but not solely because he pulled me out of the burning prison where I intended to die.

When I returned from the Battle of the Huntresses, I could taste the acrid disappointment emanating from the home full of benevolent heroes. While Saffron's daughter Jamila lay comatose and beloved huntresses like Lamb died, I survived mostly unscathed. Even as the truth of my role in the prophecy came forth, everyone kept their distance from me. They ended conversations before I started them.

All except Hephaestus.

On the day before Hattie's death, Hephaestus came into my room and asked. "Do you want to learn how to blacksmith?"

Hephaestus let me help him make the two hammers, which we hold in our hands now. He isn't the greatest conversationalist, but when he talks, it is with profound wisdom. He makes me laugh, and doesn't treat me like a villain.

"Why are you so nice to me?" I ask him.

He grumbles his response. "Few like me, either. I'm too ugly, too lame, or too grumpy. I'm avoided when I enter a room, just like you, just because of the way I look. You can't kill me with an arrow to the skull, so I figured why not see if you're bearable to be around?"

I can still hear it sometimes. The *thwack* of my arrow lodging itself into Willow's skull. I fear I will never run fast enough to escape that sound.

"And what's the verdict? Am I bearable enough to be in your company?"

He grunts. "You'll do."

Our friendship developed so fast and so naturally that I wonder if I ever had a friend before him. When I began as a huntress, Willow and Lamb were always together, too inseparable to invite a third, lonely person into the fold. Artemis was cordial, but that was the extent. Cordial, not friendly. I made small talk with a few huntresses, like Reaper and Shikari, but nothing of substance.

With Hephaestus, it's easy.

Natural.

I grin up at him. "Maybe taking a shat would be the perfect distraction. Who is going to want to fight the girl who keeps crapping all around them?"

Hypnos glances at me with disgust, curling his lip. "I do *not* want to hear this conversation."

Hart only smiles ever so slightly as she fidgets with her gold feather necklace.

We stand upon a grassy plain, where not even a hill covers the fifteen-mile radius. The grass is shortly trimmed, as if someone expected a war to unfurl here, requiring a resplendent view before the inevitable destruction. Dark green smoke, desecrated by black vines within it, swirls out of the thinly cut grass. I glance at Hephaestus, who sees the smoke, and I nod my head once.

We do not speak as the moment my destiny cements itself into history. Adrenaline pumps through my body, threatening to rip my heart from my chest, because everything surrounding our success relies on me and this moment.

I lock eyes with Hephaestus, and I run towards him. I leap into the air, and my feet land perfectly into his awaiting palms. There is only one second to think, and this glimmering moment reminds me that, for once, I'm on the right side of a war. I do not listen to pretty words and sinful smiles. Instead, I hear Hermes's last words to me in my former life on repeat.

*"I think if you could reverse your actions, you would."*

And I do, Hermes.

I reverse my actions.

Hephaestus throws me a hundred feet in the air, and my finger grazes along the teal raven emblem on my hammer. Magic thrums to life the moment my finger caresses the emblem. The hammer grows to magnanimous heights, growing larger than me. It glints a blackish teal, and I can feel its power radiating off me and coursing through my veins.

It's impossible to explain, the magic overtaking me, with any other word but power. The overwhelming power vibrating along my skin feels right, and a bellowing cry leaves my lips as a horde of bronze-beaked birds rushes towards me. They are eager to stop my fate, but they're too late. There is no fear of death or regret as I crash-land, hammer first, into the ground.

The moment the black-and-teal hammer slams into the ground, I picture a volcano of gargantuan height. Lava oozes out of the crater, and an ash cloud larger than the entire spans of the battlefield forms. I hold the thought in my mind of a volcano of my creation, and my hammer obeys the harrowing command. As soon as my hammer crashes into the thinly cut grass, I imagine a volcano, and the ground rumbles in acquiescence.

The ground trembles around my feet, but I know I'm not in danger. This hammer beckons to my command. It is how Hephaestus and I crafted this invention. The hammer has the ability, when it hits a surface with a force hard enough to obey the command of its owner. So, when I collide onto the ground from a hundred feet in the air, instead of death, I demand a volcano.

It cracks the surrounding ground, and a bird's beak breaks through my shoulder. I bite back a scream as it pierces my flesh, burrowing its way through to tear my arm from my flesh. A flash of light blue crashes into the Stymphalian bird, and it quickly crumbles beside me, but it isn't dead. The bird snores, sleeping soundly as Hypnos's light blue magic infiltrates the tiny, yet lethal animal.

The volcano sprouts quickly and furiously, and I lose my balance. I tumble onto the ground, my behind hitting the grass, and I stare up at my creation. The base spans farther than I can see, growing from where I stand at the western front, and all the way towards the northern edge of the battlegrounds. The volcano's cone rumbles as it grows, reaching higher and higher into the air until I can scarcely see the crater on top.

My part in the prophecy is complete, but my role in this war is not. I grab my hammer, and I scramble to my feet just as a spear spirals towards my face. I yell as I spin my hammer towards the spear. The opposing weapon crashes into a thousand pieces the moment it connects with my godly hammer, and I'm running towards the fertility god who attempted to kill me.

Around me, Hypnos manifests his light blue sleeping powder into darts, and he throws them at the Stymphalian birds. They fall around him like raindrops, sleeping soundly on the floor, but even more rush towards him with their bronzed beaks glinting in the sunlight.

Hephaestus fights against Oizys, goddess of grief, and Styx at the same time. The women are quickly overpowering him, but in a blur of pale pink, Hart sprints past us towards the volcano and captures Styx's attention. Styx raises her hands in the air, black water beckoning to her command, as her eyes lock with Hart's retreating form.

Hart climbs up the length of the volcano as Priapus rushes towards me and Styx builds her magic until it creates a wave of black behind her. Oizys moves to impale Hephaestus, but then a sound causes all three immortals to pause. I have heard many beautiful singers throughout the years. I have attended galas where the muses sing in perfect harmony, and I have lived with Willow, whose voice was so beautiful that at first, I thought she was a descendant of a muse.

But no one holds a candle to the tune floating from the southern border of the battlefield.

A deep, soulful voice momentarily dissolves Saffron's eternal scream from the winds because even the air becomes so enamored by the woman's singing that it cannot focus on anything else. Priapus's hand pauses from manifesting another spear to attack me, and Oizys drops her weapon seconds before it reaches Hephaestus's chest.

Even Styx stumbles, her black river unable to obey her commands when her thoughts are no longer her own. Styx looks between the soothing voice and where Hart flees, and uncertainty roots her to the spot. Meanwhile, the music compels Priapus and Oizys, and they walk in a daze towards the southern border where the prophesied muse sings her last tunes.

Styx frantically screams as she sprints after Hart, ignoring Hephaestus and me altogether in her pursuit towards the oracle, who ruins all her plans. Hypnos barely glances away from his fight against the birds. They scarcely acknowledge the music gliding through the wind.

Hephaestus grabs my arm and tugs. "Move it!"

It is easier to fear death than embrace it fully, and I race beside my only friend with the daunting realization that to die for the right cause is greater than the promise of forever.

# FORTY-FIVE

HERMES

Silence smothers me on the battlegrounds as we wait for Styx's army to arrive.

Green smoke, polluted with black, swirls like a tornado. It's close enough that the wind rattles our hair and causes our stance to wobble. When the mist dissipates, standing in front of us are half a dozen titans. Astraeus, titan of dusk, stars, and astrology. Epimetheus, brother of Prometheus and titan of afterthought and excuses. Eurynome, a titaness of water-meadows. Iapetus, titan of mortality. Perses, Hecate's father and titan of destruction. And last, grinning wildly, is Momus, a spirit of mockery and scorn.

Maressa stands behind us all, beginning her song as Persephone, Zeus, Cerberus, and I attack the six immortals.

*"I am the muse who sings of your brutality,*
*The daughter of the goddess of tragedy.*
*Hear my words now,*
*Immortals who bow*

*To the river of pain,*
*To the goddess of hatred."*

A gigantic *boom* echoes across the plains as a monumental volcano manifests where there was once only smooth grass. Screams surround us as Caduceus slams into Momus's face, but the most poignant sound of all is Maressa. She uses her wings, which mirror a vulture's in shades of dark gray, to gain enough altitude in the sky that Zeus's clouds can mostly conceal her form.

It is there, high above in the sky, where Zeus's storm rises to magnanimous heights; she continues her song.

*"Come traitors now, to the plains you invaded.*
*Come traitors now, to the king you betrayed.*
*Come traitors now, so you may be slain.*
*Don't you wish now that you never followed her tirade?"*

Zeus has a lightning bolt in each hand, and he bellows as he strikes through Epimetheus and Eurynome's skulls. They collapse, but they will soon rise fully healed until Saffron arrives. Momus swipes at me with his sword, which I quickly evade, while Cerberus tackles Astraeus to the ground. Two heads bite into either side of Astraeus's neck. He tries to scream, only to choke on his blood. Persephone fights, blade to blade, against Perses. He snarls threats at her, but we can barely hear them above Maressa's hypnotic music.

Music that lures gods to their deaths.

Priapus and Oizys stumble in a daze towards our side of the battlefield, venturing farther away from Styx, just as we hoped. I slam my fist into Momus's chest, gripping onto his heart, as the two immortals nearer. They do not raise their weapons or dare to fight us, but they wander towards a voice more melodic than the rest.

*"Near closer, near closer, you foolish deceivers,*
*Near closer, near closer, where there are no healers.*

*Near closer, near closer, you malevolent god,*
*So I may watch you rot."*

Perses knocks Persephone aside with the front of his shield. The Queen of the Underworld stumbles to the ground, her face a mottle of ichor, while the powerful titan spins his attention towards the source of the music. He materializes two javelins that shine obsidian, and I abandon my fight against Momus. My winged sandals soar me through the air, and Momus doesn't have the speed to grab onto my ankles.

I catch one of Perses' javelins a foot away from Maressa's face, but the second one comes too quickly. My body barrels towards the weapon, and I accept its cruel touch for her. The javelin slides through my stomach, encapsulating me with pure agony, but I bite back the scream clawing at my throat. I rip the javelin out of my stomach, now glinting with my blood, and I chuck it back at Perses.

He easily evades it, but he focuses too much on Maressa and me. Persephone barrels towards Perses, knocking him to the ground, while I spin to face my soulmate. "When this is all over, I don't just want a date. I want to marry you, Maressa Holliday."

She stumbles on her next lyric, but I fly back down against my opponents before she can deign a response. Her music floats through the air as Priapus and Oizys move in a daze towards us. Her siren voice causes our enemies' movements to slow down. Their attacks grow sluggish, and they cannot deflect as easily.

Zeus smashes lightning bolts, one right after the other, against our opponents. They crumble to the ground, fried in the center of their chest, but they eventually rise again. I spin through the air, slamming my Caduceus against enemy flesh, but their bones heal too quickly. Their skin heals as quickly as I fly away. Persephone slices at their flesh, and Cerberus pounces on the immortals with canines dripping with ichor, but as long as Saffron is away, they will continue to stand back up.

Three more weapons fly towards Maressa, and I accept them all as my penance. We wait for two certainties, Saffron's carnage against our enemies and Maressa losing her voice forever, and I pray to the Fates that Saffron arrives first.

*"I am the muse who sings of your brutality,*
*The daughter of the goddess of tragedy.*
*Hear my words now,*
*Immortals who bow*
*To the river of pain,*
*To the goddess of hatred."*

I tackle Astraeus to the ground as he chucks a spear towards Maressa's face, but before I can reach her, Zeus throws one of his lightning bolts towards it. His spear obliterates the moment the lightning bolt touches it, and I slam Caduceus through Astraeus's throat. Ichor splutters in my face, but her voice centers me.

*"Come traitors now, to the plains you invaded.*
*Come traitors now, to the king you betrayed.*
*Come traitors now, so you may be slain.*
*Don't you wish now that you never followed her tirade?"*

Perses tackles me to the ground, and I jab my elbow into the side of his face. His arm lands on my throat, stealing the air from my lungs, as I kick in between his legs. He loosens his grip as he groans, and I knock him off me.

Surrounding screams join like accompaniment to Maressa's singing, and it is a prelude to what happens next. Oizys fires three arrows from her bowstring towards my muse.

*"Near closer, near closer, you foolish deceivers,*
*Near closer, near closer, where there are no healers.*

*Near closer, near closer, you malevolent god,*
*So I may watch you-"*

She never finishes the last lyric. I fly towards Maressa, but I am not quick enough. With the sword in her hand, she deflects one arrow. Another whisks past her ear, narrowly avoiding her face, but the third arrow lands with a *thump*. The arrowhead worms into her throat, and I scream where she cannot.

Maressa's wings shudder at the pain, but I'm there to catch her when she tumbles from the sky. My arms wrap tight around her, and I defy the speed of light as I soar out of the battlefield with her. The second I look away from Maressa on our journey away from the bloodshed, I see many travesties on the battlefield.

On the eastern front, Saffron stands surrounded by millions of humans. Beside her is a puddle of golden blood, and I know it is Hecate's remains. There is a minuscule part of me who mourns the woman she used to be before desolation poisoned her like a plague.

The Hecate I once knew, who I once loved, died the moment she joined Styx's side. I loved the version of Hecate, who smiled when the rain fell and danced whenever she had the chance. I loved the version of Hecate who understood the value of loyalty, who loved her friends unapologetically, and who spun her magic for good rather than evil.

From today until the end of time, I will mourn the version of Hecate who died by Styx's noxious hatred. Today is not that day. Today, I fly over a monumentally tall volcano, where Hart sprints towards the top in a pale pink dress. Styx runs furiously behind Hart, but closely after her are Hephaestus and Raven. Styx simultaneously races after Hart and fights Raven and Hephaestus in a blur of black river water and hammers.

The last images I see before I'm too far from the battle-grounds are Diam and Dýnami running towards where Saffron waits with the humans, and the four men who stay behind. Epiales faces a horde of centaurs and cyclopes without fear, but a growing rage of shadows surrounds him. The fear I once felt for him and his shadows obliterates with his best friend in my arms, and I soar away with two wishes.

One, that Epiales destroys them all.

And two, that the Fates let me keep Maressa a little while longer.

# FORTY-SIX

## ERIK A.K.A. EPIALES

I see the green smoke surround the miles long battleground. Witness fierce monsters materialize in front of me, and I feel the ground rumble as a hammer slams into it, forming a twenty-foot-tall volcano.

Everything happens around me, but I stand still.

Too still.

Nothing makes sense, even as fragmented pieces of my former life try to click into the empty spaces in my mind like a puzzle. There are too many missing parts. Ares and his twin sons run towards the danger, their weapons slashing through the air. But even as Maressa's singing voice draws the traitorous gods near her, I cannot move my feet.

Diam and Dýnami stand back-to-back, facing the monsters nearing them with determination on their faces, rather than the fear that must play upon mine. They have lost their soulmates and all their friends, yet they stand together, as centaurs run towards them with spears and swords. How can they, who have lost so much, be more courageous than me?

Saffron told me I was her hero, but I'm a carcass of what I once was. All that remains of my former self is an exoskeleton of cowardice, and I don't know how to be the hero. A hundred centaurs surround Dýnami and Diam, and they will probably die before he can fulfill his prophecy as the seeker. Ares faces the biggest cyclops of them all, Polyphemus, while his twin sons fight a dozen other cyclopes. They cannot die, but the cyclops will surely try to kill them.

And I'm supposed to be some hero.

Have I ever known what it meant to be a hero? Because all I have seen of my true self are atrocities after atrocities. I close my eyes, and I see the moment Glasswing falls into the River Styx with Saffron. I see the moments where Hermes screams with unwavering fear and pain, while I grin with glee. Saffron calls me a hero, but I feel as if I am only a monster.

Maressa's voice is soothing across the battleground, and I want to succumb to it because I'm so tired of this world. I must have lived a thousand lifetimes because I'm drained to spend another day in this existence. My knees buckle, threatening to fall to the floor and accept whatever death this battle gives to me, but then I see her.

Saffron.

I barely recognize her blurry silhouette from the miles separating us, but I know it's her. She is a beacon my eyes always obey, even if I only remember her brown hair in the sand and her luminescent smile in the darkness.

Everyone else hears her screams in the wind, forever a fixture, but I replay the stories she's told me instead. Her soothing voice hums through the wind and the air, kissing across my exposed flesh. *"You were my first love, and gods, I wish you remembered that, too. Our love was like a fire, burning and extinguishing so fast, but as long as you remember you are not a villain, but a hero, then that will suffice."*

Phobos flies, his face covered in blood and broken bones, and he lands on the ground in front of me. His body is oddly bent, and he doesn't immediately get up and heal. He groans on the ground as three cyclops walk towards us, grunting and laughing at the distorted state of their opponent.

They are all over twenty feet tall, hideous and gripping cudgels. When they grin and laugh, their razor-sharp teeth display pieces of fresh, human flesh. Ichor stains their mouths, and my eyes flit back to Phobos on the ground. His throat, collarbone, and exposed shoulder wear bite marks.

*"When you watch one hero display an act of such bravery, you wish to become a hero yourself."* Instead of listening to Maressa's hymn, I focus on Saffron's calming voice floating towards me. *"And in this time of war, I believe we need more heroes now than ever."*

The cyclops saunter near, and in the back of my mind, I see black wisps of smoke begging me to summon them. I hear Saffron's voice, hear her laugh, and I invite the smoke to envelop me. It changes my clothes, creating an obsidian armor made solely from the smoke. It manifests an all-black sword as tall as I am, and when my hands curl around the handle, it feels familiar. The smoke snakes around my arms, but it seeps towards the floor too.

Soon, the black smoke blankets the entire floor of the southern battleground, but I can still see perfectly. There are gasps and screams of confusion, but I only hear her.

My Saffron.

*"Maybe instead of a baker who tries to make cookies in a muffin tin, you can be a hero instead."*

429

I run towards the three cyclops who approach Phobos and me, and as I slice one cyclops's head off, a memory returns. It's a kiss shared between Saffron and me inside a hut that I know I created for us. My grin shines brightest within the smoke as I plunge my sword through another cyclops's heart, because with each heroic act I make, another memory of her comes back.

Saffron dancing with me.

When I kill a third cyclops, I feel her fingertips dancing across my tattoos with reverence.

I help Phobos to his feet as he stammers. "How do you have your powers back?"

I can only grin back at him. "Go help with the remaining cyclopes. You should be able to see through the smoke well enough."

Phobos stares at me, wanting answers to his questions, but eventually he pulls himself away and runs towards his brother and father. I dart in the opposite direction, where Dýnami and Diam wait for me. Dýnami is on the floor. Blood coats most of her abdomen and legs, but even in a kneeling position, she doesn't stop fighting. She plunges her spear through one centaur's thigh, as another slaps her across the face.

She grins as blood coats her mouth. "You hit like a bitch."

The same centaur who slapped her unsheathes a sword, and my smoke obeys a command I do not need to say aloud. Daggers made of my smoke spin towards the centaurs surrounding Dýnami, slamming into each of their skulls. It takes all Dýnami's strength, but she rolls away as each of the half-horse, half-human men fall around her.

Diam fights seven of the centaurs on his own, with a curved sword in each hand and blood sliding down both temples. It is not his destiny to die on this battlefield, surrounded by nearly a hundred centaurs, but it is mine. Memories of Saffron and me swarm back with each centaur I kill, and with each heroic act. If this is my penance before my death, then I'll gladly pay it.

Because I finally see the bits of good in my former life as Epiales.

I was good only for her.

For Saffron.

I was a monster. A villainous cretin who cared only about destruction and revenge for the crimes against me, but then I met her. Then, I realized that revenge is not nearly as sweet as true love. I died for her once, and as I push Dýnami and Diam away to fulfill his end of the prophecy, I will happily die for her a second time.

I will be a hero to her one last time.

My smoke and I work together as an extension of myself, and I use it as a whip through the air. Centaurs surround me, and with each three I kill, one inflicts harm. I'm stabbed in the shoulder as I strangle life out of three centaurs with my smoke. One centaur slices the Achilles tendon on my right foot as my sword impales one centaur's eye and another's skull.

Yet, each kill I make and each injury I sustain gives me another moment with her. We were a combination of love and stories, and in my last minutes in this world, I get to relive all those moments with her like they are the first time. Her declarations of love, her kisses, her stories, her smile, her hugs, and everything about her.

I have loved Saffron, my queen, from the first time I laid eyes on her and as the final living centaur slices a sword across my throat.

My smoke grabs the centaur's neck, breaking it, and we crumble onto the floor together. My red blood creates a river around me, but I'm not dead yet. Barely, I can make out the final cyclops, Polyphemus, facing against Ares, Phobos, and Deimos. As soon as I see Ares, another memory floods in. A conversation I had with Kronos, who told me long ago that Ares was Saffron's third love. I didn't know then, or now, how he knew this information, but I knew it was the truth.

Death crawls nearer me as my body becomes so cold, and I reach out for my smoke one more time.

For my queen.

My smoke creates a javelin that soars through the air. Polyphemus, with his limited eyesight paired with the black mist I surrounded our battleground in, cannot see his death until it strikes. My javelin of smoke pierces the back of his skull and pokes out of his eye socket.

Polyphemus, the last monster in the battle, falls to his knees and dies face-first into the dirt. Faintly, someone screams my name. I realize it is Ares when he runs towards where I lay on the ground, but he won't get to me in time. I stare at the sky, wishing there were stars to keep me company in my last seconds alive because I won't come back to life a third time.

This is it.

My last story.

But I will die a hero a second time for my Saffron.

I have told Saffron that I would die a thousand deaths to ensure she never suffered one, and while this isn't my thousandth death, I know I would die more times over for her. Her smile plays in the graying clouds above me, and the last two words I hear in the wind before death takes me for one last journey is her voice in the wind.

"My storyteller," she says.

I die peacefully, knowing I was her hero once more.

And that seems like the perfect way to go.

# FORTY-SEVEN

## HART

While others wear battle armor to our penultimate war, I wear the outfit I wore when I first met Apollo. My mind has no time to ponder how unusual I look, wearing a full face of makeup, a pale pink sundress, and ten-year-old tennis shoes splattered in paint and holes. I sprint up the length of a volcano, ignoring the burning sensation in my lungs as Styx's steps grow nearer.

"You foolish, ignorant child!" Styx screams, her composure crumbling like the volcano beneath our feet. "Your ruination is coming, and I won't make it swift!"

I glance back at her the moment she whips around, momentarily stops running, and releases a wave of black river water from her hands. Hephaestus leaps in front of Raven, and he strikes the water with his hammer with a ferocious scream. The blackened river collapses under the weight of his hit, but Styx does not stop. She spins back to where I run, and she sprints after me.

Every dozen steps, she spews a threat to me, then spins around and attacks Hephaestus and Raven. Sometimes, curiosity draws my gaze back towards them, but most of the time I use her distraction to my advantage to apply distance between us. Eventually, Raven and Hephaestus will not accompany me on this journey to the top of the volcano, and I need their distraction for as long as possible.

The higher I rise to the top of the volcano, the stronger the smell of burned rubber becomes. My tennis shoes, which are old and tattered, dissolve under the rising heat. Yet, I do not slow down. Even as sweat lines my brow and my breathing grows more haggard, I keep going. My hand wraps around my gold feathered necklace, and with Aashritha and the other oracles' voices encouraging me, I run.

All around me are travesties I saw coming weeks prior. I hear every bone in Hecate's body fly out of her flesh, the thump of an arrow lodging into Maressa's throat, and the crash of Epiales's body falling to the ground and never rising again. Ares screams, mourning a man who helped shape his soulmate into the person she's become, and I know a warrior manifests from Epiales's death. Yet, the carnage does not end with those three souls.

Hephaestus screams behind me, and I whirl my head around to face Styx's rage. She is about half a mile behind me, with her back facing me. She shapes her river into three snakes, and they all race towards Raven, who uses her godly-gifted hammer to smash into one snake's head. The water dissolves into the volcano the moment the hammer touches it, but the other two river snakes attack faster than she can counteract.

While one touch from Styx's river causes unimaginable pain to gods, humans will either die or become nearly impenetrable by the water. Achilles is proof of the powers of the River Styx. When he was a babe, his mother Thetis took him to the River Styx. She dipped Achilles into the water, holding him by his heel. It made him invincible, except for the heel which his mother held as she dunked him into the cold depths. He could not die from a stab wound to the chest, but one arrow in his heel ended his life.

There is no in between for humans, and Styx's cursed river has only gifted one hero with power in three thousand years. Only Achilles, while the rest have thrashed in pain, growing insane from the river's touch, before perishing. One snake grazes her ankle, and Hephaestus yells for Raven.

In such a short time, the war has bound Hephaestus and Raven together. The two ostracized souls found kinship in each other. So, when the river grazes Raven's skin, Hephaestus grabs ahold of Raven and propels them off the volcano. He uses his own body as a shield to stop the fall from killing her, but as they flee, I'm left alone with Styx.

Styx whirls to face me, eyes locking with mine despite the distance, and I sprint faster. At first, I have distance on my side. Styx's miles' long fight with Hephaestus and Raven has drained her, and she doesn't have the strength to propel her black river far enough to touch me. She doesn't spew threats or attempt to murder me because all she can muster is the strength to catch up.

My throat burns, and the smoke from the crater cloys my lungs, but I refuse to slow down. I refuse to stop, as my fate is at the top of this volcano. I reach the vent before Styx, but her words follow me to the fiery rim.

"For three thousand years, I have prepared for this moment, and you believe you can best me? I've existed for eons. Long before your ancestors even knew how to create fire. I am wiser than you, girl. There is nothing. *NOTHING*. You can do to stop my reign from coming forth. You are a worthless, pathetic human."

Styx stops her threats the moment she reaches the top, and our eyes lock. It would be so easy for Styx to dispose of me right now. I have no weapon except the power of foresight, and I stand in front of a volcano that can swallow my body whole. Even without knowing that I am now immortal because of my marriage with Apollo, Styx is still stronger than me. She is still more powerful than I will ever be.

Yet Styx doesn't immediately dispose of me.

She takes a few more steps, prowling towards me like a lion stalks a gazelle. Lazily. Overly confident. "You are such a docile little thing, aren't you? Yet, you thought you could take the world from me. You are barely old enough to understand the gravity of who I am, yet you sought to destroy everything." Styx *tsks* at me as she nears closer, and I let her. I do not stumble away or flinch the moment her hand caresses the side of my face.

I stay eerily still as I whisper. "May I have my last words before the volcano takes me?"

"You tried to best me, but when you cannot hide behind the coattails of gods, you realize the truth." She leans closer, her nose brushing against mine, and I feel the cold, noxious caress of her breath against my lips. "That you are nothing but a human pretending to play god."

"Hubris. That is what you accuse me of," I conclude.

Styx slides her jagged fingernails down my cheek, threatening to nick my flesh. "You try to play a god's game. What other name best defines your crime but hubris?"

"Hubris is one of the worst acts a human can commit against a god. Because if a human believes they are better than a god, then what use are gods at all?"

I half expect Styx to silence me with death, but she humors my last words. I think she lets me speak because she hopes that when my speech ends, I will see my death staring back at me and find fear within its depths.

"The crime of hubris only has one punishment. Death. Not even if your pretty god will save you from that fate," Styx says.

"Oh, of that I'm certain. Apollo cannot save me now, but while I commit hubris talking to you, you have committed a much worse crime."

"You must be more specific, girl. There are many crimes a god can commit in their eons' long existence."

"Underestimation is the opposite side of hubris's coin. While I commit the crime of hubris by believing some humans are better than some gods. Like, how Lamb is better than Uranus, whose hand she cleanly and easily sliced off. Or how I believe I am better than you."

"Careful, girl," Styx snarls.

I continue. "You commit the crime of underestimation. You believe no human is better than any god. Worse, you believe no human can change the fabric of your world. Like Pyro, a human boy who Gareth French decapitated in your prison cells under your command. You thought him inconsequential because of the color of his blood, but he was one of Saffron's first friends in this world."

Styx does not hear it, but I do.

The silencing of every single titan and god at the bottom of the volcano. Saffron rips out every single one of their bones the moment Diam leads the humans to safety, where their eyes cannot see the carnage her hands can inflict. She commits mass murder, simultaneously with only a snap of her fingers, and now she flies towards us.

Styx has her back to Saffron's levitating form, oblivious to her arrival as I continue my last speech. "Like Zig, the ferryman of the Underworld, who Saffron loved like a brother. Sika, who trained Saffron when she was a scared human girl. Lamb, who gifted Artemis with the greatest friendship and immeasurable courage. Like Hattie, who Saffron loved enough to make an oath with a goddess of hatred in order to protect."

Realization stiffens Styx's body, and her hand falls from my jaw. She turns her body to face Saffron, who levitates in the air above the furious volcano vent, and she holds out her hands. All of Styx's allies bear witness to Styx's demise, as bones circle around Saffron's head like a crude crown.

"You are an instrument of hatred and decay," Saffron seethes as she paralyzes Styx with her power over her bones. "Because of you, I must live without the pieces of myself that make me whole. Because of you, I must exist long enough to forget what Zig's smile looks like. To forget the sound of Sika's laugh. To forget what Lamb's voice sounds like. I will forget details of Hattie's face until all that remains is a vague outline. And I'll forget pieces of Epiales's stories, and oh, how I love him more for the stories he told. You did this, and for that, you will die today."

I wrap my arms around Styx's body, hugging her from behind, and I whisper the last sentence she will ever hear. "All will crumble like Pompeii."

We stand on the very edge of the volcano's mouth, and I tilt my body backwards. Styx screams, trying to wrench herself from my arms, but Saffron paralyzes Styx. I tilt backwards until gravity finishes my job. With my arms encompassing Styx's body, we tumble down into the depths of the magma.

I used to fear just about everything. The dark. Clowns. Spiders. Giraffes. And everything in between.

I wore a whistle like a necklace when I was a kid, and

all my classmates would laugh at my expense. I would blow the whistle anytime something scared me, no matter how small or large. During a fire drill, I feared the possibility of smoke and fire so terribly that I would not stop blowing my whistle outside, even once the alarms lessened.

On my tenth birthday, my dad took me to a jewelry shop to replace the whistle with something better. On the way to the store, Dad told me this beautiful story about the goddess of victory, Nike. While Saffron was my dad's favorite goddess, he knew I needed a goddess like Nike on my side.

He told me that Nike had golden wings, ones that were a mile long and as sharp as blades. "She's the goddess of victory because of those wings, little Hart," my dad said with an easy-going smile upon his face. "For the golden wings have a power. Do you know what it is?"

I was eight at the time, so I didn't know that he was lying to me. My dad's eyes sparkled when they looked at me, a fake look of surprise etched on his face. "You don't?!" My dad dared to gasp, and he took one hand off the wheel to hold his heart. "It's one of the single greatest stories in Greek history!"

It was then that he spun a story that, even to this day, I believe despite knowing better. My dad told me Nike's wings would absolve anybody of their fears. Countless demi-gods, humans, and monsters alike have tried to steal just one feather, hoping to possess the ability to be fearless.

We walked into the jewelry store and waiting for us was a chain with a golden feather in the middle. My dad bent low until his lips were right next to my ear, and he whispered. "That's why I wear this necklace." Dad grips the feather necklace he wears every day and squeezes hard. "I prayed to the goddess Nike when I was your age for a single golden feather, so I could be brave, and she gave it to me."

"Do you think she would give me one, too?" I asked, my voice coming out like a whistle because of a few missing baby teeth.

Dad grinned widely. "I prayed to the goddess last night, asking for just one of her feathers for my daughter, and she said that we could come here to get you a matching one so you could be fearless too."

Even as I grew older and knew that my dad lied to me to help me, this necklace was my elixir whenever the fear became too overwhelming. To this day, the small piece of jewelry stays on my skin, and today in particular, I hold on to the gold feather for strength when all I fear is trepidation.

I keep both my arms tight around Styx's, but my eyes flicker between Saffron's sobbing face above me and the gold feather necklace. My dad may have lied about the story of fearlessness gifted to me by a single feather, but I feel fearless now. As the magma singes off my clothes, burning its way through my skin, I smile because I can feel the weight of my gold necklace against my chest.

I mouth, "Now."

And Saffron obeys.

She rips out every bone in Styx's body, but I keep my arms tight around every piece of her. It is my torturous fate. My foresight showed me every version of this war, and if I did not live in the magma chamber with Styx's remains, then someone would bring her back to life. Because I married Apollo, I am immortal, so I will not die on my mission to guard Styx's remains.

It is the only way Styx will remain gone.

The other oracles, who live inside my head, materialize in a circle around me. They hold pieces of Styx's bones, and they smile at me. We cannot speak in our eternal prism, but I swear I can hear how proud they are of me. Aashritha is closest to me, wearing an identical gold feather necklace, and she almost makes me forget about the pain.

I was so scared when I first learned I would die in the pit of a volcano, but as everything else melts away, and I hold the bones and muscles and skin that once made up Styx's remains, my gold necklace and I remain.

It stops me from fearing my eternity.

Just like my dad promised me.

# FORTY-EIGHT

SAFFRON

S tyx's death required a sacrifice on our side.

And that sacrifice had to be Hart.

Kind, artistic Hart. Apollo's soulmate. Apollo's wife.

When she first showed me the vision of the ultimate battle, I wanted to fight against her fate. She knew she would die for weeks, but she did nothing to avoid it. That is when she showed me every other alternative to the war. In every scenario where she lived, either Apollo died or it was only temporary because Styx won and destroyed us all.

Everything makes sense now, even if the truth shatters what remains of my heart.

Why I had to bring Epiales back to life, why Hattie had to be my prophesied heart, and why a cataclysmic event like the crumbling of Pompeii became our guide towards survival. I let the bones of our enemies fall to the ground, where they previously hovered over my head like a crown, as my gaze drifts to two running forms.

Diam and Dýnami, twin flames of the same broken

heart, run with millions of humans towards freedom. Diam leads the charge, while Dýnami stands in the back. Blood follows her every step, which the three remaining centaurs follow, like a trail made just for them. Epiales destroyed every other monster, and his body lays around a circle of corpses as proof. His shadows, which returned to him when he needed them most, keep his desecrated body company. They stay to protect him one last time.

For as long as the world spins, I will love Epiales. Never again will I let the world forget his existence. From today until my eternal last, I will tell the tales of the Storyteller who became a hero for one goddess.

Dýnami's wounds make her gait slower than Diam's and the other humans, so she stops. I fly towards where Dýnami stands against three centaurs, and I reach out my hand for their bones. She spins her spear and grins at the faces of her adversaries. Dýnami slams her spear into one centaur's throat, but as she rips it out and a shower of blood splatters her face, another centaur thrusts his sword into her side.

I rip out the remaining centaurs' bones the moment the blade punctures her stomach. The centaurs lay in a heap around Dýnami, and she crumbles beside them a moment later. I collapse to the ground by her, cradling her in my arms, and she surprises me with her grin. The remaining immortals, like Persephone and Ares, run after Diam and the humans to provide aid, but Zeus stays with me and Dýnami. Cerberus, Hypnos, Phobos, and Deimos join close behind.

I do not ask where Hephaestus and Hermes are, or where Raven and Maressa are. My only concern at this moment is Dýnami, who wraps her bloodied hand around mine. As she lays in my arms, I see the multitude of wounds she accumulated in the battle. She has a deep gash along her thigh that has stained her entire pants' leg red, as well as a nick on her neck and three stab wounds on her shoulder and back. It is a miracle she hasn't bled out yet, but the Fates' scissors are nearing ever closer to her thread of life.

"Do you think I will see her?" Dýnami asks. "Will Sika be there when I open my eyes again?"

Dýnami dies before I answer, and I'm grateful for this small mercy.

Because I whisper after she dies, "they won't be reunited."

"Who won't?" Zeus asks, his voice gravelly with sympathy.

He does not care to learn more about Dýnami. He didn't care to talk to her, laugh with her, or understand the gravity of her heartbreak. But I do. I know how Sika and Dýnami loved each other in a way only soulmates could, and Sika died before Hecate. Her soul left her body in a white orb, which entered Hecate's body the same way Hattie's and Zig's soul did. Dýnami's afterlife will begin in the Underworld, but Sika won't be waiting for her.

Sika's soul is gone forever.

The war is over, but at what cost?

Because with all the deaths that create a bloodied time-line of this war, I don't think anyone is the winner.

"Let's go back to my house. Dýnami deserves to be buried."

I wait for him to strike his lightning bolt in the ground between us, propelling us away from the battle where so many have died. I do not have the strength to look back at Epiales's body again, so I stare only at Dýnami, who looks so peaceful in death.

Zeus stands in front of me and softly says, "Saffron."

I look up at my biological father, who I stopped seeing

as anything but the reason behind my creation. Hades is my true father because he never wanted my death. He only wanted to love me the way a father should love a daughter unconditionally. Zeus's praise has always come with conditions and expectations too high for anyone to reach.

We barely look alike, him and me. We share the same sharp chin and lips, but that is all I can notice. His eyes are the blazing blue of his brothers, while mine are the quiet brown of my mother's. His hair is as white as snow, with no sign that he ever bore a dark shade, while mine is the color of chestnut. A shade, I have learned, that is identical to my mother's. I adopted her sharp cheekbones and warm smile, stealing all her traits. The god in front of me bears fewer similarities to me than my adoptive parents.

"I'm sorry," he says so quietly, it almost dissolves in the screaming winds. I try to find my voice, to question why he's decided that now on a battlefield is the best time for a century-late apology. But the words never come to fruition. I simply gawk at Zeus as he bows his head and whispers. "I made the same mistakes my father and his father made when I tried to kill you, and there hasn't been a moment where I have woken up without regret for that decision. My daughter, if I must lose my crown, you are the best one to pick it up. I'm endlessly sorry that it took me so long to realize that."

He walks a few hundred feet away from me, and he picks up Epiales's corpse. He created a river of red around him, but he didn't die in vain. Epiales killed a horde of cyclops and centaurs, and he died a hero. I have always known Epiales is a hero at heart, but Zeus's actions and the old world's environment shaped Epiales into a mold that never fit him.

The mold of a villain.

I hope in his last moments he realized he wasn't evil,

like his nightmares tricked him into believing. He was fractured but beautiful. A story meant to uplift rather than discourage.

Zeus carries him gingerly in his arms, like there has never been a rift between them. He looks at me and says. "I'm sorry for your loss."

Zeus lays him on the ground near me, and only then do I look at Epiales's face. Death doesn't suit him, despite suffering its touch twice. I extricate myself from Dýnami and crawl towards Epiales. I lay his bloodied face in my lap, and my tears fall silently on top of his head.

Despite Zeus being here, I lean down and kiss the top of Epiales's forehead and whisper a goodbye to my first love. "I love you today, tomorrow, and every day, my imperfectly perfect storyteller. May I always find you in the stars."

Zeus kneels beside me and whispers. "Why the stars?"

"Why do you care?" I snap back, but it holds less anger than usual.

"Because I'm a terrible father for not saying it earlier, but I do love you."

"It's how we always find each other," I whisper back. "We would always look into the stars and find pieces of each other within them."

"What shape, my daughter?"

I look at Zeus. "What?"

"It won't make up for everything I've done to you, but let this be a start. I'll put him in the stars for you. Just tell me what shape you want his constellation to be, and it will be done."

I surprise myself when I envelop him in a hug, but Zeus hugs me back tightly. He isn't the father figure I first think of because Hades is my father by love, but perhaps somewhere in our future, Zeus and I can be civil. We can even be family. Zeus squeezes me tight and places a kiss on top of my head.

"A crow," I say through my tears. "Let him be in the shape of a crow."

His corpse disappears from my arms, but he isn't gone. His soul flutters up towards the sky. I cannot see him yet, since it is daytime, but instead of transporting away, we walk the rest of the journey home. Zeus gingerly carries Dynami, and we trek through the woods back to my house of bones.

We walk until nighttime shines down upon us in a clear sky. In a space between the Hercules and Draco constellation, a crow shape appears. Zeus might not understand my love for Epiales, but he stares at the night sky in remembrance of the hero he became.

"He hated the Underworld." I do not know why I confess this to Zeus, who has never cared about Epiales, but the words pour out. "He preferred the oblivion I provided by murdering him because to him, anything was better than the Underworld. It was his prison for hundreds of years, and you finally freed him. Thank you."

Only then does Zeus transport us back to the house, where we equally mourn our losses and celebrate our bittersweet victory.

# FORTY-NINE

SAFFRON

*Five Days After the Battle of Pompeii*

For three days following the Battle of Pompeii, my home was a circus of pain and confusion. The millions of humans Diam lead away from the battlefield, who are all that remains of humankind, fill up my infirmary, my kitchen, and my dining hall with their multitude of injuries. Styx, Hecate, and their minions tortured these humans for days. Their bodies hold hundreds of mutilated scars, reminiscent of scarification marks from when I was a human slave.

We do not sleep for three days straight.

Zeus, Persephone, Thanatos, and I work on stitching every wound and cleaning every injury. Hermes, Ares, Phobos, and Deimos constantly search for more supplies. They provide food and drinks to everyone while stocking our infirmary with various gauzes, needles, and blood bags. Hypnos constantly bounces between humans to gift them with sleep, while Hephaestus and Raven dig more and more graves behind the house for the humans we cannot save and those whose bodies we brought here after the war ended.

Dýnami lays in a freshly dug grave in my background, while Hart's grave is empty, but for the first three days, I do not have the time to focus on their deaths. I cannot spare time to cry and grieve as I suture another wound and hold another traumatized human as they scream in their sleep, thrashing and threatening to reopen wounds.

On the fourth day, I finally sleep for twenty-six straight hours. Ares lies beside me, with one arm draped over my waist. We do not talk about us yet, not with Epiales's death so fresh a wound, but we sleep beside one another to stop the impending nightmares.

Now, five days later, most of the humans' agony diminishes.

My scream still exists in the wind, mirroring the heartache I feel now as the realization of everything we've lost comes to light. Ares is there, though. He stays close as I get ready for the day in a simple red tunic. He helps me put on a pair of gladiator shoes, delicately tying the back string so they don't fall.

Together, we walk to the living room, where Diam sits in a wheelchair, with a cast around both legs and the Dagger of Chains in his hands. He broke bones in both legs while running and fighting through terror to get the humans back here safely, but they're here because of him. Humanity will live because of him. Everyone who remains stands in a circle around Diam and the Dagger.

Phobos and Deimos huddle closely together, nervously waiting for their mom's return. Hermes has an arm wrapped around Maressa's shoulder as they stare ahead. A gauze bandage wraps around Maressa's neck from her near-death experience with an arrow through her throat. If she was not a demi-god, then she would have bled out. Luckily, and with a bit of mischief on her side, she survived her wound.

She has yet to speak in the five days since her injury.

Hypnos and Thanatos lean their bodies on opposite sides of the infirmary room doorframe. They refuse to stray far from Jamila and the severely injured humans, but they watch the return of their family. Hephaestus and Raven stand farthest from everyone, outcasts amongst the heroes and the gods, but at least Hephaestus is no longer alone in his ostracization. Nobody deserves to be in a world without a friend. Persephone pets Cerberus's middle head as she anxiously waits for my dad to burst free of the Dagger of Chains. Zeus stands on either side of Persephone and me, his gaze snagging between the Dagger and Ares's arm around my waist.

We all wait with bated breaths as Diam speaks the incantation that frees them all.

Dionysus flies out of the dagger first.

He collapses onto his knees, his arms wound tightly around his body, as he shivers away the nightmares awakening within his imprisonment. Persephone is quick to run to him, wrapping a blanket around Dio's thin build.

Dionysus's purple eyes stare up at Persephone with tears brimming, and he asks only one question with both hope and heartbreak. "Claudius, is he here?"

Claudius died a traitor the same night Hattie died. He was one of the few humans who came into the house intending to murder all the humans inside. Claudius was one of the nameless ten humans I killed that night in my blind rage, but none of us divulge the full truth. When silence falls, it is a harrowing answer to his question. He sobs into Persephone's chest, heaving and shaking as the gravity of his soulmate's betrayal registers.

Hypnos walks towards them and places a gentle hand on Dionysus's shoulder. "Would you like to sleep it off, my friend?"

Dionysus stares up at Hypnos with such anguish, and he simply nods his head. Hypnos leads Dionysus to a bedroom, but in the nearly quiet mansion, all of us can hear the mixture of Diam's incantation and Dionysus's cries of betrayal.

Next, Hestia emerges from the Dagger. She stumbles out, but before she falls, I catch her in my arms. Saddened eyes stare at me, pooling with tears, and she asks. "Where is Dionysus?" Her lips tremble as she whispers. "Is he alright?"

"No, he isn't." I help Hestia to her feet, and I ask. "Do you want me to walk you to him?"

"No," Hestia shakes her head. "I can hear him from here."

She follows the sounds of Dionysus's sobs, which grow louder when she opens the door and joins him. Demeter and Nike stumble out next. Their faces are deathly pale, and they both shiver how Dionysus had. Together, they use each other as support and stagger out of the throne room for much needed rest.

Hera escapes from the dagger after them. She collapses onto her knees, but her eyes are wild with determination. Her hands lay flat on the floor, while her hair covers all but her beady, dangerous gaze. For a few seconds, her haggard breathing and Diam's incantation loudly echo in the too-quiet space.

Then, in a hoarse tone, Hera growls. "I…. want…a…. divorce."

Diam stops his incantation for a moment.

I can't help it. I smile.

Zeus frowns, but says only one word. "Alright."

I stand to help Hera, but she glares at me, and I stop myself. She struggles, but she rises to her feet on her own. She wipes her hair from her face and stares at the god who ruined the sanctity of their marital vows.

"I'll have the papers drawn up by the end of the week." She flips her raven black locks over her shoulder and, as if she were never inside of the dagger, strolls out of the throne room with her chin held high.

Slowly, one by one, every immortal escapes the dagger. Poseidon, Artemis, Aphrodite, Asopus, Sinope, Amphitrite, Athena, and dozens of others stagger forward, either shivering or short of breath.

When Aphrodite emerges, Hephaestus leaves his corner with Raven and rushes towards her. He helps her to her feet, and once she stands, she stays in one form. It's her favorite form, with light brown skin and effortlessly wavy dark brown hair. She stares up at Hephaestus, captivated but fearful, as his callused hands cradle both sides of her face.

"It is me who does not deserve you," he says. "But if you'll have me. Truly have me…"

She wraps her arms around the back of his neck and pulls him in for a kiss. After eons together, Hephaestus finally kisses his wife back, and they admit the feelings they both tried to hide in vain. Ares once told me that Aphrodite ended their affair for good because she could no longer hurt Hephaestus. It was the only affair that truly broke Hephaestus's heart- the one between Aphrodite and Ares- because he thought that was true love.

And how wrong he was.

When the Muses tumble out of the Dagger of Chains, Melpomene has her hands pressed against the floor, but her eyes shoot upwards. They land on Maressa, and tears immediately pool in her dark eyes. A few other Muses look up, but I'm enraptured by Melpomene's trembling lips. She stumbles as she tries to run towards Maressa, but eventually they join in a tight embrace.

Melpomene sobs as she says. "Maressa, my daughter. My sweet, sweet daughter. I thought I'd never see the real you again."

Maressa wraps her arms around her mother and cries.

The last god to leave the dagger is Apollo, and tears immediately form in my eyes. As soon as he leaves the dagger, his eyes scour the throne room in search of the one person he will never find. Blue, desperate, eyes hunt for his wife. She trapped him in the Dagger of Chains to stop him from saving her life. In some visions Hart showed me, Apollo leaps into the volcano with Styx's body instead of her.

She couldn't live without him, and she hoped he could live without her.

Then his gaze hardens on Zeus. "Where is she?!" Zeus doesn't answer, and Apollo screams. "WHERE IS MY WIFE?!"

Tears gather in my eyes as I whisper. "Po…"

Apollo's glare whip towards me, and he sees the tears building up in my eyes. His anger quickly dissolves, replaced with an emotion so much worse; disbelief mars his appearance, and he shakes his head.

"No." His golden hair whips back and forth from how hard he shakes his head. "No, Saff! You're lying!"

He runs out of the room just as I whisper. "I wish I was."

He screams Hart's name as he searches every single space in the entire mansion. Each time he unsuccessfully finds her, his voice cracks more. He speaks with such agony as he says her name. Each time with fizzling hope. When he checks the last room, Zeus's, he doesn't close the door. We hear him opening drawers, like she could somehow fit in them, and searching under the bed like she's hiding.

When the realization finally settles, and he knows she's dead, all we hear are his sobs.

# FIFTY

SAFFRON

The next day, we have a funeral for everyone who died. We lost fifteen loved ones. Epiales is the only one of the fifteen who does not have a grave, and that's exactly how he would want it. Instead of a burial site, he will live forever in the stars, where I can visit the moment night claims the sky.

We move one-by-one to the other graves. Panda and Pyro share the same grave, but since we do not have bodies for them, we fill their grave with items they love.

I push Diam's wheelchair forward and together we toss a stuffed animal of a red panda, a spatula, and a drawing of the two of them together into their grave. Hermes comes forward next, and he openly cries for them again as he fills the rest of the grave with Panda and Pyro's favorite flower. Tulips fill it to the brim, just as both would want.

Next, there is Angel's grave. For as long as we have been apart, Angel has continued to be loyal to me. A dear friend, who used his last minutes on earth trying to come back to Nike and me. I baked some of Epiales's white-chocolate chip cookies, the ones Angel and I thought were stars, and I delicately lower them into the grave.

"I have missed you every day, my dear friend."

Nike stumbles towards Angel's grave. They had so little time together, but her love for her soulmate has never wavered. She collapses to her knees in front of his grave, her wings wrapping around her like a hug.

She whispers, as if only he can hear her. "I failed you again, my love. I'm so sorry." She rips out one of her golden feathers, and she drops it into the pit where Angel's body should be. "There won't be a day that goes by where I won't mourn you. Where I won't miss the hole you've left behind in my heart."

I help Nike up to her feet, and I hold her while she sobs.

Next, we move onto the huntresses' graves.

Artemis stares forward, endlessly crying for the women she's loved like sisters. We start with June's grave. She was always so brave, going into battle with a giant grin on her face and fearlessness in her heart. Even with one arm, she fought valiantly and without regret.

After Artemis learned about her huntresses' battle and deaths, she went to the charred remains of the prison. The weapons Iris made for her huntresses survived the rubble. Artemis and Iris hold them now in their hands. They have charred edges, or completely calcified, but it's still clear that these weapons were once magnificent, and they hold a thousand stories about the brave huntresses who gave their lives to defeat Typhon.

Iris lowers June's cyan-colored battle axe into the ground, and the ends of her hair turn the same shade as the axe. "I will miss you," Iris whispers as twin tears roll down her cheeks. "And I will always tell the story of the one-armed, fearless huntress."

Artemis lowers a quilt. The making of it was rushed, as evident by the seams already ripping apart, but every piece of the quilt bears a piece of clothing. June's clothing, I think. Artemis hurriedly made this and lowers it to June's grave.

"Because you always run too cold. I don't want you to freeze, wherever you are." Artemis wipes away the tear that stubbornly falls, and she clears her throat. "Please stay warm, my dear friend."

Hephaestus says nothing, but he places a mechanical arm of his creation into June's grave.

Hound's grave is next to June's, and Iris moves forward first. In her hands is a brand new, bright blue shield. Her arms tremble as she stands over the grave where Hound should eternally rest, and while Artemis tries to hide her sorrow, Iris allows everyone to see the way she mourns these huntresses.

"You weren't around when I made the others their weapons, but I thought of you every step of the way. May you fight valiantly in your afterlife." She sets the bright blue, godly-gifted shield into the ground and steps back.

Artemis steps forward. She lowers gauze into the grave, followed by a stuffed animal of a dog. A hound, to be specific. She says nothing, but she wipes away more tears with furious motions. The second the stuffed animal and the gauze land on the grave beside the blue shield, Artemis spins on her heels and quickly walks away like she can flee from her anguish.

Shikari is close behind Hound, as is fitting for the two squabbling best friends. I move forward first. "Jamila once told me you thought you were nothing but a shield who bleeds for the gods." I manifest a shield made entirely out of bones, dripping with my blood. "Wherever your soul is, let me be the shield who bleeds for you."

I lower it into the grave, then take a few steps back.

Iris and Artemis both place a sentimental piece into the ground for Shikari. Her bright red crossbow from Iris and a wine glass and bottle from Artemis. Raven tries to step forward, holding a shirt in her hands, but Artemis growls. "Don't you dare, you traitor."

And Raven backs up.

Then comes Vee's, and every single person in this backyard holds a book in their hands. Vee loved to learn, and it is only fitting that we fill her grave with knowledge. We each, one by one, lower a book into the ground. On top of those books, Iris places Vee's yellow throwing knives.

"Help me out of this wheelchair," Diam says when we reach Dýnami's grave. His eyes swim with tears. "Please, let me walk to her."

Dýnami is the only one who is inside their grave. Dýnami sits inside a coffin with squirrels and her scarification mark etched into the mahogany. I wrap my arm underneath Diam, and I help him to his feet. He stumbles and groans the whole trek, but we both stand in front of Dýnami's grave. I offered to heal his bones instantaneously, but the stubborn warrior wants to remember the pain he inflicted on his own body for the survival of humankind.

"I'd be dead without you," Diam says. He chokes up, then grunts and forces himself to continue speaking. "We both lost so much, and I hate losing you, too. Our friendship was short, but it meant the world to me. Thank you, Dýnami, for saving my life more times than you'd think." He produces his favorite sword, and he throws it in her grave. "Thank you," he whispers again.

I help him back to his wheelchair while Athena walks forward. Athena has always been a goddess who shows few emotions, but today she openly sobs. She holds a tub of rocky road ice cream in her hands, and she collapses to her knees in front of Dýnami's grave.

"I wish I could have said goodbye." Tears stream down Athena's face as she whispers. "I wish we could have shared one more tub of rocky road ice cream together." She lowers the ice cream, followed by two spoons, into the grave. "It won't ever melt and it will forever refill. I promise you'll never be without your favorite ice cream again."

Iris moves forward with Dýnami's magenta spear, which Sika used to kill Typhon once and for all, but she can't make it to the grave. Dýnami was one of the oldest huntresses, who always brought a level of joy to anyone in her vicinity. Iris tries to walk towards Dýnami's grave, but she stumbles and falls. She sobs onto the floor. I look at Artemis, expecting her to help Iris off the floor, but Artemis can barely keep herself upright. She hasn't stopped crying silent tears as she holds a skewer of charred squirrel in her trembling hands.

I rush towards Iris, and I wrap an arm under her. "I can help you there, just like I did with Diam."

Iris looks at me with such sadness that it almost topples me over. "Why her? She was the kindest soul. Why did she have to die? I never wanted to see the day where her smile faded." Iris sobs into my chest, and I wait for her to find the strength to stand. I help her every step towards Dýnami's grave, but when she throws the spear, she cannot speak. She only weeps.

Artemis walks slowly, but she throws the squirrel meat into the grave and whispers. "You made sure I always smiled, and now I don't know if I can without you here."

Raven holds an item in her hand for Dýnami, and as Iris collapses into Artemis's arms, I walk towards Raven. She holds a rusty knife. "Do you want me to put it in the grave for you?" I ask. "We have a few seconds before Artemis sees us talking."

Raven places the knife in my hand. "She was the one who first bested me in a knife fight. Beneath all the jokes and laughter, Dýnami was one of the best fighters I have ever seen. I just wanted to gift her the first knife she ever stabbed me with."

Tears fall down Raven's cheeks, and I walk away with the dagger. I throw it into the grave, and we all move onto the next one.

Sika.

It makes perfect sense Sika was the prophesied huntress because there is no human I have ever witnessed on a battlefield as effortlessly lethal as her. She should have become a hero among gods without dying, but the Fates are cruel figures.

I repeat one of the first words she ever said to me. "Humans are always in danger. There are always monsters, gods, titans, and primordial deities stronger than us. We are nothing but ants beneath their mighty feet. At least with a blade in your hand, and skills to use it, then you have a chance. No matter how small the chance is, with training you still have one to slay those that dare to see you as easy prey."

I place my first sword on the ground where Sika's body should be. "You taught me more in that one lesson than others have in a lifetime. Thank you, Sika, for reminding me that humans can slay the un-slayable with the right training. You will always be remembered."

Every god gifts something to Sika in honor of her defeating a monster that none of us could. Zeus gives her a crown, Hermes presents one of his many winged sandals, and Athena drops an arrow. Everyone has a story, no matter how small or large, centering on a huntress as magnanimous as Sika.

Similarly to Hound, Iris crafted a godly-gifted weapon for Sika. It is a light pink bow and arrow, but instead of just one arrow on the string, it's five. The bow is longer than any I have seen before, but that is fitting for Sika because she's the greatest huntress to live.

Iris sets it down, then we all turn to face Artemis. There are three huntresses who Artemis vocalized as her favorites- Sika, Willow, and most importantly, Lamb. Artemis walks towards Sika's grave, and she looks so hollow. So inexplicably broken.

She holds a deer antler in her hand. "I named you after a deer because they are my favorite animal. You were one of the greatest women I have ever met, and I knew you would become the greatest huntress of them all." Artemis drops the deer antler and whispers. "I went searching for the perfect gift to leave you, and a deer walked up to me yesterday and one of its antlers fell off. It was only fitting that it was a sika deer gifting you with one last parting present."

Artemis looks at the two other graves of her other favored huntresses, and she whispers. "I can't do this."

And she storms back into the house.

Iris drops her last two gifts to the remaining huntresses, Willow and Lamb, and follows Artemis. Zeus walks towards the gifts, and he picks them up. There's a scythe that's the same icicle blue as Willow's eyes and a golden apple for Lamb, and we silently move towards the final two huntresses.

First, it's Willow's grave. Zeus drops the blue scythe, while others drop apples and music notes.

Then, it's Lamb's grave.

Every single god has a story involving the most silent

huntress because, despite her meek demeanor, she is an unforgettable force. Zeus goes to his knees in front of Lamb's grave and drops the golden apple.

"Thank you for teaching me compassion. I won't ever forget those who bleed again because of you," Zeus says. "You are magnificent, Lamb."

I leave behind a drawing I found in Hart's art room of Lamb during the Battle of the Huntresses. She stands side-by-side with Willow and Sika, her two closest friends, and it is only fitting that this art piece joins Lamb in whatever her afterlife looks like.

"Thank you for saving the world, even when others didn't realize everything you've done."

Hermes gifts Lamb the sand from Ogygia in honor of her heroic actions on this island. Athena places her favorite sword in the grave because Lamb taught her compassion, just as she taught Zeus the same thing. Apollo hasn't left his room, but I hold his present from him. A lyre, so she would never forget the power of a song again.

We mourn everyone until the morning light turns to night. I cry and grieve for everyone with fervor.

We drop Zig's favorite snacks and his ferryman staff, along with stories about his kindness.

We all agree that a funeral for Hart should wait until Apollo has the strength to get out of bed, but we all whisper a thank you to the empty grave. Without her, none of us would be here right now. We'd either be dead or imprisoned by Styx. Her sacrifices, from the moment she learned she was an oracle, will forever cement our futures.

Last, there is Hattie.

"Just Saffron and me, please." Diam looks around at the gods who knew Hattie fondly, and he says. "It's how Hattie would want it."

"But I got a flashlight," Poseidon says, pouting. "Because of the time she hit me with one. It's cute."

Amphitrite places a consoling hand on her husband's shoulder. "Honey, we respect the wishes of the dead."

"But the flashlight, it's a cute idea!" Poseidon outcries.

Amphitrite leads him and the other gods away, leaving just Diam and me. We sit next to her grave, underneath a sturdy oak tree, and we hold each other. We cry and share stories and mourn the most amazing woman alive for the rest of the night, but every so often, our tear-stained eyes will wander towards the stars where Epiales joins us.

# FIFTY-ONE

## SAFFRON

*Six Days After the Battle of Pompeii*

The morning after the funerals, Diam goes to his room for rest, but I travel through my mansion for Apollo. The sound of gut-wrenching heartache guides me towards the room he shared with Hart. He holds onto a small pillow, his eyes puffy with tears, and there, atop the pillow, is her wedding band.

"Po…"

He doesn't look up.

I take a few steps into the bedroom. "Hart wanted you to know-"

"Why?" His voice tears alongside his anguish, but he still won't look up from the pillow. "Why did she do this to me?"

I say nothing until I sit on the edge of the bed nearest him. "Because she had to."

He shakes his head. "No, she didn't. She could have told me everything, and we could have come up with any

467

other plan where she stays alive with me. How am I supposed to live an eternity without her smile? I won't hear her laugh again, Saff. How do you expect me to survive this?"

He sobs so hard and so loud that it shakes the walls, and I rush him. I wrap him up in my arms. His tears coat my shoulders, but I don't care. I squeeze him tightly, and I let him mourn her the only way he knows how. He didn't have the strength for a funeral because this is all he has the strength to do. Cry and scream and think of what could have been.

We sit like this for hours, and while fatigue lays heavy on my eyes, I don't let him go. I hold my dear friend close until his breathing calms. Then, I whisper. "Hart left you a letter; would you like to read it?" He doesn't respond, and so I counteract in a soft whisper. "Would you like me to read it to you?"

Every muscle is strained, depleted from both the dagger and the despair, but he nods his head. I slide my free hand through his golden hair, while I materialize the letter Hart gave me the day before I went to Styx to begin the final battle. In the softest handwriting, with hollow, circled dots above her I's, Hart writes her last words to her husband.

*"My sweetest love,"* I begin softly as he cries again. *"You must hate me right now. I do not blame you; I would've hated you if the roles were reversed. Before I begin this letter, I want to reiterate that I love you more than I could love anything in this world. You aren't just my soulmate, but you are my confidence and my sanity. My best friend and my reason for existing. Without you in my life, I am certain I wouldn't have been brave enough to venture through the journey that is life. If you hadn't taught me the beauty of my ability of foresight, then I wouldn't have trusted it enough to save the rest of the world."*

"I don't think I can continue hearing this," Apollo says, but he needs to hear his wife's last words.

I continue. *"When Lowell stabbed me, and I almost died, I saw everything that needed to happen for us to win the war. In every other iteration I witnessed, we lost and both of us died, but in this version of reality that I saw in my vision, we were victorious. But only if I pointed the arrows of destiny in the right direction."*

*"First,"* I continue reading the letter aloud, but as I talk, my voice sounds more like Hart's than my own. The last vestige of her magic worming its way through the room. *"I had to make sure the members of the prophecy were all alive. That night, I saw Sika with a wild expression on her face as she killed Typhon. I saw Diam leading the humans away, forming civilization once again. Raven stood on the battleground with a hammer in the air, and Hattie died as the prophesied heart. But when I had the prophecy, they were dead. Victims to a cruel world. The Underworld opened its arms to Sika, Diam, Raven, and Hattie, and I had to get them back. I knew we couldn't help them escape from the Underworld, or else Styx would know they were essential in the prophecy. So, I told one of Styx's many espionages that I had a vision, detailing how we would lose if Styx destroyed the Underworld."*

I pause and let that truth settle between us.

I always saw the Underworld's destruction as one of Styx's worst crimes, but it was also her worst decision. If she had never destroyed the Underworld, then Raven, Sika, Hattie, and Diam wouldn't have been in the ending battles. If they weren't there, they would not have cemented their roles in the prophecy.

Raven wouldn't have created the volcano that currently holds Styx's remains captive.

Sika wouldn't have killed Typhon, which meant he would have been in the final battle. Typhon would have certainly killed Diam, Epiales, and the other humans on the battlefield before they could fulfill their prophecies.

If Hattie didn't come back to life only to die, then my oath to Styx wouldn't have severed, and I couldn't kill her, Hecate, or anyone loyal to them.

If Diam wasn't alive to be the seeker, then there wouldn't have been a strong human force to lead the remaining humans away.

Humankind would have died or been eternal prisoners to Styx.

*"Next, I had to make sure Epiales lost his memory."* I read this letter once before now, but this sentence still shocks me. I didn't remember Hart doing anything leading to Epiales's amnesia, but her letter clicks everything into place. *"In seventy-seven visions, Saffron saved Epiales in the arena, and in all those visions we died because no one found the Muse in time. Another fifty visions, Zeus won and killed our hero before he could achieve his purpose."*

*"Maressa needed Epiales to lose his memory, so Hermes could drop him off in her vicinity and continually check in. Hermes never killed Epiales in any vision, and every time, Hermes saved Maressa and Epiales's life long enough for them to exact their part in the prophecy. I had to ensure that Hermes won the arena for rights over Epiales. I made sure only minor gods playing for Epiales were loyal to Hermes. Or, in Heracles's case, a big enough distraction to those loyal to Saffron, so Hermes could ensure a victory."*

"She did all of this?" Apollo asks. He stopped crying a few paragraphs ago, and he stares at me now with shock and awe.

"There's more," I say and continue. *"There were three hundred and twenty version of the ultimate battle, but there were only three where we were victorious. I had to dispose of anyone who caused our demise in the other three hundred and seventeen visions. I gave the huntresses drawings of human souls to kill before the battles truly begun because each of them killed one of the main figureheads in the prophecy. Either Raven, Maressa, Epiales, Diam, Dýnami, Sika, or*

*Lamb would have died by one of those humans' hands. For instance, a pirate named Dennis killed Epiales in seven versions of the doomed visions before Hermes and the huntresses could dispose of him. Another woman, who initially joined Styx to avenge her own murder, killed Dýnami every time in the Battle of Huntresses instead of letting a god lead her away to safety. Without Dýnami, Diam would not have lived long enough to lead them to safety. Her sacrifice promised victory."*

The huntresses hated their roles as murderers, especially because Hart never told them why. I wish they lived long enough to know that each murder had a purpose.

*"Jamila had to fall into a coma to justify you and me marrying so suddenly because I had to be the one who guarded over Styx's corpse in this volcano for all of eternity. I had to make sure Jamila became a huntress, nearly died in the Battle of the Huntresses, and married Thanatos. It was the only way you would marry me without a grand wedding because Jamila and Thanatos reminded you of how fleeting a mortal life is. I wish we could have had our grand wedding, just like you wanted, but our wedding was still perfect in my eyes. Apollo, I would marry you a million times over."*

*"In three hundred and nineteen visions, you died, and my heart died with you. In three hundred and ten visions, Uranus put you in the Dagger of Chains and Hecate shattered it into a thousand pieces. Then, in five visions, Saffron didn't listen to my advice. She killed Styx on Mt. Olympus, and Hecate fled before Saffron could murder her. We would have had two hundred years together in happiness, but Hecate is the goddess of necromancy. In those five visions, Hecate brought Styx back to life, and we all died."*

When Hart first told me about her plan for victory, I asked her why I couldn't kill Styx on Mt. Olympus. She showed me a horrific version of our world. I have seen the worst version of humankind, but at the sight of a prophetic, malignant future beneath Styx's reign, I vomited.

If I killed Styx on Mt. Olympus, it would have been a temporary victory. Hecate would have vanished before I could kill her, and I would have murdered every other traitor on Mt. Olympus. We would have pretended that we had won, but Hecate was still out there. She would have stolen Styx's bones about two centuries later, and we wouldn't have seen their attack coming.

All of us died, except me.

I was the instrument of everyone's murder. Hecate and Styx found a way to poison me, so I was no longer myself, but a shell of nothingness. Gareth French was the prototype of the mayhem I became in a world where I killed Styx before Hecate.

Hattie did not come back in any version.

*"In one vision, Saffron went mad and killed you. Ripped every bone from your body."*

I wince, but keep going.

*"In two visions, the worst of them all, I told you I was destined to die. We won the war because you ordered Thanatos, who stayed behind to monitor Jamila, to ensure I stayed behind, too. He held me back as I kicked and screamed and begged you not to go, and I never saw you again. In two terrible visions, you were the one at the bottom of the volcano instead of me, and I couldn't survive your loss. I never recovered, but in this version of the world that has come true, where it is me who forfeits my life to guard Styx's remains, you recover from my death. It takes a long time, but you are stronger than me, Apollo. You can survive my death better than I can survive yours."*

His pleas for me to stop reading cease, and slowly he rises to a seated position.

*"I didn't want to leave you, but I want you to know that there was no other choice. It was my life or the rest of the world, whether the world died that day or two hundred years later. I would not let my selfishness affect the rest of the world and all that live within it. I love you more than anything else, and I couldn't live with you in any*

472

*version of this world. Our love story was not long, but it was my greatest achievement."*

With a deep sigh, I end her letter with one last paragraph.

*"You may feel as if there's no more reason to live, or that you will never find love again, but you will. I know you hope that Saffron will end your suffering—"*

I shoot my gaze towards Apollo, who whispers. "Keep reading, please." He doesn't deny Hart's claim about his suicidal thoughts, and my heart rips a little more for my dear friend.

*"But wait seven months. In seven months, on the day when the sky remains orange from morning to night, go to the mountain where I slumber. If what you find there does not fill the hole I left behind, then I understand. You may ask for an escape from a world where I do not exist. But please wait seven months."*

There is a soft pause before I whisper Hart's very last words.

*"With love, your wife, your soulmate, and your greatest supporter. Hartika Sommers."*

An owl is right outside of Apollo's window, sitting upon a tree and softly hooting, and it is the only sound that either of us can allow at this moment. We sit and stew over Hart's words until they engrave into our minds forever.

"I wish she told me." He stares down at her wedding band atop his pillow. "I wish I knew that the last day was truly our last. There was so much more I needed to say."

"While Hart may not speak, I'm almost certain she can hear you. Whenever you want to talk, scream, or cry to her, then go to her. She cannot hold your hand or respond with words." I smile softly at my friend. "But she can still listen."

Tears slide down his cheeks as he murmurs. "I was so mad at her when I came out of the dagger. She stabbed me. I had even decided that I would not talk to her for a few days after what she had done, but now I want nothing more than to hold her. To smell her honey-scented body wash on her rather than her pillow."

"Everything she did, she had to do in order to save the world." I pause for a moment, then add. "To save you."

"She was my world," his voice cracks as he speaks his own truth, and there is nothing I can respond with. "How does one live without their world?"

I can only hold him.

# FIFTY-TWO

RAVEN

*A Week After the Battle of Pompeii*

"You're leaving," Hephaestus says as he leans against the doorframe to my now open door.

His grime-covered arms cross over his chest as his squinted gaze dashes between the luggage at my feet and the hammer protruding from the satchel across my chest.

"You have some lipstick on your cheek." I bend down to zip the rest of the luggage while he wipes at his cheek with the back of his hand. There is nothing there, and his frown deepens. "You don't need me here. You have your wife to absolve your loneliness, and I have some atoning to do."

There's a long pause, and I know what he isn't saying. I have only known Hephaestus for a short while, and yet I have never known him to bite his tongue. He is a crass god, who doesn't hesitate to spew candor at other's expense.

475

Except this time, he's silent. Because he doesn't think I can do anything to atone for my past.

I grab the handles of my luggage and pick it up. "I swore to be a huntress until the end of time. She may not want me, but I'm here."

I'm one of the two huntresses remaining, but I don't say that aloud. Because the only other living huntress is lying in a hospital bed, unstirring. It doesn't look like she will ever wake, which means it is just me. The traitorous scum Artemis won't deign to look at. I am the only huntress she has left, the one she wants the least.

"Zeus told me yesterday that I'm still an immortal huntress. As long as I'm not killed, I'll be here begging for Artemis's forgiveness. Fighting for her forgiveness."

"And if she's the one who kills you?" Hephaestus asks, and I don't miss the edge of concern within his question.

I shrug my shoulders. "Then at least I died by the right hands." I walk up to Hephaestus, who blocks my way leaving the mansion, where death and revival permeate. "Thank you for being the most unlikely friend. You reminded me that not everyone sees me as an irredeemable beast."

"Quit saying goodbye," Hephaestus grunts.

"This isn't a goodbye." I force a smile for my only friend to witness. "We will see each other again, but hopefully it will be under better circumstances. We will meet each other again when there is no war to fight. You'll be next to Aphrodite, and I'll have Artemis's forgiveness."

"You're too old to be this dumb." His words are barbed, but I feel compassion within them. He doesn't want me to die in a futile effort to gain forgiveness from a grieving, grudge-holding goddess's forgiveness. "Don't be stupid. I have a nice house on earth in Greece. Stay there and-"

"And what? Pretend I didn't kill Willow?"

His mouth forms a deep frown. "You atoned for that crime in that bloody war. You hold the scars and burns of this war. Without you switching to our side, the Battle of the Huntresses would have ended differently, and you know it. The ultimate battle would have failed without you, too. Quit holding onto guilt for a death you've already paid for with your own blood."

"Maybe I have atoned," I admit. "Maybe if I didn't help them escape their shackles, the battle would have ended differently. I don't know, though. What I know is Artemis won't even look at me, and Willow used her last words to swear she would never forgive me. You see it as one death- blood for blood- but I see it as sororicide. The murder of a sister is a crime not easily washed away, and I refuse to forgive myself so readily because of one bloody war. A war that killed her twice when it was me who deserved to die again."

"You're a foolish girl," Hephaestus snaps.

I place my hand on the center of his chest. "I care about you, too."

He squints at my hand on his chest, and his jaw ticks with annoyance. "Don't let her kill you. To be a martyr is a job only for the foolish and stubborn. Promise me you won't let her kill you, and I'll let you leave."

"She won't kill me."

"Quit sounding so sure," he says back. "You have known Artemis for a few centuries, but I have known her for a few millennia. She will kill you if you step in front of her path. Don't do it, you stubborn girl."

He steps aside, and I whisper as I walk past. "I'll miss you until we see each other again, dear friend."

He says nothing as I walk to the mansion's front doors. Everyone else I see, from the healing humans and the grieving gods, avoids my gaze. I'm the pariah amongst heroes. A disease many fear they'll contract if they venture too close. My hand wraps around the doorknob, but my eyes wander to the back doors, where all the graves lay freshly covered.

My feet propel me towards the graveyard.

Two goddesses stand in the backyard, mourning in distanced silence. Iris stands nearest the backdoors, her tears the same dark blue as the streaks in her hair. She mourns the corporeal occupants of these graves, holding her dress hem as if she grips her heart in her hand. Artemis kneels in front of one grave, and her anguish is the most wretched, heartbreaking sound that has ever pierced my ears.

And we all live in a world where Saffron's scream joins the winds in mourning of Hattie.

She sits in front of Lamb's grave, the huntress she loved most. The huntress, who I thank every day for killing me for my crimes against Willow and Artemis. The goddess grips the dirt on Lamb's resting place, and she screams loud enough to shatter glass. She slams her hands against the ground, still gripping the dirt, as her body hunches and trembles.

"Why you?" Artemis says, voice cracked. "Anyone but you."

I step forward, and Iris's eyes latch onto mine. She shakes her head, but I do not listen. I advance towards Artemis as she sobs over Lamb's grave. All it takes is three steps for Artemis to remind the world why she is the goddess of the wild. She spins around; her arrow notched atop her bow, and she points the weapon directly at me.

She is one of the more radiant goddesses, with golden-spun hair and a round, youthful face. But when she glowers at me with all the hatred in the world, she could be her father, Zeus. Ready to smite me with eyes as bright as a storm. Her hand trembles, but not with hesitance. Rage paints the darkest picture upon a face that once only brimmed with happiness in my vicinity.

"Why you? Anyone but you. Yet, here you stand. Alive. Heroic." Artemis spits the last word as she latches onto the hammer sticking out of my satchel. "How dare you live when they lay dead?"

She pulls the bowstring back, and I whisper only two words. "I'm sorry."

Because I am.

"I'm sorry that I am the one who survived instead of Lamb, who was your favorite."

Artemis flinches, then screams. "Don't say her name!"

"I'm sorry that I'm the one who survives instead of Sika, who was the best among us. Willow, who was the first. Dýnami, who was the bravest. Shikari, who was the sneakiest. I am so sorry that I live instead of those amazing women, who never fell for a titan's tricks. I'm sorry that I stand here in front of you when they never fell in love with a male who only wanted to use them as a pawn. And I'm so sorry that I'm all you have left of the huntresses when I do not deserve to live."

I drop to my knees, sling my satchel off, and throw the sacred hammer towards my goddess. With my arms out wide, I accept the execution befalling me. I deserve it. My eyes lock onto Willow's grave, and to only her, I whisper. "I am so sorry."

"I close my eyes, and they are all I see. Their deaths." Artemis snarls at me, but her voice grows nearer.

I don't look at her, or the arrowhead pointed at me. My focus remains on the one I murdered, who I love like a sister. Willow will never forgive me, but if I can at least absolve Artemis's rage through my death, then it would be something.

Right?

"I blink, and I see Typhon's foot slamming into June. I close my eyes, and I see Sika falling into a vat of flames, accepting her death." Artemis's voice breaks as she comes closer and closer. The tip of the arrowhead rests in the center of my forehead, but I don't flinch. I finally draw my gaze back to Artemis, whose tear-stained face holds more haunting memories than pleasant ones. "I blink, and I see your arrow driving through Willow's skull." Tears fall more plentifully as she hiccups. "I close my eyes, and I see Lamb…"

One name, and Artemis falls into shambles. She drops the bow and arrow, and she falls to the ground. She sobs with a full body shake.

"No more," Artemis chokes out. "No more will I love. No more will I bring women into the huntress fold." She glowers up at me from where we sit on the ground, and she seethes. "Why did you have to be my last huntress when my heart cannot handle adding anymore? Why must you be the last of my legacy?"

Artemis won't kill me, and I don't know if the realization brings me relief or dread. She turns her back to me, and she crawls back to Lamb's grave. She collapses on the fresh soil, and her sobs return. Her fingers go back into the dirt, and almost too quietly for me to hear, she says. "Get out. If I ever see you again, I'll kill you. I'll rip your heart from your chest, just as you did to me."

I rise to my feet and grab my satchel. "Whenever you decide you need me, I won't be far, and I'll come. I'll follow you anywhere."

"I'll never need another huntress again. Get out."

Artemis lays her cheek against Lamb's burial ground, and I leave.

But I don't go far.

When Artemis eventually leaves the mansion with Iris, moving into the woods, I'm close behind. There will never be a day where I live unloyal to her again. I have an eternity to serve Artemis again, and I will follow her until she needs me.

I will be here even if she doesn't.

The greatest mistake of my life was turning my back on Artemis in favor of a false love with Kronos, and I will never make that mistake again. From today until my last, I will follow a few steps behind her, waiting.

What I wait for, only the Fates can tell.

# FIFTY-THREE

HERMES

*One Month After the Final Battle*

aressa Holliday survived an arrow to the side of her throat for three reasons.

First, the arrowhead slipped in between the carotid artery and the jugular vein. Although the arrowhead is larger than the space between the artery and the vein, it pushed the artery to the side without nicking it. If the arrow moved a little to the right or left, I might not have gotten Mae to the infirmary in time to save her life.

Second, Maressa is a three thousand-year old demigod, with remarkable healing skills that far surpass a typical demi-god. Since the injury did not hit any major artery, the moment Thanatos ripped the arrowhead from her neck, there was minimal bleeding. He stitched her wound with minor difficulties.

Third and most importantly, the Fates gave me a miracle.

A month after the war, after Apollo removes the sutures

and there isn't a single scar to identify her wounds in the last battle, she opens her mouth to sing, except no song joins in the wind. She is the daughter of a muse, the only half-blood siren, but she can no longer sing. According to Thanatos, then Apollo later on, her vocal chords are fine.

Yet, she opens her mouth and cannot sing.

She cries instantly.

I wrap her in my arms, cradling her small body into my own as I place comforting kisses on top of her head. Her singing voice has been her entire personality for her eons long existence, and now it is gone. A single hymn and an arrowhead steal the piece of herself that she has had her entire life.

"I'm so sorry," I murmur into her hair, squeezing her tight.

Maressa pulls her head away from the crook of my chest to look up at me. I expect complete anguish on her face, but while she is crying, she also wears a radiant smile. Maressa grins at me, and I realize too late that her sobs are with joy.

"Why are you apologizing?" she asks. "I'm no longer a monster. This is a celebration. I cannot sing anymore."

We never learn why she lost her singing voice on that battleground, but it is the happiest day of Maressa's life.

Until six months later, when I drop to one knee and ask her to be my wife.

# FIFTY-FOUR

## SAFFRON

*Four Months After the Final Battle*

Civilization regrows brick by brick.

Nearly every god stays on Earth to help clean the streets, and there is no time for other conversations. Artemis and Iris are gone, hiding and mourning in the woods, but the rest of us stay until every piece of rubble is gone and new homes can grow from the decay of the old.

Hermes is essential in the reconstruction. With his winged sandals moving at the speed of light, he disposes of almost all the rubble himself. Maressa, who now proudly displays her bird wings, helps him alongside Hypnos and Nike. They fly and dispose of everything Styx ruined. Occasionally, Thanatos helps, but mostly he stays inside with his hand clasped in Jamila's sleeping one.

Hephaestus, with Aphrodite giddily prancing behind him, starts building new houses. We begin in my neighborhood, erecting modest buildings the scarce remaining humans can call home. Zeus kneels beside them, meticulously laying each brick for a new world. Diam, as their newly appointed leader, gets the first house. Then, as the week progresses, three dozen homes are made for humans by gods. They stand proudly beside mine and Diam's.

There is no time for conversations and grief. We had one day in front of the graves to mourn our loved ones, but now we rebuild the world. We will have time to cry for our sisters, brothers, friends, and lovers later. For now, all conversations evaporate in the air. All sense of reality lay as shattered glass upon the ground that we pick up piece by jagged piece.

Ares and I share heated glances, where declarations have yet to leave either of our lips but are static in the air. It takes three weeks to reconstruct a small sliver of the world, but it isn't enough. It takes four months to create enough homes to occupy the remaining humans, as well as courthouses, for all proceedings.

Once peace seems within the humans' reach, Poseidon returns to his home in the seas. Hades and Persephone resume their roles as king and queen of the Underworld, where only a few dozen deceased souls live. All who died, either during the last battle or after from their injuries, live in Elysium as heroes.

Dýnami, I heard, is their appointed general of Elysium. They have a general in case another thunderstorm of green smoke fills the air. This time, instead of running and becoming victims of magic, they can fight against it.

It is a befitting role for a woman as brave as Dýnami.

Hephaestus and Aphrodite travel with a few other low-level gods to the other side of the world, rebuilding homes in Greece and Rome to prepare for the growing population. Zeus lets Hera, his soon-to-be ex-wife, return to Mt.

Olympus to stand in as the ruler while he remains on Earth. He continues to move through the countryside, building houses and finding compassion towards the humans.

As month after month begins and ends, a new form of normalcy takes shape. It isn't like the world before Styx's carnage, but it is something beautiful too. I can walk down a street and see smiling faces. There are fewer tears, fewer nightmares, and more twinkling stars when the night takes siege.

Ares keeps enough distance, so I know he is here, but he doesn't pressure me into talking about us. He helps me rebuild humanity, trains with me in my home, and patiently waits for when I'm ready to begin a new version of forever. A version of forever with my destined soulmate. I think he would wait a thousand years for me, and that's why I cannot wait a moment longer.

I find him a mile away from where I was, kneeling in front of a garden bed. Demeter laughs at a joke he makes, while he stares up at her with a wide grin. Demeter sees me first. She glances at me, the laugh fading in the wind that still screeches with my scream, and she knows. Somehow, without a single word, Demeter looks from me to Ares and realizes why I'm standing here.

"I'll be back in the morning to check on our gardens." Demeter disappears, but my focus remains fixed on Ares.

He stands and wipes his soil-covered hands on his tunic, then turns to face me. Ares wears a rust-colored tunic with pockets embroidered gold. His eyes roam over me. I feel his stare like pinpricks against my flesh as he looks at my hair pulled into a messy bun atop my head. His gaze lowers to the grime creating a line across my cheek, wanders down to the lilac purple sundress also covered in grime, and he smiles. Truly smiles like I am the first sight of sunlight after eons in the dark.

He shoves his hands in his pockets. "Hi."

"You told me before the war that you had something you needed to confess once we restored peace in the world." I take a step towards him.

"If it is too soon, then I can wait," Ares is quick to respond, but there's an eager cadence to his words.

The sun has newly risen, but I can still make out the scarce outline of Epiales's constellation. I can no longer hear Epiales's sinful velvet voice, but I can feel his approval as I step towards Ares. Epiales always said he desires my happiness above all else, and as he looks down, I know he is aware of my inevitability with Ares. I think I even knew, from the first time we saw each other in the arena, that destiny spun a specific, yet glorious tale for us.

"Would you wait three thousand years if I asked you to?"

"Yes," is his immediate response. "I'd wait a thousand lifetimes for you."

I stand directly in front of him, my chest brushing against his, and I whisper. "You have waited almost a hundred years already. Why?"

He reaches for me, and the moment his hand cups my cheek, I reach nirvana. There is peace that only his touch can guarantee. I have experienced peace other times, but only Ares can gift it to me every time we touch. Every time his body presses against mine, an undeniable wave of relief crashes against me.

Gods, how did I not realize earlier that he was my destined forever?

"Because even now, I know I don't deserve you. You are perfection in its truest form, and I am a god with more mistakes than accolades. The Fates should have paired you with anyone but me, and yet…"

"And yet, here you are."

His thumb smooths over my bottom lip, and I gasp as he says. "Here I am, utterly besotted with you. The Fates were cruel to gift me to you, but the Fates granted me the greatest prize with you as my third love. My destined soulmate." I run my hands up the length of his chest, and he shudders. "Every day, I will try to be perfect for you. To shed the god who I once was into a form that you deserve because I am madly in love with you, and there is no other place in this realm I want to be more than in your embrace."

My hands wander upwards until my fingers slide through his short beard. "Kiss me, Ares."

He bends down slowly, like he wants to give me enough time to change my mind, but there is nothing in this world I am more certain of than at this moment. His lips are smooth against mine, and they feel just right. I wrap my hands around the back of his neck, and I deepen the kiss. A thunderstorm lives inside of me as Ares's hands grab the back of my thighs and lift me into him. I wrap my legs around him, and I melt into his moan.

Time stops. Hearts beat too fast. Yet, there is nowhere else I want to be.

When he pulls away, his lips swollen, I whisper into them. "I love you too."

His mouth slams against mine again, and we fall into the garden full of tulips.

My destined soulmate and me.

# FIFTY-FIVE

APOLLO

*Seven Months After the Battle of Pompeii*

Every day, I reread Hart's letter, hoping for a new clue into how I can save her from the bottom of the volcano. No hope comes, but I still wait seven months as she requested. Zeus gave me the Dagger of Chains after I cried to him one night, begging for an escape that Saffron will never provide me. Zeus gave it to me in exchange for one promise.

*"Wait the seven months," he said.*

I took it and agreed.

These seven months are agonizing. Every morning, I awake to the fading scent of honey on her side of the bed. I've laid out some of her clothes where she once slept, so I can carry that scent a little while longer, but it's fading fast. Too fast. I barely leave the bed in Saffron's mansion, where I last held my wife, and I relive every conversation.

How did I not know that I was going to lose her?

I spend my days crying until Saffron convinces me to

get out of bed for dinner. Then I return, lay my head down on my pillow, and stare at Hart's side, hoping she will reappear. I fall asleep each night disappointed.

But now, the seven-month wait is over.

My steps are sluggish, filled with sorrow towards Mt. Sommers on a stormy Sunday morning. I almost turn around to go home about eight or nine times, but a sound pulls me out of all of my terrible thoughts.

It is the sound of a baby crying.

My lethargic steps turn into a brisk jog. The closer I get to the volcano, where Hart eternally slumbers, the louder the cries become. My jog turns into a full-blown sprint until the sight in front of the volcano completely halts me.

When I first met Hart within Olympus Industries, we shared a vision the moment we touched. In this future, we saw two baby girls, one with my golden blonde hair and one with her brown locks. The girl with the blonde hair has the same electric blue eyes and upturned nose as me. Meanwhile, the other girl is a replica of Hart. Not as tan, but everything else reflects her appearance. Her lips, her cheeks, and her wide-eyed expression.

There they lay, nestled together in blue and red blankets. In the world of gods and monsters, there is no rhyme or reason behind the birth of powerful creations. Athena came into the world after Zeus ate her mother, then complained of a migraine eight months later; she sprouted out of his cracked skull. Helen of Troy emerged from an egg after Zeus turned into a swan to lie with her mother, Queen Leda. Even my birthing story had no logical explanation, only phenomena. My mother birthed Artemis first, who then helped deliver me.

So, I do not question the two little girls sitting outside a volcano. I only crumble with bittersweet joy at the sight of them.

I collapse to my knees in front of both baby girls, and I sob as I pick them up. When Hart and I shared this vision over a year ago, I forgot that in the vision, I was the only one holding both twin girls. I cried in the vision, and I foolishly thought I only cried with joy at the sight of two perfect demi-gods, created with love and a promise of forever.

But the vision was a warning long foretold Hart would not be alive to share in the joy of us having twin daughters together.

"You were pregnant," I whisper softly into the darker girl's hair, which already smells like honey. "Curse you and your secrets, my beautiful, wonderful wife."

I can only laugh in disbelief as I hold two perfect babies in my arms.

One of them looks exactly like her. Her skin is slightly darker than her sister and mine, a trait given to her by Hart, while her eyes are like honey pits sprinkled with gold. Her cheeks are round and little freckles dot her cheekbones. She is her mother, and her name sputters out of me as if Hart and I decided it together.

"Melina." I hum her name and find love within her eyes just as I had with her mother.

The other daughter looks just like me. Every detail mirrors mine, except for a streak of red hair amidst the wavy golden locks.

"Pyrrha." I amorously kiss the tip of her upturned nose, a trait that she has from me before turning to her sister and kissing Melina's chubby cheeks. "Oh, my girls."

For seven months, I have wanted to fling myself into the magma, to be reunited with Hart, but now I have a reason to live that I didn't have just a few minutes before.

Thank you, Hart Sommers, for changing my life in so many ways.

# EPILOGUE

## SAFFRON

*Eighteen Years After the Battle of Pompeii*

Ares's hand is warm against mine as we round the steps to Apollo's house. Underneath my arm, I carry the girls' presents. As I knock on the door, Ares leans forward and presses a kiss on top of my head. I smile at him, still in awe of him almost two decades after we married. His lips careen to the tip of my nose, then my lips.

It isn't Melina, Pyrrha, or Apollo, who opens the door for us.

Maressa stands in the doorway with a widespread grin, with one hand on the newly opened door and another around her swollen belly. It's their fourth child, and the three godlings run around the living room with their father quick on their heels. Hermes always said he wanted a big family, and now he has his wish, and it is with the perfect woman.

"Come in!" Maressa exclaims with a smile. "We were about to play some games."

Maressa ushers us inside, and the moment we step in, Hades and Persephone rush towards me. They envelop me in a hug, threatening to break bones with how hard they squeeze me.

They have worked tirelessly with the deceased to revamp the Underworld. There are no longer acres of land where dead roam, barely remembering their former life. The newly appointed ferryman does not accept bribes; rather, he follows the code of honor Zig created. There hasn't been a moment where they have time to leave the Underworld, except for the girls' birthdays every year.

Mom doesn't even come up for spring anymore; instead, she demands that if Demeter wants to see her, she can come help in the Underworld.

Demeter does just that.

Many other immortals are here for the festivities. Zeus flirts with one muse, Clio, at the bar separating the kitchen and the living room. Clio looks unimpressed. Hera, however, stands at the far corner with a blushing Sinope giggling at every joke. Hera and I lock gazes from across the room. For most of my existence, Hera has sought to murder me because of the story of my conception. Now, she looks between her favorite son and me, and she smiles at my arrival.

She was even the officiant at our wedding.

Aphrodite, in her many shifting forms, sits on Hephaestus's lap. She twirls a piece of his orange hair, and the normally grumpy god grins at her before kissing her lips. Melpomene, Maressa's mother, scoops up one of her grandchildren and peppers their face and neck with kisses. Hermes and Maressa's youngest giggles the entire time.

Demeter laughs with Hypnos, while Athena and

Poseidon bicker on the opposite side of the house. Amphitrite, always nearby her husband, rolls her eyes in mock annoyance.

Dionysus and Hestia hold handfuls of games, but perching at the top is Monopoly. Hermes, who playfully catches one of his daughters, sees the Monopoly game at the same time as me. We are across the room from each other, but we share a smile and a fond memory of how this all began. Him and me with a Monopoly game, and a promise to always protect each other.

Pyrrha and Melina run down the steps, laughing as Cerberus chases after them. The twins look more opposite with each passing day. Pyrrha loves elaborate gowns, which always match the blazing fire that streaks one tuft of hair on her otherwise golden head. Melina, however, prefers pants and battle armor. On her belt is a plethora of throwing knives, and while none of us have seen Artemis since the huntresses' funerals, I know she's looking somewhere at her niece with pride.

Hart is smiling, too, because her daughters are perfect, and they are raised by the best god of them all. Apollo strolls down the stairs after his girls and Cerberus, laughing with Diam, and they both wave at Ares and me. Diam and Ares share a nod of understanding. It took almost a decade without their soulmates, but they are finally at a place of peace. Their shared strife brought the two close together, providing comfort for each other in a way few others understand.

Ares told Diam the truth a few years ago about his torment during the time of human enslavement. He explains how Morpheus distorted his brain until he lost all sense of sanity. It doesn't absolve Ares of his crimes, or eradicate Diam's suffering, but now he understands. They will never be friends, and Diam may always look upon

Ares as his enemy, but at least he knows the reason behind every horrible action.

Actions that Ares fights to fix every day.

Nike brings out a cake as tall as the nearly six-foot-tall girls, and we all sing in resplendent pride at the creation of these two future goddesses. All of us gods use their birthdays as a time to remember the woman who saved us all, one vision at a time. We share stories about Hartika Sommers, the prophesied oracle who sacrificed so much so her daughters could live in a time of peace.

We play board games around the expansive living room, and Hermes passes me my favorite Monopoly piece. "Do you ever regret it?" he asks.

"Regret what?"

"Me stealing you all those years ago."

I grab my Monopoly piece. "You once told me that the greatest things in life are the ones you stole. My dear friend, there is nothing about our story that I regret. It is one of the greatest parts of my life."

Hermes smiles, water misting his eyes. "I love you, my friend. From today until the end of time."

"And I love you, my friend and thief."

As Dionysus rolls the dice, starting the game, Thanatos crashes through the house. He stands directly on top of the board game, causing Dionysus to yell. "That's cheating!"

But Thanatos doesn't care. He looks between Hermes and me, and he smiles for the first time in eighteen years. "She's awake."

Zeus doesn't hesitate.

The moment those two words leave Thanatos's lips, Zeus crashes a lightning bolt into the ground and sends us all to my mansion. I kept my home of bones. It isn't as grand as my former house, which held endless stories of

Zig, Hattie, Diam, and me, but this holds enough memories to treasure.

Thanatos lives here too, with his room one door away from Jamila's. We all materialize inside her room, filling out the entire space, while Jamila blearily opens her eyes. She takes us all in, but her gaze levels on Hermes and me. "W-What happened?" she asks, voice cracked. "Did we win?"

Tears well up in both of our eyes. "Yeah, we won."

Jamila smiles, but she's not the next person to speak.

Pyrrha is.

She takes a step forward and sits in the chair beside Jamila's bed. "My wish came true." Pyrrha takes Jamila's hand in both of hers and she grins widely. "It only took me eighteen tries, but my wish finally came true. You're awake."

I lay my head against Ares's shoulder, and he wraps his arms around me.

As our wish finally came true.

### The End.

# ACKNOWLEDGMENTS

This book is dedicated to my sister, Nora Grace, because Hattie was fully inspired by her.

Nora has always been my protector, ever since I was a little girl swimming in the deep end without my floaties. She's always been my strong, reassuring presence. The person who would hurt anyone who hurt me, then comfort me right after. She was the person who stopped me from making a terrible decision when the sadness of my life became nearly unbearable, and for a million reasons, I am so grateful that I have my big sister in my life.

When I wrote the first draft for this book on Wattpad, I was newly twenty-one years old, and I'd only recently started dating my now-husband. So, when I wrote Hattie, from the first page, I knew she'd be the prophesied heart because I didn't know the magnitude of true love; I only knew the power of sisterly love. When this story first came to me, I knew that Nora and I would pull heavens apart to save the other, just like Hattie and Saffron do time and time again.

Nora, thank you for spending so many years putting me first. For being the laughter when all I wanted to do was cry. For saving me when I didn't know how to save myself. Your daughters are in the single most capable hands.

Thank you for being my heart.

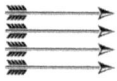

I would also like to thank my amazing editor for continuing to push me forward as I say goodbye to my dearest book series. I have written about this world for almost a decade and a third of my lifespan. This world and these characters have meant everything to me, and I am going to miss them so much. If it wasn't for my editor, I don't know how long it would have taken me to finish the final installment of the Ichor Series.

It hurts too much to part with these characters that have quickly become an extension of myself.

But Saffron is ready for her last page to be turned. Ares is ready for his rightfully deserved happy ending. Hermes is ready for a break with the love of his life. Artemis is ready to stop mourning, and Raven is ready to spend her life off the pages vying for Artemis's forgiveness. But Epiales will always look over us, the brightest star in the night sky.

Now, grab a bowl of strawberries and wine that you pretend came from Dionysus himself, and help me say goodbye to this world once and for all.

Or a temporary goodbye.

Who knows what the future will hold?

# GLOSSARY IN ALPHABETICAL ORDER

**Achilles:** Infamous hero in the Trojan War. Demi-God, son of a sea nymph named Thetis.

**Aegis:** Athena's sacred shield with Medusa's face in the middle. Known as a protective force.

**Alecto:** One of the 3 Furies, who live in the Underworld.

**Ambrosia:** Food of the Gods.

**Amphitrite:** Wife of Poseidon and Queen of the Seas. One of the 50 Nereids. Daughter of Oceanus & Tethys.

**Aphrodite:** Goddess of Sexual Love and Beauty. Wife of Hephaestus. One of the 12 Olympians.

**Apollo:** God of Prophecies, Music, Poetry, Art, Truth, Healing, Sun, and Light. Twin Brother of Artemis. Son of Zeus and Leto. One of the 12 Olympians.

**Arachne:** First spider in existence. Transformed into a spider by Athena after she committed hubris.

**Ares:** God of War and Bloodshed. Son of Zeus and Hera. One of the 12 Olympians.

**Argus:** Many-Eyed Giant. Slain by Hermes. Hera's guard in most stories.

**Ariadne:** Wife of Dionysus. Once a human princess, who helped Theseus defeat the Labyrinth. Daughter of Minos.

**Aristaeus:** God of Beekeeping, Honey, Shepherds, and Cheese-making.

**Artemis:** Goddess of the Hunt, Wild Animals, Vegetation, Chastity, and Childbirth. Twin Sisters of Apollo. Daughter of Zeus and Leto. One of the 12 Olympians.

**Asclepius:** God of Medicine. Son of Apollo.

**Asopus:** A river god with twenty daughter nymphs.

**Asphodel Meadows:** Largest segment of the Underworld. This is where almost all the dead are placed.

**Astraeus:** Titan of Dusk, Stars, and Astrology.

**Atalanta:** Famous Female Hero. Member of the Argonauts.

**Athena:** Goddess of Wisdom, Crafts, and Battle Strategies. Favorite Daughter of Zeus. First-born child between Metis and Zeus. One of the 12 Olympians.

**Atlas:** Titan condemned to hold the skies for eternity after the first Titanomachy War. Father of Calypso.

**Calliope:** One of the Muses. Goddess of Heroic Poetry.

**Calypso:** A nymph who was exiled to the island of Ogygia. Captured Odysseus on his way home from the Trojan War. Daughter of Atlas.

**Centaurs:** Half-horse, Half-man.

**Cerberus:** 3-Headed Dog of the Underworld. Child of the Echidna and Typhon. Guards the gates of the Underworld.

**Circe:** Witch Goddess. Daughter of Hecate and Aeetes.

**Clio:** One of the Muses. Goddess of History.

**Cyclops:** One-Eyed Giants known for blacksmithing, sheepherding, or eating humans.

**Daedalus:** Creator of the Labyrinth. One of the wisest men in Greek Mythology.

**Dagger of Chains:** Fictional dagger created by the

author. "Created" by Daedalus to imprison immortals. Inspired by the Tibetan Phurba Dagger from Indo-Tibetan Buddhism and Bön traditions.

**Deimos:** God of Terror and Dread. Twin Brother of Phobos. Son of Ares and Aphrodite.

**Delphi:** Delphi is a town on Mount Parnassus in the south of mainland Greece. It's the site of the 4th-century-B.C. Temple of Apollo, once home to a legendary oracle.

**Demeter:** Goddess of the Harvest. Daughter of Kronos and Rhea. Mother of Persephone.

**Dionysus:** God of Wine, Partying, Fertility, Insanity, Festivity, Orgies, and Theater. Son of Zeus and Semele. One of the 12 Olympians after Hestia gave up her spot for him.

**Echo:** Famous Lover of Zeus. Hera cursed her to only speak in others' echoes.

**Elysium Fields:** The Underworld's version of heaven. Most gods and scholars are sent here.

**Empusa:** A shape-shifting monster with a single leg of copper that is commanded by Hecate

**Epiales:** Personified Spirit (Daemon) of Nightmares. Almost completely forgotten in mythology. Brother of Hypnos and Thanatos. Son of Nyx.

**Epimetheus:** The Titan of Afterthought. Brother of Prometheus.

**Erato:** Muse of Lyric, Erotic Poetry, and Hymns. One of the 9 Muses.

**Eros:** God of Love and Sex. Son of Ares and Aphrodite. Husband of Psyche. Has arrows that, once shot, can either turn you deliriously in love with the first person you see. Or it will make you hate them.

**Eurynome:** An elder Oceanid titaness.

**Euterpe:** One of the Muses. Goddess of Music & Flutes.

**The Fates:** Three weaving goddesses, who represent the inescapable destiny of humanity.

**Fields of Punishment:** A land in the Underworld, where the worst humans are sent to suffer for all of eternity.

**Hades:** God of the Underworld and Jewels. The eldest son of Kronos and Rhea. Husband of Persephone. One of the 12 Olympians.

**Hebe:** Goddess of Youth. Daughter of Zeus and Hera. Wife of Heracles. Cupbearer to the Gods.

**Hecate:** Goddess of Witchcraft and Necromancy. Wife of Aeetes.

**Helen of Troy:** Daughter of Zeus and Queen Leda. The most beautiful mortal woman in the world with a face "that sails a thousand ships".

**Hephaestus:** God of Blacksmithing, Metalworking, Sculptures, and Fire. Son of Hera. Husband of Aphrodite. One of the 12 Olympians.

**Hera:** Queen of the Olympians. Wife/Sister of Zeus. Daughter of Kronos and Rhea. Goddess of Marriage and Childbirth. Notoriously hates all of Zeus's children outside of wedlock.

**Heracles:** God of Heroes. Son of Zeus and Alcmene. Hero is most famous for the 12 Labors. Married to Hebe.

**Hermes:** God of Thievery, Trade, Wealth, Luck, and Travel. Son of Zeus and Maia. Messenger of the Gods.

**Hermaphroditus:** God of Effeminates. Son of Hermes and Aphrodite.

**Hestia:** Goddess of the Hearth. The eldest daughter of Kronos and Rhea. Gave up her role as an Olympian for Dionysus.

**Horkos:** The Personification of Curses and Avenger of Perjury. If you disobey an oath you swore, Horkos will

come for you on the 5<sup>th</sup> day of the 5<sup>th</sup> month and
curse you.

**Huntresses:** Immortal female warriors loyal to Artemis,
who take a vow of celibacy when they join her regime.

**Hyacinth:** Famous Lover of Apollo. Killed by another
god, Zephyrus, out of jealousy.

**Hypnos:** Personified Spirit (Daemon) of Sleep. Son of
Nyx. Twin Brother of Thanatos.

**Iapetus:** Titan of Mortality.

**Ichor:** Gold Blood of the Gods.

**Ilithyia:** Goddess of Childbirth and Midwifery. Daughter
of Hera and Zeus.

**Io:** Notorious Lover of Zeus. Turned into a cow by Zeus
to hide his adulterous ways from Hera.

**Iris:** Goddess of Rainbows. Messenger of the Gods.
Specifically Works for Hera.

**Ixion:** The man who tried to seduce Hera. In the Fields
of Punishment, eternally spinning on a wheel of fire.

**Jason:** Greek Hero and Leader of the Argonauts.
Retriever of the Golden Fleece.

**Khione:** Goddess of Snow. Daughter of Boreas and
Oreithyia.

**Kronos:** Titan of Time. Son of Gaia and Uranus.
Defeater of Uranus. Fallen Leader of the Titanomachy
Wars.

**Labyrinth:** A maze created by Daedalus in Crete for
King Minos. The Minotaur lived and hunted in here.

**Lamia:** A woman who had an affair with Zeus and bore
children with him. Hera killed her children and turned her
into a monster who fed on children.

**Leda:** Lover of Zeus when he was in swan-form. Gave
birth to 4 children in eggs, including Helen of Troy and
Queen Clytemnestra of Mycenae.

**Lethe:** Personification of Oblivion. Has dominion over

the River Lethe, where the deceased souls go when they wish to forget their existence. Daughter of Eris.

**Leto:** Mother of Apollo and Artemis.

**Megaera:** One of the 3 Furies. Resides in the Underworld.

**Melpomene:** One of the Muses. Goddess of Tragedy.

**Metis:** Titaness daughter of Oceanus and Tethys. Zeus's first wife. Mother of Athena. Second child was believed to become the most powerful immortal. Killed by Zeus.

**Minos:** King of Crete. Orchestrator of the Labyrinth. One of the 3 Judges of the Underworld.

**Minotaur:** Half-man, Half-beast. Son of Queen Pasiphae and a white bull. Slain by Theseus in the Labyrinth.

**Momus:** God of Mockery.

**Morpheus:** God of Dreams. Son of Hypnos.

**Mount Olympus:** Home of the Gods. Located in the Skies.

**The Muses:** Nine Goddesses who defend the arts. Provide entertainment for the Olympians.

**Narcissus:** Mortal man, who was so obsessed with his appearance that he could not pull his eyes away from the water's reflection of him.

**Nectar:** Drink of the Gods.

**Nemean Lion:** Vicious lion with impenetrable fur. Defeated by Heracles during his 12 Labors.

**Nemesis:** Goddess of Divine Retribution and Revenge.

**Nessus:** Centaur famous for attempting to kidnap Heracles's second wife. His poisoned blood is partially responsible for Heracles's mortal death.

**Nike:** Goddess of Victory.

**Nosoi:** Personifications Spirts of Plague, Sickness, and Disease. In this story, their form is birds, but their form is ever-changing.

**Odysseus:** Hailed wisest hero of Greek Mythology. Famous for the Trojan War and his journey home.

**Oedipus:** The king of Thebes, who unwittingly killed his father and married his mother. Slayer of the Sphinx, which gave him Thebes' crown.

**Ogygia:** Island where Calypso was exiled. Known as a distant island, most could not find.

**Oizys:** Goddess of Misery, Anxiety, Grief, Depression, and Misfortune.

**Olympians:** The 12 major gods of the Greek Pantheon.

**Olympus Industries:** A fictional skyscraper building created for this story. This is where the gods met when conducting business on earth before the destruction of the Underworld.

**Οστά:** A fictional sword made by Hephaestus for Saffron, which is made entirely out of bones.

**Oneiroi:** The gods of dreams in Greek mythology. The innumerable sons of Nyx. (See: Epiales & Hypnos).

**Oracle:** A person (typically females) considered providing wise, prophetic insight. Another common terminology is a seer.

**Paean:** Physician of the Gods.

**Pandora:** The first human woman created by Zeus/Hephaestus. She opened a box that released all the evils of the world. She opened it out of curiosity, not malice.

**Perseus:** Demi-God, son of Zeus and Danae. Slayer of Medusa.

**Persephone:** Queen of the Underworld. Goddess of Spring. Daughter of Zeus and Demeter. Wife of Hades.

**Phobos:** God of Fear and Panic. Twin Brother of Deimos. Son of Aphrodite and Ares.

**Polymnia:** One of the Muses. Goddess of Sacred Poetry and Pantomime.

**Polyphemus:** A cyclops who herded sheep and tried to

kill Odysseus and his men. Lost most of his vision because of Odysseus A.K.A. Nobody.

**Pompeii:** Once a thriving and sophisticated Roman city, a volcano buried the city under meters of ash and pumice. The catastrophic eruption was Mount Vesuvius in 79 A.D.

**Poseidon:** God of the Seas. Son of Kronos and Rhea. Husband of Amphitrite. One of the 12 Olympians.

**Priapus:** Low-level Fertility God.

**Psyche:** Goddess of Soul. Wife of Eros.

**Seer:** See Oracle definition.

**Semele:** Mother of Dionysus and lover of Zeus. Hera tricked her into convincing Zeus to show his godly form. She burned to death at the sight.

**Sinope:** River Nymph. Daughter of Asopus.

**Sisyphus:** Man who tried to cheat death twice. Cursed in the Fields of Punishment to eternally push a boulder up a hill, only for it to fall to the bottom again.

**Sphynx:** Female Monster. Body of a lion, head and breasts of a woman, wings of an eagle, and tail of a snake. Defeated by Oedipus.

**Stymphalian Birds:** Bronze-beaked, monstrous birds that Heracles defeated in one of his 12 Labors.

**Styx:** Personification of Hatred. One of the Eldest Immortals. The strongest oaths are to her river.

**Tartarus:** A prison in the pits of the Underworld. Most famously holds the titans. In this story, Epiales and Uranus are also prisoners.

**Tantalus:** Demi-God of Zeus's, who believed he could trick the gods. Killed his son, chopped him up in pieces, and put him in a stew that he tried to feed to the gods. When they quickly caught him, they threw him into the Fields of Punishment. They forced him to stand in a pond but never drink from the water, and he could never reach the food, just out of reach.

**Terpsichore:** One of the Muses. Goddess of Chorus and Dancing.

**Thanatos:** Personification of Death. Twin brother of Hypnos.

**Theseus:** Famous hero and slayer of the Minotaur.

**Thalia:** One of the Muses. Goddess of Comedy.

**Tisiphone:** One of the 3 Furies. Resides in the Underworld.

**Titanomachy War:** A 10-year war between the Titans and the Olympians.

**Triton:** A sea god. Son of Poseidon and Amphitrite.

**Typhon:** Father of Monsters. Greatest Monster in Greek Mythology Existence.

**Urania:** Muse of Astronomy. One of the 9 Muses.

**Uranus:** Father Sky. Husband of Gaia. Father of Kronos. Grandfather of Zeus.

**Zeus:** King of the Olympians. The youngest son of Rhea and Kronos. God of Lightning and the Skies. Father to most Gods and Demi-Gods.

# ABOUT THE AUTHOR

Trish D.W is a woman with a lifelong dream of being a full-time author. She has dreamed of this moment since she was a little girl at recess writing scripts rather than playing on the playground. Each day, her dream becomes a clearer reality, and she is grateful to everybody who has purchased her novel.

**FOLLOW TRISH D.W ON THE WEB AT:**

trishdw.com

Instagram & TikTok: @authortrishdw